FOREWORD

Ermal Walden Williamson has blended history with a "ghostly" tale of the western past in **"The Ghost of Ginny McBride"**. His rich character development mixed with a strong storyline has created a book that is hard to put down. His addition of a few familiar characters has made **Williamson's** latest book his best ever

Kenny Keiser
2300 W. 131st St.
Olatha, KS 66061-5915
913-254-7050

Author of "**Ride the Trail of Death,**" "**Black Moon's Revenge,**" and "**Tucker Cole**".

Award winning magazine and newspaper author of 33 years. Inducted into the National Fresh Water Fishing Hall of Fame in the 2010 class as a Legendary Communicator

REVIEWS

Ermal Walden Williamson has again captured the historical perception and details with imaginative storytelling of the events after the War Between the States. The content of the story blends historical people and fictional characters with believable reality. The story flows from the ending of the fighting of the War Between the States to the beginning of the rebuilding of the Southern industries. The cooperation between the business personnel of the North and the South, working toward a unified government, is written with knowledge and understanding.

The story moves fast and is in sequence with the ending of the War, the fighting and distrust of the people with opposing ideals, the violence that results, the rebuilding of the destroyed South, the emergence of the organized outlaw gangs, all spilling over in the new Western movement.

The barroom fights and gunfights make the action move fast throughout the novel. These are based on factual events with added drama to keep the reader on his toes. The reader is drawn into the story as participant of the action much like watching a movie.

The characters are well portrayed. Our heroes remain true to their characters throughout the entire BRAZOS saga. Matt and Steve remain loyal, strong, brave, honest, using their fists and guns, fighting for justice and the rights of the little man. They are the measure of the true Western Heroes. Most of the male characters are true to the ideal strong rough hewn western men.

This is an exceptionally well written, true to history, fast moving novel that is hard to put down until the last page is read. **Ermal Walden Williamson** is the leading modern Western writer.

Marilyn G. Cates – Bergman, AR

==

Ermal Williamson's latest western novel of the *Brazos* series is non-stop exciting action. From the main character's Civil War era days to his Waco, Texas cowboy days, and finally to his Montana ranching days, Matt Jorgenson searches for his lady love Ginny, who comes to him in ghostly dreams. Matt and Ginny are star-crossed lovers in the turbulent days of the early west, who are destined to meet again, even after Ginny is wounded during the Civil War and suffers from amnesia. Read a western novel the way we fondly remembered them, with the flair of a Zane or L'amour.

—Jack San Felice, Noted Superstition Mountain, Arizona Author and Historian. Books include: ***When Silver Was King, Lost El Dorado Of Jacob Waltz and Superstition Cowboys***

==

"The Ghost of Ginny McBride" brings to light the search we all chart for ourselves. Although most people know what it is they seek, some don't even realize when they have found what they're looking for.

Ermal Williamson weaves a delightful story that follows a cast of characters in their own personal searches.

Ron Feldman – author **"Double Cross"**
www.okcorral.com
480-982-4040
P. O. Box 1082
Ouray, CO 81427

3

THE GHOST OF GINNY MCBRIDE

(The Brazos Series 6)

Reviewed by: Conan Tigard
Reading Review

I like this series and highly recommend the first three books. Two other books have been published that I haven't had a chance to read yet. If you love those books, then you may want to pick up a copy of this story and learn more about how Ginny McBride became Beth Paterson.

THE GHOST OF GINNY McBRIDE

BY

ERMAL WALDEN WILLIAMSON

Giant Shadow Publishing

Printed in the United States of America

The Ghost of Ginny McBride is published by:

Giant Shadow Publishing
www.ermal.com
Branson, MO 65616

Editors: Paula Williamson
          Marilyn G. Cates

Cover Photo: Lance Fontaine, Photographer, Springfield, MO
Horses and Background by: Bear Creek Trail Rides, Walnut
          Shadows, MO
Front Cover Design by: Caleb Wheat, Joplin, MO and Denis
McMillan, Branson, MO
Printed by: Publishers ExpressPress

DEDICATED TO

My wife, show partner and friend,
Paula Erlene Williamson
"America's Yodeling Sweetheart"
Whose tremendous drive, creative insights and
editing added dimension to this story

A disclaimer: This is an historical novel based upon facts and is intended for entertainment without any prejudice or bias. The McBride Mill is fictitious.

PREFACE

One word dominates a cowboy's life when he is seeking to resolve the disappearance of his loved one whom he was told was shot and killed; *fate.* Because he refused to believe that she was dead, his obsession was to find her.

Fate is that word which, seemingly no one can describe, yet is one of the most powerful nouns in the English language. One may call it *predestination* or *foreordainment* or simply *plain old luck.* However one calls it, the fact remains that it is real for anyone believing in and accepting it. Matt Jorgensen believed it. So did Ginny McBride.

It is told that when a soldier goes into battle, he probably enters it as a dead man, knowing that his chances of coming out alive are slim to none. If he makes it, he counts it as an act of God's mercy. When a coward goes into battle, he fears greatly for his life and puts his fellow man into constant danger.

Whether the two statements are altruisms or are the makeup of a soldier who has faced one or many battles, it could be taken as altruisms as many a soldier or coward has come out of battle with scars; a soldier with a memory and a coward with a hidden past. If a surviving soldier believed in the Divine, he or she would give the Divine the glory for his or her blessing, whereas the coward would seek solace in the bowels of his weakened spirit.

To many people, spirits are believed to be real and in essence they surround us. In this novel, the reader is invited to enter the spiritual or ethereal world with our hero and heroine for an enlightening experience that should be as entertaining as well as an enjoyable adventure. In this episode of Ginny McBride's life, she experienced the apex of her spiritual powers to be able to penetrate through space and time faster than a thought.

In the Bible, Jesus is quoted in John the third chapter . . . *the wind blows where it will . . ., so it is with the spirit.* And so it was with Ginny and Matt's unnatural experiences with one another while in search for each other.

PROLOGUE

The shot was loud and clear; reverberating throughout the woods like the sound of a hunter's shot at a wild game. Ginny McBride felt the sting of the musket ball as it hit her shoulder and knocked her from her saddle with a thud, causing her to fall to the ground in a rolling motion, settling face down.

She was a plantation owner's daughter just turned nineteen, of medium height, thin, blond hair and blue eyes. She was dressed all in black to prevent her from being seen by any Union soldier, but with a tight enough blouse to point out the features that would show her foe that she was a woman. It was early dawn and the fog hid her true appearance, and the young Union soldier mistook her for the enemy when he fired his Union carbine at her.

"I got 'im!" the soldier cried out.

From that moment on, Ginny's life was changed for she later fell into a fever, and after trying to escape from the Union camp, her weakness sent her again crashing to the ground, this time hitting her head on the cold, hard ground. Developing a rare case of amnesia from the fever and the concussion she sustained from the fall, she would lead a life of four years without knowing who she was or why she fell into a Union camp.

Her lover, Matt Jorgensen, searchers for her and finds too many conflicting reports about her being killed. Convinced that she is still alive, he searches for her.

The attending physician, Captain Doctor Henry Paterson took her case on a personal basis and had her transported to his Richmond, Virginia home where his wife attended to her needs. Emma Paterson and Ginny bonded together in a mother and adopted daughter connection whereby Ginny took upon herself the family name of Paterson, and accepted the name of Beth for Elizabeth until, hopefully, she would come out of her amnesia.

CHAPTER 1

BETH PATERSON FINDS A NEW HOME

<u>10 December 1861</u>

A young soldier boy drove the one-horse military wagon through a pair of iron gates and brought it to a halt in front of the steps of the Paterson Manor on a slight incline overlooking Richmond.

"We're here," he addressed Beth as he went around the wagon to help her from the plank seat. He watched her as she eyed the manor. "Yep. She's a biggun. Real big, if'n ya ask me."

"You sure we got the right place?" Beth asked, picking up her light luggage.

"Here, let me get thet for ya." The boy quickly took the bag from her grip and escorted her up the stairs.

At the door, he pulled the chain which summoned a black male servant to their assistance. Beth looked startled at first at the sight of a black man opening the door and bowing to her, and then she gained her composure.

A lady in her mid-thirties appeared at the door behind him. It was Mrs. Emma Paterson, the wife of Captain Henry Paterson who had been attending to Beth. It had only been a few months since Emma Paterson agreed to take her in as her husband's patient.

At first Emma was reticent about having a strange, yet beautiful young lady as a border in her house, knowing her husband to be a man of vanity. Yet, to follow her husband's demands as a professional man, she bowed to his wishes and looked towards taking her in. She also thought about having some companionship during such a frightful time as this war had become, being alone and with her husband so far away.

"Well, dear," she addressed Beth, seeing her for the first time dressed in a horse soldier's outfit and pinned for size, "you have to be Beth."

Beth nodded and smiled. "Yes, ma'am."

"Well, let's get you inside and changed from those awful looking clothes. You must be tired from your journey. I can tell from the looks of you that you must be starved."

Emma looked at the soldier boy who escorted her from the one-horse military wagon to the door of the stately Paterson manor. "Thank you, son. You can quit goggling over her and get back to wherever you're heading." She shooed him easy back down the steps in a kindly manner.

The lad gulped, and apologized, "Yes, ma'am. Sorry, ma'am." He nearly fell down the steps as he turned and hurried back to the wagon.

Penny, the house Negro escorted Beth inside the house as Jeremiah, a Negro man-servant took Beth's luggage filled with her few belongings. The act of the two servants appeared odd to her at first, then she reeled back into her consciousness and realized they were black people being subservient to their masters; something she felt connected with in her past.

"What is it, dear?" Emma asked, watching Beth changed expressions on her face at the sight of the servants.

"I . . . I don't know. I've seen niggers along the way here. That's what you call them, isn't it?" She kept her eyes on Penny.

Emma nodded and took Beth's hand from the house Negro and led Beth into the foyer, which opened to a spiral staircase in the middle. She took Beth to the right of the staircase into a large living room filled with two large divans and four overstuffed chairs. Off to the side of the living room was an expansive dining area with a large table set for eight.

"We call them that. What would you call them?"

Beth thought a while and watched the two servants as they scurried off attending to their duties. "I . . . I don't know. I have no idea. Just seems an odd name for me to remember."

"This here is Penny," Sarah pointed out her house Negro. "And Jeremiah took your luggage upstairs."

"Well, no matter," Emma continued, "we've more important things to attend to at the moment. Your room is at the top of the stairs. Would you like to sit and talk awhile, or lie down? I suspect you might be tired."

"Oh, yes, I am, "Beth agreed, "but I want to know more about this house." Her eyes grew large as she eyed her surroundings. "This is quite a house."

"Oh, my, yes," Emma agreed politely. "It's called a manor. It was built by Doctor Paterson's father and his father before him." She stopped and rested her hand on Beth's shoulder. "What kind of house did you come from?"

Beth looked around the house as if Emma were not present. Emma followed her from room to room. When Beth stopped to look into the dining room, she turned and met Emma. "It's large."

"Yes, it is," Emma returned. "As I asked before, what kind of house did you live in? Can you remember?"

Beth looked at Emma for a moment as in a daze, trying to recollect her earlier surroundings.

"I remember a living room this big," she started recollecting. "No. It was bigger."

"Bigger?" Emma returned with a surprised look. She thought to herself, *Nah. She can't have come from a rich family. Not the way Doc described her.*

"Yes. At least twice as big." She gazed at Emma as if she could look right through her. "Why did I say that? I don't know any such thing." She wrapped her arms around Emma and cried. "Oh, Mrs. Paterson."

For the first time in a long time, Emma felt a sense of being needed by another human being, having no children of her own. And, even though Beth was not yet twenty, Emma knew that she needed her, and as an added feeling, she felt the need of a *daughter*. Doctor Paterson seemed to have made a wise choice in sending Beth to her. Even though, Emma could not get the thought out of her mind that this amnesia might be faked.

She took a handkerchief from her sleeve and wiped Beth's eyes.

"My house nigger, Penny, has served up her special, smoked ham." She referred to her house Negro who had the appearance of not only being a good cook, serving up a good supper but showing it on herself as well. "If you're up to eating, that is."

While they shared the supper hour together, Emma opened the Doctor's last letter, which inquired about Beth's condition upon her arrival at the manor.

"This will be somewhat of a revelation to tell him," she conversed with Beth. "A small one, yes, but a revelation, to say the least."

Penny refilled Emma's cup of tea and did likewise with Beth's cup as Emma continued talking with excitement. She waited for what seemed like forever before Beth would start talking.

"Mrs. Paterson, I'm just not sure what I saw."

"Tell me, Beth, anything that comes to your mind. Anything will help the Doctor in speeding up your recovery." She continued to wait for Beth to talk about her vision in the dining room. "Anything."

Beth shrugged her shoulders, smiled, shoved a bite of biscuit in her lovely mouth and kept eating. She appeared to Emma to be nonchalant about herself, but the truth of the matter was, she simply could not recall anything that would be of help. So, she figured that the best thing for the moment was to get on with her supper.

****

Christmas came and it was made sure to Beth that she was treated as part of the family. She awoke that morning and walked softly through the hallway and down the staircase to the living room. There she saw the tree she, Emma, Penny and her husband, Jeremiah had brought in and decorated. Under the branches of the evergreen were presents. Upon examining them, she found one with her name on it.

Emma had followed Beth down the staircase without her knowing it, as Jeremiah and Penny watched stealthily through the opened kitchen door.

Beth sat down cross-legged in front of the tree, stared at her present and wondered what was inside. She heard a giggle come from the kitchen, looked up and saw Emma walking into the room.

"Merry Christmas, my dear," Emma said with a smile as a mother would share with her offspring.

Penny led Jeremiah by the hand and they moved in behind Emma.

"Child," Jeremiah said with glee, "you done made this heah family proud."

"Open it," Emma said as she stood clothed in her bathrobe next to Jeremiah and Penny.

Fumbling through the paper wrapping, she uncovered a dark blue dress. "Oh, my!" was all she could exclaim as she held the dress up to her bosom.

"You start finishing school the first week in January, Beth. You'll be needing these." Then, as Emma saw Beth staring as in a trance, said, "Keep going. We have another present for you."

She followed Emma's advice and opened another smaller present. It was a pair of high-laced shoes. And then Emma pointed to a bonnet tied by the ribbons to the peg that held a stocking marked *Beth* that dangled from the mantle above the fireplace.

Beth remembered those presents as being so important to her, more than anything she could imagine. She so looked forward to finishing school, although she felt she was slightly older than she should have been for that. But then, she did not even know exactly how old she really was, so she accepted the opportunity to become a lady; a task she thought was next to being impossible. After all, she evidently had not been thinking like a lady when she mistakenly dressed in the appearance of a man. Thinking she would look like a lady in tight clothes, she was mistaken for a man and shot as one. Those were the facts pointed out to her by Doctor Paterson.

CHAPTER 2

A FACE ON THE WALL

<u>20 February 1862</u>

It was a moderately cool evening when Beth succumbed to heavy sleep from a tiresome day at finishing school and having been tutored in the evening.

As she lay on her back, the appearance of a battlefield appeared to Beth in a dream. She could see the canons exploding in the near distance and men dressed in an array of different clothing, manning the canons, riding horses, walking and firing their muskets. She saw the battery of explosions set off in cadence and heard the echo vibrate throughout the woods.

And then all was quiet for a long while. She followed one horseman as he rode towards her and dismounted. As quickly as the scene of fire and smoke appeared, it disappeared as fast, leaving only the man in her vision as he tied his stallion to a tree branch and sat on a log.

He looked towards her and took a pencil and paper in hand. And then only his face appeared shrouded by a mist which enveloped his appearance to where she could not clearly see his face.

The face seemed to stand in mid air in the far off corner of her bedroom. As he began to write, he talked, and occasionally he would stare towards Beth.

She twitched and turned in her bed as she fought the fear of her nightmare. But, to her, it was no nightmare, as the face seemed to pay attention to her, as if it knew her. And somehow, she sensed an awareness as to who the man was, but could not see him or hear him clear enough to ascertain his identity. He spoke in an even, pleasant tone as one addressing his lover, softly, almost in a whisper as he wrote.

To My Beloved.

I'm still in Tennessee. The winter is cold. Bitterly cold. Eighty-four Rangers died before January's end. Only five from battle. Seems we're plagued with a really bad winter. We have less than half the men prepared for duty.

Colonel Terry's gone. So is Colonel Lubbock. Brave men, both. The Brazorian Sabers. We're still calling ourselves, Terry's Texas Rangers. God, I admired Colonel Terry! Did you know he was a rich man? He was very wealthy. But none of it went with him. Only his fame and his glory. Colonel Wharton is now in command. I suppose he'll prove to be a good leader, too. He was in command of Company B.

Whatever happens, I suppose now I have to sorta live up to Terry's legend. Don't you worry, darling., Steve and I will keep his name alive as long as this blasted war lasts.

They tell me a young girl was shot by a blue boy who had all his senses in his britches. Somewhere close by. I suppose that's why I keep coming back here, fighting and trying to figure all this out. I can't believe it could have been you who was shot. But if it was, I know you're still alive, darling. I feel it. I feel it as if you were sitting here on this stupid log with me right now.

Maybe you are.

I love you so, darling. And I miss you so very much . . .

As Beth slept, her closed eyes moved as if intently listening to each word but not understanding all that was being said. She wanted to rise out of bed and touch the words with her slender fingers. For fear of the face disappearing, she remained asleep in bed and kept her eyes shut tight, and desperately tried to hold onto each syllable.

Her lips pursed up into a smile and her fingers reached out and grabbed a tight hold of the sheet that covered her, pulling it to her body. For what seemed like hours, she continued reading the words over and over. She questioned herself as to who he was and quickly let any apprehensions waft off like the morning dew to be forgotten; simply to enjoy the moment.

Then a sense of ecstasy moved across the room towards her bed. She let go of her hold on the sheet and let it slide off of her onto the floor, exposing her alabaster body clad in a thin night gown. She felt the wisp of cool air seemingly caress her and tenderly kiss her moist lips.

Finally, the apparition left as quickly as it had appeared, leaving no trace of its having been there. Beth slept on, hoping that he would come back and tell her who he was, and possibly reveal to her who *she* was. She slept through the rest of the night with a smile on her lips.

When she awoke the next morning, she walked over to the wall where the ghostly figure had appeared. There was no sign of anything out of the ordinary having been there; nothing was disturbed. She turned and looked at her bed, messed up from her restless sleep, and then spun around in the room with her arms outstretched and a broad smile of contentment on her face.

Whoever you are, mister, she said to herself, wondering over and over what he called himself and what his message was all about. Giving up, she thought, *I'm going to see you again!*

She was quick to dress and run down the stairs where she was met by Emma.

"Good morning, dear," Emma greeted her. "Have a good night sleep, I take it?"

Beth stopped, looked at Emma for a moment, looked around the room and outside into the garden, and answered her. "Yes, ma'am. A very good sleep." Then she smiled and sheepishly said, "I've got something to tell you."

"Breakfast is on the veranda, Beth. Let's talk about it over some scrambled eggs and biscuits. Penny made them the way you like."

The two ladies sat at the table, and Penny had already started serving them breakfast. During the course, Beth told Emma about her dream.

"It was real! I could almost reach out and touch his face, that's how real it was. And . . ."

Emma waited for Beth to continue. When she kept looking as if in the distance, she asked, "And, what, Beth?"

"That face. It looked so familiar. So, so familiar. Like someone I know . . . or should know."

"Oh? Can you describe it in any detail that could help us?

Beth put her chin in her hands and placed her elbows on the table. "Handsome. Beyond words. He knew me, Emma. He addressed his letter to me. I forget what he said in it. But it was addressed to me. He . . . had blue eyes. Sparkling blue eyes. I think."

"You think?"

"Yes. Because, we don't dream in color, do we?"

"But you saw them as blue."

"Maybe. Maybe they were blue because they looked blue . . . to me. Oh, he is handsome. If I don't know him, I should. I want to know him, Emma."

"Did he say anything? Can you remember anything he said?"

Beth looked puzzled and then, after careful thought, said, "I actually do not remember. Isn't that weird?"

Emma buttered her biscuit in a hurried fashion, and took a sip of her orange juice. Then she sat the glass down, looked smiling at Beth and said, "Don't worry about it, Honey. You can be Beth Paterson until the cows come home. I'm ok with it if you are."

Emma dismissed it in her own mind, thinking that all Beth had was a dream; a realistic dream, but just a dream.

Beth furrowed her brow, and then nodded in agreement.

****

A second vision came to her within a year. It happened when sleep overcame her through her exhausted studying. She heard sudden gunfire and yelling of soldiers.

Then it hit her hard and fast. Her eyes opened and she sat up. Then she closed them tight. "Matt! Watch out! Watch out, darling!"

She saw Matt leading a charge against the Federals when, in the midst of the battle, a young Yankee had a bead on Matt's chest with his rifle. It would have been a sure hit had it not been for Beth. She found her spirit passing Matt's horse, causing it to rear and throw Matt to the ground. The musket ball missed and the horse's hooves knocked the soldier off his horse and into a ravine.

CHAPTER 3

THE CIVIL WAR IS OVER

<u>2 April 1865</u>

The bursts from a battery of cannons shook the early morning air in Virginia, but nothing was going to disturb the leaves or the squirrels in Richmond, for they had grown accustomed to the noise.

However, this day was different from all the rest. The War was over and Richmond had fallen into the hands of the Federals. As Petersburg fell, Richmond was evacuated, and so leaves fell and squirrels ran for cover.

There was no moon the night Confederate President Jefferson Davis and his cabinet escaped Richmond by taking the Richmond & Danville Railroad to Danville.

Retreating, the Confederate soldiers set fire to the military establishments and arsenals throughout town, but the wind knew no boundaries. Their intent was to keep the contents from the hands of the Federals.

As fate would have it though, the winds picked up the cinders and flames from the burning buildings and spread them across the beautiful city. The sky lit up with a bright orange and was deceived by the grayish brown smoke that carved Richmond's face into that of a melting scene befit only by a steelworker's delight when tapping a furnace. The fire consumed Richmond.

CHAPTER 4

THE LADY VS THE AVENGER

<u>7 April 1865</u>

It had been four years since Beth came to the Paterson manor in Richmond. Because of the unique nature of her illness, of which Doc Paterson seemed to have all but given up on healing her, he charged that she be transported to his home in Virginia so that he could personally tend to her illness once he returned from the War; figuring he would soon be home. However, as the War progressed, he stayed on the battlefield by choice and the War lasted longer than he expected.

The task of tending to Beth was turned over to Mrs. Henry "Emma" Paterson who at first regarded it as a duty laid upon her, but soon became attached to Beth in a mother-daughter relationship.

The scantily clad body of a beautiful woman stood at the window and looked with fear at what was happening; afraid to move.

Emma Paterson walked into the room and her shadow engulfed Beth's body as she approached her quietly.

"The fire's headed in the other direction, Beth," she spoke in a whisper. "Let's pray that God keeps it that way, and that it will go out."

That evening, Beth stood in her bedroom in the manor, tall and straight, wearing the clothes she wore when she was shot; black pants, blouse and hat with a whip and a .44 strapped to her side. She pulled back the drape that covered her window and looked out over Richmond, watching the many colors of orange fire envelope her buildings with plumes of smoke climbing up to the night sky.

Why, she asked herself, *am I here? And why now? Who am I? Why can't I remember? Why? Why can't I remember even my own name?*

A rap on the door interrupted her thoughts and she closed the drape.

"Yes?"

"It's been a while since supper, Beth," Emma Paterson answered in a soft voice from behind the door.

"Our Union Soldiers are taking Richmond!" Emma exclaimed, looking out the bedroom window. "The fires were set by the Rebs, turning tail and running, as they always do. The ruffians!"

For some strange reason, Beth felt a cringe inside her soul at what Emma had just said.

Seeing Beth for the first time in this outfit, Emma was taken aback at the sight. For the past four years, Emma had put her through finishing school and then watched her as she was tutored by the president of the   now-closed William and Mary College in law. Emma was proud of her foster daughter, a lady of refinement and intelligence. But, now with Beth looking like a hard-hitting fighter with vengeance in her heart, Emma bit hard on her lip. For the moment, she thought, *she has she recovered from her amnesia and has now become the person she was before she was shot?*

Beth saw the startled look in Emma's eyes and attempted to explain.

"This get up? I found it in my old luggage under my bed after all this time. Would you believe? I thought if I put it on, somehow it might spark something to bring back my memory as to who I really am."

"Anything, darling?"

"Not a thing, Emma," Beth responded. "Not a blasted thing. Excuse me. But somehow, it does make me think that I must have been some sort of Rebel or something. Where would I be using a whip and a gun?"

Emma watched as Beth began to undress. "You and I have asked the same question many times. I swear I don't know."

Emma's house Negro walked up and stood outside Beth's bedroom and overheard the conversation.

"Excuse me, Missus Paterson."

"Yes, Penny. What is it?" Emma asked, relieving Beth of her weapons.

"I think I might know who she be, mum."

"You what?" Emma asked, turning quickly around with the whip and gun in her hands.

"You know who I am?" Beth asked. "Who?"

"Wull, not who, but I know them things you has in yo' hands."

"These?" Emma asked. "A whip and a pistol?" She turned to Beth, and handing the gun back to Beth, said, "Oh my goodness. Is that thing loaded?"

Beth took it, opened the cylinder and examined it. "Nope. It's clean. Suspect they unloaded it when they found me."

Beth looked at Penny while Emma began helping to unbutton Beth's black blouse. "Go on, Penny. What need would I have had with them."

"Wull, miss," Penny began, pulling her bodice away from her shoulder to show scars.

"The whip?" Emma gasped. "How is it that I never saw those before?"

"Cause you neber had no cause to sees 'em. You neber uses the whip, ma'am."

"You mean to tell me that somebody whipped you?" Beth asked, climbing out of her pants.

"Why, it's obvious that she was," Emma addressed Beth. She touched the scars with her finger tips. "They're whelps, Beth."

"Yes, mum," Penny replied. "Bigger ones on my back, too. I s'pose I didn't rightly knows how to act in 'dem days, ma'am. I was a might much younger and unlearned as I am nowadays."

"Your master?" Emma surmised. "The man who sold you to us."

"Yes, mum."

"Your master?" Beth asked. "Your master did this to you?"

"Yes, Beth," Emma said, still looking at Penny's scars. "Some masters will use a whip on their slaves." Then she turned to Beth, and with wide-opened eyes exclaimed, "Oh, my gracious, could you have been a master?"

"Me?" Beth asked, slipping her arms into a white blouse that had been lying on the bed. "Me?" She laughed and then stopped abruptly. "Could I have been? Nah! Not me."

"You don't know that for sure," Emma returned. "It's something to go on. I'll write Henry and inform him about this possibility."

But the incendiary grew that night along with the fear, and by daybreak more Federals entered the city and began putting the flames to rest. Once again, Richmond stood strong and her people knew she would live. She also knew that the South was defeated.

Beth slept very little as she let the thought of the possibility of her being a slave master keep her up most of the night.

CHAPTER 5

A FLIRTATIOUS MOMENT

High on the hillside of Richmond, Emma Paterson sat on the veranda of her Richmond estate with the company of one Victoria Jamison, a lady of grandeur who had been a close friend of the Paterson family for several years. Victoria was in her thirties, medium height with a good figure and brown hair. They watched the smoldering fires as they began to slowly die down that morning.

Pouring Victoria a cup of tea, Emma seemingly enjoyed her conversation, but her mind was on Beth as she watched her lingering about in the garden.

"The Federals are putting out the fires," Emma said. "Oh I am pleased that the noise has finally stopped with the blasting off of those cannons." She continued to stare in amazement at Beth in the garden

"All this time," Victoria noted, "and you still don't know who this charming lady is, Emma?" Then as an afterthought, she asked, "It's been over three years, hasn't it, Emma?" Victoria looked chagrin at Emma while she sipped her tea.

"The war?"

"No. Since Beth has come to stay with you."

"Closer to four years, Vickie," Emma answered. "One day last week, I caught her wearing black pants and shirt with a whip and gun strapped to her side."

"What?"

"She must have been a slave owner, the way we see it. Can't be sure, but Penny suggested the possibility."

"She is an interesting person," Victoria returned.

"She's a wonderful lady. Yes, she is mysterious and yet wonderful. She is just like the daughter I never had. And you know something. I like that. I love her, Vickie." She stood up, taking her cup of tea with her, and looked out into the garden where Beth was examining the roses. "You know, that sounds silly. She's not that much younger than I." She patted the back of her hair and shyly added, "Maybe fifteen years, twenty at the most." She looked up at Victoria. "And yet, she seems to fit in so comfortably."

"You're not afraid of a little competition when Henry comes home?"

Emma paused for the moment, stared back at Victoria, and took another sip of tea. "Can't say that."

"What can you say?"

"I don't know. Oh, I know the old stories about how a doctor's patient falls in love with the doctor, and all that." She sat back down. "But you know, Vickie, I don't see that here. Maybe they had a fling back in Tennessee where he found her. I don't know. I don't really care. Really! I am an adult. I can understand what I'd have done had it been me. So why should I fear what I don't know, or what I don't want to know."

Victoria smiled.

"I just know I love Henry, and I know Henry loves me."

Victoria finished her tea and brushed off Penny' wanting to pour her another cup. "No, thanks, gal. I've had enough." She looked out at Beth, and continued. "The War's over. Henry will be coming home soon." She rose from the table and asked, "Will I be seeing you tomorrow?"

"Or the next.."

CHAPTER 6

FROM OUT OF THE ASHES

<u>14 April 1865</u>

It took a few more days before Emma felt it was safe for her and Beth to take a carriage ride down the main part of town to review the damage done. As the carriage rounded a certain part of the city, Beth's eyes opened wide as she saw the words *McBride Textiles*. She had seen them before, but looking at the devastation wrought on the days before, and looking at the burnt alabaster pillars against a beautiful sky gave her a perception she had somehow not seen for years.

In her mind, she was a small child clad in a beautiful blue and white dress with lace, and white stockings and shoes. A bow was tied in the back of her hair, and in her hands she held a fuzzy white stuffed rabbit. She saw herself running and playing through the meadow of a large yard as she entered a road that led up to a palatial house with white pillars; the same type of pillars she saw now as a woman staring at the ruins of a textile company.

"What is it, Beth?" Emma asked, motioning for her Negro driver, Simon to slow down. Simon was Emma's Negro helper, a big man with gray temples and in his early forties, towering over six foot with muscles bulging him into the high two hundreds. He was her bodyguard as well as driver and helper; and he was Penny' father. He was also a man to be feared. He cherished Emma from the day he met her. She brought him and his family to live with her as her *helpers*. She refused to call them slaves.

Simon immediately stopped at her insistence and Beth stepped down from the carriage. She walked ever so slowly into the ruins of the burned out building, careful not to stub her toe or ruin her dress on the charred remains. Emma sat and watched her.

"Shall I goes wiv her, ma'am?" Simon asked, holding the whip while steadying the horse.

"No, Simon," Emma replied softly. "Give her some time."

The building they were viewing was a burned out shell with several charred bodies lined along the walkway, covered by filthy sheets. A stench filled the air, and even Simon had to close his nostrils. Several soldiers were deep inside the building, having sifted the remains. They leaned against the bulkhead and were drinking coffee from their tins, and chewing tobacco. Beth caught their laughter as they watched her near them.

"Well, what do we have we here?" one of the soldiers said, tossing the coffee grounds from his tin to the wind. He was sandy-haired and thin, in his late teens and clinched an unlit corncob pipe between his lips as if trying to look older.

"Looks to me like a Southern filly just left the stable and is looking for her stud," remarked another tall lanky soldier with tobacco juice stains on the edges of his mouth, which made him look even nastier with his rotten teeth. They both gave out a sinister laugh.

"Wh-what?" Beth asked, putting her hands to her mouth.

Emma came up behind her with Simon by her side, carrying her opened umbrella with which to protect her from the sun. "Gentlemen," she started in with tight lips, placing her dainty hanky close to her mouth and nose to filter out the stench.. "If I should call you that. You will have the decency to keep your filthy tongues in your slobbering mouths."

"Well, now, if we don't have the teacher I never liked before," a short, stout soldier mouthed off. He walked over to Beth, sized her up with his eyes, and then turned and walked over to Emma. He looked at Simon doubling up his fists, ready for a fight. "We're jest funnin', ma'am. No cause to get your black boy up in arms. I see you fumin' in your gut, black boy." He spit out a wad of tobacco juice, and motioned for the other two to join him as he walked away towards the opening. "Best you watch out for fallen timbers. They're loose around here. Might get yourself hurt." It was more in the form of a threat than a warning.

"You gonna let thet boy keep us from havin' some fun?" the first soldier asked, smacking his hat against his leg.

"Shut up, fool," the stout man whispered. "Our captain jest came in."

A Federal officer in his early thirties walked up to Emma and Beth, doffed his hat, and apologized. "Sorry for that, ma'am. But these boys haven't seen a pretty woman in a long time. Most ladies are indoors and, well . . ."

"We're outdoors," Emma came back, removing her hanky as she talked. "I understand full well, Captain, or whatever you call yourself."

"Captain Bryce Willoughby, ma'am, at your service." He moved to stop Beth from walking in further. "We've been through the building, miss. It's not a pretty sight."

"Any worse than here?" she asked, removing his hand from her shoulder. "Is . . . is anyone alive in there?" Beth asked, looking at the captain with hurt eyes.

"These didn't make it, Miss. All that we know of, anyways." He looked into Beth's eyes. "Why are you here?"

"I know this place," Beth answered slowly. "Emma. I know this place. Just as if it belongs to me . . . or maybe I belong to it."

Willoughby pointed to the entryway. "The name over the transom reads, *McBride*."

"You must have been past this place dozens of times," Emma reminded her. "Why all of a sudden? Did you work here?"

"I – I don't know. Maybe . . . maybe because of the soldiers and the destruction. I . . . I don't know why. But, somehow, I know something about this place."

Beth did a pivot and allowed her skirt to flair out, slightly showing the edge of her bloomers beneath the hem.

"Emma." Beth turned to Emma and sobbed on her shoulder. "I feel something strange about all this."

"What, Beth?"

"Like . . ." she sobbed, "Like I am a *McBride*."

****

The following days were hard for Beth to understand, and harder yet for Emma to help her. Emma left a week from the following Sunday morning and visited the McBride mansion set up on a knoll overlooking Richmond. A steel gate guarded the mansion from intruders.

The matron of the manor, Mrs. Sarah McBride had been expecting the visit; Emma had recently contacted Mrs. Mc Bride by way of their servants.

Barnabas greeted Simon at the door. Compared to Simon, Barnabas was two to three inches taller, about the same age and build; but slightly balding with gray temples. He escorted Emma into the mansion where she was greeted by a small aged woman of fine stature as she stepped down the stairwell to the foyer.

"Mrs. Paterson?" she addressed Emma. With Emma's nod, she motioned for her to walk with her into her parlor set off to the north side of the entrance. Once inside, Barnabas closed the doors and stood inside while the house Negro, Lulu Belle prepared to serve tea to the ladies.

Emma was escorted to a lavish over-stuffed chair as Mrs. McBride sat on a divan opposite her.

"It's a lovely home you have here, Mrs. McBride," Emma observed, looking around the room.

"Thank you, Mrs. Paterson. And you too are a fine looking woman."

During the serving of tea set by Lulu Belle, Mrs. McBride asked about Beth. The talk lasted through the Sunday afternoon hour as Emma brought Mrs. McBride up to date with the mysterious Beth.

"That is Ginny's photograph on the piano," Mrs. McBride pointed out to Emma.

Emma rose and went to the piano and took a hold of the photo and looked at a lovely freckled-face youngster dressed in a full rich debonair gown of the age. She recognized the face as that of Beth.

"Oh! Oh, my goodness!" She exclaimed and took the photo over to Mrs. McBride. "It's Beth!"

Emma returned home that day but did not mention right away her visit to the McBride mansion to Beth.

However Emma's conversation with Beth that evening and the next day brought out that she had stronger feelings that Beth was a McBride. She had a hard time keeping her thoughts to herself because she felt that anything at this juncture could cause a trauma to Beth and she knew she could not handle it by herself.

On the next night, Beth thought to herself. *I don't know who or anything about it, but I know . . . somehow, I know I am a McBride. I felt it the day I visited that burned out mill. I stood in the midst of the stench and smoke as if in a trance. As if someone was trying to talk with me*

Someone was trying to talk to Beth; Emma. She knocked on Beth's door and gently opened it when Beth answered. "Come on in."

"Beth, darling. I've something to discuss with you. May we talk?"

Beth sensed something serious in Emma's voice and softly answered, "Yes. Yes, of course."

Emma sat on the edge of Beth's bed and looked at the angel in front of her scantily clad in her night gown; her sheet covering her legs.

"I visited with Mrs. McBride the other day," she opened up to Beth with a slight smile.

"Mrs. McBride? And . . . and?"

"And I saw a photo of you as a young lady."

"Of me?" Beth sat straight up in bed with a delightful look on her face. "I'm a McBride?"

"It appears so, Beth," Emma answered with a tear streaming down her cheek. "You're a McBride. And . . ."

"And?"

"Your name is *Ginny.*"

Beth looked deep into Emma's brown eyes and repeated the name, "*Ginny.*"

CHAPTER 7

TWO MEN TO NACOGDOCHES

<u>25 April 1865</u>

At the same time, on the other side of the country, two troopers left their cavalry unit in Texas and rode towards Tennessee. The war was over and they were going home.

"There's no reason for us to surrender our sabers to the Yankees at this juncture, Steve," Matt said as they rode north east to Tennessee.

Matt was a young man in his twenties, topped six-four and weighed in below two-hundred pounds. He had wavy, dark brown hair, blue eyes and a smile that startled many a lady.

Steve was at six feet, brown eyes and sandy hair. He was always one step behind Matt, trying to figure out his best friend, but never succeeding.

"You've got thet right, friend," Steve answered. "Not to mention our hides. Think what they could've done to us, being Terry's Texas Rangers.

"Don't mind if we stop off at Brenda's?" Steve grinned. "Nacogdoches is on the way."

Matt returned the smile and nodded. "I look forward to a hot apple pie any day, friend."

"Thet's right. She promised you one, huh?"

The two men rode together as one, their youth hard-beaten by the Civil War that had lasted over a hundred years, but neither man was bitter; just glad that it was over and they were on their way home. Home, an ethereal place far back in the recesses of their minds where a female friend and sister watched anxiously on the porch of a small farm while the wind danced fancifully around her, kicking up dust along the dry road that stretched for miles into the horizon. The easy gait through part of Texas was peaceful and uneventful, and both men enjoyed it after the many battles they had fought.

The aroma of an apple pie sweetened the crisp morning air as it wafted gently in the breeze. A letter dangled from her hands, as she held tight to her calico apron. In the note, the words simply read, "I'm bringing him home, sis. The war's over." When Brenda Andrews read the letter from her brother Steve, her heart raced for time, for she took it to mean that Matt Jorgensen would be coming with him.

Matt and Steve stopped off at a saloon in the town of Nacogdoches to unwind from the war. It was Easter Sunday week, 1865. It did not prevent them from loosening up and winding down with some old *Jim Beam*.

When they reached a ridge the next day, each suffering through a monumental headache, they came across a small unpretentious piece of land. Steve pointed excitedly towards the house centered on it and exclaimed, "That's our farm."

"Yeah," Matt said, looking out at the farm. "I remember."

As the riders' shadows appeared through the dawning light, Brenda recognized the features and she knew right away that the two men in her life were finally home. Brenda had been a dedicated school marm in her early twenties at the beginning of the war, barely over five feet with blue eyes and light brown hair.

The men rode wearily with their heads down as if the ride had been long and tedious. One raised his head and smiled. It was Steve.

Quickly, she ran back to the house, whisked through the door and into her bedroom where she dressed and primped herself up to meet her guests.

Steve rode up to the front porch and called out, "Sis!" Matt sauntered his horse up to the house and dismounted.

Bucky went into a fast spin and began her barking and yelping, and ran towards a familiar voice.

"Brenda!" Steve called again.

Brenda walked slowly to the front room and waited breathlessly in the middle of the room as she saw the front door open and Steve bounding in.

She ran into his arms, hugged him and looked into his smiling face. Then she broke from his grip and looked behind him to see if Matt was there.

"He's outside? She asked as she pushed past Steve and rushed out the door to the porch.

Sitting on the porch swing, digging into the apple pie with his fingers was Matt. He looked up at her and smiled with applesauce all over his lips.

"I see you made two," he noted through dreary eyes.

In the meantime, Steve's eyes had caught the sight of a baby crib in the front room. His eyes widened for he had not heard about Brenda having a baby. He took his hat and threw it on the hook by the door and then walked over to the crib and curiously touched it.

Matt and Brenda entered the room with their arms around each other, but stopped short at the sight of the crib. Matt's arm dropped from around Brenda.

"A crib?" was all Matt could utter as he stood stunned. "Whose?" He thought for the moment about the time when Brenda had visited him in Rome, Georgia.

Brenda stood at the door and then slowly walked over to the crib where she picked up a small blanket and held it to her bosom. She turned and looked at Steve and then into Matt's eyes for what seemed an eternity, hoping to choose the right words.

Then she lightly spoke. "I'm married, Matt." She watched Matt's face turn ashen. "I have a son."

She sat down in a chair, caressed the blanket tenderly, and told the story to the two men. Matt stood while Steve sat on the wooden bench by the door.

"I left you in Rome, Georgia. I was in love with you, Matt. But – but it seemed that you weren't in love with me. I gave myself to you and it seemed I received nothing in return, not even a letter, to let me know how you were doing...nothing. It seemed in Steve's letters that Ginny was always on your mind. And then not long after coming home from Georgia, one day . . .'"

****

On that day, dew had lifted on the leaf-trodden road leading up to Brenda's house as the sun split her rays between the cottonwoods and streaked across the rolling hillside cutting open the curtains hanging in the kitchen window. The sound of slow-moving hoof beats broke the silence of the air and echoed against the door of the lonely home, awakening her owner.

"Keep quiet, Bucky," Brenda said softly as she bent lowly to shush him. "I 'spect they might be friendly."

Brenda threw on a light robe, grabbed the rifle that she had leaned against the bedpost, opened the front door and looked out into the woods as her pointed-ear, yelping mongrel sided her. The sounds kept coming and she knew them too well for they were those of horses moving towards her. She had heard them fearfully enough through the war, waiting to see whether the riders wore gray or blue; she was partial to the color of gray. She walked down the wagon-wheel rutted road as the rooster crowed to meet the dawn and the chickens flapped their feathers. Her cow sauntered toward the railed fence and followed Brenda with her eyes while chewing on her cud.

When the riders' shadows appeared through the dawning light, Brenda's countenance fell as she discovered the men were not the ones she had expected. Both men wore the gray Rebel uniform, but had scraggy beards and were very unkempt, saddle-worn, hungry and bone dry. Even with the few yards between them they smelled like they had been in their saddles for the entire war. Brenda covered her mouth and nose and turned her head.

One of the men looked at Brenda and asked, "Got any food?" His body was limp in the saddle as if he were glued to it. The other man eked out a small grin, exposing his yellowed teeth, those few that had remained.

Brenda turned back to the men and took her hand away from her mouth, realizing the need at hand for two suffering soldiers. She grabbed hold of the reins and led the one to her house while the other followed. Bucky yelped and bit at the hooves of the horses as if in total dislike for the muddied gaunt animals.

The two soldiers eyed one another and looked over the farm and landscape around them. As Brenda stopped the horse at the trough, she suggested to its rider, "Slide off and you can clean up here. I've got biscuits on the stove. I'll run in and fry some eggs."

The rider reached down and grabbed Brenda's shoulder as he fell from his saddle.

She winced from his grip and ran to the house as the other rider tumbled out of his saddle.

Neither man was well enough to chase her so they remained for the moment on the ground near the trough. One looked up into the sky and lazily watched the clouds form together. "Damn. Gonna storm soon, Skinny."

Skinny laid face down in the dirt around the trough. He raised himself up, threw an arm into the trough and pulled himself up to its edge where he doused his face and watched the filth muddy up the water. "Wash up, Clem. We gonna eat."

Clem, the shortest of the pair, raised himself up and crawled over to the trough where he threw himself in, clothes and all. He grabbed hold of Skinny's dirty yellow hair and pulled him down into the water, which was getting murkier by the minute. The two wrestled until they were both spit tired and fell out of the trough. The water did little good for cleaning them, but the clothes only seemed to get tougher as it soaked into the dirt. The men seemed to know every cuss word in the book as they rolled around the dirt together pulling at each other's torn and tattered uniform until the two men finally fell away from each other and passed out.

Brenda watched the pair for several minutes and finally saw her chance to walk back outside. She grabbed her rifle and walked cautiously while Bucky slowly sneaked up on the pair. Realizing that they were of no present danger to her, Benda took a bar of soap and a scrub brush from the nearby barn and tossed it at them. Neither man budged. She dipped a bucket of water from the trough and threw it on the two men in turn, who only sniffed and snorted. She sat down on a tree stump, placed the rifle across her lap and watched the pair sleep.

"You know something, Bucky. These men are deserters. They're not real soldiers. I can tell. Real soldiers keep clean. Why, their pistols are filthy and rusty even. But, they're human beings just the same and we've got to treat them as such. Yep. But we better be watchin' our backs, if you get my drift." Bucky sat beside Brenda, looking back and forth from her mistress toward the two men with understanding eyes, altering between a whimper and a low growl.

Brenda rose up and walked back to the house. Leaving the rifle in the house, she came back with a pan of biscuits and gravy and laid them on the stump beside the men. She returned to the house and came back out with two tin cups and a pot of coffee. She watched the men lay there, neither of them moving. She took her time walking back to the house, picked up her rifle, and, poking its barrel into the sky, let the burst of two bullets echo off the barn and dissipate across the farmland.

The sounds stirred the men as they jumped into each other's arms where they realized their situation and backed away from each other rather sheepishly. They looked around and saw Brenda holding the smoking rifle.

"Your food is on the stump," she said, aiming the rifle in their direction. "Eat up and then get outta here!"

****

When Brenda finished her story, she rose, placed the blanket back inside the crib, turned and looked into the faces of Matt and Steve sitting as if in a trance, absorbing what they had just heard.

Matt turned and buried his fist into a nearby post, causing skin to peel back and bleed. "Damn!" He rubbed his hand and turned back to Brenda. "Go on. Finish it. Which one did you marry?"

Brenda looked deeply into Matt's seemingly hurt eyes and continued. "They didn't leave right away. They stayed a few days, got up on their feet and had an argument. Quite a doozy, too!"

"Over you, I bet!" Matt said in disgust as he leaned against the wall, wiping his hand with his neckerchief.

"Yes," Brenda answered. "One wanted to have his way with me, but the younger one, Clem, stopped him. Both men rode away."

"But one of them . . . ?" Matt asked, haltingly.

"Clem came back a few months later. I didn't recognize him. He had returned to his unit and was now cleaned up."

"And the baby?"

Steve rose and walked back towards Brenda. "If he's about two years old with blonde hair, he's sitting a horse out here."

Brenda ran to the door and Matt slowly followed, moving past Steve. There sat Clem with a baby sitting in front of him holding onto the saddle horn.

"Matt, Steve," Brenda said as she removed the baby from the saddle. "This is Junior." Brenda smiled at Steve. "My son."

Steve walked over to Brenda and reached out for the boy. He tenderly held the boy at arms length, as if to examine him and allow his mind to grasp what he was hearing. "Oh, my gosh," was all Steve could say. "Huh. I'm an uncle!"

"This is my husband," Brenda continued. "Clem Conley." She glanced toward Clem and said, "Clem, this is my brother, Steve and a good friend, Matt."

Matt looked up at a clean-cut gentleman with a neatly trimmed beard, nothing like the way Brenda had earlier described him. He was impressed but still dismayed with the sudden news that he had been jilted; not that he had any intentions of marrying Brenda, but the fact that she was married and already a mother somewhat stunned him.

"Hello. I'm Matt Jorgensen." Then he noticed the stripe on Clem's trousers. "A Yankee!"

"7th Cavalry, Tennessee," Conley answered. Corporal Clement Jonathon Conley."

Matt looked at Clem and after a few silent moments, he broke and greeted him, "Clem," with a nod and stepped back onto the porch.

On the next day, Matt walked out with Brenda and Junior to greet the postman at the edge of the road. She yelled back at Steve, "You got some mail. A letter for you, Brother . . . From Nashville."

"Nothing for me," Matt gestured, taking a chaw of tobacco.

Steve ran down to the three-some and retrieved the mail from Brenda. "Hey, Junior," he addressed the baby, taking a hold of his hand. "It's to both of us," Steve answered, pulling his finger away from Junior.

"Both of us?"

"Yep. It's from Chaplain Bunting."

It still took Matt and Steve time to realize that the War was really over. Sharing this moment together was like mail call with them.

"Thet's right," Matt realized. "He's a pastor at some church in Nashville."

"Yep. A Presbyterian church, it says here," Steve read. "Good news about Johnston and Wharton, too."

"Wull, what's he got to say?" Matt asked, excitedly.

"He says that both Generals Albert Sidney Johnston and John Austin Wharton were re-entered in the Texas State Cemetery, Houston, Texas. Now ain't thet something. I'd say the monument was adequately placed.

"Listen to this. *I received word from Jeff Davis. He was pleased about our parade. He told me to tell you that you're a man of your word.*

Boys, I don't know how it will turn out, but our Jeff Davis was indicted for treason against the United States government. Word has it that he entered Fort Monroe, Virginia just this week for his sentence.

He continued reading. *On the lighter side. I found out that, our General Tom Harrison did get his red badge of courage at Johnsonville, North Carolina. He gave up aspiring for the Governor's seat. But I hear he's running for the district judge position in Waco.*

Steve continued to read. *Well, that's it from me for now. Write when you can or drop by when you're in the neighborhood.*

Bob

Matt let out a laugh that startled the nearby horses, and Steve joined in. "That's it," Steve concluded, folding the letter and putting it back in his shirt pocket. He took out his tobacco and joined Matt in a chewing break.

Matt and Steve enjoyed the next few days with Brenda and got acquainted with Clem Conley and a baby named, Junior. After learning about Conley's courtship with Brenda once he returned as a soldier, Matt showed his appreciation for the couple's marriage. Steve informed Matt of the work done to the farm from the last time he saw it. They learned of Conley's handy work and determination as he welcomed the role of husband and father, settling down in Texas amid men who fought his kind a few months prior.

Steve had seen the change for the good in his old home place. Brenda and Clem were making it look even better than it did in his youth. Clem had already taken up full time farming and they were already planting crops in a garden and he'd even heard Brenda giggle at Clem's tease of the possibility of having another baby.

It was Easter. He left Matt and, with Brenda, walked on the knoll toward the east of the back forty and laid flowers of their mother's grave.

Then later Matt and Steve stood on the porch and waved to the couple as they left for church just over the hill.

"Wull," Matt started in as he mounted Skeeter, "you goin' with me, friend?"

"Where we headed, pal?" Steve asked, as he hurdled the porch rail and untied his horse. He knew Matt well enough to have already sensed the restlessness creeping upon him and knew they'd soon be heading somewhere.

"Into town for starters," Matt replied. "Get muhself drunk. Reckon I deserve it. Then off to find Ginny."

"Not gonna tell Brenda?"

"Done told her." Matt pulled the brim of his hat down and said, "Don't know about you, but I'm riding."

"Whoa up a bit." Steve took a gulp as he watched Matt spur his horse back down the hillside.

The wind carried his voice across the plains and dissipated into thin air without Matt ever looking back to answer it.

Steve mounted his steed and loped behind Matt. He yelled, "What more do we know about Ginny?"

Matt reined up, looked behind and answered him. "She's a ghost right now, Steve. Jest a ghost. But I'm gonna find her. You comin' or not?"

"Nashville?" Steve asked, spurring his horse to catch up with Matt. "To see Bunting?"

"Nope! Like I done told ya. To town to get drunk."

"I knowed what you told me, but you didn't tell me where we're goin' after we get drunk."

Matt rode ahead and said to himself, "To the McBride Plantation."

Steve faintly caught what Matt had said and repeated it, "Thet's what I said. To see Bunting." He realized what he said, and then belted out, "The McBride Plantation?"

"Yep. Just a short ride. Don't need to see Bob just yet. He just got a church in Nashville. Too soon."

Steve joined up with Matt and the two of them rode off that Easter morning. The curious thing was what Steve had bottled up deep inside himself. He thought back to that night in Rome, Georgia when Brenda came to visit him and Matt, and then spent the night with Matt. He thought about the possibility of Junior being Matt's son, and not Clem's.

And now, Steve had a suspicion that was burning inside him and he wanted to talk to someone, but had no one to talk with, for he had seen the happiness in his sister's face and kept the thought to himself. *As long as she's happy; so am I.*

As if he could read Steve's thoughts, Matt looked back towards Nacogdoches, smiled and said, "Junior." They rode on to Tennessee.

CHAPTER 8

JESSE, FRANK, AND COLE

2 May 1865

While Matt and Steve headed further east in their pursuit to find Ginny, another small group of soldiers clustered together in Missouri. With the Civil War over, soldiers on both sides were mustered out of service. Some gave up their arms. Some quit without surrendering and rode back home. Matt and Steve were two who felt no need to be officially mustered out when all they had to do was to ride away.

Since there was no general amnesty for guerillas, some, like William Quantrill and Jesse James chose to fight to the end even if it meant death. Quantrill was killed in Kentucky. Jesse was wounded in Missouri.

"Hold it, mister!" the Union soldier yelled at the three running Confederate soldiers who attempted to escape their arrest. One man, Archie Clements called *Little Arch,* barely twenty was short and stocky, but could outrun anyone firing at him. The other one was a muscular man with dirty, sandy hair covered with as dirty a wide-brim hat. He was Clell Miller. He was also in his early twenties. The third man was an eighteen-year old Jesse James; medium height, brown hair and hatless. The men figured that some how they could outrun their flight from being mustered out by Union soldiers.

But when Jesse heard the hammer cock on the soldier's Navy, he stopped and, with his arms raised and still holding his .38 in his hand, he turned and faced the soldier.

"Drop your gun or I'll shoot cha!" the soldier barked at the nervous Jesse. The other two men with Jesse fired back at the Union soldiers. One Union soldier did not wait for Jesse to drop his gun, but instead, out of fear of losing all three, openly fired at Jesse, hitting him once in the chest.

"Cheeze!" Little Arch yelled out as he saw Jesse fall. Both he and Clell continued to fire upon the Union soldiers who in turn retreated in haste to escape the flying bullets. Clell picked the bleeding Jesse up in his arms and ran with him through the bushes as they made their way to safety.

"Keep still, Jesse," Clell whispered as they rested on the other side of some down logs and inside some bushes. He held a rifle and pistol aimed through the bushes and waited to see if the Union soldiers had pursued them. After a few tense moments of silence, they breathed a sigh of relief.

"D'ya think they're gone?" Little Arch asked in a whisper as they kept their posed position in the wet bushes.

Clell opened Jesse's shirt and, examining the wound, pressed his dirty bandana into the hole. After a while, he answered, "Makes no matter. We've gotta get Jesse safely outta here."

"How bad is he hurt?" Little Arch asked as helped carry Jesse further through the woods.

"Real bad. The bullet went straight into his chest, and I ain't gettin' the bleedin' to stop none. Well, maybe some, I reckon."

It was a great while until they found a house where they laid Jesse up in safety. The owners were an elderly man and his wife; confederate sympathizers.

"Where's the nearest doc, mister?" Clell asked as he looked down upon a weakened Jesse.

"Quite a ways off," the owner answered. "Let me have a look see."

He brought the lantern for Clell to hold while he opened Jesse's shirt. "You're a lucky man, son," he said, wiping the dried blood away for a better look at the wound. "You've got a busted rib and the bullet is lying right . . . there." He looked around for his wife and told her, "Heat up the knife, deary. We gotta help this man."

The flattened bullet was impregnated in between the broken rib and had stopped short of hitting any vital organ.

"Is he going to be ok?" Clell asked, holding another lantern he had taken from a table while Little Arch held another close by.

"I'm no doctor, but the bleeding has stopped and all I can do now is bandage him up so that he can heal. How good it will hold, I don't know.

"What about moving him?" Little Arch asked.

"If you two will ride in the back with him, I'll take him to Kansas City in the wagon."

"He's got folk north of Kansas City," Clell said, looking sadly down on the unconscious Jesse. "We can take him there."

"What if the soldiers come, Clell?" Little Arch asked, nervously.

"You're right. We've gotta get out of here, mister."

"You're safe for the night, son," the owner answered. "I don't think anyone will come on this side of the valley. How you men made it this far with him in his condition is a miracle."

"Then we'll stay 'til daylight," Clell answered as he looked around for a place to sit down. Little Arch sat with him and shortly both men were asleep while the owner and his wife attended to Jesse's care.

"What do you plan on doing with the youngster, John?" his wife asked, turning the wicks down in the lanterns.

"They're good men, Martha," John answered. He was a well-built man from farming his 160 acres by himself for forty years. Martha was a small, charming woman with dark hair pinned back into a neat little coil at the back of her head.. "He's got some family just north of Kansas City. We can get a start in the morning. God willing, and the Yankee soldiers don't catch up with us, we'll get to see Dr. Lankford tomorrow evening."

"You'll get him to see the boy? Is he up to traveling?"

"These two men can help keep him still for the trip. It's his only hope. Yeah. I'll have to get Doc to see him. I just have ta."

Before the sun was up the next morning, Jesse's two friends took what food Martha had fixed for them and, with John, prepared to head out with Jesse in back of the wagon..

"We're headed towards Kansas City," John reminded them.

"Yep," Little Arch agreed.

"So you've got a gal outside Kansas City, Jesse?" John remarked as he helped Little Arch and Clell carry him on the bedroll-stretcher Martha had rigged up. They placed him gently into the straw-strewn bed of the wagon.

"The boys told you? Yep," Jesse answered in a strained voice as he eased into the hay. "Cousin of mine. Cute as apple pie."

"Well, talkin' about pie," John said. "Martha has some fixin's for us." He gave Martha a kiss and then climbed up into the driver seat and took hold of the reins. "We'll ride slow and easy, Martha. It'll take us a while, the way I see it. I'll be returnin' to ya most likely tomorra'. Best keep that rifle handy, and you might even wander up to your sister's for a visit."

"I'll be a waitin', John. You best be takin' good care of yourself as well." Then she looked over at Jesse and added, "You sleep as much as you can, son. And you boys keep him quiet."

The slow bumpy wagon ride took them to north of Kansas City, Missouri close to Jesse's home town in Clay County.

"That's it," Little Arch yelled out as they neared a two-story house. "Zee's dad's boarding house. He'll be ok now, John."

Zee was a young lady, two years Jesse's junior and his first cousin. The two grew up together and were in love from the time they first learned how to kiss.

As John brought the wagon to a halt, Zee and her father and others were there to meet them.

John looked at Zee and back at Jesse. "You're right, son," he said. "Cute as apple pie."

Jesse smiled weakly.

Dr. Lankford came by that same day and looked in on Jesse's condition. He was just over five feet tall, neatly dressed with a suit jacket over his arm and a worn hat on his hat. He was the country doctor.

After examining Jesse, Doc told Zee and the rest of the men, "He's plumb lucky to have friends like you. I can tell he hasn't eaten in days. He has lost a lot of blood, and had you not got him here in time, he would have died."

"We did what we had to do, Doc," Clell informed him.

"Will he live?" Little Arch asked, watching Zee wipe Jesse's forehead with a soaked towel.

"He'll live," Zee answered without looking up. "He'll live 'cause he's m'man."

At times, Jesse still coughed up a little blood. Even Zee almost gave up hope that he'd make it.

"Jesse, darlin'," Zee said as she fluffed up his pillow and wiped his forehead with a damp cloth. "Doc is here."

Doc Lankford entered the room and saw the blood in the bucket next to Jesse's bed. He immediately took the bandages off and examined Jesse's chest. "Good job. You do it, John?"

"Best I could. The bullet's still in there."

"Yep. Yep. I can see it. I think I can get it. Hand me my forceps, John. And someone keep him sedated as much as possible."

"He's full of whiskey, Doc," John informed him.

It took several sweaty minutes until the sound of the bullet hitting the tin pan gave relief to those around the table.

"Got it!" Doc said with a smile that stretched his moustache another inch across his face. He put the forceps down and took up his needle and thread.

He looked down at Jesse's face and watched his eyes move from side to side. "I'm gonna to sew you up, lad."

After he finished with Jesse, he washed his hands in a basin and looked over at Zee.

"Sit for a spell, Doc. I've got supper."

"Wasn't thinking of leaving, Little Lady," Doc answered as he sat at the small kitchen table.

Doc stayed with Jesse a while longer until he felt he was out of the woods. When he saw Jesse open his eyes, he said, "You're a sick man, Jesse. More than you know."

"What can we do, Doc?" Zee asked, twisting her fingers.

"Keep him in bed. Little movement. Almost none at all."

"Almost none, Jesse," Doc answered, checking Jesse's temperature and pulse beat. He smiled and added, "You're fine, Jesse. You'll make it." Then he looked over at Zee and said, "Keep him warm in these cool nights and he'll be ok."

She smiled and answered, "I know how to keep him warm."

Jesse's eyes lit up and the Doc packed his bag and left.

"I love you, Jesse," Zee said as she went back to the wood-burning stove and put a pot of soup on.

Summer was around the corner and Doc kept a daily check on Jesse throughout ensuing weeks. And then one day, he found Jesse on the porch, enjoying the fresh healing air that seemed to come only from Missouri. It was a good day for Jesse, for the fresh warm spring air was drying out his lungs. He yearned for the day that he could ride again.

CHAPTER 9

DOC COMES HOME

<u>12 May 1865</u>

A fine figure of a man walked up to the Paterson Estate and stopped short of the front door. He was a tall man in stature, appeared old in features, yet carried himself well as a gentleman. He turned and viewed the burnt-out city from the hillside of the manor.

Upon seeing him at the door, Simon opened it and waited for him to turn towards him. When the tall man did turn, Simon asked, "Yes, sir. Is there sumpthin' I can help you wif?" And then just as quickly, recognizing who it was, he said as he opened the door wider for the man to enter, "Why, Mr. Doctor, sir." A smile sprang to the black man's face and he reached to draw the man of the house inside, "It's so good to have you back at home, suh. Come! Come inside, suh! Come inside!"

Emma saw the man from her window, gasped and ran down the stairs. "Henry! Henry!" She cried, almost loosing her dignity as she skipped down the stairs.

Simon stepped aside to let her greet the doctor.

Henry doffed his hat, placed it on the hat rack next to the door. He swept Emma up into his arms and off the ground. "Emma, darling," he whispered, kissed her gently and held her in a fond embrace.

Beth had followed Emma down the spiral staircase and to the door to fill her curiosity as to who was there. When she saw the Confederate uniform from behind, she knew it had to be the doctor who had saved her life.

The captain saw Beth from an angle and smiled at her. "Beth!"

"Yep. It's me, Captain," she replied with a smile.

"It just occurred to me that it's been a few years since I've seen you."

"Is she the same as she was when you first saw her?" Emma asked, wondering what Henry was thinking.

"No. No, she's not. She's a refined lady. A very dignified lady.' He looked at Beth and said, "I'm sorry. I just hadn't pictured you this way before." He turned back to Emma. "She was tough, and skinny. She spoke, well . . ."

"Yes, very vulgar. But look at you now."

Emma turned her attention back to Henry, took him by the hand and led him deeper into the house. "Oh, Henry, it's so . . . so good to see you. Let's not dally. Come on in. We've got lots to do. Lots to talk about. Simon. Simon, fetch his things and bring them into the master suite."

Obeying, Simon quickly walked to the carriage which was waiting at the end of the steps where he was met by another black servant lifting a couple of bags from the back of the carriage.

The captain put his arms around Emma and walked into the house, staring at Beth most of the time. "Is she . . .?" he asked with a smile.

"We'll talk later, honey," Emma came back smartly. "Oh, Henry. We've got so much to talk about. And, yes, Beth is recovering. Slowly, but she's recovering."

Later that evening, after a full meal and time to be alone together, Emma and Doc sat and convened in the parlor.

"Do you know who she thinks she is? A McBride."

"A McBride? The textile company? Well, hot ziggity. We're onto something. This means . . ."

The next morning came like a river after a storm, with the sun beaming through the porticos of the house. The three people were up and sitting at a table on the veranda, having breakfast together.

"What we talked about last night?" Beth asked, smiling from ear to ear over the sight of the captain. She showed her appreciation for his saving her life simply by the radiance in her appearance. And all of it exposed her excitement that he had returned home safely. "What does it all mean, Doc?"

"Who are you, Beth?" Doc asked, smiling as he sipped his coffee from a saucer.

Beth drank her tea slowly, looked over the brim of her cup at the Doc, and then at Emma who was sitting on the edge of her seat, beaming with curiosity. "Well," she started in. "Well, I'm still Beth."

"She won't tell me who she thinks she is, Henry," Emma sided in. "Maybe she'll tell you."

"What do you know, Beth?" he asked, as he started to light up a pipe he had filled with tobacco earlier.

"Let me light that for you, Doc," Beth came back. She knew she should not call him by his first name, although the two of them had been on a first-name basis from the hospital camp where he attended to her during the war. And she tired of calling him *Doc* all the time. Standing up, she took the match and struck it against a wooden post. She lit his pipe and watched him puff away to get it started, and smiled. "What do I call you, now? *Doctor? Doc? Mr. Paterson?* Is *Captain* all right? Oh, no." Looking at his epaulettes, she corrected herself. "You're a major, now." She turned completely around and jokingly asked in a whisper only Doc could hear with her finger to her lips, "Or should I call you Henry? ?"Doc smiled, looked at Emma and said nary a word.

"Call him *the Major,* Honey, until he stops answering to it, of course," Emma returned.

Over the period of several weeks, after he had hung out his *M. D.* shingle to set up practicing medicine once more, Doctor Paterson felt more and more like a guardian to Beth. He attributed his new feelings to the war, aging him prematurely. And perhaps to Emma's accepting her as an adopted daughter.

His love for Emma strengthened every day, feeling that she knew she did not have to compete with Beth for his affection any longer. He was back home!

Emma knew he was her man because she kept one step ahead of Beth, in dress, stature, and in the bedroom, the one place that Beth had never even thought to venture. She knew she had nothing to fear, except the fear that she would eventually lose Beth. Beth had become the daughter they never had.

Walking to the edge of the garden one quiet morning, Beth turned and swirled her loose dress in a carefree fashion, and smiled. Henry and Emma came out and sat on the veranda and watched her.

Seeing them, Beth said, "I know I belong here, Emma, Major." Then she turned away and looked towards Richmond's scarred face. "They're gone, Major."

"The McBrides?" he asked, crossing his legs while he packed his pipe.

"The McBrides are gone." She turned and folded her arms in front of her like she was fighting off a chill in the air. "Some at the mill. Some in the War. Some by disease. Some by old age, I reckon."

"We did a little snooping once we found out who she might be," Emma added. "It seems that I've known her grandmother for several years. She lives in the McBride estate up on the hill, east of town." A quiet came over the threesome as Penny filled their cups with tea. Emma gently took a sip and seemed to ponder what she was saying.

Laying his pipe down, Henry rose and walked over to Beth and took hold of her hand.

"I'm all right, Major," Beth assured him, putting her hands to her face. "It seems I can't cry, for I don't know actually what to cry about, or whom to cry for."

He noticed her grammar was different than that which she had the day he met her some four years before, and her appearance in her new surroundings and her mannerisms were delighting him.

"Stop staring at Beth like that, Mr. Paterson. She'll be alright. We've just got to let her figure things out for herself. She's waking up at her own pace," Emma warned him.

Beth broke away and ran to her room.

"She'll be back." Emma stood up and walked towards Henry.

Putting his arms around Emma, Henry said to her. "Emma, you have no idea what this girl went through."

"Oh yes I do," she retorted with a sly look on her face. "You've written me dozens of letters about her, and she herself has brought me up to date with her being shot by some blue boy.

"As you know," Emma said to Henry, using her right index finger to itemize the things she was saying, "she went to finishing school for ladies, as you suggested, and she's finished her law degree with our friend, Benjamin Stoddard Ewell, the president of William and Mary tutoring her. She's passed the bar and she's now an attorney."

"An attorney?" He walked away and turned back into Emma. "Fine! Fine!" Then he looked startled and asked again, "Why an attorney?"

"You suggested she select a career, darling. She did!"

"I suggested she should get married, too. Did she?"

"Well, no, she didn't. Not yet, any way. There is the matter of an eligible young man, which has been very scarce during the war.

"Now, it's up to you what you want to do next with her?"

"Oh? What do you mean?" he asked with an astonished look.

"I mean, are we going to keep her, send her back, or let her find out on her own just who in the world she is?"

Henry picked up his pipe and looked out beyond the walls of the estate towards the smoking hills of Richmond.

As she watched Henry, Emma continued, "Like I said. I visited Mrs. Sarah McBride and we talked for a good while. She showed me a photo of Beth as a young girl."

"Was it really Beth?"

"Yes. And her real name would be Virginia McBride. They call her *Ginny.*

"*Ginny?*" was all Henry could say for the moment.

"Ginny wants to see her grandmother. With your permission, I'll arrange it for sometime soon."

Henry rubbed his chin, looked at Emma and after a moment of silence said, "I don't see why not."

CHAPTER 10

VENGEANCE IS MINE

After an hour or so, Beth returned fully clad in her original black clothes that she wore when a Federal soldier felled her, still with the hole of a musket ball in the upper right shoulder from four years earlier. Strapped to her side was her Colt revolver, and she held her whip in her hand. Her hair was pushed back nside her hat.

She stood, framed in the doorway that led to the verandah as an avenger. She walked out to the edge of the garden and unfolded her whip with a loud whack.

As Henry stood up, Emma followed and felt his strong arms surround her shoulders. "Beth!" he exclaimed alarmingly. He could find no other words to say.

"Beth, Major?" she answered. "You asked me who I thought I was. This is who I am. Not Beth. But, Ginny. Ginny McBride."

She turned from the doorway and ran through the vestibule and out the front door, leaving it wide open for Henry and Emma to watch her.

"Simon!" Emma called out, loudly.

Simon was quick to answer as he came from the back of the house onto the veranda. "Yes, ma'am?"

"Get the buggy and follow her," Henry ordered, pushing him towards the front door. "Be sure she's all right."

Once Simon equipped the buggy, he trotted the horse a short distance behind Ginny as he followed her to the gate. Seeing him, she stopped and waited for him to catch up to her. Once he did, she stepped up to the carriage without his assistance and ordered him to drive on. "Back where we were the other day, Simon. The mill."

"Yes, ma'am," Simon replied and whipped the horse into a steady gait.

The bodies were no longer lined up along the walkway, and the place seemed less littered than before. The smell of smoke still filled the air with a black stench from the charred remains. The same three soldiers were outside the ruins, but the captain was nowhere around.

Ginny jumped from the carriage before Simon brought it to a halt. "Stay here, Simon!"

The soldiers saw her coming, but because of her attire, they did not easily recognize her. Once she was within a short distance of them, and eyeing Simon in the background, they began to piece together that it was the same young lady visiting them once more.

"Well, well, well," the tall, lanky soldier surmised as he walked towards her. "You came back after all."

"And without the mean schoolteacher," the other solder added, siding the lanky one.

The short, stout soldier pushed the other two aside and approached Beth with lusty eyes. "You're not the same gal you were the other day. What gives?"

Without saying a word, Beth let out her whip with a snap that cut across his chest, removing one of his brass buttons.

"Whooey!" the lanky one shouted and then started laughing. "Never saw it comin'."

"Thet's good," the other soldier agreed. "Thet was real good."

The stout soldier angrily bent over to retrieve the button when another snap from Beth's whip caught him in his buttocks, ripping open his trousers. He straightened up, checked his uniform from behind and then reached for his Army Colt revolver closed tight in its holster.

Beth recoiled the whip and let it sling out again, ripping at his hand. Blood squirted from the top of his hand and he quickly fell to the ground, cuddling his hand to stop it from bleeding and hurting.

The lanky soldier ran to Beth before she could recoil the whip another time, but she drew her revolver and shot his hat off. He stopped fast, turned to pick up his hat, and just as quick, straightened up and left his hat alone, remembering what had happened to his fellow soldier.

The third soldier reached for his revolver, but Beth had already uncoiled her whip again and snapped it around his neck. Jerking it, she brought the soldier down in a prostrate position, asking for mercy.

"You won't be getting any from me, you viper!" Beth shouted with grit teeth.

When the stout soldier rolled over to retrieve his revolver, Beth stomped on his wrist with her boot. She brought the handle of the whip down across his head, sending him to sleep.

The sound of crunching, burnt timbers on the ground alerted Beth to know that someone was slipping up on her from behind. Without any hesitation, she turned, and with her readied whip in the air, saw the captain. She let the whip rest in her hand.

"You expect to lick the whole U. S. Army, miss?" Captain Willoughby asked. Then, recognizing her from before, he doffed his hat, and smiled. "Well, I'll be a sock-eyed mule if it isn't that pretty little maid from the other day."

"My name's McBride," Beth returned.

"And, what in tarnation are you doing to my men, may I ask, Miss McBride?"

"You saw how they acted the other day!"

"Yes. And I can't say that I blame you for being angry. But right now, I'd say you've more than evened the score. Can we let it go at that?"

Simon slipped up on Willoughby to protect Beth, but waited for a sign from her. He recognized it when he saw her eyes tell him to do nothing.

"Who can I blame for killing these people?" Beth asked. Pulling her Colt, she cradled it in her hand while her whip remained uncoiled and dangling.

"Is that what's bothering you?" Willoughby asked, as he helped the stout soldier to stand. "Better keep your back away from her, son," he told him, showing the tear in his trousers and his red long-johns showing thru.

He then took Beth by the hand and turned towards Simon. "Could your man here drive us up the road a piece, Miss McBride?"

"Where would you take us?"

"I've got something to show you that might clear up a lot of your questions."

"Certainly. Climb in. Simon, drive us on."

The ride took quite awhile and Beth had no idea what was on Willoughby's mind, but she was grateful that he was taking an interest in helping her. Then she saw a sight she knew she would never forget. It was a stockade filled with Confederate soldiers, muddy, bloody, wounded, and sick. Some were still in good health, but they were the minority.

"These are your killers, Miss McBride," Willoughby told her.

She leaned to step out of the carriage when Willoughby urged her to sit back down. "Don't get out!" He gently pulled her back into the seat next to him while Simon steadied the horse. "Not my men. Oh, my men are a bit rowdy. No doubt about that, Miss McBride. But, like I told you, they hadn't seen a pretty woman in a long, long time. And, if I may be so bold as to say it, you are one heck of an attractive woman."

"These men?" she asked, disbelievingly as she looked at the prisoners in the stockade. "Why do you say these men are the killers? They are Confederate soldiers."

"I don't think any of it was intentional. They were raiding the arsenals and warehouses so that when we took over, we would have nothing to gain from them. That is to say, if we actually needed anything."

"But how did all those people in the mill get killed?"

"Winds, Miss McBride. The fires got out of control. Houses went up. Inns, too and of course, the mill. When we got here, people were beyond recognition; burned and lying on the grass as well as inside. The fire was that much of an incendiary."

Simon turned in his seat and faced Beth. "He's right, Miss Beth. I knows. I saw lots of it from the hillside. And I even went down to help some a da 'folks. Did some. Didn't others, Miss Beth."

Willoughby looked puzzled at Simon calling the girl next to him, *Beth*. "Beth? Why did your boy call you that?"

Beth removed her hat and let her hair hang loose around her shoulders. "Take me home, Simon."

On the way back to the mill, Beth was comforted by Willoughby's shoulder. "I'm sorry I had to show you that, miss."

Once back at the mill, Willoughby stepped out. And then he had to ask again, "Why did Simon call you Beth, if I may ask you again, Miss McBride?"

Beth looked away and ordered Simon to drive on.

Willoughby removed his hat, scratched his head and gave Beth a casual salute as he watched the carriage being driven back to the Paterson Manor.

When Beth walked into the hallway of the Paterson home, she could hear Emma and Henry still talking on the veranda. She caught the grist of their worrying about her leaving and was startled at what she was hearing. She stared at the two and broke into their conversation, embracing Emma.

"Oh, Emma. I could never leave you. Never."

She released her grip on Emma and turned towards the doctor. "Major. I'd like to visit my . . . Grand Mama."

Henry and Emma got quiet while they saw that Beth had returned. She was a little messed up, but they sort of expected that, seeing how set and determined she left a few hours before.

Henry looked for a sign from Simon who stood behind Beth. And, seeing Beth was not ready to talk, asked, "Simon. What happened?"

"Oh, she's okay, now, Mistah Doctor, suh," Simon answered, showing his large white teeth in a broad smile. "Yes, suh. She's done okay, now. She licked the tar outa coupla 'dem boys she ran into th'other day, Miss Emma," he reminded her. "You'se 'member dem?."

"You mean she went back to the mill?" Emma asked, sitting down.

"Yes, ma'am. And she took her whip and done what for on all three of 'em. Thet is, 'til the Capt'n came up and we un's went over into the Confederate stockade and saw 'dem mens thet done done thet to the mill people. You knows what I means, don't cha, Miss Emma?"

"I do, Simon," Henry returned, putting his arm around Beth,

"I'm okay, now," Beth assured him. "I'll change and come right back down."

When she returned, Henry and Emma went to her and escorted her to a chair in the parlor. Joining her on a sofa next to her, Henry began. "I'm just as anxious to visit your grandmother as I suspect you are, Beth. And, we're going to. But first, let me help bring you to the present"

"How?"

"That's my first question. How?" He looked at her, stroked his chin and searched for words. "OK?"

Beth smiled and nodded her approval.

"All right, then. From your own lips, tell me what you've been doing and thinking about these past four years?"

"I kind of think we went over that so many times already."

"Yes. Yes. But that was before you sort of woke up a bit from your amnesia." He looked at her shaking her head and quickly added, "I know . . . I know, you're just coming out of the woods, so to speak. And at this juncture, it is so important that we feed upon this as much and as quickly as possible so as not to lose what we have gained."

She nodded again.

Henry looked intently into Beth's eyes like he was studying her, and then asked, "What do we call you? I mean. Are you Beth or Ginny?"

Beth smiled and then said without hesitation, "Beth."

"Why not, *Ginny?*"

"Because, I'm not comfortable with you and Emma calling me by any other name other than *Beth*. So, for the time being, please fulfill my wishes and still call me *Beth*."

"For ever?"

"Well," Beth said with a slight grin, "for a while, anyway. Just until I can get used to hearing my real name, *Ginny* again."

"I have an acquaintance coming to the house. A colleague-friend of mine who is a psychiatrist. I think he can help put the pieces back together again. Can you tell us now how you feel about your past as much as you can? Maybe something will strike a familiar note and we can help you recover more. Or at least, be a bigger help to my colleague."

Beth's story seemed long and tedious to herself, but she told it again, trying to shorten it the best she could. When she found a place to stop, she took a cup from the table, poured herself some hot tea and sipped on it.

Henry and Emma listened, having been careful not to interrupt. And then Emma could hardly restrain herself. As she started to say something, Henry was quick to tell her, "Let her finish."

"But, Henry. It was I who helped her become an attorney."

"And I asked you then, and I'll ask you now, why? Why would she want to become an attorney? It just doesn't add up to me."

The two continued to talk while Beth watched the two pare off at each other like a ping-pong match without involving her. Finally, she quietly broke in, sipping her tea from her cup with a saucer under it and her right pinky up in the air. "Well, if one would really want to know what one would want to be, I suppose one should have asked one. Wouldn't one?" And she continued this kittenish attitude while the married couple continued their discussion about what should become of her.

Then, Emma froze her gaze at Henry, listened to Beth more intently and told Henry to, "Shut up. What are you saying, Beth, honey?"

Beth put her cup down, took her napkin and spotted her lips. "Why don't you ask me why I wanted to become an attorney?"

Emma saw that Beth was going to be all right. She looked and appeared to be her own self again. *Heavens,* she thought, *if she ever puts on that outfit again, I hope I never have to see it. It scared the blazes out of me.*

"Oh. Alright, Beth," Henry answered, "tell us."

"Yes, Beth," Emma agreed, not fully into the realm of the conversation, yet.

Beth rose from the table, walked to her spot at the edge of the garden, turned to the couple still sitting, and said slowly and distinctly, "Because I do not believe that there is a woman attorney as of yet, and I think I could make a pretty darn good one. There, I said it. And, I'll say this, too. I'm just as much a part of this family now as . . . as you are. And I don't think I'm ready to be put out to pasture. Not when I've got two of the best parents a girl could ask for."

Henry's thoughts of ever loving Beth as a sweetheart quickly dissipated after listening to her singling him out as a parent.

While Henry and Emma retired to the front room out of the chill of the evening air, Beth remained in the garden for her solitude. *Matt, my darling,* she thought to herself, looking up into the evening sky. *Matt! . . . That's your name!*

The moment of their meeting unfolded to her. *If only once more I could feel the excitement with you that we felt as we found each other on the bank of the Tennessee River that day. I can't explain it, darling. It was like the millions of stars that danced in the sky, or like the myriad of heartbeats that rhythmically blended into one.*

It was another notch in Ginny's psyche that was bringing her back to her reality of who she really was.

CHAPTER 11

A LOOK AT THE PAST

<u>2 June 1865</u>

On a warm spring morning, a portly gentleman who appeared to be in his sixties was received from his carriage by Simon and walked up the cobblestone path to the front door. He sported a well-trimmed moustache and goatee of silver, and wore a pair of pincers around his neck. He was dressed in a suit with vest and coat, a watch chain hung from his vest pocket with a time piece stuck inside the pocket, and a high top hat sat neatly on his head.

Simon opened the door and motioned for the man to enter, "Yes, suh. May I help you, suh?"

"My name is Doctor William F. Harris. I'm here to see Doctor Henry Paterson."

"Yes, suh. If'n ya'll will follow me, I'll let the master know you're heah."

Simon escorted him into the house as his son took care of the horse and carriage.

"If'n ya'll sit heah in the drawing room, I'll fetch the doctor," Simon suggested to the man and walked away towards the back of the house where he found Henry with Emma and Beth having a light dinner.

"A gentleman heah to see ya, suh," Simon reported to Henry, awaiting his reply.

"Yes. Yes. Thank you, Simon." He wiped his lips with his napkin and looked at the two ladies. He addressed Emma and Beth. "Ladies, if you'll please excuse me." He arose and went to greet the gentleman in the drawing room.

"Doctor Harris?" Henry addressed the gentleman as he opened the doors.

"Hello. Doctor Paterson?" the gentleman responded, rising to greet Henry.

"Thank you for coming, and please remain seated." Henry sat down in an overstuffed armchair opposite Harris. "Some of my colleagues recommended you to me. I'm happy you could come. Yes, I'm Doctor Paterson. Please, I'm Henry to my friends. You may call me that also, if you don't mind."

"Thank you, Henry. I am William. You said something about a young lady with amnesia."

"Yes. Yes. We're just finishing up dinner. Would you care for something?"

"No thanks."

Henry motioned for Simon to leave as he stood in the door frame awaiting further instructions. He then pulled two cigars from his vest pocket and offered one to Harris. "Cigar?"

"Yes, thank you," Harris replied and accepted the cigar. After receiving a light from Henry, he exhaled a puff of smoke that wafted away and gave the room the odor of men seemingly about to discuss an important issue together.

Henry looked at Harris, lit his cigar and smiled. "You are older than I expected you to be. That is, for a psychiatrist."

"I'm perhaps the oldest in the country," Harris responded with a gentle laugh and a smile across his lips.

"Then, I think I have found the right man in which to help me. I have an adopted daughter and she's a very attractive young woman."

Harris broadened his smile and then eyed Henry curiously.

"She was shot in the shoulder four years ago while I was serving in Tennessee, and I brought her back to health."

"And?"

"Well, she was all right when she came to, but then she rode off and later returned after developing a bad case of pneumonia. By the time I brought her back from near death, she seemed to have lost all remembrances."

"Amnesia?"

"Yes."

"Are you sure it's amnesia? A lot of my patients, who claimed amnesia, faked it for one reason or another. You know, amnesia is sometimes just a word people use to feign a sickness of identity."

"I'm sure," Henry agreed. "But I've worked with her from day one when she was wounded. I'm pretty sure she's not faking. However, I'll await your examination. That's why I called upon you."

"Well," Harris harrumphed and fiddled with the watch on his chain. "Yes. Yes. And now, I'd like to ask; how critical was the shoulder wound?"

"At the time, it seemed to be only a severe abrasion. But the incident knocked her to the ground where her head impacted the cold hard ground. This lead to a contusion, which bled."

"Not a concussion?"

"I thought it might be at first, but, after a thorough examination, I concluded she was out of the woods from a blood clot to the brain. I was prepared to go in if I had to, but she responded rather well to my superficial treatment as a simple head wound, and I decided surgery was unnecessary."

"A thorough examination, Henry?"

"As far as I could examine, with my limited equipment on the battlefield. I had to await her situation to play out before I could make any type of conclusion; if I may call it that."

"A head trauma, as you well know, Henry, is not so simple. Often times it can lead to other serious effects."

"Yes. I'm aware of that. But as I said, at the time, she responded quite nicely to my treatment."

"For how long?"

"A few days. A week. I forget. Then she decided to leave our detention and rode off on a cold morning without food and supplies. I don't know what got into her, but something did."

"Who shot her?"

Henry stood up, took a puff of the cigar and walked over to the fireplace. He turned and said, "One of our young recruits. He had just heard a story about some of our guys shooting at their first enemy, and I guess he thought this was his first. She rode up in an early morning mist and he mistook her for the enemy."

"A woman?"

"Well, she was sort of dressed up like a man."

"Uh, huh. Go on."

Henry knew that Harris was playing the *Devil's advocate*, and he was good at it. But he knew that Harris had to know everything about Beth to be able to help her. Even if it meant agitating him the way he seemed good at doing.

Henry continued. "Well, she returned to camp for supplies and that's when she fell into unconsciousness and became delirious with pneumonia."

"I can see why. As I said, no head trauma is simple. Had she had sufficient time to have recovered from both the shoulder and the head wounds, the chill might have developed into a slight case of pneumonia and you could have had a healthy patient."

"Yes. But, in your vernacular, it was a complicated case brought on by a serious head wound."

Henry took another puff, exhaled and said, "One more thing, Bill."

"Yes?"

"My wife recently visited Mrs. Sarah McBride up on the knoll. Beth has had an intuition that she was a member of the McBride family. Emma found out through a photo that she indeed was a McBride; Ginny McBride."

After moments of bringing Harris into the world of Ginny's as a McBride, Henry asked, "Would you like to meet her now?" He threw his cigar butt into the fireplace as he began to leave the room.

"Ginny McBride? I am anxious to meet her. Should I address her as *Ginny* or let her inform me as to whom she really is and call her *Beth?*"

Henry smiled and answered, "That's your call."

Harris stood up and waited for Henry as he left the room. "I'll be right back."

In a few moments, Henry came back though the doors with Beth on his arm. "Doctor Harris. This is Beth Paterson."

"Miss Paterson." Harris rose and bowed slightly as he addressed Beth. Taking her hand, he led her to another overstuffed chair beside the one that Henry had previously occupied. She sat down to face him. Henry reseated himself as Harris sat back down.

"Paterson?"

"Yes, Doctor Harris," Henry replied. "We gave her my grandmother's name as we did not know what to call her."

"I see. Miss Paterson. May I call you *Beth*?"

"I don't see why not," Beth replied, looking at him curiously and then eyeing Henry as if to ask, *What's going on?*

"Doctor Harris," Henry informed her, "He is the psychiatrist I mentioned earlier. I asked him to come and see if he could be of some help in finding out who you are."

Beth looked bewildered at Henry and, after a long while, saying nothing, looked with consternation at Harris, and stated, "I am Ginny McBride, but you may call me *Beth* while in this manor. That's simple, isn't it?" She smiled and blinked her bright eyes at Harris. "I thought it was." She looked at Henry again and asked directly, "May I be dismissed now, Major?" She stood up to go and Henry stood up with her.

"If you wish. I just thought we could try another route to help you some, darling." Henry removed his glasses and laid his cigar down in an empty ashtray.

Beth stood still for a moment and then stared at Harris. Without looking at Henry, she asked, "What does he want to do with me?"

Harris stood and answered her with his cigar tightly grit in his teeth, "Merely, at this time, to simply get to know you. Who you are, now. A little at a time." And then, removing his glasses and wiping them with his handkerchief, he said, "I'm sorry, Beth if I seem to come across a little rough with you. I hope you can understand. I want to find the cause of your dilemma. And to do so," he harrumphed again. I might have to be a little rough. It comes with the territory." He threw his cigar in the fireplace and said, "Smell things. Hate them."

Ginny smiled.

It took a little lawful thinking on Beth's part before she condescended to be analyzed by Harris alone without the presence of Henry in the drawing room; but she did. The time slipped by the next morning and another morning came for the two to spend time together. After a time, the visits became friendlier and Beth felt more at ease with his visits.

As they walked through the garden one warm fall morning, Beth looked very content with her appearance as a young lady dressed in a summer outfit, slight and very fit to her frame to show her feminine features. She no longer feared Harris or his questions but was rather free about talking out her emotions.

"How do you feel about your life right now, Beth?" Harris asked as he began his questioning. "Right this moment? This exact moment?"

Beth stopped walking, clasped her hands behind her back and looked up at the sky. "Happy! I suppose."

"Beyond being happy. Who are you, Beth? Who are you?"

Beth unclasped her hands, spun on her heels and spread out her arms. "Who am I? I'm a bird." She chuckled as she watched the flight of a bird overhead as she said it. Then she looked at the rows of flowers. "I'm a flower. A bud. I'm whatever God made me." Then she stopped and looked at Harris. "I'm Ginny. That's who I am."

The two resumed their walking and Harris kept asking questions, taking notes and listening to Beth expound on her life being *Ginny* and no one else.

"I'd like to expand our visits, Beth, if you will allow me."

"Why . . .Why of course. When?"

"Tomorrow. I'd like to do an experiment with you."

"It'll have to be the day after. I have a case in court tomorrow." Beth was enthused at his willingness to go further and looked forward to the experiment that Harris would perform.

When the day came, Harris met her in the south parlor where she noticed the drapes were pulled shut.

"Please, may we talk here?" he asked, suggesting a couch for her to lie on.

"If you like," she answered, sitting down on the divan.

"How'd your case in court go?" he asked.

"Fine. It was a business merger issue. A contract. I had already done the preliminaries. The court was simply a matter of procedure that involved the Judge's opinion."

"Good to hear." He smiled as if to lessen the tension. "Relax, Beth. I'm going to do a hypnotic experiment with you. Make yourself as comfortable as you can."

Beth looked into Harris' dark eyes and hesitated a moment. "A what?"

"Hypnosis. I want to put you to sleep. A simple sleep, where I can ask you some questions that your psyche might help reveal some answers.."

"I'm sure I'm not familiar with all this. Will it hurt?"

"Not at all, Beth. Not at all."

He asked her to lie back and relax and then proceeded to put her into a trance. The more she became susceptible to his suggestions, the deeper he found her willingness to go.

In a few moments she went back into time when she saw Matt about to be shot by a young Yankee soldier. She yelled out as before, "Matt! Watch out! Watch out, darling!"

She witnessed Matt's narrow escape from a bullet that apparently had his name on it.

****

Matt quickly rose to his feet, grabbed the reins and remounted his steed. He stopped another Yankee with his pistol, firing at the man's chest. And then the fight was over. Matt looked around as Steve joined up with him.

"I thought for sure you had bought it thet time, friend," Steve said. "I can't for sure tell ya, but that boy had your number notched on his handle. You were dead, Matt. You were dead."

Matt looked back at the field of battle, took off his hat and wiped his forehead. "I saw it comin', pal. There was nothin' I could do. I heard the pistol cock and I looked right into its barrel."

"How'd you get your horse to rear so fast?"

"I . . . I don't know. It was . . . like I didn't. I felt a cool breeze as it whisked by my face and the next thing I knew was a musketball missing me and I fell to the ground. I thought I was hit. But I wasn't. When I got back on my horse, another man came at me, but I was with pistol in hand and ready to shoot."

"I saw that. The rest ran."

"What about the boy that shot at me?" Matt asked, looking towards the area where he fell.

"That him getting up?" Steve saw a Yankee horse soldier climbing up the embankment, running towards a horse.

"Could be."

"Well, I've got him in my sight."

"No, Steve!" Matt yelled out. "Let him go. I was saved from his bullet. By what, I don't know. But something or someone saved me. Put the hammer down."

Steve complied, released the hammer and watched the boy run scarily across the field.

****

Beth sighed a breath of relief. Her eyelids showed the movement of her eyeballs as she seemed to remain in a world not of her own.

"Beth!" Harris called out sharply but tenderly. "Come back, Beth."

Beth opened her eyes and laid back down a moment longer, looked around and then sat up again.

"Where were you, Beth?" Harris asked, staring at her in stark amazement.

"I . . . I don't know. It seemed like I was in a battle."

"Your friend, Matt? You called out his name."

"Matt? Yes. Yes."

"What happened?

"I don't know."

"You don't remember?"

"I don't. It seemed like it happened but then it didn't."

"What happened?"

"It's this recurrent dream of mine. I seem to have saved Matt's life. I don't know."

"You've had this dream before?"

"Yes. Several times, it seems. But . . . who is he?"

"That might be a key to finding out who you are, Miss Paterson."

With that, the session was closed.

CHAPTER 12

BACK TO THE PLANTATION

<u>3 June 1865</u>

The ride from Nacogdoches, Texas to Memphis, Tennessee was slow and almost boring for two inebriated ex-Confederate soldiers, weary of fighting but glad the war was over. How to come down from battles that caused the adrenalin to run fast and the blood to run hot was not easy. Few words were said over the campfire at night while the bottle was passed, and sometimes less was said on the trail. All that was in the mind of Matt Jorgensen was finding his sweetheart alive and somewhere along the Tennessee trails, or her body in a grave if she were killed, as Matt refused to believe. He was not a man to take a story lightly, especially one about Ginny McBride. Matt knew the McBride Plantation was on the way to Memphis and so he planned his route accordingly.

Being in on Matt's plan, Steve Andrews rode alongside Matt and watched the leather-faced cowboy stare into space and every so often glance from side to side as if to blaze a look through the trees. Matt knew they were nearing the McBride Plantation where he first met Ginny when they came across the Tennessee River and headed north.

"Whatcha thinkin' about, pal?" Steve asked as he attempted to see what Matt was looking for through the trees.

"We're nearing the plantation, Steve," Matt answered. He looked in the distance and saw a tree planted on top of a knoll. Matt rode up to the tree and plucked some moss off it. His mind roamed back to when he first saw Ginny McBride, barely a woman in her twenties; him being not much older back then. Her blond hair hung down around her shoulders under her Stetson that hung from her neck with a stampede strap. She wore a tight-fitting blouse unbuttoned at the top three buttons allowing her breasts to accentuate themselves quite naturally. She sported a good figure sitting on a horse for Matt to enjoy, had he had the time to do so. He had saved a slave from a beating but received a whipping from Ginny herself when she caught up with him napping under a shade tree. When he escaped from under her spell and the beating he had received from her and her two hired hands, the two rode together towards the river. Her ride was if she was doing penance for his beating and the river would be the cleansing of her soul.

* * * * * *

"Follow me to the river," Ginny commanded in a friendly way, leading out with her horse. "It's a hoot-and-a-holler over this way. We'll get you cleaned up, and you can be on your way."

Matt followed, for the pain began to increase, and he wanted to ride out from this country. The Tennessee River wound shallow onto the Tennessee land from Knoxville through Chattanooga, whereas flatboats had to be used for travel. It was murky in the middle, but clear up around the shore.

Once at the river, both Matt and Ginny dismounted and dropped down to its edge. Matt took off his shirt, and with his bandanna, he applied the cold water to his wounds. It was much more soothing than the warm water from his canteen.

Ginny wet her bandanna and applied it to Matt's' shoulders.

"What do you do, cowboy?" she asked.

"Just thet," he answered. "Being a cowboy."

The moment was quiet, and then he continued. "I herded cattle in Wyoming. Worked on a few ranches down this way, driving cattle. When we'd sell them, I'd get my pay, and move further south."

"How long you been away from home?"

"Home?" he pondered "Two years, more or less, I reckon."

"Where you headed?"

"Don't recken I really know," Matt answered, looking around at the beautiful rolling scenery of Tennessee."

Matt stopped her from continuing with the wet bandanna, and picked up some of the moss he had scraped off the tree with his pocket knife. "Here," he said. "Put this on my cuts. It'll heal 'em real good." Looking into her deep blue eyes as she responded to his suggestion, he added, "Of course, had someone been more patient with the whip, we wouldn't be here now."

While Matt did the same to the back of his hand, Ginny started packing the moss lightly into his wounds, and gave him a slight smile. Matt winced a little at the sting as she applied it across his shoulders and slightly down his chest. He re-tied his bandanna around his hand to keep the moss in place.

After they finished with the moss, he stood up. Taking his shirt, he slipped it back on, feeling the pain easing, but not showing her any outward signs of it. He left the front unbuttoned.

Lying back down, he rolled over on the grass and leaned his shoulder up against the nearby tree trunk. Ginny moved over in front of him and put her bandanna back around her neck.

"I'm sorry I whipped you," she said, rubbing the front of his boots with her hand.

"No man has ever whipped me, and certainly no lady."

"Thank you."

"For what?" he asked, looking puzzled at her remark.

"For calling me a lady."

Matt leaned forward and grabbed her hand gently. "You are a lady. Oh, that whip don't take that out of ya. It's the way that you handle yourself. Your dress. Your hair." Matt's eyes surveyed her whole body, resting once in a while on her breasts.

"You like what you see, huh?"

Matt let go of her hand and leaned back again, slightly embarrassed. Looking at her more intently, he said, "Your hair reminds me of spun gold. Your eyes are like sparkling blue sapphires."

This elicited a laugh from Ginny. "You're a poet. Who'd a thought?"

"Nope. Just read it somewhere," he replied.

Ginny laughed a little, and looked more into Matt's matching blue eyes, wondering what kind a man he really was. Certainly a well-built man, six-foot four inches, solid muscle from working with cattle. A tanned man, certainly, for working in the sun. And a gentle man, with blue eyes and wavy chestnut hair.

"Your real name is Lefty?" she asked.

"Could be, now," he said, motioning to his injured hand that he had wounded earlier at the end of her whip.. "No, it's Matt. Matthew. I was named after the first book of the New Testament," Matt said, watching the ripples in the river play with one another while the fish were jumping near by.

"See thet?" he said enthusiastically as he saw a fish jump, and another one and another. Then he settled back a little against the tree again to adjust his injured back.

"I know the Bible," she said. "He was a tax collector."

"See. I knowed you were a lady, right off," Matt answered. "You probably went to Sunday School every Sunday.

"Yes," she agreed. "Every Sunday."

"Prim and prissy. You had to be."

"And you never did?"

"Oh, Ma would read the Good Book to us. She'd explain all about our names, and how we got 'em."

"Wasn't a tax collector kind of a sissy?" she asked Matt.

"Thet's where you're wrong, Miss Prissy," Matt interjected. "He had to be tough. Tough as nails. You see, a lot of people didn't like paying taxes back then." They both laughed. "You don't think Pa would let Ma get away with naming me after some sissy, now do ya?"

He returned to watching the fish play in the river and listened to the quietness of the air.

She let him listen, wondering what he would talk about next.

"My brother's name is Lukas. Third book." Matt continued. "He's dead. Measles, or somethin' got him."

Actually, Lukas was killed in a fouled-up freight company robbery he attempted with another idiot companion in Montana, whom Matt was mistaken to be. Now, to stay alive, Matt was on the run and had an alias. He was safe, as long as it was believed that he was killed and buried backing Montana along with his brother, Lukas.

Matt leaned back against the tree again and looked straight into Ginny's blue eyes. "You named after someone?"

"Virginia,", she quickly answered.

"The state?"

"And what's wrong with being named after a state?" she asked, sitting straight up with her hands on her hips.

"Nothin', I suppose," Matt replied. "Kinda like it." Then after a moment of silence between the two, he asked, "Are you?"

Ginny's eyes shot up straight at Matt. "That, sir, is something you will never find out." She stood up and looked away from his presence. "What a thing to be asking a lady, and our first meeting."

"I've never taken advantage of a lady." Matt rose to his feet and stood beside Ginny. "Many times with a woman, but never with a lady, and you . . . are a lady." He stooped to pick up a stone, and skipped it across the river.

A broad smile came across Ginny's face but Matt did not see it. "Really, I think I was named after my great-grandmamma."

"Hmmm." He looked at her and then looked away. "And thet's another thing. You call them 'niggers'. I ain't never heard these terms exceptin' down here."

"What do you call them in Wyoming, Matt?" Ginny asked, picking a leaf off the tree and playing with it with her hands as if to tease Matt to want to talk about something else besides slaves. "I'm curious, that's all."

"Negroes," Matt answered. Colored people, maybe. But, not niggers."

"It's short for 'Negroes', Matt," she answered. "And if we want to bring them to attention when we're talking to them, the term *nigger* hits them right between the eyes. It's like calling someone you hate, a *son-of-a-bitch*."

Matt's eyes widened when he heard her say that, causing him to laugh a little. "I'll be dang," he said, grabbing her by the wrist again. "You swore."

"I did, and I often do," she replied, releasing his grip on her wrist. "We're not in Virginia where the ladies are ladies and the men look after them. We're in the midst of a plantation where we have to be tough."

Matt watched her fume without trying to abate her moment of anger.

She walked over to her horse and put her hand on the saddle, but left the reins tied to a branch. She pulled a .44 out from a holster attached to her saddle. She walked to the edge of the river, turned downstream and fired it at a branch sticking out of the water several feet from shore. Clipping it, she said, "And I hit what I aim at, too."

Matt got up, buttoned his shirt, and tucked it in. Then he walked over to where she stood. He grabbed her arms and turned her around, and bringing her lips to his, kissed her passionately.

Ginny responded by dropping her pistol into the dirt, and placing her freed hands around the back of Matt's neck, bringing him tighter into her lips. He felt pain from his wounds, but ignored it for the pleasure of the moment.

Without warning, he picked her up and placed her upon her horse. "I like you tough," he said. "But I want to get to know your gentle side before we get to know each other better."

Ginny sat her horse and held her quirt lady like in her right hand. She wanted to start showing Matt this side of her. She grabbed the reins with her left hand, and, looking down at Matt, she asked, "Does that mean you'll be staying awhile with us?"

Matt bent down and retrieved her .44, wiped it off with his shirt, and placed it back into her holster. "You asked me if I could take his place," Matt replied. "I was always taught, 'an eye for an eye, and a tooth for a tooth. I'll ride back with you and, for the moment, let's say, I'll consider it. After all, work is work, and right now, I ain't got none.."

"Then follow me," Ginny commanded, and waited for him to saddle up. She rode fast and swift and Matt followed on his gelding. When he had just about caught up with her, the dust from her horse's gait blew in his eyes. He brought the brim of his hat down and wiped the dust from his eyes. When he looked up, she was gone.

* * * * * *

Matt kept his horse at an even pace until Steve's voice brought him back to the present.

"You reckon we can hold up a while and rest a bit," Steve asked, rubbing his leg.

Matt's eyes focused to attention at Steve's voice and brought his horse to a halt. He looked around the terrain and motioned with his hand to a spot near the Tennessee River. "Over there!"

It might not have been the same spot where he and Ginny had their first relationship, but Matt sort of hoped it was.

"We'll make camp here for a while, friend." Matt reined up, dismounted, tied the reins to a low branch and removed his saddle.

After a meal of beans and ham, Matt rested against a tree and put his feet, boots and all, into the river. Closing his eyes to the sun, he let Steve's chatter lull him to sleep.

Minutes traveled across the clouds as they billowed and a streak of lightning opened Matt's eyes. Immediately, he saw the face of Ginny McBride staring at him with her charming blue eyes. As quickly as the lightning left, so did the apparition.

Steve's voice got him to his feet. "Looks like we're in for some rain. How far did you say the plantation was?"

Matt looked around for Ginny, and then out onto the Tennessee River. With another crack of lightning and roar of thunder, he arose and was quick to run towards Skeeter.

Matt placed his saddle back on Skeeter and cinched it quickly as if he were back in the cavalry. "Close. Real close.

"Then what say we ride?"

The men were in their saddles with precision timing and cantered down the road, leaving the Tennessee River. The rains came in huge drops as they rounded the curve and rode down the hill towards the plantation.

"That's it," Matt pointed out, pulling his collar up around his neck.

They rode past rows of corn on one side of the road and cotton fields on the other side that seemingly covered a thousand acres of land. Eyeing the plantation, Steve saw it was a lot bigger up close. The house now seemed to Matt to be ten times the size, though it was not. It was a three-storied house built of pine boards, with two brick fireplaces, one on each end of the house, and a portico in front. A weathered white picket fence enclosed the yard around the house, a large barn and led away to enclose some out-buildings out of sight.

As they approached the front of the house, Jeremiah and his wife Nancy along with a few Negroes walked out to meet them. They were ex-slaves who stayed on to help run the plantation when Jim and Ginny were there. They were not covered, as they did not fear the wetness of the rain.

Sylvia McBride walked out onto the porch as she watched the two men ride into the yard. She was the widow of Ginny's father, being a few years younger than he, shorter than Ginny herself but about as thin.

"Matt!" Sylvia cried out as she watched him stop, "It's you!"

He dismounted, turned and looked wearily into her eyes with a thanksgiving-type stare.

"Sylvia!" Matt returned, embracing the short woman. Matt stepped back, looked at her and smiled. "Oh, eh, Sylvia this is Steve."

"Take their horses, Benjamin," she ordered as she pulled her shirtwaist up around her neck to keep dry from the rain. "Get inside, boys. They'll take care of your horses."

Matt and Steve quickly dismounted, handed the reins to Benjamin and ran into the house. Benjamin led the animals quickly away into the nearby barn.

Steve reached out and grabbed a gentle hold of her hand. "Mrs. McBride. I've heard a lot about you."

"Well, Steve, I hope it's all good. Matt here is king of this plantation. He can do no wrong."

"He never told me that," Steve returned as he looked around the inside of the mansion. "You've a big place here."

"For one woman, too big."

"Where's Jim?" Matt asked

Sylvia froze for a moment, then turned her face away and as tears filled her eyes said feebly, "I'm afraid he's gone, Matt."

"Jim? How?"

"Oh, Matt," Sylvia cried.

"Easy there, ma'am." Matt cradled her head in his strong arms. "How'd it happen?"

She broke from his grip, took a hankie from her skirt pocket and wiped her eyes and nose, looked up at Matt and continued. "The Yankees came in and called us Southern sympathizers. Jim walked away from them, trying to ignore them. We gave them everything we had to eat and drink. But it weren't enough, Matt. It weren't enough. They hit him. Beat him. Roped and tied him." She sobbed furiously.

Matt walked to her side again, bent down and then, taking her hankie, wiped her eyes. "Easy, Sylvia. Easy now."

"I – I have ta tell ya, Matt. I have ta." She took her hankie from him, wiped her small nose and continued uneasily. "They drug him through the plantation 'til he weren't even a human any more." She looked down into her lap. "We buried him on the hill over by the river next to his first wife."

Matt let go of her, stood up, turned and slapped the side of his leg with his hat, then threw it across the room. He walked to the opened door and stood there, trying to recover from the shocking news.

"Easy Matt!" Steve grabbed Matt by his arms .

Then Matt rose and walked into the rain. Steve and Sylvia stood and watched him. They could see him walk up the hill to the Family Cemetery plot where he bowed his head in reverence. . Matt fell to the ground and knelt there for a long while. There he stayed til the rain eased and gave way to a rosy pink sunset.

"I'd best be gettin' up there with him, Miss Sylvia," Steve said as he slowly turned toward the hill to join Matt. "We'll be back."

"I'll have my house Negro put something on for supper, Steve," Sylvia said, putting her hankie back into her pocket. She back inside the house as Steve walked up the hill.

It was after the sun set that the two men walked slowly back to the house where they were met by Sylvia standing just inside the door, waiting for them.

"Thank you, Matt," she said with an honest smile. "We're keeping supper warm inside for you."

Matt hung his slicker on a hook. Steve followed and did the same with his slicker.

The three sat down at the table to a hearty home-cooked meal and, after Sylvia returned grace, Matt looked up and asked, "Ginny? Any word on her?"

"Ginny," Steve echoed. "I've heard of nothing else throughout the whole war. I've been waiting to meet her and her family."

"Any more word about her disappearance, Sylvia?"

"Not a word, Matt. Nothing. I've pretty much resigned myself that she's been killed. Else, we would have heard something by now."

"No!" Matt said defiantly. He rose from the table, knocking the chair from underneath him. He smacked his fist hard against the palm of his hand. "She's alive. Somewhere, she's alive. I know it."

He stood for a moment in silence, and then turned, picked up the chair and sat back down.

Sylvia knew and accepted Matt's defiance as his way of life for she felt the same about losing Jim. "I'd like nothing better than to agree with you, Matt. Sometimes I wish I didn't know Jim was up on that hill. . . . especially at night time when I'm all alone."

After supper, Sylvia allowed Steve to ease her chair back and help her up from the table. Then she turned to Steve and showed him into the front room where the three of them sat in opposite chairs around a burning fireplace. Her house Negro, Naomi, cleared the table and turned down the lamps in the dining area. Naomi had been with the McBrides since Bertha was killed; just before the Civil War began. She was slim for a house Negro; nothing like Bertha had been.

"I've never seen you as a quitter, Matt, in anything," Sylvia said in their quiet hour together. "Why Steve, I remember the time Matt went after a man who killed a slave on this here plantation. Most men, I suppose, would have let the man go for such a deed, but not Matt. He saw the man as a cold-blooded killer and it was his responsibility to bring him to justice."

"I did what I had to do. Nothing more," Matt mumbled. "Nothing less."

****

Matt's mind went back to the time that he set out to catch a killer. He felt he had a personal interest in capturing him and Ginny tried to stop him. He could still see her standing between him and his horse.

"Well, Mr. Jorgensen," Ginny started, then corrected herself and politely said, "Matt. I have a feeling you're going somewhere, and that somewhere is without me."

"I laid awake all night thinkin' about Bertha," Matt said, reloading his pistol.

"So?"

"Well, Gin," Matt said, sliding his Colt back into its holster. "In Wyoming, we don't let someone get away with murder without gettin' him. We call that, retribution."

"An eye for an eye, again," she reminded Matt.

"Yep. 'Suppose so."

"Didn't I tell you that the marshal is working on it?" Ginny asked.

"Yep," Matt answered. "You also told me that he didn't find him."

"And you think you can?"

"Got to try, Gin." He took a gentle hold of her arms and looked deep into her eyes. "I love you, Gin. And I want to marry you."

****

"You're thinking about the time you went after Bertha's killer, aren't you?" Sylvia asked as she watched Matt's face twitch.

Matt nodded.

Sylvia looked at Steve and continued. "Bertha was our house nigger and well liked by everyone. She was killed by Jim's ex-foreman and Matt went out after him.

"I know," Steve replied. "We caught the killer in Nacogdoches. That's when I first met Matt."

Breakfast was most pleasant For Sylvia, it was a treat to have company at the table so she had Naomi prepare her favorites and spared no food, eggs sunny-side up, sausage and gravy, biscuits hot out of the oven, and plenty of coffee.

Sylvia explained that it had taken some time to rebuild supplies after the war with most of the slaves leaving and then the raiders coming through the plantation; plundering and pillaging.

"They'd taken all a' th' chickens, two of my butcherin' pigs, my best milk cow and nearly cleaned out the cellar of canned goods and hams hanging from overhead. The bushel baskets of nuts and fresh and dried fruits and vegetables stored there were taken; baskets and all. We just the same as had to start all over!"

"What do you plan on doing next, Sylvia?" Matt asked, cleaning his plate with a biscuit.

After she drew in a long breath, she answered, "The plantation is mine, now. It hasn't been easy rebuilding, but I owe it to Jim to make it good again. It'll take time. We salvaged some brooding eggs and incubated them and started stocking the hen houses all over again. It'll take all summer to get them up and really going again. We usually don't butcher 'til Fall, but we did a spring butchering and actually butchered a coupla yearling piglets to last until the only other two sows can raise their new litters.

"It's been hardest on salvaging enough dry goods for both planting another crop and using it until the new crop can be harvested this late summer. But then, we have only me, the few house slaves and a coupla dozen or so that stayed on. They were married and are slave-families here. We have always given our slaves the lower pasture to live on and let them marry and have their cabins down there. We have always done right by our niggers and some of the best ones have been faithful to stay!"

Steve looked over at Matt and motioned for him to go outside.

"Excuse us, Miss Sylvia, while Matt and I do some chawin'. We'll be right back."

Steve took Matt by the arm and led him outside to the porch.

"What's on your mind, pal?" Matt asked, straightening his shirt sleeve from Steve's mishandling.

"Don't you see, Matt?"

"What?"

"She needs help and we're here, and well, there're crops, and you know this place. We don't have to go galloping off looking for Ginny right now; do we?"

"You mean...?"

"Yeah! I mean we stay awhile. A few weeks. A coupla months or more and help her get everything back in shape again."

Matt took off his Stetson, squinted into the sunrise with the Stetson hiding the light from his eyes as he looked out upon the plantation he knew so well. He put the hat back on, smiled at Steve as he nodded his head and said, "Let's tell her."

The two men went back into the house, sat down at their plates and acted as if nothing was said.

"Well, gentlemen. What was that all about?"

"What?" Steve asked. "Oh, we jest done decided that since you've got so much food to last a month or so, and you have a bunk house and no one to bunk down in it, that we'd sort of stay awhile and help you get rid of all thet food."

"What he's tryin' to say," Matt interjected, "is thet, you need help, and by dang we're gonna stay a while and help you."

Sylvia's eyes lit up and a smile broader than the kitchen spread across her face. "Matt. Steve. What . . . What can I say?"

"Say nothin', ma'am," Steve answered, "and toss me another one of those biscuits from thet there pan. It looks like we've got a lot of work to get started at today, ma'am."

"Well," Matt added with a grin. "Slap some bacon in that biscuit and let's get movin'!"

Later that evening, Matt, looking out of the opened kitchen door, caught a horseman riding up.

"Got company, Sylvia," Matt said, rising to meet the man.

"That's Olaf coming up," Sylvia acknowledged, "with his two boys. "You remember Olaf, Matt. He owns the ranch next to ours. Biggest in the county."

Olaf turned the reins of his roan over to a slave boy who took the horse and tied it to the hitching post. He walked tall as he entered the house while Jeremiah opened the door. He was a big man with a slightly protruding belly, large bushy eyebrows, and a grin that heightened his persona as a loving and caring man.

"Olaf," Sylvia greeted him. "This is Matt Jorgensen. You remember him."

"Yes, by golly, I certainly do. Matt, my son. You've weathered the war well, it seems."

"Yes, Olaf," Matt returned, greeting Olaf with a strong handshake.

Sam and John Gustavson, the sons, joined in and shook hands with Matt. "Good to see you back," John said. "Never got to meet you on personally. You bein' too busy at the time." John was the bigger of the two.

"Yes, by golly, Matt," Sam greeted."

"Thank you. And this is Steve Andrews, my friend who rode in the war with me."

"Mr. Olaf. Sam. John." Steve rose and returned the greeting with a handshake to each.

"Gustavson, my boy. But, call me *Olaf*. I was just talking with Matt about my plantation. He asked me what my plans were."

Olaf looked at Sylvia with a twinkle in his eyes, twirled his heavy moustache with his right hand and smiled. "I have plans for my plantation, Matt. Many plans." He looked over at Sylvia and smiled. "I'd also like to help get this plantation up again like it use to be. And much more."

"He's talked some about them," Sylvia added. "But he hasn't made them for certain."

"Oh", Matt came back. A certain smile from Sylvia gave Matt the feeling that a certain connection had crossed between them.

"Son," Olaf returned.. "We're talking seriously about joining our efforts and partnering the plantations."

"We'll talk more," she replied with a light smirk on her lips. "Now the boys are here and we've been talking about the plantation."

"That's all right with us, Sylvia," Matt came back, looking at Steve. "Let's just see how we can all help each other while we're here."

Sitting back at the table while Olaf held her chair, she motioned to Naomi to bring more coffee. "More coffee boys?"

"He's still searching for Ginny, Olaf," Sylvia informed him. "He won't let her go."

"I've seen her," Matt interjected. I know she's alive, somewhere."

"You've got it bad, don't cha? Where 'bouts, boy? How?" Olaf asked.

"Many times."

"One time," Steve interrupted, "she saved his life from a blue boy's musketball."

"In battle?"

"I didn't see her then, sir. I felt her. Some how I knew it was her, because I fell from my horse and brought the boy down with me. I suppose by the way he ran that it would be his last battle."

"He saw her face, too," Steve continued as he slurped his coffee from a saucer. He looked at Olaf and then at Sylvia. "Really!"

"I saw her up close once, maybe twice." He took his cup and sipped some coffee and then continued. "I can't explain it. Once I saw her lying in bed while I read my letter to her."

"You saw her while you read a letter to her? You were awake?"

"That's just it. No, sir. I was sound asleep. But I saw her, and she was beautiful. I read her the whole letter."

"And did you see her while you were awake?"

"I believe so, sir. Don't really know."

"Could she be a ghost, son? Seems like it almost has to be."

Matt put his coffee cup down hard, and bit his lip. "She's not a ghost, sir. Some how . . . I know she's alive."

"I'm sorry, boy," Olaf returned politely, looking at Sylvia.

Sylvia put her hand in Olaf' hand and smiled at him.

"No, sir," Matt replied softly, rising from the table. "I should apologize." He looked at Olaf and then turned to Sylvia. "I'm sorry, Sylvia. Maybe she is dead. Maybe she is. And maybe I'm keeping her memory too long with me."

"Well, son," Olaf returned, "working with us might get your mind off the situation for a while, as I see it. Get yourself some rest and I'll be over in the mornin'."

The next morning Olaf found the two men up and already working as he brought his wagon to a halt in the field.

"You know everything there is to know about this plantation, don't ya, son?"

"Yep," Matt replied, starting up the cotton gin. "Who ya got there?"

" A couple of my men. They're gonna help ya some."

"Good. We can use the help."

Matt and Steve welcomed the men and the work began. Matt and Steve, Olaf and Sylvia gathered all the Negro workers they could and divided the work so that all could do as much as possible; men, women and even the older children. The eldest Negroes were sent to work in the house and gardens doing the lesser chores and teaching the children how to help too, so that the stronger men and women could work the fields; each doing as much as could be done.

Each Negro worker would receive a portion of earnings from the crops plus their housing and food allotments. By working together, they were learning a new way of preserving each other's way of living.

Throughout the summer and into the harvesting time of Autumn, the plantation began to take shape; not like it had been when Matt had helped his precious Ginny, who was in charge of a hundred slaves, but decent enough to show much growth and renewal. The crops were harvested with extra care and stored for use in the coming winter and spring. There would be plenty of seed now for planting next spring. It had taken every slave and their family members old enough to carry a tool, but they worked together to rebuild their plantation; each field, the orchard, the remaining livestock and the gardens.

Not all the fields were back in use, but in proportion of man power, the land used would sustain those working and living on it. The lower fields were given to them for their allotment.

Then came the time for Matt and Steve to leave and ride the trail north. The breakfast was as best that Sylvia could make, and Olaf showed his approval by taking his fill and then some.

"Thank you, ma'am for puttin' up with us for such a while," Matt said, as he pushed himself away from the table and plucked his hat from the wall.

Steve put down his saucer and rose with Matt. "We should be going anyway, Miss," he said as he also pulled his hat away from the wall rack.

"It's a long ride, and I feel some how what we've done here will help settle things for us; or at least for me."

Then he eyed Olaf with a serious look and said, "I figure to find some answers back in Richmond. That's where the McBride Mill is."

Olaf placed his knife and fork across his plate, rose and shook Matt and Steve's hands. "You're determined to find her? I'd do the same, son. I'd do the same."

Sylvia had Naomi fix some food bundles for Matt and Steve and handed them to the two cowboys. They stuffed them into their saddle bags and waited for Olaf and Sylvia to bid them their goodbyes.

"Tiz'nt as much as I'd like it to be," Sylvia informed them. "But it'll keep you for a few days, Matt. Steve. Come again, the place will be beautiful and thriving again."

Matt caught her up in his arms and hugged her. She left his grip and gave Steve a similar hug, while Olaf grabbed Matt's shoulders with his huge hands. "You keep yourself safe. You hear? And come back and see us when you can."

Matt pulled himself into the saddle, leaned over and gave Olaf a strong handshake. "We'll return. You guys gonna get hitched or what?"

Sylvia walked around the other side of Skeeter and brought Matt's ear down to her lips. "You know, he's got a big bar-b-q planned for October. Wish you fellas could stick around for it. We're planning on a small ceremony afterwards."

Matt smiled and said, "Congratulations. Wish we could. But ... gotta keep lookin'." He looked over at Olaf, tipped his hat

and said to Steve, "Let's ride, pal. Adios, Sylvia. Olaf, we'll be back."

"Yep!" Steve agreed.

They spurred forward with one look back and a wave of their hats.

"Where to now?" Steve asked.

"To see our old friend, Bob Bunting."

"Oh. Well, it's about time."

They pulled their Stetsons down and spurred their mounts forward to another rung in the ladder of destiny for a man in search of his true love.

I know you're alive. Ginny. I'll find you. If it takes an eternity, I'll find ya.

CHAPTER 13

THE HEART AND THE MIND

<u>9 June 1865</u>

It was another warm day in Richmond. Henry and Emma were on the veranda having their usual tea time when Dr. Harris and Beth stepped up to meet them after another walk through the garden.

"Did you enjoy your walk this morning, Beth?" Henry asked as he rose to greet the couple.

Beth stopped as she approached Henry, turned and smiled at Harris and pointed towards Henry and said, "See. Even the Major recognizes who I am."

"Yes. Yes, I did." Harris harrumphed..

"I hope you came up with a name for your imaginary young man," Harris suggested.

"I only remember him as *Matt*," Beth responded to Harris' question as to who the man in the vision was. "I don't remember his surname."

"Don't?" Harris asked. "Try, Beth. Try."

"I've tried so many times lately, and I simply can't. I'm sorry. I'm sorry."

"What can you remember about him?" Henry asked. "I heard you crying to him when you were shot. And you sounded like you were mad. Mad like you were shot by the . . . the *enemy.*"

"Enemy?" Beth returned. "Who?"

"Well," Henry said, rubbing his chin and smiling at her, "It was one of our boys who accidentally shot you. Stands to reason that we were . . . the *enemy* you were referring to."

"Oh, pshaw! There's no truth in that. I know." She stood up, shook her dress loose from the wrinkles, looked over at Emma and said. "We're not the enemy. Are we?"

"No, Beth, darling. We're not the enemy," Emma answered. She walked over to Beth and brought her arms around her. She continued. "Certainly not."

"I'm afraid I might be right, Emma," Henry interrupted.

"How do you mean, Henry?"

"Just plain intuition I got from the first time I met her. Just plain intuition."

"Then put that plain intuition in your pipe and smoke it," Emma suggested, wiping a wisp of hair back from Beth's eyes. "You can see she's got just as much blue blood in her as we have. Yankee talk, that is."

Harris interrupted. "Will you ladies please excuse us while Henry and I talk?"

Harris harrumphed and took Henry's arm and led him into the house where they convened in the drawing room.

"Well, Harris, what have you found out so far?"

Harris walked over to the fireplace and turned to face Henry who stood at the bar, pouring himself a glass of bourbon. "Pour me one, too."

Henry complied, poured another drink and gave it to Harris. The two clinked the glasses together and sipped their drinks.

"Henry, I must admit, I've never dealt with a case like your daughter's. You contacted me nine months ago now. I've examined her and up to now have researched all I could get my hands on about such cases. And I've discussed the symptoms with some of my colleagues. The best in the field, as far as I'm concerned."

"And?"

"Well, if you want the skinny of it. We just don't know. First of all, I don't believe she's faking it. I'm convinced thoroughly that the condition exists and that she has amnesia. This I can unequivocally confirm. I just don't know how to snap her out of it at this juncture."

"What did you learn from your hypnosis of Beth?" Henry asked, handing Harris a fresh cigar.

"We've gone through that already. I almost got her back to her embryonic stage, but she cringed. It was like she was stuck somewhere in time."

"Time! That's it, isn't it, Harris? Time?"

"How do you mean, Man?"

"She's stuck in time. Back to when I first met her."

Harris pondered on what Henry was saying and dismissed it. "I don't know. She goes back so far and . . . and then she stops. She remembers meeting you. She told me how amorous you were at first. And then how you got more and more serious with her until you sent her to be with Emma."

Henry showed embarrassment at Harris' words, lit Harris' cigar and then his own and stared into Harris' eyes. "Did she tell you anything else . . . I mean, about me?"

"She divulged as much as she wanted to divulge. I'm certain that she didn't hold anything back. You look a little peaked, Henry. Is the bourbon getting to you?"

Henry bent over and caught his breath and answered, "It was a moment in the war and she came into my sight as a beautiful angel from heaven and for a moment, just for a moment mind you, she was mine. I held her in my arms and felt her breathing, faintly, ever so faintly. I knew then that I must forget myself as a man and treat her as a doctor, but it was difficult. So awfully difficult."

"And, did you? As a doctor?"

"I did. But I still had feelings as a man." He poured himself another drink and drank it down in two gulps. "When I sent her away, I felt as if my whole being ached for her. She gave me back my youth. My energy. My reason for living. For being."

Harris held out his empty glass for Henry to fill it. "And now?"

Filling his glass, Henry replied, "As a daughter, Harris. Strictly as a daughter. I don't know if you know that, but it's true."

"I can empathize with that, Henry. She is a raving beauty. Sometimes she gets to me, too. I maybe paswt my prime, but I still have those feelings. Only sometimes."

"But it only takes a moment, doesn't it, Harris?"

"Like you, Doctor Paterson, she is my patient. And that is all she is."

Henry sat down and Harris followed him to his chair. Taking a puff on his pipe, he asked, "So, where are we now?"

Harris laid his cigar in the ashtray, looked over at Henry and said matter-of-factly, "Dissociate amnesia."

"Dissociate amnesia? What the heck does that mean?"

"As I see it now," Harris answered, fiddling with his watch. "she might have two personalities."

"Two personalities?"

"Yes. Beth, the lady. And Ginny, the fighter."

"A dual personality?" Henry asked. "Two persons in one?"

"But they're just personalities. I'm working on the theory that she developed these personalities over a period of time. Not necessarily just when she was shot."

"Before that?" Henry asked, wrinkling up his brow as he packed his pipe.

"It's evident from when she took over as master of her plantation. A source of power. It seems to me that she came from a fairly wealthy family and was put in charge of managing a bunch of slaves on a plantation that was hot and dirty most of the time. Not like the refines of her new home here in Virginia."

"Yes. Yes, that sort of makes sense," Henry agreed, relighting his pipe.

"Now, let me address it this way. For openers, Henry, it has to do with a three-point diagnosis I've developed of her situation; illness if you'd prefer to call it that. I prefer to relate it to a psychological condition."

"Is she in need of medicine of any kind?" Henry asked.

"Maybe. If so, I'll prescribe what I think would be suitable for her." He took a large sip of his bourbon. "Now, as to the three-point diagnosis. You say that she was shot in the shoulder?

Doc nodded his head while he shook his pipe and repacked. "Like I said, she probably compounded her injury when she hit the ground. I didn't have any type of equipment to check her on this. Her eyes were all right. And there were no other symptoms of any kind that would have alerted me to probe deeper. I was satisfied that she would heal in a normal and satisfactory manner."

"That's point number two. Supposing she did compound the injury. You said she did respond to your questions in a very alert fashion; did she not?"

"Yes. And without any symptom of having amnesia."

"At that time. Yes. For all intensive purposes we'll say she was well. OK?"

Doc nodded, lit his pipe and puffed away, showing intent interest in what Harris was saying. He assured Harris, "She appeared every bit the person in good health. No reason to doubt it at that time."

"Being well then, she rode off on her horse, came back and contracted pneumonia. This complicated matters to the extreme. Point three."

"Yes. I actually thought I would lose her. But she rallied."

"And this is where she developed amnesia?"

"Right. I'm sure of it."

"OK. Now she's been telling me about her visions; about seeing a man in a uniform in battle as clear as day. Do we know this man?"

"No, sir," Henry answered. "I know about the visions. She has told them to Emma and me frequently, trying to figure out who he is."

"I think I know who he is."

"You do?" Henry came back, laying his pipe in the ashtray. "Who?"

"Well, not exactly *who* he is, but I'm certain he's the third point in my diagnosis."

"How's that?"

"It's her boy friend, husband, lover; someone so very close to her that she feigned amnesia to protect him."

"Matt?"

"That's what she called him."

"Then you think that maybe she feigned amnesia? She faked it?"

"No. She developed it, all right. But afterwards. Unconsciously. Her *id* so to speak, as Freud would say, wrapped its identity so deep into her psyche that she went into a deep state of amnesia."

"I recall that she did mention something about the South," Henry added.

"The Confederacy? Then, it pretty much adds up, now, doesn't it?"

90

"Matt must've been a Confederate soldier?"

"Yes. And she was also on the side of the Confederacy, too. Not as a spy, I'm sure, but as a patriot."

"And because of her loyalty to the South, she slipped into a state of amnesia to protect both herself and this Matt.. Is that what you're saying?"

"Precisely. There are several types of amnesia that our field describes that are associated with one's mental condition. This is one in which the patient is totally or partially unable to recall remote or even sometimes recent experiences. However, it's not totally associated with a physical condition, such as Beth received with the bullet, or maybe not even be when she came down with pneumonia. It could be a combination of many factors. To my mind, it's extremely psychological combined with her physical condition. The only thing that I can ascertain at this time, and it's not for certain, is that when she awoke the first time after being hit with a musketball, she must have sensed imminent danger in what was happening and that she was in enemy territory; viz-a-viz, a Yankee camp.

"At this juncture, she wanted to get up and leave, but she couldn't. When she tried to leave, it only intensified other disorders such as an acute stress she couldn't handle."

"The injury to the shoulder accompanied with a blow to the head and the pneumonia conditions brought on these disorders?" Henry asked. "Is that it?"

"Possibly . . . More than likely. I just don't know. It could cause one to totally lose all memory as to who he or she is; the part of her memory that we classify as *autobiographical memory.*"

"How does she come out of it?"

"Again, I don't know. I don't really know if this is what caused her loss of memory. It comes the closest. I've just never had a case like this. Nor have any of my colleagues."

"She claims she has seen visions whereby she is on a battlefield. And in this battlefield, she sees a man; a lover. She remembers only that his is name, *Matt.*"

"*Matt?* That's all I could get out of her, too. Did she describe him?"

"No. Not really. Only that he was about to be killed and her spirit, like one causing a thing to happen in a dream, brushed the boy who had a bead on him, causing him to fall out of his saddle. Almost as if she were writing the dream herself."

"Then it was a dream?" Henry returned. "I suppose you won't know until you delve deeper into her psyche?"

"No. No, Henry. More like I'd have to dig deeper into mine. I just can't answer you on that right now. To her, it was reality.

"You see, Henry, part of amnesia deals with who one is, what she or he did, what was said, where he or she went. What was thought. All of the senses play an integral part in a person's amnesia. Sometimes all that the person ever learned, even though forgotten, continues to influence his or her behavior.

"What she did or said in the past comes alive in their psyche when they experience time gaps or memory gaps. When the person becomes aware of something from the past, it triggers a memory and the person with amnesia begins to awaken. Sometimes it takes days, weeks or months. In Beth's case, years. She is now recognizing that she has lost some time and she has been trying to recover it. Maybe, desperately trying. Like I said, this is what we call *dissociative amnesia.*

Henry sat his drink and pipe down on the mantle. He looked at Harris for the longest moment as if contemplating on what he had just heard. Then he asked, "Will she ever come out of it?"

Harris downed his last drink in the glass, sat it down next to Henry's glass and answered, "Most likely, in time."

Then he sat down, looked at Henry and pondered on what he was about to say. "I just don't know. It could be the shock or recognition, such as the burned out mill. Maybe it's time she met some of the McBrides. Of course, are you sure you're ready for her to remember who she is? After all, she might cease being your daughter when she realizes who she really is."

Henry frowned, studied what Harris just remarked on, stared at him with a puzzled look and said, "Then, that's just a chance we'll have to take. I'll make the arrangements right away,"

CHAPTER 14

BETH MEETS GRAND MAMA

<u>12 June 1865</u>

The day came for Beth to meet her grandmother, Sarah McBride. Sarah was in her early eighties, small in stature and shrewd in mind. The rains came, but they didn't stop Simon from driving Beth and the Patersons up to the McBride estate. Simon fitted the carriage with enough protection to keep the rain from soaking in, and then drove them several miles beyond the city to the south east and up the massive rolling hill.

The McBride Estate was typical of Richmond's finer early nineteenth century dwellings. It was a two-story tall, plain gray stucco neoclassical mansion with a slate flat roof. The main floor featured a parlor, drawing room and dining room, while the bedrooms were upstairs. A kitchen and servants' residence were located in an adjoining outbuilding. A garden decorated the remaining land, with terraces down the hillside to the east overlooking the Shockoe Valley. Close by was the mansion of Jefferson Davis.

The McBride Mansion was one of the largest estates in Richmond, having had many slaves and workers at one time. Now, however, because of the ravaging of Richmond and the mill, many of the slaves had fled to the north. The road north still showed signs of the exodus as Simon pulled the carriage to a halt at the gate.

Flicking the lines, he continued forward as he put the twin horses into a trot, climbing the road as they entered the estate. He reigned up at the front door. Taking out an umbrella, he sided the carriage where Emma and Beth were and escorted them into the house. Henry had his own umbrella.

Lulu Belle held the door open for them to come in while Simon helped Henry escort the ladies in.

"We could put three of our houses in this one room," Henry mused.

Beth thought, *More like five or six.*

"Mrs. McBride is in the living room, suh," Lulu Belle said, closing the doors and showing them the way inside.

Beth was the first to enter the large living room. The sight brought back a flood of memories, too many for her in one moment, and she slumped in a faint.

Henry caught her and carried her into the room and placed her on a settee that decorated the front picture window in the south parlor. "You're alright, Beth," he said, gently removing his arms from around her.

Her eyes opened and looked into his, and then at Emma as she, too, came to Beth's aid. And then, as if in a fog, she looked around the room and caught the faintest glimpse of a beautiful aged woman walking towards her. It was almost as if she were looking into a mirror. The woman was strikingly beautiful, with long ringlets adorning her poof of blonde-gray hair, swept back into a mother-of–pearl clasp. She wore a long velvety green simple, yet elegant gown decorated with an ecru lace collar, which was adorned by a matching tatted-lace jacket, and low black boots.

"I am Mrs. Sarah McBride," she addressed them, offering her hand to Henry. "You are the Patersons, no doubt."

"Yes," Henry answered, accepting her hand in exchange. "This is my wife, Emma."

The two ladies exchanged looks and smiled at one another.

"And this is Beth."

"Of course. My little Virginia McBride all grown up," she said with a wide smile and a twinkle in her eye. "Of course, your Grand Mama would know you anywhere, child."

Emma looked at the remarkable likeness between Sarah and Beth.

Sarah smiled and reached out her hand to cradle Beth's chin as she seated herself on the settee beside the young lady. "She's a McBride alright," Sarah said. "No doubt about that. The high cheek bones, the slim nose, the large eyes, the long neck. Yep. I'd a known you anywhere. It hasn't been that long ago, child. Why, just a few Christmases ago, why…hmm…."

Beth sat speechless for a while, still looking around at the room where she sat in the presence of her grandmother, and then looked back into Sarah's eyes. It was her appearance that suggested to Beth that she was in the presence of class. She eyed Sarah, looking at her long flowing gown that touched the floor and at the beautiful lace collar that adorned her slender and aged neck. She looked down the long sleeves that covered her thin arms. On her right hand was a golden wedding set with several smaller diamonds and one large one. The ring finger of her left hand was adorned with a beautiful ring displaying several colored stones, just enough to show wealth but not too gaudy.

"Grand Mama?" Beth spoke, looking back into her eyes as if she could see her past through them.

"Let me look at you, child." She reached out and gently took Beth's hand helped her to stand and turned her both ways as if to examine her slenderness. "Yes. Yes, you are our Virginia McBride. I'm so delighted to have found you again." She hugged Beth to her bosom. And then she turned to Emma and said, "Bless you, Emma for bringing her to her grandmother."

She motioned for Beth to sit back beside her on the settee. Emma and Henry seated themselves in a nearby tufted parlor loveseat, listening intently at Sarah's story of how she was lost in the war.

As she sat back down, Beth fell immediately beside her. She held onto Sarah's hand and kissed it. "Grand Mama!" She turned her head and rested it on the back of Sarah's hand. "I'm at a loss for words. I – I feel like I've known you all my life, and yet now I feel like I've just got to know you."

Beth let the tears flow gently down her cheek without bothering to wipe them away. "Grand Mama!" She bit her lip. The two ladies held hands for an undetermined amount of time, and then Beth asked, "My Mama? And Papa?"

"Oh, my poor darling. My poor, poor Ginny." Sarah took Beth's head and cradled it into her bosom. Your mother passed on when you were just six years old."

"Little Annie? Suddenly her eyes brightened. She looked at Henry and Emma and then exclaimed, "Oh, I remember Annie, my baby sister." Then she turned back to Sarah. "She was born about then?" Ginny asked, fearing for the worst.

"Yes. Your mother died shortly after childbirth. You hardly would even remember her."

"Umm." Beth sat up and looked at Sarah straight on.

"Your father . . . my boy James . . . was killed just at the end of the war."

"Papa?" Beth whimpered as she broke from Sarah's grasp. "Papa?"

"Yes, child."

Straightening up, Beth asked, "How did Papa die?"

"In a letter I recently received from his wife, Sylvia, she said he worked day and night, hardly taking time to eat or sleep and always doing what he could to salvage the plantation, the crops and slaves.

"Sylvia? His wife?"

"Oh, so much to tell you, child. So much! You see, he remarried during the war. And then, the war came and I suppose he felt his whole world had crumbled in on him.

"The war tore up the McBride Plantation. Both sides moved in and ravaged the land for food, shelter, whatever they could get. It only got worse. It was several days after the war was over and the raiders came in and ransacked the place. . . . Poor James. . The raiders beat and killed Jim. Poor Sylvia found him nearly beat to a pulp. He never woke up. She had him buried on Blue Moon Ridge with your Mama.

"I'm supposing he had a smile on his face as if he were looking into your mother's eyes as she received him home. Wouldn't you think so, dear child?"

"Papa? Oh, no! Not my Papa."

"My child. My child. How I would dearly love to have prevented you from knowing all this." Sarah took a dainty handkerchief from her sleeve, gently wiped away Beth's tears and continued. "Sylvia, his wife, ran but a Reb caught her. Somehow, I don't know, some of the boys got into it, and Sylvia got free and ran to Olaf up the hill."

"Olaf?" She remembered the name. "He had a plantation, too. Not far from ours. Yes." And then she realized the enormity of what Sarah was explaining to her. "Not him, too?"

"No, dear. They knew better. He had fortified his plantation and chased the Rebs clear to Hades I suppose. They never came back."

"Oh, Papa," Beth sobbed, laying her head onto Sarah's lap. "My dear, lovely Papa." Then she stood up, and with grit teeth she said, "Had I been there, he'd still be alive!" Beth looked deep into Sarah's blue eyes, trying to see herself come alive in them.

"Perhaps, dear. Perhaps. One never knows about fate."

"Fate! Fate be damned!" Beth apologized to Sarah first, and then to Henry and Emma. "Oh! I'm sorry. I'm truly sorry."

"That's all right, dear. Emma! Major! You see, that's the true McBride coming out in her."

"We saw the McBride in her yesterday, Sarah," Emma reported. "It wasn't a pleasant sight."

"I think she'll get better the more she stays with us, Mrs. McBride," Henry added. He looked at Beth, smiled, and continued. "She knows that she's loved and needed. "I'm having a collegue and doctor friend of mine counsel with her. He's been doing a marvelous job."

Beth sat back down on the cushion beside Sarah, with her elbows on her knees and her hands hiding her face.

Sarah took her hankie again and handed it to Beth. "Blow your nose, child and wipe those tears away."

It was a while before Beth could compose herself to ask any more questions. Emma and Henry had remained quiet. Sarah eventually continued, knowing that Beth wanted to know more.

"Both your brothers are back from their positions with the war and are beginning efforts to rebuild the mill.

"My brothers?" Beth asked in astonishment. "Oh, my word! Oh, Grand Mama, where are they? When can I see them?"

The whole world came alive to Beth in that moment.

"Yes. In due time. They're in North Carolina now with plans on rebuilding our mill there."

"And Annie? Wonderful Annie. My little sister?"

"Annette, child. You'll meet her. Soon."

The rest of the day was spent in total excitement for Beth so much that she had wearied Sarah to the point of excusing herself and retiring to bed.

It was the next afternoons before Beth regained her composure and had the Patersons drive her out again to the McBride Mansion. Once received into the house by Lulu Belle, she allowed Sarah to lead her alone into the garden of the estate while the Patersons stayed in the living room as guests.

Beyond the gardens along the backside of the ridge was a fenced memorial garden. She led Beth past the tallest sprawling oaks to the gates and the trellised roses, adding their beauty and fragrance to the hallowed knoll.

"My parents are here, Beth." Sarah pointed to their gravesite, a beautifully carved monument inscribed with their names and dates on it.

Then Ginny caught sight of another marker close by. It read:

James McBride,
Son, Grand Son, Father
1818 – 1864 R.I.P.

Next to it was another marker that read:

Geraldine Annette McBride
Beloved Wife and Mother.
1817 – 1848.

"Mama!" She knelt and fell silent. Sarah allowed Beth her moment to calmly cry her soul for her deceased parents. Then, she gently placed her hand on her shoulder and helped her up from her kneeling position.

"Your mother and father are buried in Tennessee on Blue Moon Ridge. I had this monument made and placed here so that I might bring my beads to them."

"Oh!" Ginny read aloud. "Mama died in 1848. So, I was only six then?" Beth asked as she wiped her tears with her hankie.

"Yes. That would make you . . ."

"Twenty-four years old; thereabouts."

Sarah put her arm around her and then added, "June second, dear. You're so young. Yet you've lived a whole life time it seems." She watched Beth still looking at the gravesites and smiled.

The hours that day seemed to vanish ever so quickly and the Patersons stayed for dinner. Eventually the evening sun told them it was again time to leave.

"So, you will take care of yourself, Ginny, or Beth as you are now called," Sarah said with a smile. "After all, you are a McBride." She concluded with a Scottish lilt.

Beth nodded with a smile.

"We will, too," Henry answered politely with a smile. "As a patient, too . . . That is, until she has fully recovered."

"And a daughter," Emma quickly added.

"I predict that you will see her recover and become both the tough McBride heiress and yet the gentle Paterson woman-lawyer you've educated her to become all in one beautiful package."

"I'm happy to work with her. She is a remarkable case, and I think with proper care, she will once again be the grand-daughter you know so well."

"And I'm so happy that you understand that I am too old a lady to be helping her the way she needs help. Oh, of course, she will be a part of this estate, and she will inherit part of it, seeing how I am the oldest survivor of the McBride clan. You know, we Scots are very . . . well, very very . . ." She filled the air with her laughter as they shared their thoughts once more before leaving. "You do not know how relieved I am to know that you've brought her back to us. It was heartbreaking to lose my son, but we thought we'd lost Ginny too.

Emma looked deep into Sarah's blue eyes and knew that Beth must become the person she really is as both Ginny and as Beth.

"And she will move into this estate with you, Sarah?" Emma asked, almost reluctantly, but knowing that it was the inevitable.

"If she so chooses. Yes! By all means. I would like that. She is part of the estate as she has been all her life . . . and from this day forward.

"Beth. Is that your decision?" Emma asked, shyly.

Beth looked at Emma and then at Henry, and with all the enthusiasm she had in her, said, "Yes. Oh, my yes. I am home, Emma. I am home."

She put her arms around Henry and Emma and continued, "You made all this possible, Major, Emma. I am so grateful to you."

"Then," Henry acquiesced., "it's settled."

"And I expect you to visit her and she with you at all times," Sarah interjected. "Please. You know, you have become part of our family now, too."

"Odd, isn't it?" Emma said as Beth stepped to her side. Beth looked startled at the two ladies and smiled like a distant smile as if she were waving at two friends from a train. She left Emma's side and went to Sarah, taking her aged hands into hers, kissed them and left them stained with her tears. "Oh, Grand Mama."

"If that is what you want, child."

Beth turned her head and looked back at Emma who gave her an assuring smile. Then, as she looked up into Sarah's sparkling eyes, she said, "Yes, Grand Mama. Oh, yes. I've got to find out more about myself."

She rose and walked slowly to Emma and Henry as they took her into their arms and cradled her. She turned and smiled at Sarah. "I'll be back, Grand Mama, early tomorrow with some of my things.

Emma took her hand and the three of them walked slowly toward the door as Barnabas held it open. Beth looked back one more time and then walked briskly down the stairs and out the door to the awaiting carriage.

Emma waved to Sarah, as did Henry as he walked away in front of her. "We'll see you tomorrow, Sarah."

100

"And you, Emma dearest."

The rains had left the hillside and a beautiful sunset painted the horizon as the carriage rolled along the rain-slicked streets back to the home of the Patersons.

In Danville, President Davis and his staff planted their new capital. After a few days of meetings of grave concern, they deserted Danville and fled to North Carolina where President Davis was finally arrested and imprisoned.

CHAPTER 15

THE McBRIDE CLAN

<u>25 June 1865</u>

The day came a couple of weeks later when the McBride clan came together to meet with the newly-found member of the family.

Sarah stood in the doorway of the Great Room as Ginny walked anxiously, but with reserve down the stairway and stood next to Grand Mama. Grand Mama placed her arm through Ginny's and said with a regal voice, "Ahem. May I introduce you all to Miss Virginia McBride. Your sister, Ginny."

Sarah smiled as she introduced each one in the fine living room of the McBride Mansion to meet their long-lost sibling. "She may look all too dainty to belong to this group, but let me assure you, she has the temper and the stamina of a full-grown tigress. And she knows how to snap a whip!"

The clan showed their approval with their laughter and lit-up faces, showing their eagerness to embrace the lovely Ginny. Before this, they had trepidations about Ginny's amnesia. However, the meeting alleviated their doubts to some degree.

"This is Gerald and his lovely wife, Martha, Ginny. The youngsters playing in the garden belong to them. You can meet them later.

"Kenneth and his lovely wife, Barbara; their little one is asleep with her mammy, upstairs.

"And this is your sister, Annette."

The reunion was one for all eyes to have seen. The smiles and the laughter echoed throughout the empty halls of the mansion,

102

bouncing off the corridor walls and resounding cheerfully in their ears.

"Jerry," Ginny said as she hugged him. "You are my oldest brother. My goodness, you're a grown man."

He tipped his head as his hand stroked his dark, well-groomed moustache.

She looked at Martha and paid her compliments. "You are lovely, Martha. How long have you two been married?"

Martha stood almost a foot shorter than her six-foot husband in his black dapper suit with a thin black string tie making him look even taller with his dark hair parted and slicked back. Her off-white calico gown was patterned with leafy sprigs that perfectly matched her green eyes and auburn hair that was tucked under a straw bonnet with a matching green plume, while long auburn ringlets cascaded down her shoulder. She was petite and dainty with freckles, a warm smile and a sweet southern accent. "We got married a year after the war started. We invited you, of course, but your father didn't know where you were."

"And you, Ginny," Jerry interrupted. "You have most undoubtedly grown into a beautiful young lady beyond compare. I haven't seen you since you were twelve or thirteen."

"More like eleven. I was tall for my age."

"Yes, Ginny," Kenneth replied with an extra hug as Gerald let go of her.

She returned Kenneth's embrace. "You're still older than me, Kenny. But you look so much younger than me . . . than I." She smiled and put her hankie to her mouth and said, "I've got to watch my grammar."

"The *I* is appropriate, my dear." Sarah turned to her company and explained, "Ginny has not only been through finishing school, but has just recently earned her Law degree from William and Mary College. She still has some of that hard edge about her that Father let her have, I'm afraid. But time will cure that."

"And this is my lovely wife, Barbara," Kenneth informed her. "We've been married just two years this past month."

"Barbara," Ginny shook hands with her. "Yes how lovely you are."

Barbara was almost as tall as Kenneth, lacking about three inches. Kenneth, with his brown wavy hair, parted and combed to the side was less than Gerald by two inches, but thinner in his navy, double-breasted suit with a watch fob in it's little pocket.

She was a brunette with brown eyes and long hair that coiled into a Victorian twist with a tiny spray of satin ribbon flowers tucked into it. The simple strand of pearls adorning her bare neckline made her appear to be taller, but her pink floral print gown gave her a gentle, feminine appearance and accented her pink lips that melted into a soft, dimpled smile. She was a bubbly happy soul that reflected in Kenneth's cheerful manner.

"Gerald was in charge of the mill until it burned down, Ginny," Sarah informed her. "He plans on rebuilding.

"Soon," Gerald added. "Very soon. We've also got to revamp our plantation in Tennessee."

It stuck a nerve with Ginny as she winced at what Gerald said. "Plantation" Tennessee?"

"Why, yes," Gerald continued. "The one you and Papa were in charge of. You don't remember?"

"Yes. Yes, I do remember," Jerry. "But only vaguely. I'm sorry. It'll come back to me, I'm sure." She apologized and took the goblet that Kenneth offered her.

"The mill," Ginny approached Gerald again. "How did it happen to burn down? I saw the granary, too. It too was burned down."

"Our own people," Gerald interrupted. "The Confederate Army. They burned buildings around it as they left, hoping I suppose, to destroy anything that they had built up so that the Yankees couldn't get to any of it. The wind came up and tossed cinders and burning embers around town and set fire to many of the buildings."

"Could they not have realized that the wind would take cinders to other buildings; like ours?" Annette asked. Then she added as if absentmindedly. "I'm Annette, Ginny," she introduced herself. "You used to call me Annie and I guess it's stayed with me all my eighteen years."

"Oh, my yes," Ginny answered. "Annie. My baby sister! My, you're anything but a baby now. Just look at you. Last time I saw you, you were headed off to Ms. Marie's School for Young Ladies." They hugged and giggled like schoolgirls for a brief moment.

"Ginny." Annie interrupted, her honey-blonde curls tied into a bow and tumbling down her back. Her sapphire blue eyes radiated happiness from her bubbly smile as she wrapped her arms around Ginny and said, "It's been too long, sis."

"Yes, it has." She looked at her in her plum colored gown, with matching cape, shoes and gloves and seeing no one with her, she asked, "Are you married?"

"Nope. I'm looking though." She smiled and asked, "Like I said. What were they thinking? Sixteen of our employees were incinerated."

"Yes," Ginny returned. "I know. I saw the burnt-out structure. And I've talked to some of the rift-raft soldiers down there.?"

"You went there?" Kenneth asked, pouring himself a drink from the bar. "Those were Yankees, Ginny. Yankees."

"I know. I whipped one just for looking at me. I suppose I shouldn't have, but . . ."

Her siblings laughed while Sarah smiled.

"You hit him with a whip?" Annette asked,

"Now, if we have got past the point where we all know each other . . . once again," Kenneth said, holding the decanter high.

"I've poured one for each of us. Gerald, if you will, please."

Once each person had a drink in their hand, Gerald honored Ginny with a toast. "Here! Here! May I offer this toast to our long-lost sister, Virginia McBride. May this *prodigal child* be blessed from this day forward and showered with a ring on her finger, one on her toe, and a tiara on her head."

This was chorused by the rest. "Here! Here! To our sister, Ginny."

And from Kenneth, "To our wayfaring sister."

"If I have any more names, I'll never find out who I really am," Ginny joked.

"Ah," Sarah alerted her clan. "Lulu Belle is beckoning us to dinner. If some handsome, strong grandson would escort me, we should all go to the dining room for an excellent meal.

"We're coming, Lulu," Kenneth gestured as he helped Sarah to her feet.

"Mistah Ken, you knows better than to calls me thet. M'name's Lulu Belle." She turned and went back into the kitchen and continued talking to herself. "Lulu is kids stuff. I ain't no kid no mo'ah."

Kenneth stared at Lulu Belle and asked, "Why is it so important that we call you by your whole name? Can't *Lulu* be good enough."

Lulu Belle turned and looked sternly in Kenneth's face. "'Cause, Mistah Kenneth, suh, *Belle* means *beautiful*. You must admit, I is beautiful." She smiled and giggled as she turned and walked ahead of him into the dining room.

Sarah smiled and watched Kenneth's stern face turn into laughter.

She kept up her appearance that night and enjoyed every moment of her visit with her family. But as they sat around the table, talked, laughed, ate and drank together, Ginny's mind was still on the face she kept seeing in her dreams. *Matt! That has to be his name. Well, Matt,* she thought, *now that I'm starting to find myself, maybe I can find you, too.*

CHAPTER 16

A REVELATION

<u>12 July 1865</u>

After several weeks of counseling with Ginny, Harris and Henry came to the conclusion that their continual counseling with Ginny to bring her back into reality as to her being Ginny McBride had drawn to an end. With Sarah's blessings, they condescended that she was truly, Virginia McBride.

However, her continual quest still went on. *I'll find you, Matt my darling. Given time, I will find you.*

In concluding, while sitting in Doc Paterson's study, Harris addressed Henry. "Her visions, I feel, were and I suppose still are real. That is, to the point that she wants them to be real. The way I see it, Henry, is that she wants this lover of hers to be a *real entity . . . a real lover.*"

"Don't we all?" Henry gestured, biting off the end of a cigar while handing one to Harris. "But what about her amnesia? What do you suppose brought that on?"

"It *was* real. When she found out that she could not escape and find her Matt, she became the other person, like I said before, whom she ostensibly always wanted to be.

"Beth?"

"Beth. The lady. Not Ginny, the fighter. However, as I see it now, she still has both personalities. "

"A dual personality?" Henry asked. "Two persons in one?"

"But again, like I said earlier, and I'm more certain now, they're just personalities. We all have such manifestations. In Ginny's case, there is nothing more to worry about. Don't we all want to be two persons? The real person that we believe we are, and the imaginable person that we would like to be; a swashbuckling hero disguised as a bookkeeper."

"Then, what you are saying, in her case, she became both," Henry interjected.

"That was evident when she went to the mill and, excuse the expression, beat the tar out of three soldiers with her whip and gun."

"Then she'll always have that personality; the old Ginny?"

"No longer that aggressive, I can assure you. I feel that she had to have that eruption, if I may use that term, to release her inner hostilities one last time. I believe that the real person has finally emerged."

"Ginny?"

"Yes. She'll continue with her practice, but as Virginia McBride and not as Elizabeth Paterson as is on her law degree."

"When will she give up one for the other completely?" Henry asked, lighting first Harris' cigar and then his.

"When? She already has, ."

"And you think this vision is nothing more than a dream of hers?"

"As a continuing link to her second ego, yes. I'm convinced of it."

"Will there ever be another occurrence of it; say in the future some time?"

"It could happen. If she finds this chap, Matt, she could be seen in his eyes as he first met her as the incorrigible Ginny McBride, ruler of a plantation of slaves, or as the soft, loveable and intelligent Miss Beth Paterson."

"That is interesting. In my time," Henry surmised, "I suppose I've seen the two personalities."

"Which one do you prefer?"

"I don't know. I really don't know." He looked away and then turned back to Harris and laughed. "I kinda liked the first person I met. The challenging and witty one. But, now she's so sophisticated and intelligent. I don't actually know; and that's a fact."

"Now that she knows who she is, Ginny McBride, you'll start to see both personalities merge more and more in time. She'll remain the sophisticated Ginny and with a bit of that swashbuckler that you met on the battlefield. That's when I want you to contact me. But for now, there is nothing more I can do, or would want to do, Henry," Harris finished the tea visit with Henry and Emma, puffed once more on his cigar and rose to leave."

Ginny walked out on the veranda and, interrupting them, greeted Harris. "I just came over for a visit with my two special people, Dr. Harris. Did you need to see me about anything?"

Dr. Harris stood by the chair, shook hands with Ginny and said, "No, Ginny. And you *are* Ginny. As I told the Major this morning, I don't feel there is any more I can do. The Major will keep his eye on you, and if there are any further developments that I need to be brought in on, he'll know where to reach me." Then he said with a tip of his hand to his chin, "Except, I would like to have the opportunity to visit you when I feel it necessary. To kind of put a finishing touch on my studies with you. About amnesia." He gave an assuring smile.

"Why, yes, Dr. Harris. I would be amenable to that visit. Let me know when."

Dr. Harris kept in continual touch with monthly reports about Ginny's progress through Henry. The personal visits took place at random periods, and his notes were printed in the American Medical Journal the next year with a favorable report about the recovery of his patient, *Ginny McBride*, which he aptly entitled, *The Ghost of Ginny McBride.*

CHAPTER 17

THE REVEREND BUNTING

<u>25 September 1865</u>

The ride to Nashville, Tennessee was still a painful ride in the saddle for two cowboys who had a lot of thoughts about the war because they fought many skirmishes throughout Tennessee. But a refreshing thought was that they would soon be visiting with their company chaplain, one Reverend Robert Bunting.

Having left the military, the Reverend Bunting was accepted to a pastoral position at the First Presbyterian Church in Nashville. It was a rather large building with many members, and they looked only for a top of the line preacher; and Bunting was their man; one who could help rebuild the spirit and the moral of their parishioners after the turmoil and devastation of the war. Bunting met their needs.

"There it is, Steve!" Matt exclaimed as they reined up at the road crossing that led one road towards the church and another long winding one towards the town of Nashville. "Let's ride up and see our ol' friend, Bob."

The two men walked their horses gently to the front entrance, dismounted and tied them to the hitching rail. Matt walked to the front door and found it locked. He walked around to the side entrance and found an open door.

The church office was the first thing that he saw when the two men walked inside. A lady in age greeted them.

"May I help you, gentlemen?" she asked pleasantly with a smile on her lips.

Matt took his hat off and Steve did the same. "Looking for Chaplain Bunting, ma'am," Matt said, looking around the inside of the church.

"He's in his study. If you stay here, I'll get him for you."

"No, no," Matt returned. "We're friends of his from the war."

"Oh. I could tell when you called him *Chaplain.* Well, he's down the hall, first door on the right. I don't think he'll mind."

Walking down the hall, the men saw a sign depicting the *Pastor's Study*, and moseyed over to it. Behind the desk sat a good looking man sporting a moustache with dark wavy hair. On his desk was a sign that spelled out, *The Reverend Robert Bunting.*

As Matt leaned against the door jam, he rapped three times on the door lintel to let Bunting know of his presence.

"Matt!" Bunting exclaimed with over-exuberance of excitement at seeing his comrade of arms. "Matt Jorgensen. You ol' horse dogger."

"Bob," Matt returned with a strong handshake.

"Me, too!" Steve interrupted as he came around Matt and shook Bunting's hand.

"Steve Andrews. Good to see you two. What brings you to Nashville? Good news, I hope. We're through having bad news."

"About what?" Matt asked.

"The ship that went down. So many. So many drowned."

"Who?" Steve asked.

"Soldiers on both sides going home." Bunting looked at the two men and ushered them into his office. "Haven't you heard?"

"Little news crosses our path out on the prairie, Bob." Matt took an overstuffed chair and sat down followed by Steve as Bunting took his seat behind his desk.

"Where's my manners" Bunting said, bouncing out of his chair. "Let me take you fellas for a tour."

The tour lasted only a few minutes. It was plain to Bunting that Matt had no interest in a fancy church as he had no mind to be in a church in the first place.

"He's come to see you, Bob," Steve said as they re-entered Bunting's office. It's been nice to see you again, but I think I'll tend to the horses and leave you two to your talkin'.

"Well, sure, Steve. It's been a pleasure, Steve."

Steve sauntered back outside as Matt turned back toward a suddenly very serious pastor.

"Gotta talk with you, Bob," Matt said, rubbing the sides of his dungarees.

"Spiritual?"

"Kinda, I suppose. Don't know, really."

"Then let's pull up a chair and talk. Plain talk. You know I'd never preach at you, Matt. You're too good a man to be preached at, and I think I know your mind probably more than you do. Been with you the whole war, just about." Then he smiled and said, "Frankly, my job is to keep you from going to hell."

"Yep." Matt sat down and stared around the room, not knowing how to bring up the subject of visions when he noticed a cross hanging behind the chair where Bunting sat. He stared down on the desk where some carved wooden hands were clasped as if in prayer.

"Well?" Bunting asked, after waiting for Matt's eyes to focus on him.

"Jesus."

"Cussing again, or asking?"

"This Jesus fella. He's for real?"

Bunting smiled, clasped his hands and rested them on his thigh. "Oh, yeah, he's real."

"He is . . . or was God?"

"That's our belief . . . the Christian belief. God in the form of man."

Matt stood up, walked towards the window and looked out. "I'm having problems."

"What kind of problems?"

"I'm not what you call a *Christian*. Never was. Never believed in it. Just some kind of religion and I never cottoned to it." He turned and faced Bunting. "He died?"

Bunting sat back into his chair and focused in on Matt's eyes. "Jesus died."

"God?"

"Well, yes, in a sense, God died. As a man, he lived, was crucified, died and was buried and rose from the grave three days later."

"I don't have a problem with your believing in all that," Matt suggested. He meandered back to the chair and held onto its back while he stood in front of Bunting.

"What do you believe, Matt?"

"Me? Let men live their lives. The way they want to. A man's gotta be a man or he's no good to nobody."

"Then what problem are you wrestling with?"

"It's stupid. I know it's stupid." Matt slapped the back of the chair and walked back towards the window. He turned and stared at Bunting for a while before he continued. "What kinda body do you suppose he had after he rose from the grave?"

Bunting sat back into his chair, a little bit shaken with this question, coming from an ex-Confederate officer with no Christian experience. "Did your mother take you to church?" he asked.

"Oh, we stopped by a church back in town from time to time. She was a fine Christian woman too. Still is, I suppose. She lives in . . ." Matt stopped for he felt he was revealing too much about his past, being brought up in Montana and partial to Yankees. "I aim to see her soon." He knew in his guts, he'd probably never see her again, and it hurt for him to say what he did.

Bunting sensed an ill-feeling on the part of Matt and tried to put his mind at ease. He was good at doing this, having counseled many men as well as members of a large church. "What do you suppose?"

"He climbed up out of the grave, and just went through some rock they say a couple of angels rolled away."

"You have a problem with that?"

"A lot."

"Tell me."

"Well for openers, I can't figure anyone coming through a rock or a grave with any kind of body. And I don't believe in angels . . . I suppose . . . I don't know. It's that body thing that bothers me. If people saw him, then he must have had a real body, not something they couldn't see."

"Is this your problem? You want to know how Jesus rose from the grave and was seen by people and touched by some?"

"More'n that."

"Tell me, Matt. I'm here to listen."

113

"I'm not one to deal in religion, Bob. You oughta know that by now. But I'm experiencing something strange in my life, and I can't figure it out."

"Like what?"

"Like," Matt took a deep breath and when he let it out, said, "A ghost!"

"A ghost?" Bunting echoed with his eyes opened wider.

"I know it sounds crazy, but so does this thing about Jesus sound crazy to me. I don't believe any of it. Haven't from day one. I'm sorry. But . . ." Matt froze and stared into Bunting's dark brown eyes.

"Go ahead, Matt."

"I'm haunted by a ghost."

Bunting put his hands in his pockets and sat still for a moment, hoping to find the right words to say. "A ghost?" Then he adjusted himself in his chair. He pondered at what Matt was saying. He felt Matt was a puzzled man and might be having hallucinations from the war. "Any one I know?"

"Yep."

Then it suddenly dawned on Bunting who Matt might be talking about, for he had talked with him about her throughout the war. "Ginny!" he exclaimed with wide-opened eyes.

"She's real, Bob. As real as you and me. I've seen her."

"Dreams?"

"Not dreams. No. Real life."

"She was a person, Matt."

"Yes. Yes. But not just *a person*. She talked with me as if she wanted to . . ."

Bunting waited for Matt to finish, but when he saw that he was searching deeply, he asked, "What, Matt? She wanted to, what?"

"She wanted to hold me. To kiss me. I wanted to do the same, but we couldn't."

"Why not?"

Matt returned to the window and looked out into the distance before he answered. "She's supposed to be dead, Bob. Like I've told you so many times before."

Bunting closed his eyes as in prayer, opened them and then looked up at Matt. He knew Matt was perplexed with a haunting. "How is it that you saw her?"

"I don't know how to say it. Like a brush against me when no one was there. I felt her presence. I even sensed her smell. A smell I'll never forget. Like when I first met her and we sat down by the Tennessee River and she patched up my wounds. That smell will never leave me. I smelled her."

"That's it?"

"No. I saw her."

"How, Matt?" Bunting was so excited about his conversation with Matt that he could hardly restrain himself from wanting to know more . . . more if it were real, or if he was simply seeing an illusion of a loved one. He had read about many people having such illusions, yet he didn't want to put Matt into that category. He had talked with him on many occasions during the war, but he had never preached at or to him about his faith, for he felt he would lose Matt's friendship. And losing Matt, the great hero of the war, which he was, would be as devastating as if he were to get killed.

"Can you believe it, Bob, if I told you?"

"It all depends, Matt. I've talked with bereaved people who have lost their loved ones and felt that they, too, experienced seeing them, again."

"Were they telling you the truth?"

"What they believed was the truth, I suppose, yes. I couldn't swear that they did, but I believe that they experienced something that was real *to them*. And, that, Matt, I couldn't and wouldn't take away from them."

"You believe I might be like one of them."

"Could be."

"Then I'm not a good candidate for your way of life; your way of believing. 'Cause, Bob, I actually saw her."

"Did you? Did you touch her?"

Matt turned his eyes from the distance back to Bunting. "Would you believe me if I told you I did"

"Maybe."

"Well, I didn't. But I wanted to. She wanted to touch me. I know she did."

"Did this happen more than once?"

"Two, maybe three times."

" Which is it?"

"Well," Matt said, stuttering, "two times I saw her visit me. The heck of the thing, Bob, is the other time, I visited her. Dang it!"

"Visited? How do you mean?"

"Just thet. Like in a dream. Yet more real than a dream. I saw her . . . like in a fog. She was in a bedroom; a large bedroom, one I had never seen the like of. Sleeping. And there I was looking down upon her."

"In a dream?"

Matt paused, turned towards the window again and looked out. "One would think so. Like a dream. But it was real. I saw her. So beautiful, just sleeping there. I kinda talked to her like I was reading one of my letters to her."

"Did she see you?"

"Funny thing, Bob. It looked to me like she was looking right into my eyes, but her eyes were shut. No, open. I don't know. It was too real, like I could just touch her, but I wasn't allowed to. Does any of this make sense?"

"Do you want it to?"

"Well, yeah." Matt turned and looked away. Wouldn't any one? I mean. Is this normal?"

"What about the other two times?"

"I felt her in passing, like I said. Like as if she brushed up agin' me. I turned and for a moment saw her face. Just for a moment. Only for a moment and then she was gone. But I saw her."

"When was that?"

Matt sat back down in the chair, folded his hands in front of him and stared above Bunting, looking at pictures hanging on the wall. "In a battle. A Yankee came at me with his rifle. Steve was next to me and he saw what happened. He told me what he saw."

"Which was . . .?"

Matt looked away from the wall and out the window, catching sight of nothing as he continued to speak. "This Yankee. A young kid. My back was turned and he had a good bead on me. When he brought the rifle at my chest, I knew I was a gonner. Then, all of a sudden , my horse reared and I was knocked out of my saddle."

"By Steve?"

"No, sir."

"Then who knocked you out of the saddle?"

"Ginny!"

"Ginny?" Bunting drew a deep furrow in his forehead, squinted his eyes as if in disbelief and swallowed hard. "You actually saw Ginny do this? Steve saw it?"

"That's the moment I told you when I saw a glimpse of her. Just a glimpse. I felt her more than I saw her. You see, her ghost or spirit spooked my horse and knocked me out of the saddle."

Bunting stood up, walked around the room in an absent-minded circle, his index finger tapping his top lip and his mind completely engrossed in his thoughts.

After several moments he sat down on the edge of the desk, his arms folded across his chest, and said nothing as he continued to look in Matt's direction. However, he did not stare at Matt. Instead, he looked as if in a blind direction; looking for an answer.

"Tell me more."

"Not much more to tell you, Bob. Have you ever heard of such a thing?"

Bunting sat straight up, unfolded his arms and then answered him. "Yes. Yes, I have. Some experiences like the one you have had I've heard and read about. Stories where someone was in danger and, by some miraculous event, stepped away from the danger."

"Like what?"

"Like, someone stepping off a cliff and, at the last moment, falls down as if someone or something had tripped him. Maybe per chance a log or a branch on the ground. Sometimes nothing would be there at all. I've heard of heroes in the war escaping death by falling on the ground for no explainable reason. Yes, Matt, I've heard of such. We call that *God intervention,* where

God steps into our history and intervenes on one's behalf." And then he added, "But you say you saw her?"

"Just a glimpse. You say it could be God intervening for us?"

Bunting opened the Bible as if to read it, and then looked up at Matt with a more serious expression on his face. "Yes. Let's look at it in a practical way. Say that what you saw or think you saw was an apparition."

"A figment of my imagination, Bob?"

"No. Something real. An apparition can be a vision or a ghost. It can be real or false." He released the Bible and stood up. "Matt, it's like you seeing your Ginny in a mist or a fog. Right?"

He watched Matt's face cringe as he nodded. "I've read and even talked with some people who have had an experience with seeing a vision; a glimpse like you say out of the corner of their eye. A person, say. And when they turned to see the person, he or she wasn't there."

"And what I saw then, when I was knocked out of my saddle, was an apparition?"

"Maybe."

"Matt," Bunting said with a half-way grin as he came around his desk to join Matt, "I've a theory on that."

Matt turned towards Bunting and looked puzzled. "A theory?"

"Just a theory. Want to hear it?"

"You bet! Shoot, Parson," Matt said as a gesture. He was listening all attentive to what Bunting had to say, not wanting to miss a word. He slid his hands in his back pockets, turned and stood beside the chair.

"It's only a theory, but, as I come to believe, and I may be wrong, it mostly applies to the dead."

"The dead?"

"Like I said, I could be wrong. It could explain Ginny's appearance to you. But then, on the other hand, it would not explain your appearance to her." He stepped around his desk and continued, "It might seem a little confusing to you." He took the Bible in his hand, stood up and walked around the desk to the window.

He turned and looked at Matt with strong determination and a concentrated thought on his mind. "I believe that the spiritual body can manifest itself at will any time and any place it desires. This would be an illusion to the living and a heavenly experience to one having eternal life."

"But you said it only applies to the dead. What kind of experience did I have? I'm not dead. At least I don't think so." He gestured, "Sometimes I wish I were. If it would help me find Ginny, I'd wish anything."

Bunting put his hands on Matt's shoulders. "The word, *ghost*."

Bunting's mind worked overtime for he was having a discussion about ghosts with one of his dearest friends. *The very word stirs up one's imagination*, he thought as he listened to Matt. *Does such a thing really exist? Did it ever exist? Is there such a thing as a ghost? I believe it, but how do I, a minister of the cloth, talk to a non- repentant sinner about spiritual things like these?*

""I've known you as a cavalry officer", Bunting went on. "All you probably know is that you're very much in love with a girl who has been shot and presumed dead. You feel within your soul that she is alive and that some day, somehow you're going to find her. And now you've met with unexplainable phenomena that confront your suspicion about ghosts. And if she were dead, you wonder if her ghost would haunt you? And I suppose you could care less because you're in love, and this is where love abides. Am I close?"

Matt looked glassy eyed at Bunting, but took in everything he was saying.

"Matt," Bunting continued, sitting back at the desk, "nothing is without merit. Anything is possible, and since it happened in the Bible in several places, then it stands to reason that it can also happen today. We're not that far away from God that He can't do things for us that will bring us together into eternal life."

"Can it be otherwise? I don't believe she's dead."

Bunting tapped the desk with his knuckles, rose and walked away. "The hardest thing I ever did in my ministry was to tell a mother that her son was dead, when she depended on me to pray him back to good health."

"What's thet, Bob?"

"I'm trying to tell you that in all probability, Ginny is dead."

Matt walked to the closed door. Grabbed the door handle and stood there. Releasing the handle, he hit the lintel with his right fist and swore, "Damn!"

"I know you don't want to accept that explanation. But, Matt. The apparition. And the experience of you falling out of your saddle for no apparent reason. All that you've been telling me leads me to believe that she's probably dead!"

Matt turned around and looked sternly at Bunting. "What good did it do for me to come talk with you? What?"

"You're a soldier, Matt. A good one. You follow orders. Follow this one. Let her Go! If she's dead, let her rest in peace!"

Matt grit his teeth and replied with tears in his eyes, "No, Bob! Never!"

Bunting kept quiet for a long period of time while he saw Matt throw himself into the chair in front of him and bury his face in his forearms. Bunting rose and put his arms around Matt's shoulders

"Then I'm with you, Matt. If Ginny were my girl, and I was so deeply in love with her as you are, I would be convinced of nothing else than the idea that she was still alive."

"How?"

"How? I would imagine her being alive if I'd see her in everything that was connected to her being; like the aroma of her skin, the look in her eyes, and such."

"And then, seeing Ginny sleeping in that bedroom could mean that she's alive?"

"Now, you've gone into another dimension." Bunting rubbed his chin, looked away for a moment as if in deep thought of how to answer Matt, and then said, "I most certainly would, Matt. I have to step aside from my theological training for the moment and step into the shoes of a brilliant officer and say, I'm pretty much like you. I must admit. If I did that, then I would have to believe she's still alive."

Bunting looked at Matt as a broad smile came across Matt's face and he thought, *Well, Reverend Bunting, whether you believe what you just said or not, Matt's believing it. And, Lord, I hope he's right. I certainly hope that he's right.* Then with a smile, he asked, "Is she still as beautiful?"

"More so," Matt answered with wide eyes and a manly grin. "More so. But she was sleeping, and I suppose she'd have to look beautiful." He rose, stared into Bunting's eyes and added, "And I'm going to find her."

"Can I help?"

"You can. Pray that I find her."

Bunting smiled and said matter-of-factly, "Then you do believe in the power of prayer?"

Matt took his bandana, wiped his eyes and said with a smile, "You said it, Parson!"

"Matt, you've gone just about as far as any man can go with what is obsessing you. You've traveled through a war. You've covered your routes from the time you met Ginny."

"No!" Matt interjected enthusiastically. "No I haven't, Bob. Steve and I are on our way to Richmond. And we're going to find Ginny!"

"Richmond? Is that where Ginny is from?"

"Yep." Matt grasped his hands together with Bunting and walked around him towards the door. "You see. I've not gone to Richmond. If she is alive, I've asked myself, wouldn't she have gone to Richmond? And I promised her I'd see her in Richmond, and by God and all His might, I think I just might meet her there."

Bunting looked pie-eyed at Matt, smiled and said, "Yes, I think she would have gone to Richmond. If she's still alive."

"Still alive? Bob, I know she's alive." He shook Bunting's hand and darted out the door.

Steve was on the lawn, leaning against an oak when he saw Matt bolt out the door. "What's up, pal?"

Waving back to Bunting, Matt ordered Steve, "Get in the saddle. We're gonna ride."

And ride they did.

"Where're we headed to now, Matt?" Steve asked as the two refreshed cowboys rode away from the First Presbyterian Church in Nashville, Tennessee and Rev. Robert Franklin Bunting. *Perhaps the last time I'll ever see Bob,* Matt thought to himself. *Good man. Good friend. But don't know nothin' about my Ginny being alive. Ghost? Ha! No way in heaven.*

"Like I done told ya afore, friend," Matt replied, gritting his teeth as he rode slightly ahead of Steve. "Richmond."

Steve caught a bit of what Matt said and answered to the wind, "Richmond? Did I hear you right, Matt?"

Matt grunted and kept riding.

"Thet's sure a long ride from here," noted Steve.

"Yeah. It'll be shorter once we get ourselves drunk," Matt answered. Pulling the brim on his hat down, he spurred Skeeter towards Richmond.

Steve proved to be right; it was a long ride. But Matt was determined to either find Ginny or end his search at the last place he knew to look; the McBride Textile Mill in Richmond, Virginia that she had told him about while working on her plantation.

CHAPTER 18

THE BANK ROBBERY IN CLAY COUNTY

Winter, 1865

One evening that winter in Missouri, far from Richmond, several room-and-board members joined Jesse James while his cousin Zee and her father served them dinner at a long table accommodating eight people. The group this day was made ujp of the Youngers; Cole, John, Jim and Bob, Clell, Little Arch and Jesse's brother Frank. Another paying couple sat with them.

"You're still lookin' mighty peeked, Jesse," Frank said with a big smile and a good hold on a fried chicken leg. "It's a good thing ya had Zee to take good care of ya. What'd ya get down to?"

"Thanks, Frank," Jesse replied. "I needed thet. Don't know. Maybe a hundert and thirty."

"I knowed ya lost a good deal, bein' as skinny as you are."

"I also think about those two as my best friends in the hollow; John and Martha. They tended to me so's I could get up here. I wanna repay them somehow."

"How?" Cole asked, chugging down a swallow of buttermilk from a thick glass. "We're poorer than the poor folk."

"Been thinkin' on it, Cole. I've got a plan on how to make some money."

"You're not gonna get a job 'til you're well and on your feet, Jesse," Zee said adamantly as she poured more buttermilk in his glass. "And thet ain't a goin' to be 'til sometime after Christmas just before the snow's gone pretty much. We know how to ride in the snow. Our advantage."

"Darn right I'm not gonna get a job. This here war owes us somethin' and I aim to get it."

"Don't know what ya mean," Cole said, lookin' around the table at the others.

Jesse looked at the other couple eating and immediately shut up tight lip. "Later."

Later was in his room that same night with Frank, the Youngers, Little Arch and Clell, joining Jesse and Zee.

"You're our friends, right? " Jesse asked as he pointed to the men."

Cole spoke for the rest as the men nodded in agreement. "We've come a long way together. Shucks, we grew up together.

"Well. A certain bank owes us. Right, Frank?"

"We've been a talkin' for some time about thet," Frank returned. "Just gotta a yen for more buttermilk, Zee."

Zee looked at Frank and said, "I'll get some more." Then she looked sternly at Jesse and left the room.

While she was out of the room, Jesse called the gang together closely and announced, "We're ready to hit the bank."

Clell asked, "What bank you have in mind, Jesse?"

"You all know what bank. The Clay County Bank right around the corner."

Zee readily returned and after listening some more, about robbing a bank, she exclaimed, "You ain't gonna rob a bank!" She set the milk pitcher hard on the table, spilling it. "You ain't!"

"You bet I am. And with these men here. You know how it is, Zee. None of us never did get along with the bankers. Never once would they lend ma and pa a hand when they needed it. Now they're dead and it's cause of them. Now, I figure the bank owes us somethin'."

"You want us to hold up a bank?" Cole asked as he stood up and looked down at Jesse. "Can't be done. We'd be caught for sure, us runnin' our horses through the woods at night. And I know – I know about us out runnin' them in the snow and all."

"That's just it, Jim," Frank came back. "We're planning on doing it during the day time."

"Day time?" Clell stood up alongside Cole. "Can't be done."

"Why?" Jesse returned, sharply eyeing Clell. "Because it ain't been done. Thet's why. But, Clell. And the rest of you. It's gonna be done.

"Think about it." Jesse told the men. The rest leaned in, curiously.

"It's a sound bank, Jesse," Clell came back. "Solid through and through. It'll be a tough job."

"Yeah? Well nothing good ever comes easy." Jesse continued. "Frank and I know thet bank through and through. Over the next few weeks, you men will have a chance to view the bank."

Frank interrupted. "You've got to heal first, Jesse."

"I'm ok now. Don't pay no mind to Zee, Frank. I'll be better in a few weeks. It'll give us some time to smooth out our plans," Jesse returned.

"He ain't teather!" Zee came back. "He needs more time."

"Hush, Zee!" Jesse remarked with his finger at his lips. "I'm fine. And like I said, I'll be better in a few more weeks. Gives us a chance to take a good look at the bank."

"You know me, Jesse," Little Arch same back. "This bank is owned by Republicans who are Yankees. And officers to boot. I'm all for it."

"Sounds good," Bob Younger agreed.

"It can be done, Jesse, I reckon," Cole came in.

"It will be done" By us!" Jesse looked at every man in the room. "I'm sure you can round up a few others who might come in with us. The way I got it figured, maybe, twelve or so of us can do it. It's gonna take several good men."

"Over my dead body!" Zee came back. "You're not gonna do it. I'm serious, honey. You're not well enough."

"Oh, Zee, hush!" Frank said with a smile, assuring her that if it was ok with him and the rest of the men, it should be with her, too.

"Like I said. Ten or twelve of us. We'll have the numbers. And nobody, but nobody's gonna think of anyone brave enough to rob a bank in daylight. We ride in, go inside, and rob the bank. We go out, climb back on our horses and hightail it out of town before the town knows what happened." Jesse outlined a plan with a chicken leg on the table.

"We come back here?" Little Arch asked.

Jesse shot back, "No!"

"You got somewhere else on your mind, Jesse?" Clell asked.

"Yeah! It's crazy, but if we go this far, we might just as well go the distance."

"Meanin?" Clell asked.

"Texas!" Jim Reed chimed in, slamming his fist on the table in front of him.

"The hell you say?" Clell returned. "The war's over. We're in Missouri."

"Right!" Jesse came back. "But I like what my Jim here has to say. He tells us that May Shirley and her dad are in Texas. Sycene, just outside-a Dallas."

"We heard about them leavin'," Clell came back. "They were run off same as us."

"Well," Jim continued, "Now they've built an inn and saloon there. I was on my way there until Jesse found out and talked me out of it."

"You know the way, don't cha, Jim?" Jesse asked with a smile.

"Sure enough do. She's wrote me enough times."

"Men?" Jesse asked.

"I knowed about it, but I ain't a goin', though," Frank returned. "I figure with the amount of money we get from these rich Republicans, I can retire and live comfortably here in Missouri. Not Texas. I'm agin it."

Clell and Little Arch agreed with Frank. "We're Missourans, Jesse, like you and Frank. And we'll stay in Missouri. I kinda like the terrain."

"Cole?" Jess asked.

"Texas suits me just fine. Brothers? You with me?" Of course Cole had an ulterior motive for wanting to go. He also had a liking for May Shirley, and when he heard from Jesse about going to Texas, he set his mind to it and made sure his brothers would go, too.

126

"I'll speak for myself," Bob Younger returned. He looked at Jesse and then at Cole, smiled and said, "I'm a goin'. Any where but Missouri will suit me jest fine."

The other brothers nodded and Zee embraced Jesse from the back. "You're crazy, Jesse. But if these fellas say so, I'm with ya. When do we go?"

Jesse chewed on the chicken leg, looked up at Zee and then said, "You're not goin'!"

"What? I am so. If'n you go, I go."

"Once we make it, and we will . . . big time. I'll be back for ya. We'll talk later."

Zee kept a hold of her man and knew that he spoke the truth. He would return for her.

"How soon do ya figure on robbin' this here bank, Jesse?" Cole asked as he and his brothers walked towards the door.

"After Christmas."

"After Christmas?" Clell came back.

Like I done told ya, it'll give me time to rest up and heal some more. It gives you a chance to look the bank over."

The men eyed each other and then looked back at Jesse. "What do we do in the meantime, Jesse?" Little Arch asked.

"Do whatever the hell you wantta, Arch, like you've been doin'."

"Drinkin' and playin' cards, mostly," Clell came back. "Nothin' more to do."

"But hang close by," Jesse added. "We'll hit it when I say we're ready. Not before."

It was a good evening for everyone, but for Jesse. He still felt the pain in his chest.

February 13, 1866

He called the time to hit the bank; two months later. And hit it they did; all twelve of them. As Jesse predicted, the day was cold and the snow packed the roads. A typical winter Missouri day, keeping most of Clay County's citizens indoors. A few dared outside with rain gear and umbrellas, but not enough to keep Jesse from his goal that dreary day. It was actually in his plan.

He was still not up to riding, but he did his part. After the twelve men rode up to town, they looked the place over carefully, noting the partially empty streets.

"Jesse told it like it would be!" Cole exclaimed as he sat back in his saddle.

The gang had done their study of the town well. They rode over to the bank and dismounted. It was a solid two-story brick bank building that appeared to be impenetrable. Jesse, Frank and the Youngers walked inside while the rest stood outside sort of meandering to take away any suspicion from any bystander.

Jesse himself walked boldly inside the bank ahead of the rest and announced himself. He was right; the bank was practically empty this time of day. "I'm Jesse Woodson James and this here is my brother, Frank. These men are all my friends, and we've come to rob your bank." He looked at the startled people and commanded them. "Get down on the floor and you won't get hurt. We just want this bank's money. Not yours."

At first the startled people did not know whether to laugh or faint. A woman fainted. A man grabbed her and eased her to the floor.

The bank manager bolted out of his office and ran his face directly into Frank's Navy.

"On the floor with the rest, mister!" Frank ordered. "We're taking your money so you can take a vacation."

Frank looked at the woman who fainted and her husband who cradled his wife. "That's right, mister bank man. Stay down there with her. The rest of you get on the floor, too. That way no one gets hurt."

"You, too, Jerry!" Jesse ordered a young teenager who he quickly identified.

"Sorry, Jerry. Get down and you won't get hurt."

"No, sir!" he came back at Jesse. "You ain't gonna rob this here bank. I know you, Jesse." The boy looked around at the people on the floor and yelled, "He's Jesse James! He went to school with me! He's not tough!"

Cole took this .45 and clobbered Jerry across his head, sending him to the floor.

"Anyone else wanna try?" Cole asked, pointing his two revolvers around the room at the remaining three or four customers. They stayed on the floor while the gang vaulted the rail and went into the tellers' booths.

"Fast, boys!" Jesse ordered, holding his two revolvers on the tellers. He kept a third revolver tucked inside the front of his pants; a trick Quantrill taught his guerillas during the war to prevent running out of bullets and having to reload on the run.

Jesse and the Younger brothers grabbed the money bags and ran outside with their revolvers pointed in the air.

Frank looked at the other riders and ordered them, "Get the hell out of here! I'll bring Jesse along."

Cole looked at the bank door where a dazed Jerry stepped out with a gun. As he raised it, Cole quickly fired at him. The bullet found its mark and brought Jerry down; dead. He fell face down into the watery wagon tracks where blood flowed from his body.

"What the hell did'ya do thet for, Cole?" Frank asked, getting into his saddle at the same time, making certain that Jesse was all right.

"He had a bead on ya, Jesse," Cole answered. "Thet's why He turned his horse, yelled out, "Let's get the hell out of here!" and swiftly rode away, as the rest of the outlaw gang caught up with him.

"You ok, Jesse?" Frank asked as he helped Jesse into the saddle, making sure his feet were solid in the stirrups. "You alright?"

Jesse kept looking at Jerry's lifeless body until Frank slapped Jesse's horse into a gallop. "If you ain't ok now, little brother, you will be!" Frank's horse was fast and he kept Jesse's going through town.

Frank ordered Cole as he caught up to him, "Fire over their heads, dammit, Cole. No more killing."

As soon as Cole saw people paying undue attention to them, he obeyed Jesse and fired over their heads.

"Stay with me, Frank," Jesse said as he gripped the saddle horn.

"I'm with ya, Jesse. Yah!"

After more than hour of hard riding and now feeling safe from any posse, the men rested down by the Missouri River above Sibley in Jackson County.

"Anyone hurt?" Jesse asked, dismounting.

The men examined each other and claimed their victory over being shot, dismounted and washed their heads in the cool Missouri River.

"How much we got, Cole?" Jesse asked as he passed out some cigars and lit one for himself.

"Some notes here, but figure over twenty thousand in cash," Cole came back, fingering the money.

It came to over $62,000 total, which they divided among themselves; Jesse kept the larger amount.

"Woo whee!" the men shouted. Jesse and Frank were more than elated at the amount; never dreaming they'd see that much in a life time. Jesse's thought at the moment was brief and to the point as he shouted it with a clinch fist. "If only Quantrill could 'av been here to see this."

He looked at the smiles on the faces of all of his men and then interrupted them, saying, "Now, don't any of you shoot off your guns," Jesse warned them. "We're still running."

Then he looked around as the men began getting into their saddles. "Whose riding with me?"

"Little Arch and I are headed north but like we said, we're gonna stay in Missouri, Jesse," Clell answered. "It's our home."

"And me," Frank answered, letting the cigar smoke waft into the cool Missouri air as he sat his saddle. "They know you, Jesse. But I'll be up in the hills and no one will know. Trust me."

Jesse gave Frank the nod. Then a sad countenance came upon Jesse as he thought about Zee staying behind. "I'll keep watch over her, little brother," Frank assured Jesse. "You ride to Texas. Like we talked, you get things organized, and I'll join ya when ya come back to Missouri. The South shall rise!"

The men split up, going their own directions while Jesse, the Youngers and Reed rode towards Sycene, Texas.

No one was hurt or left behind, and it was the first time a bank had ever been robbed in the daylight. It took Clay County,

Missouri a while to get over the fact that they had in deed been robbed; and by Jesse and Frank James and the Youngers.

Little did they know that their paths would soon be crossed by two professional soldiers and now simply long-legged cowpokes, riding to Texas, across the Brazos to help a general resurrect his ranch.

CHAPTER 19

AN END OF AN ERA

4 March 1866

"**W**ell! Well! Well!" Gerald McBride exclaimed as he poured himself a glass of bourbon from the bar of the McBride Estate.

The McBride family had congregated in the west parlor to brief Ginny as well as one another as to the future of the McBride Mill. Gerald and Martha, Kenneth and Barbara, Annette, Ginny and of course their matron, Sarah.

"We're all here. So, Ginny, I suggest we get down to business immediately," Ralph gestured as he swirled his bourbon in a round goblet. "We had a mill. Everyone in consensus of that?"

"It was destroyed. I saw that," Ginny answered as she stood next to the bay window with a drink in her hand. "What's next?"

"Mrs. McBride?" Gerald gave the floor to Sarah.

"Well, to bring all of you up to date on what has happened and what we look forward to, I'll put my two cents in, whatever it's worth." Sarah smiled and went on as she sat in an overstuffed chair.

"My husband, Mr. Jonathon McBride; your grandfather, was a man with a vision. When we were married here in Richmond, we started off with a store   Then he had the opportunity to buy some land in Tennessee, which of course he did; the McBride Plantation. We rented out our store and moved to Tennessee to oversee the plantation. Of course, the plantation was nothing more than a large farm at that time. We got the idea that cotton was going to be, how you say it, *king* some day. Well, we bought ourselves some slaves and rolled up our sleeves and dug right in. We didn't have the gins that we have today. Oh, no. We barely scraped by, making the farm pay for itself.

"That's when your father came in. We didn't plan it. It just seemed to happen. Times were rough. We bought more land as we could for the getting. James and his brother Jonathan grew up. Your mother came along and married your father

"Jonathan?"

"Your uncle. He was a rebel from day one, I reckon. He rode out west. None of has heard from him since."

"And I was born on the farm?" Ginny came back.

"You weren't the last one. Annette was born there, too. And, Ginny, you helped take care of her when you were knee-high to a grasshopper."

"Do you remember any of it, Ginny?" Sarah asked, motioning for her to sit on a stuffed chair next to her.

"Some, maybe. Not much."

"Do you remember …..?"

Ginny sat down and looked puzzled at Sarah. "A cousin or something?"

"Your mule, chocolate brown. His name was Grizzli . . . or something like that. You rode her every day. She dumped you down at the bend of the road one day. She wanted to drink from the mud hole and you wanted to ride. Remember, Ginny?"

"Can't say that I do, Grand Mama. I'm trying. Honest, I am."

"You carried a switch with you and you were warned. Yes indeed. You were warned never to touch the mule's ears. And you did. You reached over and swapped the switch to your other hand and accidentally touched her ear. She went up and you went down. You came walking in, holding your arm and crying. You busted it. Right arm, too, as I recall. You had to write left handed in school for several months. Remember?"

"Wish I could, Grand Mama. But, I just don't."

"What do you remember?" Gerald asked, reaching into the cuspidor on the mantel for a cigar. "Me and Kenny here chased you through the corn field."

"Maybe. I do remember something about Papa getting real upset because someone chopped down the pop corn instead of the regular corn. Was that you, Kenny?"

"How come you to remember that?" Kenneth came back with a grin.

"Because . . . Because I remember you getting the belt and . . . then we all sat around the fire in the one room and all I could hear that night was the clicking of a clock. We just sat there real quiet. I guess you guys were maddest. Didn't bother me none that we didn't have any popcorn. I think. Am I right?"

"You're right, dear," Sarah answered with a sweet smile. "James wrote and told me all about how he wanted the land free of the corn stalks and Kenny cut down the popcorn instead."

"Well, it all looked the same to me back then," Kenneth defended himself. "In fact, Papa made me chop and haul all of those corn stalks, shucks, cobbs and all and load it into grain barrels to feed the mule with. You know we never wasted anything.

"So, child," Sarah continued. "You do remember some things?"

"I guess. And the mule thing is coming back to me now. It was a mud hole. I remember that one of you two boys got a horseshoe magnet and gave it to me. It was there I lost it in the mud hole and I went down there to look for it."

"Ever find it?" Kenny asked, watching Gerald light his cigar.

"Any one else want a cigar?" Gerald asked.

"Nope. Never did. I don't think I ever thought about it after that."

"Well, dearest," Sarah added, "some things will come back to you.

"Your Grand Papa and I left James in charge of the farm. He had a lot of slaves to work it. Your brothers came with us back to Richmond and helped us get our store back in order and finish their schooling. It was your Grand Papa's dream for their education." She looked at Gerald and Kenneth and added, "You two ran deliveries for us in the evenings and on Saturdays."

"And me?" Ginny asked.

"You, child and your sister Annette here stayed behind on the farm for awhile. You wanted to stay and help your dad since your mother had passed away. You couldn't do anything for your sister, so James up and brought her here to us."

"Well, it wasn't all together my fault," Annette argued. "Ginny, you were the tom boy. I didn't care to ride mules and I certainly didn't care to pick cotton. Grand Mama and Grand Papa took me in and made a lady out of me."

"It wouldn't be because you two could never get along together, now would it?" Sarah asked with a lilt to her voice. "You two were as opposite to one another as two sisters could be."

"And us?" Kenneth asked, taking a cigar from Gerald. "How did Jerry and I fare?"

"Not much better, I must say," Sarah returned. "Of course, however, you were boys and you played rough with each other. That left Annette by herself so we sent her off to a private school where, as she said, she became a lady."

Annette turned red and faced away from the group.

Sarah continued. "People depended on us for textile. And, then we had the opportunity to build a mill."

She stopped, took out her dainty handkerchief from her sleeve, wiped her eyes and continued. "Then, your Grand Papa died and this filthy, dirty war began. Our mill was destroyed.

"Letters have come from my brother and your cousins that they are working in North Carolina now with hopes of us building our new mill there."

Sarah looked tearfully into Ginny's eyes and added, "You, darling, are our final touch. God blessed the day when you came back to us. You can help make our mill grow like your Grand Papa would have wanted."

She kept looking intently at Ginny, waiting for some type of answer. Ginny kept silent, waiting to learn more from Sarah, whose eyes stared into Ginny's, feeling her vibes.

After what seemed an eternity, Ginny said, "It's a wonderful dream, Grand Mama." Her thoughts went to her dreams of Matt, and then she continued. "I'm sure we McBrides will resurrect our mill to Grand Papa's expectations. I'm glad God saved me for this moment."

Gerald brought out the glasses and, after filling them with fine brandy, gave each of them one and made a toast. "To our new mill!"

CHAPTER 20

MISS GINNY McBRIDE

<u>20 March 1866</u>

Slowly over time Ginny began to discover more, not only as to who she was, but intuitively who she would eventually become. She no longer saw herself as the rough and tough girl with a whip and a gun, but now she carried a law book and an umbrella to keep the sun from burning her alabaster skin.

Every once in a while she would walk in the garden of the McBride estate in Richmond and listen to the wind whisper her name and call her to a far off land. The name *Matt* haunted her from the time she realized that she was a *McBride.*

And many times she would sit at the side of Mrs. Sarah McBride and talk to her about him. She never felt this easy spirit with Henry or with Emma that she felt with Sarah to talk about her lover, for fear that they would have thought she was a spy during the war, and come to dislike her. Still, she knew deep in her heart that she was simply being silly about suspecting any such thing. But, she felt much more comfortable talking with Sarah just the same.

"Tell me, dear." Sarah asked one day with a lovely and caring smile. "What's disturbing you?"

Ginny looked into the grayish eyes of a matured woman and then looked down. "I'm having trouble with visions, Grand Mama."

"Visions, child? What kind of Visions?"

Ginny fidgeted with her fingers and looked around the room and outside the window into the moonlight. Then her head turned towards Sarah and their eyes met. They stared into each other's eyes for seemingly an eternity without either of them blinking and then Ginny asked, "Do you believe in ghosts, Grand Mama?"

Sarah looked away, stood up and walked over to the window to be next to Ginny. After looking out into the vast emptiness of space she returned, took the teapot which sat on the table next to her chair and poured a cup of tea for both Ginny and herself..

"It's a quiet time like this that I like to share a cup of tea with someone special." She looked at Ginny with a shine in her eyes. "I think you're very special."

Ginny returned her look and pondered on what she had said. "Do you, Grand Mama?"

Sarah sat down, took her cup and sipped the tea slowly, looking into Ginny's face at the same time without as much as a blink.

Ginny felt the kindness in her eyes and began talking about her dream.

"Tell me more about these visions, dear."

"Oh, like a dream. Only it wasn't a dream. It was a vision. As if I were awake and looked upon it."

"Were you awake?"

Ginny looked down, took her cup and sipped some tea and then said, "No. I suppose not. But it seemed like I was awake. I remember it so clearly and I don't always remember ordinary dreams. Do you kinda know what I mean?"

"I think I do, child. Tell me about your visions."

Ginny returned her cup to the table and began talking. "I see a man's face. It's a familiar face but I can't make out who he is. It's sort of blurry. And, and then I hear him read a letter to me. I can make out some of the words and sentences at times but then when I wake up, I can't recall what they were exactly."

"Yes, dear. I do believe in visions. The good book tells us that we shall have visions. Think, child. Think back to the visions."

Ginny looked back into her past, trying to remember something that would help Sarah see what it was that she was trying to remember. "That's it. When I awake, I seem to see the place where the vision was, and when I walk over to touch the wall, it's gone."

"Can you recall any of what he said or how he looked?"

"Nothing, except that he was a soldier."

"A soldier? A Union soldier?"

"No. No. He is . . . he's dressed like a Reb. He's got rank, though," she said with a smirk. "I can tell by the way he stands." And then she looked at Sarah and said, "I think."

They laughed together and Sarah poured them both some more tea.

"That's enough for now, Ginny. Let's finish our tea and just relax here. I'll tell you some about James."

"James?" Ginny asked, taking her tea cup gently to her lips.

"Yes, Ginny. Your Papa." She smiled, looked off into the distance and continued a long story about her son that brought warmth to the both of them.

"When your mother passed on from diphtheria, Annie was young then. James gave up managing the mill to your brother Gerald, and the legalities and paper work to your brother Kenneth. He then took you and headed back to Tennessee to keep us in material for the mill. Cotton! He left Annie here in Virginia to go to finishing school."

Bits and pieces began to emerge in Ginny's subconscious.

You werfe so headsgtrong, you felt you would be better off on the plantation.

And, once more Ginny began to find herself again that Indian summer, resigned that she was no longer in any hurry to really learn who she was. Soon, Sarah introduced Ginny to her ophthalmologist for fitted glasses. She also made an appointment with her personal tailor to have some of Ginny's attire refitted to make them more suitable to a McBride as Sarah confided to Ginny and lastly to a millinery. In one fell swoop, Ginny became a different person; refined and quite feminine. The world was a happy place for her and she was content in keeping it that way.

On the morning of the next day, on the veranda of the McBride estate, an aged lady of society gave sage advice to a young lady in search of her lover who was lost in the Civil War. The young lady, Ginny McBride, not knowing that she was being sought by her lover at the same time she was seeking to find herself, relied in part on her grandmother's prophesies for her destiny.

"Young Ginny," Sarah said as she sipped her morning tea in the drawing room; a grand room where she and her husband had sat and held conversations with all the elite that had visited them in the many years gone by. Now, only the two women of different generations sat and chatted in the same room.

"I am allowed to continue to call you that; am I not?"

Beth smiled and nodded. "From here on out, I shall always have my baptized name, *Virginia McBride*. Maybe it'll help bring both my lives together in some sort of an order to me. Of course, Grand Mama, I shall always be *Ginny* to you. And I'll be Beth to them. And that's okay, too."

Sarah smiled, took a firm hold of Ginny's hand and said, "Yes. Yes. My Ginny."

Ginny stood up, twirled around in happiness and laughed to herself and to the world. And that day, that hour, that precious moment, she felt she was home.

"My, my, my how you have grown." Sarah remarked. She took a deep breath and continued. "I can't tell you how grateful I am to God for leading you back to me. Yes, I remember . . . I remember the day you were born. Yes, and the time you pricked your finger on one of my special roses in the garden. Yes, yes, yes."

Ginny smiled and walked to the other side of the large room to look out the window. The garden came up to the edge of the house and she could reminisce about the roses.

"They're beautiful, aren't they, girl?" Sarah asked with a smile as she walked up to Ginny. "They weren't always like that. Oh, no. At times they were weak and bending. Other times they looked wilted. Barnabas had pruned them so that they would grow strong and proper."

Ginny listened to the sage words of the wise old woman as she leaned forward against the railing and looked out into the garden.

"You're referring to me, aren't you, Grand Mama?"

"If the shoe fits, dear, wear both pairs! I look at you, child, as a woman of distinction. And then again I look at you as a daring soul in search of her man."

Ginny turned her back to the railing and looked at Sarah. "You know me too well, Grand Mama. You're saying that I'm still two people? Is that what you're saying?"

"Are you in love with your Matt, dear?"

"Yes! Oh, yes! You know that I am!"

"Then, why are you here?"

"Grand Mama?"

"Your Father and Mother, God bless them, were pioneers. Your Grand Papa and I were pioneers. We let nothing stop us from doing or going. Nothing. And you, my dear, dear child, are the product of our pioneering days."

Ginny wrinkled her brow and looked sternly into Sarah's eyes. "Am I that much of a disappointment?"

"Only to yourself, Virginia."

"What are you saying, Grand Mama?" Ginny stood and waited for Sarah to answer, and then said, "What? What can I do?""If my Jonathan was alive and out there somewhere and I were here, I'd ride to him."

Ginny's eyes widened and her lips parted as she tried to answer Sarah.

"You called me *Virginia.* Why all of a sudden?"

Sarah smiled and answered her. "You are Virginia. You are the lady. You are me when I was your age."

"But you want me to . . .?

"Go after your man, dear!" She smiled and winked at Ginny, showing her the assurance of a sage old woman that she could find him, if she tried. "Don't let anything or anyone stop you!"

Ginny turned and walked away. She stopped, pondered on what Sarah had just said and did a pirouette with her gown flowing outward. "You turned me into a lady, and then . . . just like that you want me to ride out on my own and find Matt."

She remembered the time she rode from her plantation in Tennessee to meet Matt in Richmond as he was to ride in a parade in front of Robert E. Lee. It was on this momentous ride that she was shot by a young Yankee soldier.

When Sarah continued talking, Ginny's mind raced to the present and she listened intently to what Sarah had to say.

"You'll always be the lady. And, in all probability, you'll retain your spunk to be the woman Matt fell in love with. The Ginny McBride. Find him before it's too late.

"Where do I start?" Ginny asked without moving.

"You're an attorney, Miss McBride. Surely you can check out his whereabouts. Why not start with your plantation? Contact Sylvia. She saw him last."

Ginny looked down at the floor, turned and walked away, patting her cheeks with the tips of her right index finger. Sarah looked on as she disappeared, and smiled.

CHAPTER 21

CAPTAIN BRYCE WILLOUGHBY

<u>24 March 1866</u>

It was not long after that a gentleman caller, dressed in a Yankee Captain's outfit, approached the McBride mansion. He was met by Barnabas at the front door.

"Yes, suh?" Barnabas addressed the gentleman, keeping him at bay with the door ajar.

"Would you please announce to the lady of the house that one Captain Willoughby would like to visit with her."

"Captain Willoughby? Yes, suh. You're askin' for the Missus McBride?"

"She's married?"

"Was."

"Was?"

"Yes, suh. Was. He done up and died ten year ago."

"Ten years?" Willoughby frowned and wondered at Barnabas' remark. "I see. Well, could you announce my presence? I could wait in the front room. That is, if you would allow me."

"I could, if'n I knew what a front room was, suh," Barnabas returned. "If'n, suh, you are referring to the drawing room, it is in the middle of the house. That is where most people meet when they come into the mansion."

"The drawing room? Well, of course. Please allow me to wait in the drawing room. And, if you will, please let Mrs. McBride know that I am there."

"Yes, suh. But, thet is if'n you don't mind awaitin'."

Willoughby was amused at Barnabas' manners. He nodded his head and followed Barnabas down the long corridor to the drawing room. It veered off to the right with two large doors at the entry way. Barnabas opened the door and took the captain's hat as Willoughby gave it to him.

"Yes, suh," Barnabas came back. He closed the doors and walked back down the corridor.

The time slipped by and Barnabas had not shown up for a while. Willoughby looked around the room, found a shelf full of books and picked one out. He sat down and began reading.

After several more minutes passed, and no Barnabas or the Mrs. McBride, Willoughby rose, put the book on a table and opened the huge door to the corridor. Seeing no one around, he walked out and to the far end of the house, looking into each open door as he passed by.

At the end of the house, he saw a figure moving about on the patio. He went to the door, opened it and stepped out onto the veranda.

Ginny turned and looked towards the intruder.

"Oh! And who are you?"

"Well," Willoughby said, apologetically. "I'm Captain Bryce Willoughby, Madam." And then, correcting himself almost adamantly, he said, "Of course you know that." Straightening up his attire, he stood more at attention and continued. "I have come to visit with you and I might say, I have been waiting in the . . . drawing room for quite some time. You could have at least had the decency to tell your servant that you did not wish to see me."

"You came to see me?"

"Yes." He came down from his formal position, bent to her height and continued. "We met some time ago at your mill." He straightened up again and finished, "I was called away to Washington on another assignment, and now I've returned. I have wanted to call upon you for quite some time. But I didn't realize you were married."

"I remember you. Yes." Ginny sat down and offered a chair to Willoughby. "Well, sit down, Captain . . .?"

"Willoughby."

"I've been away myself," Ginny added. "Just returned the other day.

"Oh? Where did you go, if may ask?"

"We're looking at other mills."

"Oh. May I ask if you have the time to visit, as I've already been here for the better part of an hour." Willoughby thought of Ginny as married and felt uncomfortable.

"You told Barnabas you wanted to see me?" She sat down at the table.

"Yes." He sat down opposigte her with his hands folded. "I told your servant man that I would like to visit with you. I suppose he got lost some where."

"Barnabas? Oh, no," Ginny laughed. "He's been on these grounds from day one, I suspect. But he never came and told me that you were here."

The door to the veranda opened and, when the captain turned around, he saw Barnabas helping Sarah out onto the patio.

Willoughby rose to greet her.

"I left you in the drawing room, suh. What are you doin' out heah?"

"You came to visit with me, Captain?" Sarah asked as she walked out onto the patio. "Please. Sit down, Captain. Please ask Lulu Belle to bring us some tea, Barnabas."

"For him, too, Missus?"

"Captain?" Sarah asked. "Would you like some tea? This is usually the time that Ginny and I have our tea."

"Well, no, ma'am," Willoughby replied, totally confused.

"Then, how may I help you?" Sarah asked, as Ginny helped her to her chair. "I was taking a nap when you called."

"Oh. Well, I'm sorry. I really was asking for Mrs. McBride."

"You found her", Sarah returned. "She's sitting before you. I am Mrs. Jonathan McBride."

"Yes, ma'am. I mean. I guess I'm confused. Please excuse me. Well, for starters. I'm Captain Bryce Willoughby. And I've come to visit with Mrs. McBride, if I may." He gestured toward Ginny.

"Certainly, my good fellow. Sit down. Sit down. Let's visit."

"Yes, ma'am." Willoughby looked at Ginny, pulled out another chair from around the table and offered it to Ginny. "Mrs. McBride?"

Ginny took the chair and sat down. "Thank you, Captain. But, I think you're addressing the wrong person. She's Mrs. McBride. I'm Ginny McBride."

"Oh. I see. And you prefer to be called Mrs. McBride, also?"

Ginny grinned. "No. No. I'm not married. You may call me Miss McBride, if you so choose." Then, Ginny realized what was happening. "Oh. I see. You thought I was Mrs. McBride, didn't you?"

"Well, yes. That is, your man servant said that you were."

"He probably misunderstood who you wanted to visit. This is the lady of the manor, Mrs. Sarah McBride. I'm her granddaughter, Ginny McBride." Then she stopped, brushed a loose strand of hair back out of her eyes, and looked up at the captain as he was sitting down. "What is the nature of your visit, Captain Willoughby?"

The captain hemmed and hawed for a moment, got his bearings at what was happening and laughed. "I'm sorry. I thought. Well, whatever I thought, I'm glad that I'm visiting you, Miss McBride." He eyed Sarah for a moment and corrected himself. "Not that I didn't want to visit with the two of you."

"Captain," Sarah addressed him. "You've dug yourself a hole. Now quit throwing manure on yourself."

"Yes, ma'am."

"I believe the gentleman is seeking a private audience, Ginny. If you will please excuse me. Why don't you take Captain Willoughby for a walk through the garden?"

Sarah smiled and accepted the cup of tea that Lula Belle had been pouring for her. "Run along, child. When you return, your tea will be ready."

The couple stepped out into the garden path and walked a distance before Ginny asked, "And, Captain. What is it that you wish to discuss with me?"

Willoughby looked at Ginny and then back at the lonely figure at the table sipping her tea and watching them.

"It's rather awkward, but like I said, I had to go to Washington on business. I've been away for quite some time but thought about you. I mean. When I returned, I thought about asking you if I may take you to the military dance we're having down at the hall this coming Saturday."

"A dance?" Ginny returned "Why, I think that would be exciting. I've not been to a dance in a long time, but I bet I could still remember the steps of a few."

"Then, you will allow me to be your escort?"

"Why, yes, Captain."

They walked through the garden and acquainted themselves with each other for several moments before returning to the veranda to have tea with Sarah. And then Capt. Willoughby excused himself and left the mansion.

The night of the dance wore on quite well for the couple and especially when the Caller sang out, "And now, ladies and gents. The Virginia Reel."

If Ginny had thought that she forgot how to dance, she showed the people that evening that she still knew how. She fell into the rhythm of the Virginia Reel as the couples lined up and did some fine dancing. Every time she came back around to Willoughby, her eyes lit up to show that she was having the time of her life.

And what better way to spend an evening, she thought, than to be on the arm of a captain. Never did the thought enter her mind that she was dancing with a Yankee, until he took her home in his carriage.

As she leaned against his chest, she asked in a melancholy way, "Where're you from, Captain?"

"Me? Michigan. Born and raised just outside of Ann Arbor. Went to the University there just after the depression of '57. That's when the Cincinnati's Ohio Life Insurance and Trust Company was rumored to have ceased operation. War came and I had enough college for them to muster me in as a Lieutenant."

Ginny broke away from him for the moment and with hands on her hips looked him in the eyes and, without thinking said, "A Yankee!"

"Well, yeah!" Willoughby began but Ginny stopped him immediately.

"You stop this ride this instance, you hear?" She pulled up on the reins and with his help, commanded the team to a halt. She climbed out of the carriage and began walking away.

"Ginny! What's wrong with that? You knew before that I was a Union officer."

"Yes, but I kind of forgot." She picked up her dress and marched up the hill towards the McBride Mansion. Without turning she shouted back at him, "A woman can forget if she has to, you know." Her second personality apparently kicked in as if she were back on her plantation with the slaves, and not the lady of the evening coming home from a ball.

Willoughby drove the carriage up to Ginny and talked with her while driving it. "Climb in, Ginny. Please."

"I will ride with no Yankee!"

"But you have been dancing with one all night and his whole company I might add."

With her nose slightly upturned, she marched on with her arms folded firmly across her waist, holding her shawl around her tightly with the ringlets bouncing at the nape of her neck, making her look all the more attractive to the young captain.

When she arrived at the front gate of the mansion, Barnabas was there to meet her on the front stoop.

"Barnabas!" she called to him. "Please see to it that Captain Willoughby is stopped from following me through this gate."

Barnabas scratched his head and answered, "Yes'm, Miss McBride." He opened the door for her and then waited for Willoughby in his carriage inside the gate.

Ginny went inside, turned and watched Barnabas as he took the bridle of the main horse and turned him around. "Miss McBride done said to get you off these here grounds."

Willoughby hopped out of the carriage and bolted up to the door where Ginny attempted to shut it. Barnabas tied the horse to a hitching post and ran to Ginny's rescue

"You are not welcome here, Captain," Ginny said, pushing on the door to shut it against Willoughby's might.

"May I just have a word with you, Ginny? Just one word."

Barnabas cried out as he ran as fast as his aged legs would carry him. "Please Captain, suh. Miss Ginny don't want to be bothered. She told me to chase youse away."

Ginny looked into Willoughby's confused face and answered. "What would that one word be . . . Captain?"

"I've had a terrific evening tonight. A wonderful evening. The dancing and all. And I apologize for whatever caused you to be angry at me."

Barnabas came up behind Willoughby and, as he was about to grab him around the shoulder, Ginny ordered him, "Wait, Barnabas. I'm letting him have one word with me." She showed an interest in what Willoughby had said.

"The moon is full tonight," Willoughby went on as Barnabas stepped back. "Would a walk through your garden be too inappropriate for us to talk?"

Ginny thought for the longest moment while Willoughby stared down on her. "A walk? A small walk?" "Alright" She sighed. "But I don't think it's going to do you any good. I hate Yankees! And you are one."

She opened the door and allowed Willoughby to walk with her down the corridor to the veranda and outside. The path in the garden was long and the flowers on each side were fragrant and high. The moon lit the path as if to pave the way for the couple to walk.

"I understand that you were born and raised here in Richmond. Your folks were rich. The owners of a cotton mill."

"And a cotton plantation before that," she added.

"My folks are not poor. Not rich like yours by any means, but I had a good upbringing and schooling. I majored in mathematics and studied to become an engineer. That's what brought me to Richmond. I am here to help reconstruct what I can. I plan on making the army my career. Reconstruction throughout the South is going to be a monumental task. I'd like to be part of history. Soon, there won't be anything such as a Yankee or a Rebel."

Ginny listened to her suitor's plea for a second chance at her hand and, for the moment, liked it. As they walked, they approached a concrete bench. Willoughby motioned with his hand for her to sit.

"Only for a few more minutes, mind you," she returned, pointing to the light in Sarah's window. "You know that she's been watching every moment we've been out here. And the sound carries right into her bedroom window."

Willoughby smiled and caught her smile as he looked into her eyes. He removed his hat and placed it on the edge of the bench. "May I?" he asked, taking a hold of her hand.

"Just as long as you don't go any further."

"No intentions of doing any such thing, I promise you."

The promise was broken within a few moments as the couple shared their laughter together. "You've quite the gift for talking, Captain," she acknowledged as she allowed him to take both of her hands in his.

"I don't mean to. I just need to be understood."

"You certainly don't seem to be a man of mean intentions," she came back. "I've not been kissed in a long time, if that's what you're leading up to."

"I was thinking about it, but you said not to go any further."

"You've got both of my hands, Captain. I'm helpless."

"Bryce. Please, call me Bryce."

He leaned into her, wrapped his gloved hand around the back of her head and brought her lips to his. A spark went though her and she broke away as Matt's face appeared in her mind for a brief second.

"What's the matter?"

Ginny rose and said quickly, "I'm sorry, but I can't."

"Why?"

"I'm in love with another man," she confessed without looking at him.

"I thought you were single and unattached," Willoughby asked, being more than a little perturbed.

"You know nothing about me, Captain. Bryce," she said defiantly.

"No. No, I don't. But I want to know everything about you. Are you engaged?"

Ginny turned and looked into his eyes. "I'd like to be."

"With this man, I mean?" he asked.

"Yes. Oh, yes. I know you can't understand what I'm talking about. Maybe you should go now."

He took her in his arms and addressed her softly, "Not until you tell me about this man. Your lover?"

She attempted to pull away from his grasp, and then she let him hold onto her without too much restraint. She looked down and gasped a little. "He's a memory. Or, or missing. Or something."

"I don't understand."

"He's not real. He's in my dreams. I see him on occasion. Oh, I don't know how to tell you. You wouldn't understand."

"You say he's not real. Yet, you see him. How?"

"I met him before the war. We were separated and lost each other. He's probably dead now. I don't know. But I've seen him over and over and over again."

"In your dreams?"

She broke loose from his hold and ran towards the door. He followed her and caught her before she went inside.

"Tell me one thing, Ginny. Did my kiss mean anything to you?"

Ginny stood there almost breathless, wanting to let him hold her, to let him kiss her and to be with him for the rest of the night. She fell into his arms and sobbed. "I can't love you, Bryce." She broke away, ran inside and closed the door behind her.

From up in her room, she heard the carriage drive away. She fell onto the bed and cried herself to sleep.

CHAPTER 22

A NIGHT OUT FOR GINNY

The next morning, Lulu Belle and the nurse, a woman in her fifties in a nurse's outfit complete with hat and cape, assisted Sarah to her spot at the table for her morning tea. She had missed breakfast but felt strong enough for her tea.

Ginny had returned from a short ride, rode up to the verandah and dismounted. Barnabas was there to stable the horse.

"Thank you, Barnabas," Ginny said as she walked up to the verandah. "Good morning, Grand Mama."

"Good morning, Ginny." She pointed to the lady beside her and introduced her. "Ginny. This is Nurse Nelson. Dr. Paterson has been gracious to have her start regular visits with me."

"Nurse Nelson. It's a pleasure to know you. And, it's so good to see you up for your tea, Grand Mama."

"Not that I'm feeling feeble or anything. It's just that he's so understanding and knows my needs."

"She had a good night's sleep," Nelson replied, standing next to Sarah. "I thought the day would be good for her. Lots of Vitamin D, you know."

"I'm alright, Ginny," Sarah assured Ginny. "I've got a good nurse." She patted Nelson's hand as it rested on her shoulder. "And I had to come down to have tea with my favorite grand-daughter."

"Thank you, Grand Mama," Ginny replied as she sat at the table. Lulu Belle saw to it the ladies, including Nelson, received a good cup of hot tea with their biscuits.

"You may leave us, Nurse Nelson,' Sarah suggested with a whisk of the hand. "I'd like to talk to Ginny alone."

"As you wish, Madam. I'll be in the parlor." Nelson replied and left the two to be alone.

As Sarah sipped her tea, she smiled and said, "Now, Child. About this Willoughby fellow."

"Oh, Grand Mama. I'm not in love with him."

"No? You were in the garden with him last night. You've never been in the garden with any man before. And, at night. I heard you giggling."

Ginny blushed and replied, "I hope that's all you heard."

"Never you mind. What you say now may come to haunt you later."

"What? I just said I don't love him."

"And . . . you just might some day . . . whether you think so or not. It happens more times to two people in love than you might think."

"I just had an evening with him."

"Did you enjoy yourself?"

"Well . . . I can't say I did and I can't say I didn't," Ginny came back, shyly eyeing Sarah.

With her right index finger pointed at Ginny's nose, Sarah stated rather sharply, "Ah ha! It's like I say. Once you let your so called . . . ahem . . . defenses down, metaphorically speaking, you can wind up being Mrs. Virginia Willoughby." Then she topped it with, "Ugh!"

"Grand Mama!" Ginny laughed. She stood up, turned around once, twice, three times and said each time she turned, "Never! Never! Never!"

"Then let me tell you, child. Your heart is set for Matt. I know. And his heart is set for you. Don't let anything or anyone distract you from your calling.

"But shouldn't I see someone else in the meantime, Grand Mama?" Ginny asked, bowing to her.

"If you must. But remember what I said, young lady. *Keep your defenses up!*" She smiled, sipped her tea, took a bite of her biscuit, and then finished, saying, "Watch out for that Willoughby fellow. I don't trust him."

This was not the last time that Sarah brought up the subject of Willoughby's intentions. And it was not the last time that she talked about Matt. Ginny was to be escorted to other dances by gentlemen callers of distinction, and Sarah would size them all up and pitch them against Matt whom she saw and knew through her intuition and gift of prophesy. But it was exhilarating for Ginny to sit and listen to her rant and rave about who should and who should not have her hand.

However, when Willoughby came calling, it seemed that Sarah kept the conversation with Ginny in her bedroom, lingering just to agitate the young man to want to give up and leave while waiting; which he never did. It was enjoyable for Ginny to see Sarah pit her skills of wisdom and wit against one Union captain. And it was annoying to see how a man of such *a simple sort of character* could put up with her shenanigans. "After all," she told Ginny, "he's a *wimp*."

Ginny simply sat at the vanity and brushed her hair as if to ignore Sarah's remarks. But, at her last remark, she had to break out into a laugh. "A wimp? " She pondered for a moment and then exclaimed, "Indeed not!"

"See!" Sarah said, sitting on her bed. "You think so, too."

Sarah saw Ginny fully dressed up with a fine coiffure and knew. "You've a date with a gentleman tonight?"

"You're quite observant. Yes, Grand Mama. Another social dance and he's due here any minute."

Sarah thought for a moment, put her hand on her chin, sat straight up and asked, "the wimp?"

"Oh, Grand Mama! I love you so." She stood up, walked over to the bed and sat down. Taking her hand, she caressed it ever so carefully and said, "You are my life!" She walked to the doorway and looked back at Sarah. "Yes. Willoughby. But . . . I'll keep my defenses up!" She smiled, showing her shiny white teeth and the dimples in her cheeks.

Sarah simply folded her arms and said in disgust, "Bah!"

Ginny threw her a kiss from the door way, turned and walked away. "I'll be home early."

Sarah looked towards the doorway as she heard the click of Ginny's shoes as they descended the stairway. Her face of disgust turned into a smile, she went to her room and slid down into the bed for a good night's sleep.

CHAPTER 23

CAPTAIN WILLOUGBY COMES A COURTIN'

<u>Spring, 1866</u>

The toll for taking care of Sarah, staying up with the mill's legal matters and building her own law accounts prevented Ginny from having too much of a social life.

Willoughby's constant calling on Ginny was a welcome rather than a hindrance to her as she needed special attention whenever and wherever she could get it. Willoughby was fascinated by her beauty as well as her talent to manage a large mill. To him, Ginny was liken to a Greek goddess. She could do no wrong.

Not having time to enjoy his company, Ginny's refusal to go on any dates frustrated him to no end. To her, his love was nothing more than an infatuation. To him, it was real.

It was a Saturday evening, and he had told her many weeks before about a shindig in town that he had planned to take her. As usual, she had forgotten about it; or better yet, completely put it out of her mind for staying with her law cases. He remembered and came calling, wearing his full dress captain's uniform with cape.

Barnabas showed him in when he arrived at the mansion and escorted him to the famous west parlor. When Ginny came down the stairs, he was there to meet her. Seeing her beauty was his delight, but she was not dressed for the occasion. In fact, she was attired in a night robe and bare feet and held a law book in her hand.

"Willoughby?" she addressed him nonchalantly at the foot of the stairs. "Was there something you wanted to see me about?"

His mind went blank for the moment; he turned around and then turned back towards her with his hand rubbing his chin.

"Eh, yes. Yes. You forgot again? Didn't you?"

"Forgot? About what?" And then came the dawn. "Oh, my gosh. The shindig. Bryce, will you ever forgive me? I'm not prepared to go to any shindig."

Willoughby's face dropped and Ginny watched a little boy begin to pout.

"Oh, alright! It'll take me a second to change." Then she asked herself, *What to wear?* as she walked back up the stairs. She stopped, looked back and said, "It's a shindig. I'll wear something simple, if it's alright with you, Bryce."

Bryce' face lit up again and he nodded in agreement. "Yes. Oh, my yes."

It was a full hour until Willoughby, having paced the hallway and the path to the west parlor in anticipation of her appearance, witnessed the angel with which he was in love.

"Am I presentable, Bryce?"

With his hat in hand, he bowed to her beauty as she took his arm. "As pretty a lady as I've ever seen."

And *pretty* was a slight word for her as she waltzed across the floor of the community hall with her date for the evening. She was not dressed in a simple dress by any stretch of the imagination, for her evening gown draped the floor with each step and flowed with each delicate movement. She was indeed the belle of the ball, though the ball only happened to be a Saturday night shindig.

Willoughby was not the only partner she had for the dance that night. Many a man asked for his chance to dance with the prettiest miss on the floor. It kept Ginny busy, but she enjoyed it. It also was a way to keep her mind off her work and to let her enjoy a social life for a change.

As usual, the country boys spiked the punch bowl with their homemade brew. Ginny knew about it and kept her drink to a minimum, setting a glass down before each dance and never picking it up when the dance was over. However, Willoughby had not thought about it, and kept his drinking while he watched Ginny dance away with other gentlemen.

He did get in the last dance with Ginny, as she made certain that he did by warding off other offers. She waited for Willoughby to walk over to her as her partner walked her off the dance floor and back to his side of the floor. He placed his drink down and, feeling the effects of the alcohol,, staggered to her side with his hand held out for her to take. Being the officer and gentleman that he was, he did his best to show that he was not inebriated but in full control of his person.

When he pulled up to the mansion with Ginny clinging to his arm, he sat still for the moment and looked somewhat steadily into Ginny's eyes.

"You haven't said two words to me since we left the dance, Bryce," Ginny observed. "Are you mad at me?"

Willoughby coughed up a smile and apologetically answered her. "Mad? Me? At you? No way, Ginny. I couldn't be mad at you. You must know that."

"Well, sir, a gentleman usually holds his date's hand, or better yet put his arm around his date's shoulder." She smiled, took his arm and put it around her bared shoulders. "Like this."

He looked into her smiling eyes and felt the moment right to kiss her. He inched his lips towards her while he watched her close her eyes and wait patiently for them to touch hers. His kiss was tender to the touch at first. He tested the waters. When she did not resist his attempts, he pushed further and kissed again.

She threw her arms around his neck and brought him in closer as she enjoyed the moment immensely. Willoughby was proving his manliness and she was enjoying it. As it had been awhile since she had experienced a vision, this was a release from the captivating of Matt's persona.

His hand began its journey in an attempt to touch Ginny's blouse, hoping beyond hopes that she would allow his fingers to wistfully play with the frills, which he hoped would lead further to a sensual touch of her breasts. She stopped his hand once she felt it on the first ruffle of her blouse. His attempt again to touch it was not resisted as she was wrapped up in his kisses.

Barnabas came out of the mansion to take care of the carriage when he witnessed the pair. He stopped, turned around and went back inside. A few moments later, throughout the ordeal, he peeked out the side window to see if his services were needed.

On a second look, he found that they were for the carriage was empty. He opened the door, looked down the path that led to the garden in back and saw the couple disappear around the corner, walking hand and hand.

Ginny heard the whinny of the horse and the wheels of the carriage on the cobblestone as Barnabas drove it to the stable. She paid no mind to it but walked slowly with Willoughby to the garden. Once in back where the moon shone upon a path in the garden of flowers, the couple stopped.

"I come here often when I want to get alone and be by myself," Ginny said softly as she stood with him holding his hands.

"You're lovely in the moonlight, Ginny. Arc you glad I kissed you?"

"Yes. But you shouldn't be trying to rush things. Let's just enjoy the hour."

The hour? It might have been an hour but to the young couple, the minutes froze and their hearts intertwined. He leaned in and kissed her again, bringing her body into his. There was no resistance on her part again, and she put her arms around his neck, bringing him in closer to her body.

She felt the fullness of his manliness and began to enjoy the experience as he whispered in her ear. "I've waited so long for this moment."

The kiss became more passionate as his hands brought her body closer to his to where his knees bent and he gently brought her to the ground. The moon appeared to be throwing her beams upon the couple through the leaves of the nearby apple tree. The chirps of the crickets and an occasional howl of the hound baying down the road seemed to orchestrate the lovers' syncopating rhythm of the beating of their hearts.

When Willoughby's moment of sensuality came, Ginny's eyes opened and she felt as if Matt's spirit were in their presence. Instantly the words formed in her mind that brought a smile upon her face. *Darling Ginny. My love. How I yearn to be in your arms. Stay, Ginny! Don't throw your love for me away!*

As quickly as the words came, just as quickly they dissipated into the evening air. Ginny pushed Willoughby away, rolled over, stood up and ran to the mansion.

157

No lights were on yet so she knew no one was watching them. She stopped when she reached the verandah and paused, waiting for Willoughby to catch up.

Willoughby ran as fast and as clumsily as he could, redressing himself on the run. When he caught up to Ginny on the verandah, he turned her around and into himself, but she pushed him aside.

"I'm sorry, Bryce."

"Ginny. Are you angry at me? I . . . I don't understand."

"No, my dear Bryce. I've enjoyed the evening. I've enjoyed what we did. I know that I've needed that moment for a long time."

"Then. What?" He leaned forward to bring her into his arms, but she again resisted, turning her back on him.

He stood there, watching her motionless body as the moon lit upon her bared shoulders and the wind played with her rustled hair. After what seemed an eternity, waiting for her to turn again, he said, "It's him! Isn't it? Mr. Matt! Isn't it?"

She turned slowly and, with her eyes looking downward, said, "I know you can't understand, Bryce. If you can't now, you never will."

"Did you see his face? What was it like?" he asked angrily and defiantly like a boy who has been refused his candy stick after it was taken from him by his mother.

"No. I didn't see his face," she answered as she slowly walked towards the door. "I heard his voice."

Willoughby dropped his jaw and stood there helplessly while Ginny opened the door and disappeared inside. "Do I get to see you tomorrow?"

"Maybe," she responded as she opened the door again. "And if I were you, I'd button up." She closed the door and silently disappeared into the mansion. Lulu Belles' lantern broke through the darkness and led her to her room while Willoughby met Barnabas at the side and the two strolled towards his carriage.

"I took care of your carriage, Captain," Barnabas said with a smile as big as the moon itself for he had witnessed the pair on the verandah. "And suh, I'd do what the lady said."

Willoughby looked at Barnabas and then at the opening in his trousers, and shyly buttoned them.

"Didn't mean to be, but suh it comes to be my duty to care for your horse and buggy. And I naturally knowed you be needin' them some time soon. I stayed in front 'til I heard Miss Ginny go inside."

"Oh. Of course." Willoughby walked ahead of Barnabas in a heated way and said, "Damn!"

"Yes, suh."

Turning the reins over to Willoughby, Barnabas stood there and watched a disgruntled, yet extremely satisfied man drive away. "Yes, suh. You is one mixed up captain. You sho is." He looked up towards Ginny's window and smiled; his teeth lighting up the portico as he danced back inside the mansion.

Sleepy-eyed Ginny, met Sarah on the verandah the next morning for breakfast.

"You look too pretty for breakfast, my dear. As usual," Sarah said as she watched Ginny curtsy over to the table in her morning light tapestry flowing robe and take a chair. "You certainly take your time getting ready to meet the day."

"Good morning, Grand Mama."

"I see you've had an interesting evening. The dance go alright?"

"Who told you?" Ginny asked in a puzzled way as Lulu Belle poured her tea.

"Well, no one really, but Barnabas has a silly grin on his face, so I figured he got it from last night." She put sugar in her tea and stirred it. "Fact is, I heard you on the verandah. My window is just above it, you know, and it was open."

"Oh, Grand Mama. You are a sly one."

"You will see the young man again, won't you?"

Ginny smiled and answered her. "Those are my intentions."

"Then, I'm happy. So let's eat breakfast."

The morning was happy for Ginny and she eagerly awaited for Willoughby to call on her again; perhaps that morning.

It was early afternoon when he did call, and the two drove away in his carriage for a short drive. She made up for the past evening with a lot of sugary talk that complimented the rumble of the wheels as they bounced along the road. As the lady she was, she kept the sun from burning her skin with a brightly colored parasol.

When they returned to the mansion, Willoughby stepped out of the carriage and ran to the side to escort Ginny down to Barnabas' consternation. With Ginny on his arm, he eyed Barnabas, smiled and said, "I'll be just a minute, so leave my carriage as it is, Barnabas."

Having a hard time not to laugh, Barnabas simply smiled at Willoughby's ostensibly uncontrollable personal habit with his pants.

Ginny caught it and looked embarrassed at Willoughby. "Again, Bryce?"

After Willoughby left, Ginny went up to Sarah's room. When she entered, she found Sarah in bed, sleeping. She carefully closed the door, not to awaken her. But the littlest sound did awaken her.

"Is that you, Ginny?" Sarah asked, looking towards her with half-opened eyes.

"I didn't mean to wake you, Grand Mama. I didn't know you'd be in bed at this time of day."

"Oh, I got rather weak and knew I needed a nap. I'm alright." She smiled and asked, "How was your drive?"

Ginny walked over to the bed, sat down and took Sarah's hand. "Wonderful, Grand Mama. He is like a pussy cat. He can't do enough for me. We went to town. He purchased a gift for me; a small purse that I've had my eye on. He was so nice."

"Did he say anything about your abruptness last night on the verandah?"

"Oh, Grand Mama. Nothing until I brought it up. He liked that. And, yes, I let him kiss me again."

Ginny looked again at Sarah as she closed her eyes and was fast asleep. She whispered, "Grand Mama?"

Sarah slept with a smile on her face.

CHAPTER 24

MATT GOES TO RICHMOND

<u>12 October 1866</u>

After several uneasy and boring months on the plains, Matt and Steve finally rode into Richmond down the water-filled wagon ruts in the road as rain came down. The battle scars left to Richmond were being healed, but remnants of the war still remained and both men felt the grimace of the hour as they continued to lazily ride into Richmond.

After asking several people along the way, the cowboys found the broken-down sign that bore the name of the McBride Textile Mill in front of the burned-out ruins. For what seemed to Steve an eternity of silence, he watched Matt staring intently around the ruins. The rain trickled down his face. Then he slid down from his saddle and walked through the ruins as Steve dismounted and followed him.

"This was a huge place, friend," Matt whispered through the rain as he kicked a burnt plank out of his way.

""You're thinking you're not going to find her, friend," Steve said to Matt as they examined the rebuilding of Richmond.

"I've jest about given up, pal," Matt said.

"Well, as I see it. There's no sense in staying, Matt," Steve suggested, looking around the ruins. "You can see. No one's here."

"Yeah."

Matt turned, walked back to his mount, climbed back into the saddle and rode slowly away, almost dejected for not having found Ginny.

"She's got to have a home around here, Steve," Matt exclaimed as he brought Skeeter to a halt. "It's the home that we should be looking for."

They rode further down the road until they came to a tent that housed some Union soldiers playing cards. Matt dismounted and walked inside the tent. There he found four men sitting around a pork barrel turned on its end, playing poker.

"Tell your friend there to climb down and come inside," one of the soldiers suggested to Matt. He was the older man of the four soldiers and held a lit cigar butt between his teeth. He was bareheaded with salt-and-pepper hair and beard that looked like they hadn't seen soap for a month. He wore three stripes on his sleeve.

"Thanks, Sergeant," Matt answered politely. "Just wanted some information, if you could help us."

"Sure. Sure. What can we do for ya?"

"We're looking for the owners of the McBride Mill that burned down."

The sergeant stared up at Matt and removed his cigar from his mouth. "The McBride Mansion?"

Matt suspected the man knew something and felt uneasy about pushing his luck. "Yes. I suppose you might call it thet."

"What ya want to know fer?"

"I'm looking for a person. A girl. Thought she might be there."

The sergeant appeared to be tense and uneasy about answering Matt. "Give me three cards and keep the game going," he ordered the dealer, a much younger man.

To Matt's dismay they continued playing poker without answering him right away. Once the soldier took a look at his cards, he smiled, put his cigar back into his mouth and said, "You a Reb?"

"What's thet got to do with findin' the McBrides."

"This gal. She a Reb, too?"

"If she's who you're talkin' about, yeah."

"Your girl?"

"Could be. Why all the questions, mister?"

The sergeant took the cigar from his mouth, wiped his mouth with the back of hand, spat and answered Matt. "Can't help ya, mister."

Matt sensed the air was getting thick and there was no further need for discussion, so he bid the soldier *good bye* and left the tent. As he did so, he heard one of the soldiers say, "Why did ya tell him that? You know where the mansion is."

The sergeant placed a bet and said, "Shut up and play. I call."

Matt turned quickly, pulled open the flap of the tent and went back inside. "Mister, I heard the young man. Why are you hiding a simple address from me?"

Looking a little agitated, but without getting up, the sergeant answered him defiantly, "He didn't know what he was talking about. Now play, boy! Raise me or fold 'em!"

Matt looked at the man whom he thought had said what he had heard and asked, "Son. Do you know where the McBride Mansion is? It's important to me."

"Mister!" The sergeant shouted as he rose and threw his cards down on the barrel. "I answer for these men, and I said we don't know about a McBride Mansion."

"Then how come you called it a *mansion?*"

"'Cause you said it was," he answered, chewing on his cigar.

Matt's patience ran out and his fist plowed the cigar back into the sergeant's mouth. The other three men began to draw their revolvers when Matt quickly slapped leather. "Don't go there!" was Matt's quick command.

The men froze but watched their sergeant rise to the occasion with a fist that swung past Matt's face. Matt returned it with his pistol to the man's stomach that caused him to double over and sit back down in his chair. Matt pinned his arms down to the sides of the chair and looked sternly into the man's eyes.

"You wanna change your answer, old man?" Matt asked with grit teeth.

The sergeant looked up at Matt through his now swollen eyes and, feeling the blood run from his mouth, answered Matt sheepishly, "On top of the hill, north east of town."

"Thank you, kindly," Matt answered and let the man go.

As Matt walked away, the sergeant broke a whiskey bottle and came at him with the jagged neck piece.

A shot rang out that busted the remnant of the bottle into pieces that flew through the tent. Steve held his revolver pointed at the bearded man.

"Thanks, Steve," Matt quickly added as he stared into the startled man's face. He walked over to the man and back-handed him across the mouth. He watched the man hit the floor and bounce.

"I see you haven't learned your lesson."

"No more!" the man whimpered.

Matt turned and mounted his horse and, with Steve rode away.

The young dealer helped his sergeant to his feet and asked, "Why didn't you just tell him where the mansion was? Seems to me you could have saved all this."

The sergeant walked over to a pan of water, grabbed a rag and soaked it. While applying it to his face, he answered the young man. "Because Willoughby's marrying that there woman he's looking for. And he ain't goin' to be a happy man when he finds out about a dang Reb looking her up."

"Then what should you want us to do?"

"Nothing! I ain't aimin' to go up agin' him again. The dang captain's been a courtin' her all these months and she a tellin' him about this here Reb and all. And now he shows up in person. Uh uh! Let Captain find out for hisself."

Without any further hesitation, Matt and Steve rode out of town and headed towards the mansion. When they neared the mansion, Matt reined up and sized up the mansion.

"Thet is one heck of a house. Wouldn't you say, Steve?"

"Whoo whee!" Steve returned. "Looks to me like we're bitin' off more'n we can chew, friend."

"I'm inclined to agree with ya. I've never seen a house thet big. Do you suppose we got the right place?"

"One way to find out," Steve came back. "Go on up there."

The two men spurred on and rode through the gate to the stoop at the front entrance. They dismounted and tied their reins to the hitching post.

Matt walked up to the door and knocked on it. "What do we do, pal?" Matt asked with his hat in his hand. "What if this isn't her?"

"But what if it is?" Steve returned.

"Yeah!"

Barnabas answered the door and asked, "Yes, suh?"

"Well," Matt started in. "I don't know how to ask this, but do you have a young lady by the name of Ginny living here?"

"Who shall I say is calling?" Barnabas returned.

"Who is it?" A masculine voice came from behind Barnabas.

Barnabas stepped back and answered, "Two gentlemen, suh."

Captain Willoughby came around Barnabas' side and eyed Matt and Steve. "It's ok, Barnabas. I'll see if I can be of help to these men."

Barnabas bowed to the captain's wishes and left.

"I'm Captain Willoughby. How can I help you?"

Matt looked at the uniform and answered, "We're looking for Ginny McBride."

"Ginny?"

"This *is* the McBride Mansion, isn't it?" Matt asked, trying to look past the captain.

"And, just who are you?"

"M'name's Matt Jorgensen and this is Steve Andrews."

Immediately, the captain identified Matt as the man in Ginny's visions. *Mister,* Willoughby thought to himself, *you finally arrived. I've won her over her remembrance of you. And there is no way I'm going to give up my love now.*

"I'm sorry, Mr. Jorgensen. Mr. Andrews. You have the right Mansion, but the lady you are inquiring about no longer lives here."

"She did live here?" Matt asked, dejectedly.

"It is rumored that she was accidentally killed in the war."

"We've heard the same thing. Is there any one here that can help us. Fill us in as to what happened?"

"I'm afraid not. Her grandmother lives here alone and she's old, tired and resting. I'm sorry."

Matt looked at Willoughby with distrusting eyes and asked, "Why are you here, if I might ask?"

"I'm a friend of the family."

"Family? I thought only her Grandmother lived here."

"She has two Grandsons and a Granddaughter who visit with her. I have become rather close to them and so I visit here quite often to check up on Mrs. McBride."

Matt grew more leery of Willoughby's answers. "We've traveled all the way from Texas. I'd like to come in and sit down, if you'd let us. There might be a picture of her or something."

"Who are you, Mr. Jorgensen? That is, in relation to this Ginny?"

"I am her friend. We fell in love."

The captain felt indignation at Matt and started to close the door on him. "I'm sorry, gentlemen. That's all I can help you with. Your coming here would only add to this family's grief of losing her, sir, I must ask you to have mercy and let them alone."

Matt stopped the door from closing and opened it with a strong shove against Willoughby. "Somehow, Captain, I don't believe you."

Steve pinned Willoughby to the door. "It wouldn't do to make him mad, Captain," Steve warned him. Steve's pistol was out of its holster and pushing against Willoughby's ribs.

Matt went inside, looked into the hallway at photos, and then ran upstairs. He looked inside each bedroom and found no one at home. He came back downstairs and went into the drawing room where he found wedding gifts stacked neatly and decorations all about the room.

"Someone getting married?" he asked Willoughby.

"Yes. I'm getting married and we're using this mansion as our wedding reception.

Matt walked over to where the presents were stacked and rummaged through a few. Seeing the names, Beth Paterson and Captain Bryce Willoughby on them, he tossed them down and walked away.

"And your home?" Matt quickly interjected sarcastically.

"Did you find anything, friend?" Steve asked, still holding his pistol on Willoughby.

"I found a photograph of a young girl that could be Ginny on the piano in one of those big rooms and another in a bed room. Was that her room?" he directed to the captain.

"Yes. Mrs. McBride has kept it the same way since she left."

Barnabas returned to the front entrance after hearing Matt rummaging throughout the house. "Is everything all right, Mistuh Captain, suh?"

Steve hid the pistol from Barnabas' sight and smiled as Barnabas looked at both him and Matt.

Feeling threatened by the pistol in his ribs, Willoughby answered, "Yes, Barnabas. These gentlemen were just leaving."

"Yes, suh." Barnabas left and walked back down the corridor.

"Where's Mrs. McBride? The Grandmother?"

"She's with my fiancé in town."

"Uh huh. We're leaving, Captain. But we just might return if we find out you're lying to us. Do you read me?"

"Fully. I'm truly sorry that I can't be of further help. I can understand what you went through. You were on the Confederate side?"

"Thet's right. Terry's Texas Rangers. Ever hear of us?"

Willoughby cringed for a moment and then was relieved when Steve returned the pistol to its holster. "Who hasn't? They were one of the best cavalry units in the war."

"The Best!" Steve answered. "On both sides."

Matt and Steve left the mansion, mounted their horses and rode off towards town. The rain had quit and the sun was drying the mud when they rode up to the Purple Garter Saloon. They dismounted, hitched up their horses and walked towards the door.

167

The two men entered the room and walked over to the bar where the bartender met them. "What'll it be, gents?"

"Whiskey!" Matt ordered and stood at the bar with Steve.

"Did you buy all thet, friend?" Steve asked, holding a glass for the bartender to fill.

Matt threw a coin down to cover the cost of the drinks. "We'll take the bottle." He grabbed Steve by the arm and said, "Let's sit down."

"Well. Did you?"

"Don't know. I picked up the photograph." He took the photograph of Ginny from under his shirt. "She is beautiful. Younger in this photo. But there was no Ginny. Wish I could have talked with her Grandmother."

Matt poured the two a round of drinks and swilled his right down.

"What good would it have done?" Steve asked, downing his drink. "He said she was killed."

"*Probably* killed. Apparently they don't know either."

"So where do we go from here?" Steve asked, watching Matt pour him another drink. "It's too early in the day to get drunk, I'm a thinkin'."

"Yeah." Matt poured his and toasted to Steve. "Here's to finding Ginny." He swallowed the drink in one gulp and added. "Let's get out of here. I've got to think."

CHAPTER 25

A GLIMPSE OF GINNY

The two cowboys rose from the table and waddled back outside. Matt leaned against the post and watched people riding and walking through the mud. He reached inside his vest and pulled out a piece of beef jerky. Taking his knife, he cut a slice for Steve.

Then it happened. As he cut a piece of jerky for himself, an expensive looking carriage drove by with two women in the back; both holding opened umbrellas over their heads. Matt looked intently at the two ladies, took a bite out of a plug and chewed on it. He smiled at the ladies and tilted his hat in a salute to them as they rode by. The younger of the two ladies was beautiful beyond compare and it caught his attention. He turned to walk away and then turned back. All of a sudden he said under his breath, "Thet's Ginny!"

Steve looked at him, took the plug and knife from Matt and gazed into Matt's astonished looking eyes. "Who?"

"Her."

"Where?" Steve asked, looking all around.

Matt stepped off the sidewalk and into the mud. He slipped and fell into the mud face down and slipped twice more trying to climb to his feet. He fell against the hitching post, grabbed a hold of the saddle on his horse and looked towards the direction the carriage had gone.

"She's gone!" Matt exclaimed as he looked up and down the street.

"And you're drunk. Look at cha."

"Did you see the carriage?"

"What carriage?" Steve looked down the street and back up the street where he saw several carriages. Another of your visions, pal?" Steve asked, looking with Matt up and down the street. "There are lots of carriages here."

169

Neither man saw a carriage with the two women in it. There were some buggies and a few carriages, along with riders and people meandering in the mud, crossing the street, or simply walking down the boarded walkways. But, there was no carriage with two women in it.

"Let's check it out, friend," Matt said to Steve. "It's gotta be her."

With his mud-covered body, Matt climbed into his saddle and, with Steve by his side, rode up the street to, but to no avail.

"No carriage with two women up here," Steve noted, sitting high in his saddle and looking both ways.

They rode the other direction, looking down the side streets. "Nope!" Matt came back.

After spending time riding the streets of Richmond, Matt reined up on top of a hill that overlooked Richmond. "It could have been her. It could have been my imagination."

"Probably your imagination because you're thinking too strongly about her."

Steve turned in his saddle and caught sight of a carriage with two women holding parasols.

"Matt!"

"What?"

"The carriage. I see it, too. Could it be?"

Matt turned and looked where Steve was facing. "It's the carriage. By gum, we found her!"

He rode fast to catch up to it and heard Steve yelling behind him.

"If it's her, you'd better shave some of thet mud off your face."

Matt caught up with the carriage, but the driver kept his pace with the set of horses and refused to stop at Matt's commands. Matt rode up to the side of the carriage, leaned in and jumped upon the rail, falling at the feet of a couple of women.

"Wha? Who in tarnation?" one of the ladies cried out.

The other one drew her legs in and sat upright on the seat. "Who are you, sir?"

Matt turned over and sat up. He smiled as he stared at the two beautiful and charming ladies. Then he realized that he *had* made a mistake and changed his smile to a face of embarrassment.

"Eh. I'm . . . I'm sorry ladies." He sat up, wiped his face with his hands and looked meekly into their faces. "Is either of you, Ginny?"

The ladies looked at Matt as the driver kept his pace with the horses. Both ladies giggled and pulled a fan to their face.

"Why I'm Ellie and my friend here is Bernice. My, my, my but we do like the way you introduce yourself. Mr. . . . Mr.?"

Matt stood up in the carriage and smiled at the ladies and apologized. "M'name's Matt and I'm lookin' for Ginny. But, I suppose neither of you know her."

"Ginny? No. Did she ever work at the Purple Garter? That's where we work."

Matt suddenly realized that he was in the midst of two soiled doves, apologized and looked around for Skeeter. Steve held Skeeter's reins and rode up to the carriage. Matt bid adieu to the two ladies with a tilt of his hat, turned, and jumped into the saddle. "Sorry ladies."

"Come down and see us sometime," one of the ladies yelled back.

"Yes, ma'am," Matt answered and rode off with Steve who was laughing so under his hat 'til he found it hard to stay in the saddle.

"Wanna go back to the Purple Garter, pal?"

"Shaddup!" Matt replied, and the two rode off.

"Which one was the grandmother, pal?" Steve asked, still laughing. "And the other could have been the captain's fiancé? Haw! Haw!"

The two men rode back to the Purple Garter Saloon and took a table across the room from the piano player who seemed to be enjoying playing especially loud for some reason.

Once settled down with a bottle, Steve looked up at Matt and said, "You gotta admit it, pal, thet was the silliest I've seen you since I've been ridin' with ya."

"Yeah? Well don't laugh too loud. Your turn will come some day." Then aside he said, "You're the one who pointed out the wagon with the parasols."

"Now I know you're serious about seeing Ginny in dreams and such. But just how did you see her this time in a carriage as Ginny?"

"I . . . I don't know." He rose from the table again and walked around to the bar, stopped and rubbed his hands together. "It was Ginny. I don't know how. Don't ask me. I just know. Like when I saw her lying in bed in this massive bedroom. That, too, was Ginny. My beautiful, beautiful Ginny."

He continued his tirade back to the table, and spent the rest of the hour drinking. When the bottle became empty, he rose and walked over to the bar for another bottle. He continued talking about not finding Ginny and about the carriage incident.

By this time, the men at the bar and adjoining tables were deeply engrossed in Matt's carrying-on as he tried to explain what he had seen and how he was looking for a ghost. "Have you ever lost a beautiful woman in your life?" he asked one of the men at an adjoining table in a not too soft voice so as to be heard over the loud tunes coming from the piano.

Matt looked around at the tables, and then at two men standing next to him at the bar. "Well, it happened to me."

He took a shot glass of bourbon from the man standing next to him and sloshed it into his face. "You don't look at me like I'm some crazy . . ."

Before he finished his threat, the man wiped his face with his bandana and hurled his right fist into Matt's face, sending him across the saloon floor and under the doors. Steve went to rescue Matt as his partner rose to rebuke his opponent.

"Get thet stinkin' ol' bum out of here," the man said as he poured himself another drink. "Make him clean thet mud off him afore he takes another man's drink."

Steve walked over to the man who hit Matt, picked him up by the shirt collar and before he could say a word, a bottle slammed against his head, sending him down to the floor where he rolled, stopping at the feet of the inebriated Matt.

172

Matt got to his feet and walked straight to the man who hit him. The man rolled back his fist and brought it around to Matt. Matt dodged the fist and came back with a haymaker that caused the man to sit down hard on a spittoon.

The bartender came to the man's revenge with an empty bottle. But before he could connect, Matt's hand grabbed his and catapulted him over the bar, smashing him into the nearest table.

A second bartender came around the corner with rolled up sleeves. At the same time, four customers of the saloon who had been playing cards joined in the donnybrook. Matt caught the second bartender and tossed him back over the bar and onto the floor.

Two of the gentlemen from the table grabbed Matt by the arms and pinned him against the bar. Steve rose groggily to the occasion. While trying to assess the situation, another man brought his fist across Steve's face and sent him sprawling across the broken table next to the first bartender.

A tall, skinny man pummeled his fist into Matt's rib cage, causing Matt to cough up spit. Unfortunate for this man, he was the recipient of the slop. Matt brought his knee into the man's groin that caused much pain to the man and sent him down next to the other man who had sat on the spittoon. Matt took the advantage and brought the other two men toward each other, butting their heads together.

Steve got back up, shook his head and watched the first bartender start to get up. He reeled off a fast fist and knocked him back down. As another man from the saloon came behind Steve, he swirled around and gave his opponent a hard elbow to the chest. The man spun around and spread-eagled across the nearest table, collapsing it.

A few more of the saloon's patrons came to their party's defense and brought Matt up to salute the chandelier. Once up in the air, they let him fall to the floor, pinned his shoulders to the floor and punched him in the face. Steve took hold of a chair and brought it up and smashed it across the backs of the two men who were on top of Matt.

Matt rolled over and away from his attackers. He rose to his feet and pulled his Navy with lightning fast action.

"Hold it!" he commanded everyone in a loud and masculine voice. "My friend here says to stay! Any of you move and you'll wish you hadn't."

He looked over at Steve picking up their hats. Steve dutifully placed one properly on Matt's head, topped his own head with his hat and pulled out his Navy.

"Sorry for the ruckus, gentlemen," Matt said as he walked backwards toward the saloon doors. "But this party's getting a little bit too rough."

He placed a dozen silver dollar coins in the hand of the first bartender who, at this time, was standing close to Matt and rubbing his jaw. "If these don't cover the damages, let them make up for the rest." He pointed to his assailants lying on the floor.

The bartender looked at the coins, smiled at Matt and said, "Thanks. Good party."

Matt laughed and Steve joined in as the two men turned and casually walked out of the saloon.

"Where were the girls?" Steve asked as he mounted his horse.

"Girls? Thet's right! Dang if I know. Probably stayed in their rooms." He looked back at the Purple Garter and added, "Dang shame. That one was a pretty good lookin' filly."

They both laughed and rode away.

"Where to now, friend?" Steve asked as he took a chaw of tobacco and rolled it around his mouth to ease the pain in his jaw.

Matt grabbed the plug, bit off a bite and said, "We're goin' back to the mansion after we rest and clean up a bit. I wanna meet this guy's fiancé."

"You sure?"

Matt gently touched his sore chin and looked away. "Nope. I'm not. I'm not sure of anything right now."

They walked back up the sidewalk where Matt took an empty chair and sat down outside a general store. Steve joined him in a second chair and the two men sat there for a long time, staring into space and thinking.

A day later, clean and sober, Matt and Steve mounted their horses outside the Purple Garter,

"And, too," Steve came back. "If thet's the case, then the other woman could have been the Grandmother." He looked at Matt's face and asked, "You ready to go back to the mansion and find out?"

"I don't know. What are we goin' to find out? We've already made fools out of ourselves with the captain. If we meet the grandmother, she'll tell us the same thing, and that'll just make me madder."

"Then?"

"Then . . ." He thought for a brief moment and then with grit teeth and a clinched fist said, "Let's get madder." Matt spurred Skeeter towards the mansion and Steve followed.

CHAPTER 26

A SECOND TRIP TO THE MANSION

<u>14 October 1866</u>

The carriage that Matt had seen before was driven back to the stable and parked there for the night, out of sight. Ginny and Sarah were escorted to their rooms by Willoughby, and Barnabas who carried the boxes the ladies brought home with them.

Several couples who drove up to the mansion were welcomed by Barnabas who led them through to one of the two parlors where a young lady and her husband met them.

"Good evening," the young man addressed the guests. "I'm David Southerland and this is my wife, Maggie. She's Bryce' sister. We're from Michigan."

Willoughby came down and welcomed his guests to the McBride Estate. He caught the tail end of the introductions and put his arm around his sister.

Both were in their thirties. David was a well-dressed gentleman with glasses and light brown hair. Maggie was as tall as David with her long hair neatly coiled up on top of her head with long strands hanging across her shoulders.

"I see you've met my lovely sister and her husband. Well, the party is just beginning. So, drink up and have yourself a wonderful time. I'll be roaming around welcoming the rest."

Then he looked at Maggie and David and said, "Could I talk with you two for a moment?" He led them into the drawing room.

"I have to beg your pardon for me taking you away from the party as it's just beginning, but I've a very important favor I'd like to ask of my sister. If you both don't mind."

"Certainly," Maggie answered.

"What is it, Bryce?"

"Well. It's rather personal. May I borrow my sister for a moment? Just for a moment. Afterward, you two can go back to the party.

"Certainly. Am I to do this favor, too?"

"Of course. I need the help from both of you."

"Yes," Maggie answered. Of course we will. But it had better not take too long."

David and Maggie looked strangely at Willoughby. "Now," Maggie said, dangling a petite hankie from her fingers. "What kind of favor, Bryce? You act so mysteriously."

"Well, to tell you the truth, I feel rather mysterious. You see, Ginny had a boyfriend some time back. And, well you know from my letters that she had suffered a serious attack of amnesia. And, well, it's been almost five years now, I suppose and now this supposedly boyfriend of hers has shown up at our door."

"Oh! How utterly marvelous. It sounds like a story from one of the novels I've been reading."

"Sis. It's a true story. She did suffer amnesia and she did have a love affair. But it was a brief affair. She was only in her teens. The first pretty face she met and thought she was in love with him."

"And he?" David asked. "Is he still in love with her?"

"Oh!" Willoughby turned and walked towards the window and looked out. "Impossible. He's been out to war. The wrong side. He's been a killer. Probably a rapist. He's got to have known a lot of women in that period of time."

Maggie walked over to Willoughby and touched his arms. "You don't know that? Why, haven't you killed some during the war?"

"No. No I haven't. I'm an engineer. I didn't have time for killing. But now I've found my one true love. I love her and she loves me."

David looked intently into Willoughby's eyes and kittenishly asked, stroking his chin, "And what is the favor you want from Maggie?"

"Maggie. Dearest Maggie. Please do this one favor for me."

"Lie? You know I won't lie. I'm a Christian and I do not lie."

"No. Not lie."

"Well, then what, Bryce?" David asked, looking extremely puzzled.

"I've heard that he intends to come back here."

"For what?" David asked, watching Willoughby fidgeting with his hands.

"He's not all together sure that I told him the truth this mornin'," Willoughby answered.

"About what?" Maggie asked.

"About Ginny?." He looked again out the window and then back to Maggie. "You see. He came looking for her here. Well, she wasn't here. I recognized him by his name."

"Oh!" Maggie said as she walked to the window. "He told you who he was. And that he was looking for his sweetheart. And you lied to him?"

"Yes, I lied to him. I'm in love, sweet Maggie. David. For the first time in my life, I'm in love. I'm in love with the most beautiful and the most mysterious girl that ever crossed my path. Can you understand that?"

"Well, sure. Certainly I can," Maggie answered. Then she looked out the window herself. "And he's coming here to find her?"

"Yes. I'm afraid so. I don't want to have to fight him."

"It kind of looks that way, doesn't it Bryce?" David surmised. "I mean, you will have to defend your honor."

"I don't mind that. I'd probably get killed because I'm no match for him. But you know I'd fight for her."

"Then," David continued. "have Barnabas and a few others chase him away."

"No. No. If she got wind that he was here, I'm afraid she'd never marry me. She'd probably run to him."

"Are you sure of that?" David asked. Putting his hands in his pocket, he followed Willoughby around the room.

"She seems to be all smiles and beaming in your direction," exclaimed Maggie, trying to reassure her brother.

"And you want a favor from us?" David asked again. "I'm curious. Just what kind of favor could you ask of us that would resolve this issue? You're going to marry her tomorrow?"

Willoughby went to the window one more time and then looked back at Maggie. "Time is not on our side at this moment. I'm afraid he's arrived."

"Well, what do you want us to do?" Maggie looked out the window again, hoping to get a glance at the gentleman in question.

"Remain here. And you, sis, will pretend to be my fiancé."

"What? You're out of your mind. She's prettier than me. Younger than me. I couldn't get away with it."

"Yes you can, Maggie. He's never seen my fiancé and he's been told Ginny is dead. He simply won't find her.

"He'll take our word for it, collectively; yours, David's and mine, that you are my fiancé and then leave. There will be no mention of Ginny."

"Barnabas is walking down the hall, now. How do we handle it?" David was excited and extremely nervous.

"I've instructed Barnabas that if he should show up again, to bring him into this room, which he'll do. And when they do show up, you, David, go out of the room. Get a couple of drinks and bring them in. I'll introduce Maggie as my fiancé. You come in with the drinks and confirm it by congratulating us some way."

"Some way?"

"Yes." He looked at Maggie and asked, "Can you do it?"

"I'll not lie for you."

"Dang it, sis! Just stand there and say nothing then and I'll do the talking." Then, seeing David walk out, he yelled out to him, "David! You can lie, can't you?"

David looked at Willoughby, nodded his head and answered, "Yeah!"

Willoughby ran up the stairs to make certain Ginny would not be interrupting his plans.

When Matt and Steve rode up to the mansion, they were met at the front gate by the soldiers they had met at the McBride Mill, standing and armed. Willoughby was not with them.

They reined up and sat their saddles as they confronted the Yankee line.

"What's your business?" the sergeant asked, waving a rifle at them.

"You're really pushing for punishment, aren't you, Sarge?" Matt asked as he pointed at the man's rifle.

"We're told you were trying to mess up a wedding party. And we don't cotton to party breakers. Now our advise to you is to turn around and git!"

The talk got heavier as Matt and Steve sat their horses without any intention of turning around.

Inside the house, Ginny heard the men outside with the two riders.

"What's happening, Bryce?" she asked, as she continued readying herself in her bedroom. She was putting the last of her hair in place as she stepped toward the window, "I see your men are talking with two riders. Friends or not?"

"Not really. Troublemakers. They were down at the mill and busted up my sergeant. Now they want to pick a fight and I had to bring more men in to assure that they would be protected. After all, honey, Sergeant Mayberry is our best man, and I didn't want to have to step in to help him at the cost of messing up our wedding entirely."

"Well, get rid of them and let's finish what we have to do. The wedding's in the morning and Grand Mama and I are not entirely ready for it. Are you?"

Willoughby went to Ginny, put his arm around her and said, "I'm as ready right now as I'll ever be. Let me run along downstairs and chase away this riff-raff so we can move along with our bridal shower."

"Mister," Matt shouted to the sergeant. "Move out of my way!" Matt moved Skeeter onto the grounds, and pushed the soldiers to the point that they jumped upon Skeeter and knocked Matt to the ground.

Steve rode in with his Navy and backed the men off of Matt. "He said to move. And I'm telling ya'll. Move or else!"

The men moved out of Steve's way, but some other men came around from behind and knocked Steve out of the saddle.

Barnabas was at the door, watching the fight, left the door open and went to address Willoughby who was descending the staircase. "Suh," Barnabas announced to Willoughby. These gentlemen you said would be heah are heah."

Willoughby went out and called to the men. "Let 'em up!"

"Sir, they were intent to break up the party," the sergeant answered with a salute.

"They've come to see me. Bring them in."

Leading the men to the parlor where Maggie and the rest were waiting Willoughby put his arm around her. Smilingly, he whispered to her, hoping in his heart that she would do this favor, and without having to lie to convince the men that she was his fiancé.

"Mr . . . . ?

"Jorgensen," Matt answered, wiping his face with his bandana."

"Of course. And Mr. . . . ?"

"Andrews. Steve Andrews," Steve answered as he and Matt walked into the parlor.

"And this is my lovely fiancée, Maggie."

Matt looked at her and then at Willoughby. "Miss. . . ."

"Southerland, Mr. Jorgensen," she answered. "Maggie Southerland. I'm from Michigan as is Bryce. We were born and raised just outside of Ann Arbor, Michigan."

Willoughby sweated throughout the introduction, hoping that Maggie would curtail her conversation. He was afraid she would go too far and, without lying, reveal to Matt who she really was. He was doubly concerned about any other guests walking in on them and revealing her real identity. He had mentioned to Barnabas earlier that he should not in any manner be disturbed while entertaining Matt and Steve.

"Miss Southerland. I'm pleased that you and the captain here are getting married. Steve and I just came by to give you our best wishes."

"Well, thank you, sir. Bryce will make a charming husband, I'm sure," she gestured, giving Willoughby a teasing look.

David entered with three glasses of Champaign, which he offered to Willoughby and Maggie.

"Oh, I'm sorry. I didn't realize we had more guests." He caught Barnabas standing by the door as if in preparation for a fight and told him, "Barnabas. Please bring in two more glasses of Champaign for these gentlemen."

Barnabas nodded and answered, "Yes, suh." He looked at Matt and Steve with a frown as if to say, *something wrong goin' on heah,* and walked away.

"And how did you gentlemen meet Bryce?" Maggie asked, taking one of the glasses from David.

"Oh, eh, they came to Richmond looking for the lovely Ginny McBride. Well, I told her what we have been hearing all these many years that she's missing and probably killed. Isn't that right, Maggie?"

Maggie almost choked on her drink.

"Maggie?" Willoughby repeated, hoping that she could get around his question without lying."

She answered, "Yes. Yes, that's what we've *been* hearing all these years." Then she straightened up and asked Matt, "She was your sweetheart?"

"Is. Yes she is. I don't believe she's dead. Missing, yes. But not dead. I know somehow, and don't ask me how, but I know she's alive."

"And you still love her after all these years since she's disappeared?"

"More and more every day."

Then she looked slyly into his eyes over the top of the Champaign glass, as devilish as she could and asked, "Always been faithful?"

Matt hemmed and hawed for a moment, and then Barnabas brought in the two glasses of Champaign for him and Steve.

"Thank you." He raised his glass and said, "May I present a toast?

Willoughby looked at Matt nervously and in thought said, *Git out while you can before you blow my whole scheme. I don't want to have to fight you.*

Matt caught the grit in Willoughby's teeth and seemingly enjoyed it.

"To two wonderful people. May your marriage bring forth good fruit and happiness."

"Well," Maggie added, "thank you, Mr. Jorgensen. You'll probably be half right."

"Matt to my friends, Miss Southerland."

She smiled and gave a humorous gaze at Willoughby.

After the toast, she asked, "And you will continue to look for her?"

"Until I find her."

"One way or another?"

"Alive, Miss. Southerland. Alive."

"I must say, I like your tenacity, Mr. . . . Matt. I hope you find her. I really do." Then she looked around at Willoughby and David and added, "We all do."

"Thank you, Maggie. Mr. eh, I didn't get your name."

"Yes. Johnson. David Johnson."

"David," Matt continued. Then he turned and attracted Willoughby's attention. "Captain Willoughby. We won't be staying."

"No. No," Steve chimed in. "Fact is, we've got an engagement back in town at the, eh, hotel."

"Oh?" Maggie smirked. "Why don't you bring them back with you and join our celebration? I'm sure we would all enjoy your company." She gave a hint of flirtation to Matt and he received it well.

He looked over at David and smiled; but the smile was not returned.

Steve was dumbfounded at Maggie's quick return for he realized that she knew he was making an excuse for leaving and could be a cause for their staying.

Willoughby furrowed his brow at hearing Maggie but felt at the moment he had to cover it with, "Yes. By all means. Why not go and get your, eh, business and bring them in. I'm sure the rest of the guests would be delighted." Then, as for a scare tactic, he added, "The sheriff and a couple of his deputies and their wives are here, along with Judge Jacobson. You'd be quite welcomed."

Matt and Steve caught onto the gist and excused themselves one more time. Matt swallowed the rest of his drink and continued, "Oh, no. We can't. But . . ." He brought a box out of his coat pocket. "We bought this in town as a wedding gift. Hope you like it."

Maggie accepted it and curtsied for Matt and Steve. "Why, how thoughtful. You boys sure you can't stay?"

Matt looked at her and for a moment, just a moment, felt that she was continuing to play a game with him. Then he looked at the trio and again excused himself and Steve.

"Thank you, Miss Southerland." Matt bent forward, kissed her hand and looked into her lovely eyes. He again sensed a smile of loveliness towards his mannerism. "It's been a short, but pleasant evening."

"You never answered me, Matt." She said softly for only him to hear.

He answered, "You do have a sense of charm about you, Maggie."

He smiled, rose and shook hands with David who finally gave him a smile; perhaps of being comforted with the knowledge that they were leaving. Then he shook hands with the trembling captain. "Captain. It's been a pleasure. Sorry for all the confusion."

"Thank you, Mr. Jorgensen. I sincerely hope that you find your true love. Wherever she might be."

"Ginny?" Matt replied. "Yes. I'm certain that I will some day."

Barnabas overheard Matt and echoed it to himself, *Ginny*?

Willoughby, walking by, caught Barnabas by surprise and told him to answer the door. "More guests are coming."

"Yes, suh. But , Miss Gin , . ."

Willoughby was quick to interrupt Barnabas. "We've more guests coming, Barnabas."

Willoughby escorted Matt and Steve towards the front and Barnabas opened the door. Other guests were welcomed into the mansion by Barnabas and Willoughby as Matt and Steve slipped by them.

Once on their horses, Steve turned to Matt and asked, "Are you satisfied, pal?

Matt looked back at Barnabas who was busy ushering in other guests and said, "For the time being, friend. For the time being."

"Where to now?" Steve asked as they walked their horses out the main gate.

"For tonight, it's not back to the Purple Cow."

"Purple Garter, friend."

Whatever. I need to get out of Richmond. We'll find some place on the way to bed down. I'm beat."

"About thet little gift you pulled out of your pocket. I don't remember you buying anything in town," Steve asked.

"Just a little something I picked up at the table, Mr. Andrews. Two cards. A queen of hearts and an ace of hearts."

"Two face cards. Why?"

"Maybe something just to irritate our good friend a little. He'll wonder why for a long time to come, I reckon."

They rode out from the mansion onto the main road and out of town. Matt repeated what Barnabas had said under his breath, *Ginny*.

CHAPTER 27

TO WED OR NOT TO WED

<u>14 October 1866</u>

The evening at the McBride Mansion went well after Matt and Steve left; that was until Ginny entered the scene. She was to be preceded by Sarah McBride down the spiral staircase on the arm of David Donaldson. The fifty some guests, the Judge and his entourage, and other town dignitaries stood in quiet admiration of the matron of the manor.

The guests waited for the entry of Miss McBride. Instead, she remained sitting on her bed in her room while Maggie stood beside her.

"Do you still see this *Matt* in your sleep?" Maggie asked while looking out the window, almost as if hoping to see Matt on a white horse. She was acting as the jealous matron of honor; not enamored of the groom, but of the man who rode away. She turned and walked over to Ginny.

"I can tell you this. If I had a man such as your Matt whom I loved and felt he was still alive and searching for me, I'd wait for him."

Ginny looked up into Maggie's face. "Five years, Maggie. I've waited five long tortuous years. Can you understand how I feel?"

"Yes, my love. Yes. You can know this that I understand perhaps more than you can ever realize."

Ginny rose from her bed and looked intently into Maggie's eyes. "You seem to be hiding something from me, Maggie. What is it?"

"Well, if I am, it's for your own good. I just feel that Matt is a man who could make you feel like a woman again. Make you feel like you're an important person."

"So can Bryce."

"Bryce? Bryce is a worker, Ginny. He is loyal, faithful," and here she turned her face from Ginny and continued. "He's trustworthy. Matt sounds like a man who would take you to the edge of the world and ride you on clouds of adventure. You came from a background of slavery; a whip and a pistol. You lived and breathed excitement. Now, you're going to settle for a mundane life of having socials and dances and dignitaries of all kinds who will mob all over you. I know. I'm there now. Michigan. David is a professor at U of M. He teaches physics." She turned and looked at Ginny and gave her a frown. "Boring! I see him when I can, with other people around us. We never leave the campus, or Ann Arbor for that matter. This is the furthest we've come since we met."

"What would you do if you were me, Maggie?"

"Well, I'm not you." Then under her breath she said to herself, *If I were, I'd find Matt and sail the wind with him to wherever he'd take me.*

"But what would you do? I know it's not fair. I'm marrying your brother in the morning. But just what would you do?"

"You and I are different in age, Ginny. I know where I am. I married too young, just before the war. Because of the war, we opted not to have any children as of yet because of his career. He stayed at the university. I worked there at times. I'm pretty much contented with my life and family."

"You have a good life."

"Yes, and so do you. I understand that a tutor from the closed-down William and Mary took you on and that you've graduated as his law pupil."

Ginny interrupted. "Yes. The dean in fact. And Kenny and Gerald are on top of getting the mill up and running again. It's going to be a big job, restructuring the mill in North Carolina. But, they're great at getting things done."

"You've got the world at your feet."

"So, what are you saying?"

Maggie walked over to the window once again and looked out. She saw no knight on a white horse so she turned, looked at Ginny and answered. "Don't marry Bryce. Not if you still love Matt."

She walked over to Ginny and, as Ginny stood up, she put her arms around her and said, "Honey. I'd love to have you as a sister. I'd love it. But I'd rather have you as a friend whom I know somehow I helped."

Then she quickly added, "Now please don't get me wrong. I love Bryce. As a brother, he's got great ideas. It's just that I don't see him making you the husband that you really want and more importantly, one that you need. I know Bryce."

It was several moments after Sarah walked down the staircase that the door to Ginny's bedroom opened. Maggie walked out first and descended the staircase.

"Ladies and gentlemen," Maggie began and introduced Ginny to the awaiting guests. "Miss Virginia McBride"

Ginny stood at the head of the staircase in all her glory, dressed in an evening gown that accentuated her eyes, her hair and most importantly, her body. The people gasped as they saw this beauty, gracefully enter their realm in all her dazzling array.

Sarah smiled.

The evening went on with everyone wanting to dance with the lovely and beautiful Miss McBride. Willoughby danced the first dance with her, turned her over to Doctor Paterson for the next dance, and then got drunk. He saw very little of her that evening.

The evening moonlight covered the sleeping beauty majestically in her bed as her eyelids moved from side to side. She saw the man who stood at the hitching post in front of the Purple Garter Saloon. And then, as she awoke, the vision of her lover appeared again on her bedroom wall in front of her. As it did, her dream vision of the man in front of the saloon slowly enlarged and emerged into one and the same face. Her eyes began to open wide and then she covered her face and screamed. The scream flowed throughout the bedroom, out the opened doors that led to the outside balcony and down below to the veranda. Again the scream reverberated under her bedroom door and traveled ever so fast down the corridor and bounced from side to side against the walls. The notes of the shrill noise slid into Sarah's bedroom and awakened her.

Sarah put on her robe and as she opened her bedroom door to investigate the cacophony, she was met by Barnabas and Lula Belle; both clad in bedclothes haphazardly thrown about them and an oil lamp in Barnabas' hand. Lulu Belle wore a robe with a shawl.

"What *is* it, Missus Sarah?" Lula Belle asked, taking her by the hand.

"I don't have the slightest idea, but it seems to be coming from Ginny's room, Barnabas suggested.

They looked down the corridor and walked quickly towards the noise that penetrated the night with fervent vigor. When Barnabas knocked on the door, the scream got louder.

"Open it, Barnabas!" Sarah ordered, holding her housecoat together tightly in her small bony hands.

Barnabas opened the door and allowed Sarah and Lula Belle to enter it first and he entered immediately following them. Ginny was standing in her nightgown in front of the bedroom wall with her hands covering her face.

"That is all for now, Barnabas. I'll take it from here," Sarah said as she stood inside the doorway, not wanting to frighten Ginny any further. "Lula Belle, you may pour her some water from the pitcher on the wash basin stand and then return to your quarters."

"Yes, ma'am," Lula Belle faintly whispered. "Kinda looks like Miss Ginny's had herself a nightmare, ma'am."

Barnabas covered his eyes, turned and lit one of the lamps on Ginny's bureau, then picked it up and walked back to the corridor and waited.

"Ginny?" Sarah motioned quietly as she walked up to her. "What is it, child?"

Ginny removed her hands from her face and looked frighteningly into Sarah's eyes. "It's him!" she screamed. "It's him!" She clutched onto Sarah's housecoat and brought her close into her body. "It's Matt, Grand Mama!"

"What is? The vision?"

"Yes. No, it was him. I saw him in town. Remember when we drove down the main street. A man stood just outside the saloon. What was it? *Purple* something or other."

"Oh that awful place?" Sarah returned.

"Yes. Oh, yes, Grand Mama. He stood there and smiled at us as we drove by. Remember?"

"Yes, child. I remember a man chewing tobacco and smiling at you. That awful thing. He looked drunk to me."

"He was charming and handsome, Grand Mama. Remember? He smiled and tilted his hat at us. At me. Oh, Grand Mama. It was him! Matt! It *was* Matt!"

The darkness broke into dawn when the two women finally went back to sleep only to awaken shortly afterward to prepare for the breakfast to be served for the family and guests before the wedding that day.

That morning was about to wreak havoc on everyone from the maids and butlers to Lula Belle and Barnabas. It also was to include David as the Best Man and Maggie as the Matron of Honor; not to mention the Groomsmen and Bridesmaids and also the Flower Girl and Ring Bearer. They and others hustled back and forth to make sure that the wedding would take place without a hitch.

Sarah stayed with Ginny and sat on her bed as Ginny prepared herself for the wedding.

"I'm not going through with it, Grand Mama." Ginny sat at her vanity, making sure her make-up was on properly while Sarah brushed her hair.

"Are you sure, child?"

" That vision I had last night, Grand Mama." Ginny rose, walked over to Sarah and sat down beside her.

"I know, Ginny." Sarah wrapped her hands around Ginny's. "But, you haven't had a vision in over a year. Why now? "

"He was there. Looking at me. His face looked tired and worn. Yet, still handsome as ever. But he looked forlorn, as if he were giving up on finding me."

"Oh, he can not ever do that."

"What does it mean, Grand Mama?"

Sarah looked at Ginny lying on the bed. She sat down and brought Ginny to her bosom. "There, there, my dear child. You're giving up on him by going through with this wedding!"

190

"Yes. You're right, Grand Mama. I can not love another man."

"No, you can't," Sarah answered. She took her hankie from her sleeve, put it in Ginny's hand and said, "Here. Blow your nose!"

As they continued talking, Ginny rose, embraced Sarah, and asked, "Grand Mama. How did you and Grand Papa meet?" She let go of Sarah and looked at her wonderful aged face. "I mean, did you fall in love right away?"

Sarah returned the smile, sat on the bed and folded her hands in her lap. "Jonathan? My Jonathan? Love at first sight? Oh, no, my child. He had some competition, he did. You've seen the painting of me as a young lady that hangs above the fireplace. I wasn't always this old. That was made just after we were married. I was almost as pretty as you are," she said gracefully to Ginny with a wink.

"Matt and I fell in love right away."

And then Sarah added, matter-of-factly, "Matt is still searching for you, dear."

"Matt?" Ginny's eyes opened wide and turned to Sarah's. "How? Where?"

"I don't know, dear. But by you having visions of him, I only have the deep, deep feeling that he has never given up."

"Do you know something that you're not telling me, Grand Mama?"

"Child. You have the deep perceptions that I had when I was your age. Mine have grown and I can somehow see into the future.

"Yes, I am holding back on you. You see. Your lover's name is . . . *Matt,* we all know that."

"But, how? What do you know about him?"

"Your father wrote about Matt's visit to find you during the war."

"Matt? My Matt?" Ginny asked excitedly. "What, Grand Mama? When? Tell me everything."

"Well, according to your father's letters, Matt was poorly when he visited him, but didn't let on about his health." She smiled as she looked into Ginny's wondering eyes. "I understand that he had deserted his unit just to find you."

"My Matt?" She clutched at her breast.

"Yes, dear. Your father said that he was not the same Matt that he knew before the war. He was thinner, dirtier, in need of a shave and a haircut but most of all in need of a real bath." She laughed a little that turned into a precious smile.

"Oh, my wonderful Matt."

"Your father was not in good health, either, child. Else he would have gone with Matt in search for you. He had already spent weeks looking for you before.

"He's out there. And you're here. Somehow, somewhere, some day, you will find each other again. Of that, I am certain. Our God has a way of making things turn out. Sometimes we call it *fate*."

"Oh, Grand Mama. Grand Mama." Ginny leaned again against Sarah's bosom and wept gears of great release.

The organ played a beautiful song later that morning, and the lawn outside was filled with guests waiting for Ginny to enter. She never did. Instead, Sarah made the entrance on the arm of Barnabas.

The guests hushed as Sarah walked up to the front where Willoughby and the wedding entourage stood. She turned and after a few moments of quietness, said, "I'm sorry, Ladies and gentlemen. Judge Jacobson. Sheriff Pleasant. But our Ginny has told me to tell you that she will not be getting married today."

Willoughby dropped his jaw and looked up towards the upstairs window, hoping to catch a glimpse of Ginny.

"She told me to tell you, Bryce that she would prefer not to see you at this time. Maybe later."

The crowd dispersed quietly as well as did most of the wedding gifts. Willoughby sat on the veranda, comforted by his sister and her husband. Sarah sat close by.

"No point in me going upstairs and talking with her?" Willoughby asked, dejectedly.

Ginny walked out the door and answered him herself. "I'd appreciate it if you left me alone for a while. I'm truly sorry, and it was unfair to embarrass you in this way, but I need some time alone, Bryce."

"Darling, darling Ginny. Why?" Willoughby asked, stretching out his arms to take her into himself.

"No, Bryce. Maybe later. But certainly not now. I love you. I really do. But not the way that I should if I were to marry you, and I'm not ready for that step at this time."

"But we've planned it."

"You planned it, Bryce. I only helped and I shouldn't have led you on, but things have happened since."

"What kind of things?"

"She saw a vision again last night, Bryce," Sarah spoke up without rising. "She's still in love with Matt."

"Matt! Matt! That son-of-a . . ." Willoughby stood beside himself, slamming his fist into his other hand.

Maggie smiled within herself, walked over and embraced Ginny. She whispered in her ear so where no one would hear. "Congratulations, Ginny. Find Matt, or let him find you. It'll be worth it." Then she turned and walked over to put her arms around her brother to console him.

It'll be worth it! The words echoed in Ginny's ears the rest of the day and into the night. As she slept that night, no visions appeared and there was a surety in her heart where turmoil had been the night before. But she talked through the night to the man of her dreams.

If you can hear me, my darling Matt, know this one thing; I love you. And I will always love you.

The night was cool and Matt and Steve slept under the stars, each rolled up inside a blanket to keep warm. A dream kept Matt tossing throughout the night and the words haunted him as they repeatedly said, *If you can hear me, my darling Matt, know this one thing; I love you. And I will always love you.*

CHAPTER 28

A DYING MAN'S CONFESSION

<u>3 January 1867</u>

As hard as Captain Willoughby tried, he could not get into the mansion to see Ginny. She never took the carriage to town except on business matters; instead Barnabas and Lula Belle did the shopping.

"Are we going to town to spend some of our money, Captain?" asked the sergeant. He knew better than to step on Willoughby's toes with talk about Ginny. "You've been like this for weeks. It's time to unwind."

Willoughby stood up, strapped his Army revolver to his side and picked his hat off the rack.

"Let's go, Jack," he said. The sergeant and ten other men from his company mounted and followed on their horses. It looked like a gang was going to hit Richmond. Instead, they rode like army gentlemen.

When they reached the Purple Garter, they tied their horses to the hitching post and the whole company went in. It was a night for them to frolic and let go of one's inhibitions. The whole company was bent on getting drunk, including Willoughby.

Willoughby sat in on a game of what he thought was a friendly game of five card draw poker. The game went on for a couple of hours until two men walked in and sat at an adjoining table.

"Well, it looks like the whole Yankee infantry has landed, boys," one of the men observed, looking at the twelve uniforms sitting around at different tables. The man was mean looking, a lot of bulk under his opened face shirt that showed off his dirty union suit. He had a scrubby beard that made his face look even meaner with a scar that ran along side his nose.

The other man was almost as mean, skinny as a rail and puny to boot. His bald head appeared to be laden with infested sores that matched those on his cheeks as if he had not taken a bath in months.

"You boys here on business or you planning on losing some of your hard-earned money," the bulky one yelled out. "Give us some whiskey, bar keep."

They leaned up against the bar and observed what was going on as they drank down their first shot. "We'll keep the bottle," he said indignantly.

"No trouble, mister," the bartender warned as he gave him the bottle.

The two gals came out and began their routine with six other gals on stage to the tinkling of the ivories by a gentleman in a derby hat with a garter on his sleeve. The number was livened up with the two men howling.

"Keep it down, mister, while the gals sing," the bartender warned them again.

"We're here to play poker, get drunk and visit some purty women. Now you tell us to keep it down again and we'll shoot up this place."

Willoughby heard the man and said as he read his hand, "You heard the bar keep. Keep it down if you want to have a good time tonight. We want to hear the girls sing."

The mean one threw his chair out of the way and walked over to Willoughby. "You ain't got no cause to interfere with our pleasures, Blue Belly."

"War's over, mister. Best you sit this one out," Willoughby suggested with a gentle and steady voice.

The sergeant watched from his table as well as others around him.

"You got your fellas around you to keep you safe, don't cha, Blue Belly? I don't think you got nerve to face me down." The bulky one took a knife from his boot and showed it to Willoughby.

Willoughby drew his Army .45 and shoved the barrel in the man's direction. "I don't like wasting time with a knife. You put it away and you'll live, mister. Now!"

"What? What is this? We come in for some fun, and you want a fight." The bulky one sheathed the knife, sat back down and downed another drink.

The two men turned their backs on the company and rested at the bar.

Three other men came in and sat down at a table close to the front to watch the women. The saloon kept peaceful while the girls danced and the men started up a game of five card stud.

"Care if we sit in?" the bulky one asked as he walked over to the table where the three men sat.

"Sure. Why not?" One of the men at the table accepted them. "We'll start the game as soon as the ladies finish their song."

A round of applause sent the women back to their rooms behind the stage as the men began playing poker.

"You gotta watch these Blue Bellies," the bulky man started up as he received his cards from the dealer. "They play for keeps."

The dealer looked back over his shoulder and saw Willoughby at the table behind him. "Well, well. If it isn't the captain. Come here for some female entertainment, did ya?"

"Just playing cards, mister."

"Yeah. I heerd about your weddin'. Fact is, the whole town heard 'bout how you got stood up at the altar. Har! Har!"

"What?" the bulky man asked as he received his cards. "He got stood up at the altar? Mister Blue Belly?"

Willoughby kept silent and stayed in the game. "I'll see you and raise you a dollar."

"Who was he a'gonna marry?" the bulky man came back with more sarcasm. "Some frilly little maid?" The two mean men laughed devilishly.

"No," said the dealer. "He had his hooks in one o' the richest maids in all of Richmond."

"A rich one, huh?" the bulky man asked, eyeing Willoughby.

"What's the matter? Too rich for us poor cowboys? And she turned you down? Why?"

"I'll tell you why," a second man at the table interrupted. "She's in love with another man. A dead man."

"A dead man?" the bulky man asked, throwing down two cards as the dealer came around again. "I'll take two. And make 'em good 'cause I got me three aces in here."

"You gentlemen better make some peace over there," the sergeant warned from the table up front. "We're here to have a good time and we don't want anyone messing around with our captain."

"Oh, we ain't messing around, Mister Three Stripes," the bulky one answered, taking a swig of his whisky. "You need lessons on how to get a woman, Blue Belly?"

The laughter at the table grew, and so did the sergeant's anger. He rose from the table and walked over to the bulky one.

"Now you pulled a knife on the captain and now you're trying to test his anger," the sergeant said, standing straddled with tight fists.

"Sit down before I knock ya down, Blue Belly," the bulky man came back, taking another swig of his drink.

"I'm in on this, too," the skinny one chimed in, nervously.

"Well, I'll tell you what," the sergeant informed the two men. "I'll take the two of you on right now."

Willoughby threw his cards down and walked over to the table up front. "Hold it, Sergeant. We didn't come in here to fight. Let's leave."

"Har! Har! The captain's a chicken," said the bulky one, pouring himself another drink. "Your Blue Belly three striper says he's gonna take us two little ones on. Ain't thet right?"

"Let's go, gentlemen," Willoughby waved his men to get together. "That's an order, gentlemen."

The bulky man stood up and, with a big arm, swung his fist at Willoughby, connecting to his jaw. He sent Willoughby back across the room and under the table where he had been playing cards.

The sergeant brought his fist hard against the bulky one, almost to no avail. The bulky one smiled, spit out part of a tooth and backhanded the sergeant.

This brought up the rest of the company of ten men to the rescue of their two leaders. The skinny one stood up but was accidentally knocked backwards by the bulky one's big arm that swung away to get better leverage.

Immediately, two of the men were thrown over and against the bar while the bulky one stood and laughed at the rest. "Bring on your best, Blue Bellies. I done killed more of you than you could count anyhow. I can take you to the devil if you aim me to do so."

The bulky man brought out his knife again and showed it around to the other soldiers. A shot rang out that broke the bulky man's hand. The company looked and saw the captain's gun smoking.

"I told you before to sheath it and I meant it. I'm an army captain, and I'll kill you in the act of duty if you so as much threaten any of my men again. Do you understand me?"

The bulky man took his knife in his left hand, turned as if to sit back down. Instead, he swiftly turned and threw the knife at Willoughby that stuck in his right thigh.

The soldiers, seeing the bulky man was unarmed, attacked him in full force and brought him down to the ground. The skinny man ran to the door but was stopped instantly by the sheriff who had been summoned by the bartender.

"Break it up! Break it up!" the sheriff ordered as two of his deputies backed him up.

"The bulky one is the one you want to lock up, sheriff," the bartender informed him.

"Our captain is injured, sheriff," the sergeant said, pulling the knife out of his leg.

"It's my knife," the bulky one admitted. "Give it back to me."

"Shut up, mister, or you'll get it like you did to the captain," the sheriff ordered him, shoving a shotgun in his belly. Take the two of them away, boys," he told his deputies.

He walked over to Willoughby and checked on his condition. "How is he, fellas?"

"It went in deep," the sergeant informed him, tying a tourniquet around his thigh. "He's losing a lot of blood."

"Get him over to the doc right away!" The sheriff told them, watching the soldiers form a human litter to take him out. "Closest one is Doc Paterson up the street. Get 'im up there!"

The night was confusing to the soldiers as they looked for a wagon to take Willoughby up the hill. When they did commandeer a wagon, they found that the mud was thick and was cause to fight the wagon wheel from the ruts.

The road was rough, but they arrived at Doc Paterson's office and quickly took Willoughby from the wagon and placed him on the table. The Doc took a look at Willoughby's leg and began cleaning it up.

"He's lost quite a lot of blood," Henry said as he cleaned up his thigh and applied a tourniquet. "But thanks to you boys getting him here as fast as you did, well see if we can save him."

Willoughby was awake but weak when Henry began working on his leg. "Will I make it, Doc," he asked, trying to watch what Henry was doing.

"We have no assurance, son," Henry came back, tearing back his pant leg from the wound to see if he could suture it. "You've got to be weak as a kitten right about now."

"I am, Doc. I don't think I'm going to make it."

"We'll try, son. Hold in there." He looked at the sergeant and asked for assistance. "Can you and another of your men get a couple of lanterns together for me to see with in here?"

Quickly, the sergeant and another man had two lanterns lit and fully bright within minutes. Willoughby hung in there while Henry continued his preparation. "Once I've got the bleeding under control, I'll patch him up the best I can and see what happens."

"It was a filthy knife, Doc," the sergeant told him.

"Thanks. That makes my job a whole lot easier," Henry came back, being a little sarcastic. "We'll treat it with iodine."

"Doc," Willoughby whispered weakly. "I'm Catholic. Can you get a priest?"

"Do any of you boys know of a priest?" Henry asked. "I'm a Baptist."

"No, sir," Sarge answered, as he squeamishly watched Henry at work.

"I've got to make my confession, Doc." Willoughby whispered again. "I've got to have absolution for my soul."

"Well, son, I'm no priest. But I'm going to try and save your life and your leg."

"Can I confess to you, Doc? You're a religious man. You go to church."

"As often as possible."

"We don't have to listen, Doc," Sarge said, plugging up his ears.

"That's ok, boys. As soon as I've got the bleeding stopped, I'll listen to you. Is that all right with you, son?"

"Yes. But, hurry, Doc. I don't want to meet my Maker with sin in my soul."

The tourniquet worked and the bleeding stopped. Henry continued cleaning the area and applying iodine. "There. Now the bleeding's stopped. I'll sew it up. So, go ahead, son. Confess."

"Come closer, Doc. Please."

Henry bent closer to Willoughby's lips and listened to his confession.

"I told a lie a few weeks back. It's been gnawing on me all this time. Maybe that's why I got struck tonight."

"What's the lie, boy? Do you want to tell me?"

"Yes, Doc. I made up a lie to prevent another man from knowing that his girl. . . . The one he thought got killed in the war."

Henry listened closely because he knew that Willoughby was talking about Ginny.

"Go ahead, son."

"He came to the mansion."

"Who came, son?"

"That man. The one who was looking for the girl."

"Did you get his name?"

"Oh, yes, sir. That's why I knew who he was. His name was Matt. Matt Jorgensen."

Henry stopped working on his leg and swallowed hard. "This man was here in Richmond?"

"Yes, sir. He came to the McBride Mansion,"

"You saw him?"

200

"Yes, sir. I talked with him. I told him at first . . ." He grunted for a moment. "The pain, Doc. The pain. It hurts."

"I know, son. Let me work on it."

"No. Not yet, Doc. Let me finish."

"Go ahead." Henry began his suturing as Willoughby continued confessing. He thought, *His talking might help keep him from feeling too much pain,.*

"He left, thinking she was dead. At least I hoped so. But he came back later. I figured he might be coming back, so I got my sister and her husband to lie for me. No. That's wrong. My sister didn't lie. She wouldn't. . . . The pain, Doc. It hurts."

"Yes, I know, son. Keep talking."

"They helped me convince this Matt that she was my fiancée and we were getting married."

"Your sister?"

"Yes. No. She pretended to be Ginny so that way he wouldn't suspect she was living there at the mansion."

"Did he believe you?"

"Yes. For all intensive purposes. I think he believed us." He laughed and then cried out, "Doc, it hurts!"

"Get one of your men to bring me some whiskey. We're going to have to get your captain drunk, or else."

"Loose the leg?" Sarge surmised with great reluctance.

"Not if I can help it. Run. Get some whiskey."

"I have some on me, Doc," the other soldier, standing next to Henry, revealed.

"Why didn't you say so, boy?" Henry scolded.

"Didn't know you'd need it. Guess I weren't a-thinkin', Doc."

"Give it to him in small swallows. Let him drink the whole thing."

"The whole thing?"

"Yes, the whole thing."

"It's a big bottle, Doc." The soldier began administering the whiskey to Willoughby.

Henry brought his ear back to Willoughby's lips and continued listening to his confession. "Go ahead, son. I'm listening.

Willoughby slipped into a sleep and then came back out of it when pain returned. The soldier gave him another sip of the whiskey.

He continued his confession. "They convinced him that she was marrying me. Not Ginny. That way he had no reason to believe that Ginny was still alive and living there. You see what I mean, Doc?" He coughed a little and then continued. "We fooled him. And I . . .another drink! The pain! Oh, God! The pain!"

The soldier administered another drink to his lips.

"We kept him from seeing her, Doc . . ." His words trailed off.

Henry kept sewing as Willoughby kept talking and drinking liquor. "Do you feel at peace with your Maker now, son?"

"Will you say a prayer over me, Doc . . . absolving me from my sins."

"I can't forgive you of your sins, son. God does that through Jesus Christ."

"I know, Doc. But if you don't pray for me, and I don't make it . . . Doc. The pain! Please!"

Henry continued praying while suturing, asking God for forgiveness for Captain Willoughby. "He's confessed all so we ask, in the name of Jesus, that you forgive him. Amen."

Willoughby felt that he had become the officer and gentleman he once was, He felt for the moment that he was exonerated for his lie, took another sip of whiskey and passed out.

"He's lost a lot of blood, but I've got it stopped. I'll finish patching him up."

"He'll live, Doc?" Sarge asked, looking down at his commander.

"As far as I know, he'll live. Leave him here. That's as much as I can do for now. I'll take care of him."

Willoughby lived and Henry kept the confession to himself. It was a dying man's confession, and even though Henry felt that Ginny should know about Matt's visit to the mansion, he felt the secrecy between Willoughby and his Maker was more important; even though Willoughby was still alive.

On his last visit to Henry's office, Willoughby said, "You did all right, Doc," "Once I I get rid of this cane, I'll feel better."

"One thing," Doc interrupted him before he left his office. "Do you remember anything you said while you were on the table?"

"I said something?" He looked over at Sarge who was there to help him into the carriage. Sarge looked at Henry who gave him the high sign not to mention anything.

"Well, son. You probably just mumbled some things. Not important. I just thought you might have said something that I needed to know."

"I don't think so. I really don't remember."

Henry smiled and watched Willoughby step up into the carriage. As he drove away, Henry said under his breath, *Another case of amnesia.*

CHAPTER 29

GINNY RIDES ALONE

Before dawn, a rider in black rode from the McBride stables towards east. The ride took Ginny into the afternoon when she reined up on the shore overlooking the Atlantic Ocean. She dismounted, held onto the reins and walked her horse on the beach where she looked out onto the vast blue waters.

She tied the reins to the limb of a large piece of driftwood and sat down on the sandy beach. She stared out onto the large white waves as they rolled upon the shore chasing the sea gulls inland.

After a long while, she took the canteen from her saddle and drank her fill. She wiped her lips, took her Stetson off and poured some water into it for her mount. She then put the cap back in place and returned the canteen to the saddle bag. Then she turned and walked to the edge of the shore line and stood straddle-legged, strong with a determination building within her breast.

"Matt, darling!" she yelled out. "I'll find you if it takes the rest of my life!"

She bedded herself down for the night and rode back to the McBride Estate the next morning. She walked loud with the clicking of her boots on the hallway tile and found Sarah in the large parlor.

"Grand Mama," she said as she stood in front of Sarah like a tired rider in need of a drink. "I plan to ride to the plantation soon. Right now, I've got too many loose ends to tie up."

Sarah grasped Ginny's hand with a strong grip and looked at her with the assurance of a wise sage whose dream was coming true. "So, where did my lovely grand-daughter ride off to?" Sarah asked.

"To the ocean."

"Why?" Sarah asked with a frown. "Why there?" She had expected her to ride on to Tennessee.

"Because I had to find myself. My courage. My determination. And that's as far as I could ride east. I don't know, Grand Mama. To leave you. The Patersons. My practice. My family. I suppose while I'm still just beginning to remember who I am."

"So! What did you decide?" Sarah looked down and straightened her shawl.

"I'm going to take your advice, Grand Mama. If he's alive, I know I must try to find him. And I shall!"

"When you find him, bring him here."

"And if I don't find him?"

Sarah looked up and answered her. "Oh, but you will, Ginny. You are a McBride and you will find him. I know. You'll find him. He is your destiny, my child." She looked into Ginny's tear-filled eyes and continued. "It might take some time, but I know you won't stop until you find him!"

Ginny smiled and walked away towards her room.

After a moment of listening to Ginny's boots click down the hall way, she asked, "When will you be leaving?"

Ginny stopped and without turning said, "I've got to meet my family first to find some answers before I leave." She smiled to herself and walked on with pride in her steps. She knew who she was now and what she needed to do. For the first time in many years, the answers were coming to her. "Hmm. My destiny . . . Hmm," she said to herself.

CHAPTER 30

A LADY NAMED MAY SHIRLEY

15 May 1867

The ride to Texas was long and dry with little rain in sight to ease the tension felt by two cowboys headed to the Brazos Bar M Ranch south of Waco to help a friend chase encroachers, rustlers, rebels, killers, thieves and all around bad guys from the ranch of their former general and friend, Ted Mitchell. The night crept upon them sudden-like as they decided to bed down in a small clearing somewhere in north east Texas.

Exhausted, Matt and Steve slept easily once they had filled their bellies with beans, sowbelly and corn nuggets. As the fire flickered out, leaving the smoke to waft across the two bodies, a pair of figures approached the camp on foot without the crackling of a twig or a dried leaf. After assuring themselves of the condition of the two cowboys, making certain they were asleep, they unhitched the two horses and walked them softly away. Once in the clearing and a good distance from camp, they climbed upon their horses. Taking a hold of the hackamores, they slowly led the stolen horses down a trail and once in the clearing, ran them towards Sycene, Texas east of Dallas.

When the morning sun awakened Matt, he rose and threw another log on the smoldering ashes. He relit the fire with kindling that laid around and fanned the smoke in the direction of Steve's slumbered body, wrapped in a blanket.

When Matt stood up and kicked Steve with his boot, he turned and noticed that their horses were gone.

"Steve! Wake up! I think we've got a problem."

Steve grumped and rolled over, rubbed his eyes and then sat up. "Mornin', Matt."

Matt ran to the place where they had tied their horses and saw that they had been taken.

"Dang! We've had visitors!"

"What? What'cha talkin' about, pal?" Steve asked, walking over to Matt and looking at the place where the horses stood that night. "Where're our horses?"

"It looks like they've been taken during the night while we slept."

"How?" Steve came back. "We had them tied up. And, and we slept right here. We would'a heard 'em."

"Yep. You're right. But the fact is, they're gone and we didn't hear a thing. Son-of-a-buck! I guess we were so dead-tired . . . but I didn't know we slept thet sound.

Steve slapped his hat on his head, pulled it down tight in the back and said gruntingly, "What're we supposed to do now?"

Matt knelt down, blew on and stoked the embers to strike a brighter fire, and then took the coffee pot down by the creek. "Find some water for coffee. At least we've got some grounds left."

After a bleak and tasteless breakfast of bacon and beans, the pair kicked out the fire, picked up their bed rolls and headed out to look for any signs left from their horses. Matt picked up the hoof prints left by the thieves.

"Looks to be just a coupla horses along with ours. Two people. Knew what they were doing, I reckon. Didn't make any noise like they were well trained Rebs. Come on, friend. Let's haul our butts out and see what lies ahead."

What lay ahead was a long and tedious trek for the two men. They had a load to carry; their tack. They picked up their saddles and gear and headed towards Sycene, a town neither man had ever heard of before, and never cared to visit. But this time, they were bent on revenge and getting their rightful property back; even if it meant violence. Both men were well-trained to meet that challenge.

It was evening of the next day when two tired cowpokes approached Sycene, a town of less than three hundred people. As they walked down the wagon-gutted street, Matt counted three saloons on each side, a church on the far end of town and a school further down the road. Together with twenty-six businesses, six saloons and a wagon factory, the town proved to be wild and rough.

The evening sun rested just above the horizon as Matt's steely eyes scanned the long wagon-rutted street.

"Reckon we'll find 'em holed up here some place?" Steve asked as they walked past the first two saloons.

"Keep walkin'. Don't look nervous or think about pickin' a fight. Just keep lookin'. If they're here, we'll find 'em."

By the time they reached the far end of town where a few people had found their way around the saloons, neither man had spotted any evidence of the thieves or their horses.

Matt looked down the back street, pushed his hat back on his head and said, "Let's head towards the smithy's."

The smith was closed and cold. Steve looked further down the road at the livery stable. "It's a chance," he said and the two men rambled towards it.

When they reached the stable, they found the door partly opened and walked on inside. A friendly voice came from behind a stall.

"Can I help you gentlemen?" the woman asked as she brought her head into sight from around the stall. She was a young lady, her light brown hair tied back, and she wore men's clothing; denim pants and a plaid shirt. Matt noticed her pretty hazel eyes and gulped in surprise at the sight.

He straightened up, removed his hat and suggested to Steve to do the same. "Yes, ma'am. I mean, Miss."

"It's Miss, Carol Jenkins". She straightened up, pushed her hair out of her eyes and asked again, "Now, I ask again. How can I help you, gentlemen?"

Steve kept looking at her while Matt's eyes caught the sight of Skeeter's rear. His trained eyes roamed the floor and bulkheads of the stable and found both saddles perched on the stall gate.

"That there animal you just brushed is my sorrel, Miss Jenkins," Matt informed her as he walked around the horse and patted him.

"Don't bet on it, mister," Carol retorted as she watched Steve looking agape at the horse next to Skeeter.

"And that's Toby," Steve blurted out as he walked around Matt and rubbed down the horse with his gloved hand.

"Mister, these horses belong to a man who just bought them and brought them here for care and grooming. If they were yours, he bought them from ya."

"Well, Miss Jenkins, they're ours. My name is Matt Jorgensen, and my initials are here under Skeeter's lip." He pointed to the two initials *M J*. "And trust me, I didn't sell anyone m'horse. We just walked twenty-four hours to get here."

A creek in the front door brought attention to the two men as a tall man entered with a shotgun in his hand. Another man sided him with a cocked Navy pistol.

"You've got a problem?" the tall man asked Carol as they entered the stable.

"Yeah!" Matt answered, watching the tall man with the shot gun. What amazed Matt most was the fact that the tall man was dressed as a gentleman; dress coat with vest and tie. He was not the ordinary cowboy or crook that Matt figured he would encounter. The little man was the typical cowhand, dirt and all. After a moment at sizing his opponents he continued, "These are our horses. How'd they get here?"

"These are the owners," Carol said, pointing to the two men who just walked in.

"In thet case, Miss Jenkins, we've just found the horse thieves."

"You're a liar, mister," the tall man called out as he approached Matt. "We found those horses roaming the plains. We searched all over and found no one to claim them; so we did. And the law of the plains is simple; losers weepers finders keepers."

He sauntered up to Matt, threw the barrel of his shotgun into Matt's gut and said with tight lips, "And no one calls me a horse thief."

"Yeah!" his companion drawled. "You got anythin' to say, get it out now or leave while ya can."

Matt sized up the situation fast and brought his hand against Steve's hand as Steve began to reach for his gun.

"Smart move, mister," the tall man suggested, cocking the hammer on his shotgun. "You just saved your friend's life." He looked at Matt and punched him again with his shotgun. "Now, step aside, mister!"

"You could get a man killed quite accidentally with thet cocked gun of yours."

"Thet's the idea, stranger."

The two men with their guns on Matt and Steve walked past them, eyeing Carol as she simply watched the two men take charge. They saddled the horses, mounted them and walked them out the door.

"You got something up your sleeve?" Steve asked Matt as his fingers itched to reach for his pistol.

"You see," the tall man said, looking down at Matt, "they're our horses. They know us." The two men mounted up and rode out without looking back.

Matt and Steve walked out with Carol.

"If they were your horses, they surely would have noticed you."

"Yes, Miss," Matt answered, rubbing his chin. "You'd think."

Matt watched them ride out further and then placed his fingers into the sides of his mouth and gave out a shrill whistle. Skeeter stopped, reared up high and straight and threw off the horse their. The tall man's shot gun discharged. Immediately, Toby followed Skeeter's move and threw his rider off as well.

The tall man rose to his feet and picked up the shotgun only to be knocked aside my one of Skeeter's hooves, which skinned his forehead. The tall man sank to the ground as blood spilled from his forehead.

Matt gave another whistle and both horses rode back towards them.

"Does that tell you anything about our horses?" Matt asked Carol, catching hold of Skeeter's bridle as he stopped in front of him.

Matt and Steve mounted and rode over to the men still lying on the ground. The saddle pal to the tall man made the mistake of going for his gun when Matt's Navy was out of its holster. The man hesitated and Matt shot the man's pistol, causing the pistol to ricochet to the left and the man to flip over backwards. He grabbed at his hand and cursed loudly.

"Your mistake, mister. Lie still and you'll have time to tend to your hand afterwards." Matt looked at the other man lying in the street with his bandana in his hand covering the blood on his black wavy hair.

Steve kept his pistol aimed at the man with the injured hand while Matt dismounted and went to the tall man's side, "You won't have any need for your weapons, so I'll just lighten your load." Matt picked up the men's guns and threw them into a nearby horse trough filled to the brim.. "Let them find them." Then he looked at Steve and asked, "Ready to meander, friend?"

"Not yet," Steve answered with raised hands. "We've got company."

"That's right, mister," a woman's voice answered behind Matt. "You do like your partner here and you'll live."

Matt turned around and found a young lady sitting side saddle astride a large bay. She was draped in a tight black velvet skirt with high-topped boots, a man's wide-brimmed fawn-colored beaver, turned up in a curl with a black ostrich plume billowing from within the curl. What impressed Matt the most were her twin ivory-handled pistols pointed at him.

"What happened to you, Jim?" the woman asked, keeping her pistols pointed at Matt and Steve.

"They jumped us as we rode our horses out of the stable," the tall man said, standing. "Shoot 'em!"

"Looks to me like you made a mistake, friend," the woman said, looking at Matt. "You busted up my boyfriend's head and shot up a friend of mine?"

"Nope. Horse busted his head. I shot the man's hand 'cause he aimed his gun at me. It was either him or me. I could-a killed him."

She gazed over at the tall man and asked, "Why? What happened?"

Matt looked at the two injured men walking up to the woman on the bay. "'Cause they're horse thieves and liars."

"Shoot 'em!" the tall man barked again. "Nobody calls me a liar."

The woman looked at Matt and liked what she saw in the handsome man. "Is this true?" she asked Matt.

"'Cause his horse kicked me in the head. Shoot 'em both!"

"Don't look to me to be any reason to shoot him," the woman observed. "Looks to me that your head ain't hurt none too much for me to have to kill a man." She uncocked her pistols and hung them loosely in her gloved hands while her wrists rested on her saddle horn. "Especially one as good lookin' as this one." She referred to Matt.

"Gentlemen, you can put your hands down." She smiled at Matt and repeated what Matt had said. "They stole your horses and then lied to you about it?"

Matt and Steve brought their hands down and Steve dismounted while the tall man grunted, went over to the water trough and retrieved his shot gun. Aiming it at Matt, he yelled out, "I'll kill the son . . ."

At the same time, a pitch fork pricked his coat with a poke from Carol as she yelled out, "It'll be your last breath if you don't drop it."

"No one talks to me like that. The tall man drew limp and let the shotgun hit the trough and splattered water. "What's wrong with you, May?" He turned quickly and plowed into Carol, knocking the pitchfork from her grip.

""Hold it!" the horsewoman commanded. Holstering her pistols, she brought the horse into the man's way. "You stole these horses, didn't you Jim?"

Jim looked up into May's eyes, and then said defiantly, "They called us horse thieves." He turned his head away from May. "You know we don't steal horses, May. They were loose on the prairie and we found them. It was night fall and we couldn't see anyone around, so naturally we took 'em."

May watched him and suspected he was lying "They're good horse flesh. Real good. Thoroughbreds, both."

"The best, Miss," Steve came back.

"And I suppose you can prove that they are your horses?"

Matt rubbed his chin with his gloved hand and walked over to Skeeter. He turned Skeeter so that May could see the underside of his lip. "Read it! *M. J..* Those are my initials. M'name's Matt Jorgensen."

The woman looked at the horses again and then back at Reed and said, "You did steal them! And you lied about it. Now, you know, Jim, I don't mind some things you do, but I don't appreciate your lying about it. Get on down the road with ya!"

"I didn't steal 'em! Like I done said, I found 'em out in the field. They musta got loose or somethin'. But I found 'em"

"Then why didn't you believe them and give them back to them? No Jim, you lied."

"Didn't want to cause any trouble."

"Well, you made a fine job of trying not to stir up trouble. Now git!"

The two men hobbled away and disappeared around the corner, still nursing their wounds. May looked down at Carol and said, "You're a brave one for being so young."

"I'm older than you by a few months, Miss Shirley" Carol came back. "I'm eighteen, and I can handle myself."

"You also work for me. Remember that. Better watch yourself if you still want to keep your job."

May looked at Matt and Steve, and then back at Matt again.

"You own this stable?" Matt asked.

"This and a few others in town. My father owns the Shirley House and the blacksmith down the road."

"Well, they're horse thieves," Steve said, holding tight to his gun grip. "We hadda right to kill 'em."

She stared into Matt's blue eyes and said, "You want to press charges, or leave it be?" She smiled and added, "I'd leave it be. You got your horses and saddles. No bloodshed, except for my fiancé's bruised head."

"Your what?" Matt asked as being bewildered.

"You're kinda cute. You hitched?"

"Nope," Matt returned. Carol mused herself while watching May flirt with Matt and Matt seemed to like the flirtation.

"Figurin' on stayin' a while?"

213

"Nope!" Matt answered as he walked over to Carol and shook her hand. "Thank you, Miss Jenkins."

"I'm the one who you should be thanking, mister," May advised Matt.

"Yes, ma'am," Matt returned, cordially, tipping his hat. "But he could have discharged thet shotgun of his and killed me just the same."

"Well, maybe. Maybe not. The shotgun was all wet." She looked at Steve and acknowledged him. "You're a Reb. Can tell by your talk. But you," she looked at Matt. "Where're you from?"

Matt stared at Steve for a moment and then up at the woman on the horse. "We just won a war against the north. Does thet tell ya anything? And I do want to thank you for saving our necks."

The woman eased her body up on the saddle a bit and a part of a flag appeared on her petticoat. She saw Matt's eyes as they widened a bit at the sight.

"What's the matter, mister? Ain't cha never seen a petticoat afore?"

"It's not the petticoat, Miss, thet caught my eye. It's the stars and bars on it. Mighty pretty."

"Thank you. I'm for the South, true enough. Me and some other gals waved them at the boys, both sides, whenever they marched by up in Carthage, Missouri. That's where I'm from. Ne'er a man can go agin me on thet. I done my part, much as you'ns.

"Anyhow, take your horses and if'n you're gonna stay, stop by at my place, the *Shirley House,* for a drink on the house."

Matt turned his horse to ride out but was stopped by May, moving her horse into his path. "By the way. What's your friend's name, Mr. Jorgensen?"

"Him? Oh, he's Steve." He stopped, eyed May for a fresh time and asked, "Jest what caused you to come to our rescue anyway?"

"No secret. Jim told me about the horses. I came over to size them up. Was gonna sell 'em tomorrow. I just wanted to get another look at them and knew Jim would be up this way."

"What?" Matt asked, looking back into the woman's dark eyes that matched her dark tucked under her hat and strung loosely down around her shoulders..

"Your horses. Jim has a good eye for horse flesh. He likes Kentucky horses for breeding and horseracing. And I must admit, yours are the finest Kentucky breeds I've seen in a long time."
And they were, for the horses were brought in from Kentucky for Matt and Steve's forage in Texas before leaving their company. They made it a point to ride Kentucky bred horses during the war; a trait taught to them by General Albert Sidney Johnston

"Good thing you came along when ya did." As she tipped her hat with her fingers and rode off, she said, "I had a hot buyer."

Matt watched her disappear around the corner and stood there with his jaw hanging loose.

"If thet don't beat all," Steve remarked, slapping his Stetson along side his leg. "A young girl. No, no. A woman bigger than life. Who is she?"

Carol smiled and walked back into the stable. "Some one you won't want to go up against . . . again."

Matt took Skeeter into the stable and handed the reins over to Carol. "Will he be safe here?"

"I'll watch them. Put yours back in his stall, mister," she ordered Steve while she walked Skeeter into his stall. "They've been fed and watered. I'll take good care of them."

Matt took a dollar piece from his vest and started to hand it to Carol, but Mary stopped him. "They've been paid for, Mister Jorgensen."

"Jorgensen," Matt returned with a smile and put his dollar piece back into his vest.

"The question is," Steve interrupted emphatically, "will we be safe?"

"Who is the man?" Matt asked, looking at Carol as if trying to compare her good looks with those of Ginny's.

"The tall man, Jim. Like she said, he just happens to be her beloved. They're gonna be married soon. So that might change your intentions a bit, mighten it?"

Matt realized that she was playing coy with him and went along with it. "He sure didn't look the marryin' kind."

"His name's Jim Reed, a childhood sweetheart, from what I heared. They're from up Missouri way. They kinda grew up together."

"Why'd they come to Texas?"

"Accordin' to her, she had a brother, Bud, who got killed fighting with Quantrill." She looked at Matt as he listened to her every word. "You know . . . Quantrill?"

Matt nodded and tilted his Stetson.

"She and her mother retrieved his body and buried him. She got so mad that she gave enough information to the Rebs to win a battle. One that made her and her family to have to leave her hometown 'cause they were ready to rampage the town."

"Where in Missouri?"

"Carthage. She and the others came down here and kinda took over our small town while the Rebs burned their hometown."

"Carthage?" Matt mumbled to himself. "The Rebs did thet?"

"Uh, huh. War, Matt. Anything and everything goes, I suppose."

"I can attest to thet," Matt came back.

"Any how, they ups an came down here to get married. Many things cause many people to do many silly things," Carol said rather sarcastically as she turned her back on Matt and walked away.

Steve held back his laughter with his hand as he closed the stall on Toby.

"Her dad owns the Shirley House down the street. That's her name, too. May Shirley. It's a saloon and an inn. Real fancy."

"Where 'bouts?" Matt asked, looking down the street as if trying to eye the place."

"You can't miss it. It covers a whole block. The rooms are upstairs. She'll treat you fairly," Carol returned.

Steve kept his eyes on Carol, noticing that her eyes were still on Matt except for when Matt turned her way. "You're sure a pretty sight, Miss Carol," he interjected with a bashful smile. "I mean, for a stable hand. One wouldn't have guessed it."

"It's family," Carol came back. "Judge Shirley owns all of this, and a black smith shop, too. Pa don't work too much now So my brother and I tend to it mostly. Russ is the blacksmith."

"Too old? I mean, your pa?" Steve asked, walking up to Matt.

"Pa. Nah! He just got too roughed up, trying to help out here in the stable. We have all kinds now that the war's over; they come here from all over. Mainly for the South. They're still fightin' the war. If'n Pa didn't get the horses right with them, or like tonight, when you claimed they were stolen, there'd be fightin' and squabblin'. Your friend, Matt, here shot the other fella. Didn't kill him though. Well, others weren't quite so lucky, and once in a while pa got the brunt of it."

"That bein' the case," Matt stepped in. "why're you here taking care of the place by yourself? Bein' so young?"

"Brother Bill? He's in town gambling, same as most. Not much doin' on a week night. So's he has me clean up. I'll close up now thet you're through and the horses are bedded. I was on my way to suppere anyhow when you showed up."

Matt watched Carol take the lantern and close up the doors to the stable as he and Steve lent her a hand.

"Thank you, gentlemen. G'night to both of you." She smiled and walked across the way to a house where she entered and disappeared.

"Well, partner," Matt said to Steve, "let's saunter down the road to May's and see about getting' ourselves a room."

"You figurin' on us stayin'?"

"Yep."

"How come, all of a sudden?"

"Thet May intrigues me. Never saw anything like her. Probably never will again." He looked out towards the main street and added, "Besides, she did offer us one on the house."

"And she's gonna marry thet?" Steve asked as he walked away, scratching his head.

"Thet? Who?"

"Thet pretty Miss May. And thet Jim fella."

Matt smiled and outpaced Steve's steps towards the Shirley House.

CHAPTER 31

THE SHIRLEY HOUSE

The Shirley House, owned and operated by Judge John Shirley as an inn, saloon and bawdy house, was in the middle of town and catered to most of the rough cowpokes in town; many of whom had refused to lay down their arms after the war, but kept them in their belts and knives in their boots. These are the ones who ruled the town. Others rode in, busted up a joint or two for the fun of it and rode out with a Rebel yell.

When Matt and Steve entered the saloon, they felt dangerous eyes following them as they meandered up to the bar. Matt almost wished he had listened to Steve for once and kept riding on through town. He looked around the room for the young lady who had saved him and Steve, but failed to find her.

"What'll it be, gents?" the bartender asked as he leaned into the two strangers.

Matt turned to face him and ordered, "Whiskey," while Steve motioned for another one for him. "This here's May's saloon?"

"Yep," the bartender answered, pouring the two drinks. "She'll be out soon. Friends?"

"You might say."

The bartender took Matt's coins and walked away with the bottle. He looked back at the men who remained, eyeing the saloon for a friendly face.

"I heard you," a young man's voice spoke softly as he approached the pair, walking with a slight limp. "You know May?"

"Just met her," Matt returned, downing his drink. He turned and faced a young teenager with blinking blue eyes. Matt noticed that the man was dressed as the tall man at the stable was; in a suit coat, vest, dress shirt and tie. "Who might you be?"

"A good friend, you might say. We watch over her safety."

"A body guard?"

"Yep. And more. How'd you meet her?"

"She saved our lives a few minutes ago."

The young man smiled, pushed back his expensive beaver and laughed. "You the one who shot up Bruce's hand? Made Jim run?"

"They stole our horses."

"Whoa! Uncinch your girth, mister. Don't say thet too loud. We don't cotton to horse thieves in here. Jim and Bruce are hard workers. Why, Jim and May are n'tendin' to get hitched real soon. Kinda makes you out to be a liar, and we don't like liars, either."

Matt turned and looked around the room slow and easy and quietly said to Steve, "Kinda looks like we're in a room filled with a bunch of teenagers, Steve. I don't see one man in the place. And none too tall." He faced the young man and looked down sternly into his eyes, seeing him agitated by his threatening words. "Sonny. You draw thet pistol and you'll be dead before you hit the floor!"

The young man turned his smile into a frown, looked over at Steve and asked, "Your partner in this?"

"Nope," Steve returned. "He's fast. Why, I've seen him shoot a man twice before my glass hit the floor." He looked the man down and then asked Matt, "Want me drop it, Matt?" Of course Steve was merely playing along with the stand, but he knew Matt could outdraw him. He just wanted to scare the man a little more.

"Thet right?" the young man asked Matt.

"You wanta find out, mister, tell him to drop the glass."

The young man froze, which gave Matt time to quickly slap him hard across the face with his left hand while his right hand came up with his Navy.

"Does thet answer ya?"

The man shook his head from the slap, rubbed his cheek, eyed the Colt in Matt's hand and then smiled. "How'd you do thet?"

Matt saw that the young man had no intention of fighting him, so he holstered his pistol. "You've got three guns on ya. You would have had to take time to figure out just which one to use. I didn't have to. Makes it easier to get the drop on you."

The young man pulled his pistol, and before he could cock it, Matt cupped his hand around the barrel and twisted it away from him. He handed it to Steve who stood behind him and then grabbed the man by the shirt and lifted him up where his boots barely touched the floor.

"Sonny. You're itchin' to get yourself killed. You tired of livin' or what?"

May entered the saloon from the top of the stairs that led to the sleeping rooms. "Put him down!" she ordered Matt as she pulled her gown free and walked daintily down the stairs.

Matt let the man down easy and watched the young lady sashay into the saloon.

"Twice in one night, mister. And with two of my best men. Now, this is Daddy's saloon and he don't like his saloon being messed up with brawls and such. So take your hands off of Jesse and let me buy you that drink I promised you."

It didn't take any time at all for Matt to comply with May's command. The young man retrieved his pistol back from Steve who handed it to him while standing behind Matt.

"What'll it be, gentlemen?" May asked as she waltzed gracefully over to the bar while keeping her eyes on other men around the area who stared in utter amazement. "Go back to your gambling, gentlemen," she said with a flutter of her hand. "This here's my friend . . ." She looked at Matt and asked, "What's your name again?"

"Matt Jorgensen. This is Steve Andrews. We're jest ridin' thru to Waco."

"So you'll be needing a night's lodging? Maybe two nights . . . or more?"

"Kinda, I'm a thinkin'," Matt answered with a smile.

May walked over to a cleared table and motioned for the bartender who knew to bring a bottle of whiskey for her and her party. "Tell Jake to set them up with a room." Then looked at Matt and Steve and asked, "Care to join me?"

Matt and Steve walked easy over to the table with their hands on their pistol grips, knowing all eyes were on them, but they soon found safety by merely being in May's presence.

"Mind if Jesse sits in? He's a special friend of mine."

Matt looked at Jesse as he pondered to answer him. He nodded for him to come over, and the three men joined May at the table as the bartender poured the drinks.

"This is decent of you, Miss," Steve added as he watched his friend keep his eyes on Jesse.

"She called you *Jesse.*" Matt acknowledged him.

"Jesse Woodson James, mister."

"You say that like I'm supposed to know you."

"If you don't, you will." He took his glass and toasted to May. "To the loveliest lady in all of Sycene, Texas."

May acknowledged the toast with her eyes and clinked her glass with his along with her two new friends.

"I really liked your trick at the bar, mister." Jesse smiled. "But I had one better."

Matt looked at the young man and questioned him with a look in his eyes while he downed the drink.

"You would have been dead another second had May not come down the stairs."

Matt furrowed his brow and looked sternly into Jesse's eyes.

Steve up and asked, "How'd ya figure? He done showed you how he'd a plugged ya twice before my glass hit the floor."

Still smiling and blinking his pretty blue eyes, Jesse pointed to another man on the other side of the room who was sitting at the table playing a hand of Poker.

"Another friend?" Matt asked.

"My best. Come on over, Cole."

The tall good looking cowboy folded his cards, rose to his feet and chipped in, gathering his winnings. He sauntered over to the table and stood facing Matt. He, too, was well dressed, wearing his tan beaver cocked over his left ear. He had two guns holstered to his hips under his coat and strapped down.

"I'd like you to meet Cole Younger, gentlemen," Jesse introduced them.

221

"Like we're supposed to know who you are, too?" Matt asked, pulling out a cigar from his vest pocket as an indication that he had little interest in the introductions.

"He had both of those things aimed at you and would have pulled the trigger had May not shown up."

Matt bit off the end of the cigar, took a match, struck it on the butt of his pistol and lit the cigar. Blowing the smoke into the air, he licked his lips and spit out a piece of tobacco. "You would have been the target, Jesse. I saw the pistols and they were all uncocked. If'n I heard them being cocked, you would have been between us and I would have emptied my pistol into your friend's face here."

Jesse's lips grew tight and Cole's fingers twitched as he curled them towards the pistol butts.

"My pistol is aimed at your groin Mister Younger," Matt said most calmly as he put the cigar back into his mouth with his left hand. He remembered the time he played this hand out while he started out his gun career with an empty pistol in Wyoming. This time his pistol was loaded and still in his holster but out of sight of his new found friends and under the table.

Both Jesse and Cole froze and stared into the calm eyes of one Matt Jorgensen. Steve looked down and saw Matt's empty hand under the table. He knew the bluff could work because he had ridden with Confederate Brigadier General Nathan Bedford Forrest when he pulled a bluff on another general with a larger-than-his army and captured the whole lot. And now, having learned from him, Matt was counting on his bluff to work this time.

What he did not know at the time was that Cole's older brother, John, sat on the other side of the room, ready to make a move. He was fearless and a dead shot; the best of the Younger bunch. He gave his enemies during the Kansas-Missouri border raid something to remember him by as vengeance against the Kansas red-legs who had killed their father and burned his home. Now he was eyeing Matt carefully to make his play.

"Unbuckle your gunbelts, gentlemen and we'll have a drink together. Else, you're gonna hit the floor before Steve can drop his glass."

Steve held his whiskey glass a little shaky but strong enough to show that he knew how to follow Matt's order.

"What'll it be, gents?"

A short stout man in his fifties stood behind Matt some distance and watched the cool Matt play out his hand and then, while Jesse and Colt unbuckled their gunbelts, said, "You fools. You let him bluff you. He didn't have a pistol in his hand."

Matt pushed his chair back real fast and flipped over backward while drawing his pistol. He fired it into the air before his friends could pick up their gunbelts. Steve stood up and aimed his pistol into the faces of the men in the same motion.

Jesse froze and smiled at Matt. Cole gritted his teeth, looked over at John who stood with his drawn Navy. "Holster it, John," he yelled out. "There'll be another time."

"I like you, mister," Jesse said, taking his gunbelt and gently slipping it around his waist. He sat down and held his arms over his head. "I'll not fight you. Not now, anyhow."

Cole looked at Matt and then over at May who was all smiles. Then he licked his lips and wiped his mouth with his right hand, indicating he too was through.

"Go ahead and pick it up," Matt said, keeping his pistol aimed at Cole's eyes.

Cole bent down, picked up his gunbelt and strapped it back to his hips. "I guess you did a good number on us, mister."

"Thanks," Matt returned, slipping his pistol back into its holster. "Looks like I'm the one to buy the drinks."

"Keep your money, Matt," the man behind Matt returned. "I'll buy. It was worth the show." He looked up at the ceiling where the bullet hit and said, "Just hope no one was home up there."

"Let me introduce my father to you, Matt," May said with a slight smirk. Father, this is Matt Jorgensen Matt, my father, John Shirley."

Mister Shirley was dressed like the gentleman judge that he was, proper and straight laced without a hat to show off his wavy black hair trimmed in gray around the edges. He sported long sideburns that curled up to his jowls, and a small moustache that was neatly trimmed. He looked at Matt over his spectacles that were attached to a light gold chain that hung around his neck.

"You played your cards well. I like a sharp gambler who's not afraid to call his hand."

"Mr. Shirley," Matt acknowledged while rising. "This is my partner, Steve Andrews. We're just riding through to Waco, not wishing to cause any trouble."

"Well, gentlemen, that will be enough gun play for tonight. I run a clean saloon."

"He'd prefer to be called *the Judge*, Matt," May suggested, "'Cause that's what he was back in Carthage and he is a judge."

Then, with a stern look into Matt's face, the Judge asked, "Waco? Why Waco?"

"Yes, sir. Sorry about the ceiling."

"Don't worry about it. Now tell me about Waco."

"I've got a debt to pay to a general. Seems he has a ranch somewhere south of Waco on the Brazos. Now thet the war's over, we're supposed to get it back into shape for him."

"You talk like a northerner but you're headed for Waco. Who are you?"

"Kinda wonderin' thet myself," Jesse returned. The rest joined him at the table, including judge.

"Just a tired cowboy who fought a war a hundred years ago. Yep. The South."

"The South you say. What outfit?"

The sound of spurs clanking from a couple pairs of boots in the distance alerted May's attention. Her eyes rested on Jim Reed and his partner as they came down the stairs.

The two men stopped at the edge of the stairs as they saw May and company sitting with Matt and Steve.

"Come on down, honey," May said with a laugh. "Might just as well join the party."

"What party?" Jim came back angrily. "Who's doin' all the shootin? It shook up our room some, like bashing in our door."

"Why, your friend here, honey. Matt Jorgensen."

Reed and his sidekick walked over to the table. Matt saw that he was staring at a man perhaps in his early twenties. Matt

224

had at least four years and more in experience on him. "Sorry about the trouble down at the stable,"

"Yeah," Reed returned. "Anyone can make a mistake in the dark. Those horses were loose, like I said."

Matt took the bottle from the table and poured May a drink and then one for himself. He poured another for the Judge and shifted the bottle to Steve. When May picked up her drink to her lips, and without looking at the Judge, Matt toasted to her. "Thanks, Judge for the drink. May I offer a toast to your lovely daughter?"

As Matt sipped his drink, he held his hand close to the butt of his Navy. Steve also had the edge, waiting for someone to be foolish. No one made that mistake again.

"You were saying. Who are you, mister?" May asked, eyeing her father and the rest of the men at the table. She knew they were just as eager to find out about Matt and Steve as she was. What side of the war were you on, Matt?"

"Ever hear of Terry's Texas Rangers?" Steve asked, pouring himself a drink.

Jesse's eyes opened wide and he answered, "You bet we have. You with them?"

"We trained them and fought with them," Steve answered, sipping his drink slowly like Matt.

"The hell you say!" Cole came back.

"No. No." Jesse repeated, drumming the tips of his fingers on the table. "They'd have to be, with what they just did. No one in his right mind would waltz in here among all of us and do what they jest did if he wasn't dang sure of himself to be the best gunfighter in the west. And you are the best, as far as I can see, mister."

"Why didn't ya say so, mister?" Cole returned. "We're all Rebs. Fought with William C. Quantrill. Those guys there." He pointed to a table behind him in a corner. "All my brothers. The good looking one with the fancy hat is Blackjack Kellum." He looked at Matt, winked and whispered, "He goes by the handle of *Blackjack*. Don't cross him. He kills for sport, if you know what I mean."

225

Matt eyed the men while he spoke to Cole directly, "Why didn't they take up for you?

"They know better. You see, Jesse here's our leader."

Matt looked over at Jesse and furled his brow. "Jesse?"

"Don't let his youth fool you, mister. He's smart and he knows how to use his guns. Better'n any of us."

Steve spoke up with a grin, "Don't say much for the rest of you." Then he looked at Blackjack and his grin fell.

"I like your style, Matt," Jesse broke in. "We can use you."

Matt looked at Jesse and then at the bottle.

"The bottle is yours, Matt," Jesse motioned as he picked it up and poured Matt another drink.

Sipping his new drink Matt asked, "How do you propose to use us?"

"We don't need him!" Blackjack yelled aloud as he walked over to the table with Cole's brother, James."

"This here is my little brother, James," Cole introduced.

"Don't look too little." Matt nodded.

"James here is a dead shot. Might show you up a bit, if'n you know what I mean."

"We're not lookin' for trouble and we're not interested in entering any fool contest.

"When you got time, son," the Judge addressed Matt, "drop in and see me. Sometime in the morning would be alright. I'd kinda like to talk to you."

He finished his drink, rose from the table and kissed May behind her ear. "Why don't you sing something, sweetheart?" Then he walked back to his office and disappeared.

The Youngers went back to their table with their pal Blackjack while Matt and Steve sat with Jesse. Jim Reed and his sidekick took a table closer to the stage, sat and motioned to the bartender to bring them another bottle.

An applause echoed through the saloon as May went up on the stage and sat behind a piano. Steve imagined that he saw a goddess in May; a woman with youth, beauty, manners, guts, and talent all rolled up into one. He was so mesmerized by her persona as she began playing, that for the moment he forgot that he was in the company of rough gentlemen.

Matt sat back and watched Steve's starry eyes as both men were entertained by the beautiful music. Her voice was not a soprano, but not harsh either; it was very melodic and the song reminded him of the time in Louisiana when he had heard the young lady sing *The Bonnie Blue* just before his regiment got their inspiration to become *Terry's Texas Rangers.*

May finished one number, *The Girl in the Golden Swing,* and then another, *Mama Told Me to Watch Out for a Man Like You,* and gave the audience an encore. After that, she left the stage and returned to the table where the men were standing and still applauding.

"She's something, isn't she, Matt?" Jesse asked while sporting a large grin with a cigar stuck between his teeth.

"May, you were absolutely marvelous," Matt said as he pulled out a chair for her to sit.

"More than marvelous," Steve countered. "You . . . you were simply great. Where'd you learn to play and sing like that?"

"Father's money paid off, I guess. He sent me to a private school and I just fell in love with the piano."

"See, Matt," Jesse continued. "With your talents, you too can be a part of all this."

"Let's talk about it tomorrow, boys." May interrupted, and then asked, "You gamble, Matt?"

Matt nodded, took out a new cigar and lit it.

"Honey!" she yelled out over to Jim Reed. "You in, too?"

"Not interested!"

Cole left his table and walked over to join May's group. He smiled at May and sat down. "As beautiful as ever, May. As beautiful as ever."

"Thank you, Cole. Now, gentlemen. Know this. I love gambling, almost as much as I love playing the piano." She opened a new deck of cards. "Gentlemen! Ante up! Draw Poker."

"You say your father is from Missouri," Matt asked May while he looked at his cards. "You, too?"

"Same place. Carthage. Good place until our own men burned it to the ground."

"Johnny Rebs?" Steve asked.

"Yep. I helped feed them information until they saw fit to run in and take over the town. My brother Bud was with Quantrill, too. Got killed in Sarcoxie. Blue bellies. So, the Judge and I high-tailed it here and took over. Like it quite well." She threw her arm around to show off the saloon. "Got the whole dang town to ourselves, Matt."

"And you're friends here?" Matt looked over at John Cole, Jim Reed and the gang of men in the saloon who were made up of outlaws and ex-Rebels.

"Yep. Matt. I welcome anyone who comes in my door, who ain't the law. These here are my friends. And now I've added two more."

Matt took a puff on his cigar and looked around the room as the cigar smoke rose in the air.

Throughout the night, Cole sat next to May and rubbed elbows with her from time to time. Jim Reed drank and kept eyeing May's table with a vengeful look at Steve as well as at Cole. One lady and three men for the night allowing their affections to show on the table burned into him jealously.

CHAPTER 32

A GIRL AND A BALE OF HAY

Restless and with too much on his mind, Matt walked out of the rented room quietly, carrying his gun belt and boots so as not to awaken Steve. He slipped his gun belt on along with his boots at the top of the stairs and walked down, careful so as not to attract too much attention from the men in the saloon. A few stood at the bar while another table found four men playing Poker. None of the faces were familiar so he slipped out almost unnoticed, except for the bar tender.

Outside, he took a deep breath and rolled himself a cigarette while he meandered down the street towards the stable. His mind was cluttered with what was going on in town with Jesse and his gang.

When he got to the stable, he opened the side door and walked on in where he lit a lantern hanging on the wall. He walked over to Skeeter, patted him on the head and began talking to him while he combed his mane.

"Jesse James, Skeeter. Ever heard of him? He's an outlaw. Sort of, I suppose. Heck, how do I know? I've never even heard of the kid. Says he rode with Quantrill. You know, William Quantrill and his Raiders. All a bunch of cut throats, so's I heard tell, who fought for their own bellies more than they did for the South.

"You wouldn't want me to ride with a man like thet, now would ya?"

"No. I wouldn't." A young feminine voice from behind Matt caused him to turn around and reach for his Navy. "Don't shoot, Matt. It's just me. Carol."

"Oh! You startled me."

"Didn't mean to. It's just that you woke me up. You know, you're not the brightest when it comes to lighting up a stable. The light shone right through my window from the back."

"I'm sorry. I didn't mean to awaken you. It's jest thet I needed someone to talk with by myself, and Skeeter was my best choice."

"Well, I'm here."

"But he can't argue with me."

"Try me."

Matt pulled his leg upon the gate of the stall, embraced the gate with his arms and looked into Carol's hazel eyes with a passion that had built up inside him that made him feel good to be with her. Since he met her, his mind kept going back to how she looked.

"You're young," he said with a slight grin.

"You don't look much older. Twenty five? Am I right?" She leaned into him, backed away and sat on a bale of hay.

"Something like thet. Born in '41."

"Got a gal?"

Matt looked away for a moment without saying a word. Carol hesitated but finally, not hearing an answer from Matt, asked, "She pretty?"

Matt twitched and finally answered, "Yeah."

"Yeah, you got a girl, or yeah, she's pretty."

"Both."

"Where at?"

"Oh, I don't know." He saw her look away and didn't want to hurt her. "No. Not thet I don't want to answer you. It's jest thet, well, I don't know."

"I'm sorry. I didn't mean to pry."

"You did. And you meant ta. But I jest can't give you any kind of answer except, I don't know. You see . . ." He looked away as if trying to say something to please her.

"You were saying?" she asked shyly.

He took his hands and began painting a picture with them. "You see, back in Tennessee somewhere along a Yankee camp, she was shot by a young soldier. I believe thet she might still be alive. But . . . I can't find her."

"I'm sorry, Matt."

He went back to being silent again and looked at the walls where the tack hung.

"Do you want to talk?" she asked, walking over to his side.

"More than you know, Carol. More than you know."

"Well, let's sit down and talk." She led him to the bales of hay and the two of them sat together. "Now, let's just talk."

"Thet boy in the saloon," Matt started in. "Do you know him?"

"Which one? My age? Older?" Carol asked.

"He told me his name was Jesse something James."

"Jesse Woodson James," Carol corrected him. "He's might proud of his name. Always sayin' it. Who is he?"

"Yeah."

"Well. They all served with Quantrill."

"I heard about thet. And?"

"I don't know if I should be a tellin' ya any more. Not knowin' whether ya be the law."

"Nope. Just an ol' Confederate soldier. Don't need to know no further. Just need to know how to get out of town and get to Waco. Thet's where we're headed."

"I'm afraid they won't let ya, now."

Matt looked around and said, "Yeah. You might be right. I saw eyes on me ever since I came to this town."

"Well, ya gotta be careful."

"Any way, you were sayin'?"

"It won't get me into trouble?"

"Like I said, no need to know. Naw. I ain't the law and I ain't all thet interested. Unless, of course ya wanna talk to me just for the sake of talkin'. I'd like thet."

Carol thought for a moment, turned around and said, ""Well, Jesse and Frank were close to May, and when May and the Judge moved down here, they decided to do the same."

"And so they followed May?" Matt asked, putting a piece of straw in his mouth to chew on.

"Don't let her age fool you none? She's real educated. Knows the Bible, too."

"Well, a lot of young people know the Bible."

"In the original language? She can read and write Greek and Hebrew, and somethin' else. I forget." She looked up at Matt and smiled. "She also went to finishin' school. A real lady, I'm a tellin' ya." Then she turned and faced away from Matt for the moment and added, "You can tell thet, with all the frills and laces and fancy talk."

She stood up and walked to the lantern and turned it down a bit. "Well, Mr. Jorgensen. We've talked near the whole night away about others. How about talkin' about yourself. Who are you?"

Matt grinned and watched Carol, taking in all the beauty that she possessed as she stood by the lantern. "Carol, I'm nobody in particular." Matt laughed.

Carol joined Matt's laughter, walked over and sat beside him.

"No, Carol. I met m'girl before the war began. Got caught up with Terry's Texas Rangers. Killed a few men. Almost got killed myself a few times."

"They were a good outfit, I'm told," Carol returned. "Bein' from Texas and all." She looked at Matt's face and felt that she needed to know about Ginny. "And your girl? You're still gonna look for her?"

"I went searching Yankee camps throughout the northern states, and on into other southern states. I hear about her at different times and different places. Stories about how a young girl, looking like a boy, rode into camp and a young Yankee soldier shot her."

"And you still believe she's alive?"

"They tell about how a doctor nursed her back to health, but then I lost her. After the war, Steve and I went to Richmond where her folks owned a mill."

"And did you find it?"

"I found it. Nothing but ashes. Several of the people in it were killed."

"But, you didn't find her?" She put her hand into his. This caused him to tremble slightly as he felt the warmth from her hand. She wanted to hold him and bring him to her bosom, but was afraid the timing was off, so she sat and squeezed his hand ever so slightly.

Matt felt the kindness shown by Carol and wanted ever so much to reciprocate by putting his arms around her, but he didn't. "I went to the mansion where she once lived and was told thet she was still missing; presumed dead."

"Who told you that?"

"A Yankee captain who happened to be there. I don't know any more about it. So I left, believing the Yankee."

"I went back the next day with Steve, and I searched the whole mansion for her; for some clue to her being there. But nothing."

"No photos of her?"

"One. Found it on the piano." He reached inside his vest pocket, pulled it out and showed it to her."

"Very pretty. Young." She returned the photo to Matt who put it back in his vest pocket.

"Thet was not how I remember her, though."

"And now?"

"Now? I shared my story with a preacher friend of mine who served with Steve and me in the war. He knows everything about me, just about. And he knows about Ginny."

"Ginny? Is that her name?"

"Thank you. Yes."

"Thank me. For what?"

"You asked me, *is that her name.* Instead, you could have asked, *was* that her name. Yes, that's her name, and yes, I truly believe she's alive."

"Why, Matt?" She placed her other hand in his and took her arm and wrapped it around his shoulder. "What makes you believe so hard that she's still alive?"

His body tingled with excitement and passion as he felt her presence coming ever so close to his own. He continued slowly and easily and said, "Visions."

"Visions? What kind of visions?"

Reluctantly, he removed her arm from around his shoulder and held her hands together with his own hands. "I've seen her. Just as I remember seeing her when I met her on her plantation.

233

Her lovely face. Her beautiful blue eyes. Her honey blonde hair thet hung around her shoulders. Her lovely, beautiful body."

Carol felt a little embarrassed and said, still allowing Matt to hold her hands in his, "It sounds like you'll always see her in a vision. A vision of the person you saw before she was shot."

"Meaning . . . thet if she's alive, she's not the same person today?" Matt looked strangely into Carol's eyes.

"I would think so," Carol answered. "If you left right now, I'd remember you for a long time, I suppose, just the way you look . . . right now." Then she laughed, let loose of Matt's hands and stood up. "Perhaps ten years from now you'd be sportin' some white hair and maybe grown a beard."

Matt laughed, and then a frown came on his face.

"What's the matter, Matt?"

"There was a time. A time when I thought I saw her. I really thought I saw her. In Richmond."

"You saw Ginny? When?"

"Steve and I. When we went to Richmond. There was this lady riding in the back of a rich-looking carriage. She was beautiful. And, and she had the appearance of Ginny. Just for a moment. Just a moment." He let his words trail off.

Matt frowned and stared ahead as if looking at what he was describing. "She was on the other side of this muddy road. She rode in this here carriage. Now thet's silly. But there she was. I was resting agin' a hitching post in front of the saloon and she rode by."

"Was she alone?"

"No. No. She had a driver. And another woman sat beside her. I turned to go into the saloon, thought a moment, and by the time I looked back for her, she was gone. I never saw her after that."

"What did you do? I mean, apparently you didn't go after her."

"Yes. Oh yes. We rode off and searched in three or four different directions, and still never found her."

"I just knew I saw her like I did afore the war."

"How did she look to you? I mean, in the carriage?"

Matt sat back down. "Beautiful."

"It may have been her," Carol said gently, showing much interest in Matt.

Matt smiled and stood up with Carol.

The two of them laughed together and then stopped abruptly as they had begun. Matt looked penetratingly into Carol's eyes and said nothing.

"I brought you some happiness, didn't I Matt?" she asked, taking hold of his hands again.

Matt continued to smile and then said, "Yes. Yes you have. More than you know." He wrapped his arms around her and brought her into his body.

"I'll probably never find her, Carol. Probably never will."

"Turn the lantern down a little, Matt," she said softly, not wanting to let him go. "It's still too bright for the night air outside and might attract someone's attention."

Matt obliged, walked over and turned it down. There was enough light to see Carol, and his eyes feasted on her small-framed body clad in jeans and a plaid woolen shirt. Her hair hung down to just below her shoulders. He reminded himself that it was not quite the length of Ginny's. She seemed to be the same size and dimension as Ginny, and as young and beautiful. His mind began to play fanciful thoughts within him while eyeing Carol up and down.

"I'm not trying to take Ginny's place, Matt," she said, standing with a little light on her to accentuate certain beautiful parts of her body.

Matt saw that she was all woman to him and he wanted so desperately to hold her, to kiss her and to make love with her. He walked back to her, took her hands in his and set her back down on the hay bale and sat beside her.

"You asked me if I had someone. Now I ask you. Do you have someone?"

She smiled with her eyes and answered with her soft lips, "No, Matt. Oh, I've had dates with a couple of nice boys. And I've been fondled by one or two of them who had no good intensions at all and I simply up and walked away."

"I'm . . . I'm not thet kind of guy, Carol."

"What kind of guy are you?"

Matt looked deep into her eyes and said, "Don't ask me. I don't know why I'm talking like this to you, a perfect stranger who I knowed jest a few hours ago, standing in a smelly stable and now someone I want to kiss."

"Well?" She asked, squeezing his hand.

He felt passion swelling up within him, looked at her and brought his hand up and placed it on her shoulder. She moved into his body and at the moment of touch, he released her hold on his hand and walked away.

"No, Carol," he said gently as he walked to the door. "Not now. I'm sorry." Without looking back, he stumbled through the door and back to the Shirley House.

He kicked a piece of sod in the road and, with grit teeth, said "Dang!"

CHAPTER 33

THE YOUNG OUTLAWS

The next morning found Matt and Steve walking inside the saloon, looking for the Judge.

"He's been expecting ya," the bartender said as he swept the floor close to the bar. "I told him you had probably been over to the stable."

Matt looked at the bar tender for a moment and remembered that he had seen him leave the inn alone earlier that morning and again with Steve. "Yeah! We'll be leaving this morning. Just wanted to make sure everything was alright with our horses."

"Well, the Judge is in his office over yonder."

Matt and Steve followed the direction of the bartender's arm and came to an office with the door closed. Matt knocked on it and a woman opened it from inside.

"Come on in, gentlemen," she said as she motioned with her hand for them to enter. "I'm Mrs. Judge. Eliza Shirley."

"Careful, boys," the bartender warned. "She's a Hatfield."

"Oh!" Matt came back with a smile as he removed his hat. Steve followed suit. "I sure hope you're on the good side."

"Yep," was her reply with a smirk on her lips. "The Martins were the bad 'uns."

"Sit down, boys," the Judge motioned as he stood at their entrance.

Once each was settled in a chair, the Judge asked, "I certainly hope our hospitality was good for the night. The room? The food?"

"You didn't have to go to all this trouble, Judge," Matt replied. "Everything's perfect. But we have to leave today."

"Today?" the Judge asked, taking a couple of cigars from the cuspidor on his desk. He handed each of the men one and then continued. "Well, I suppose it's for the best."

"We just went over to the stable to check on our horses."

Matt smiled at Steve and then shyly said to the Judge, "You said you had something to tell us."

The Judge sat down behind the desk.

"Thank you," Matt returned as he accepted the cigar. He bit off the end, struck a match and lit the Judge's cigar first and then Steve's before lighting his own.

"Well, yes. I suppose you'd want to know about those men you were with in the saloon last night."

"It did peak my curiosity some," Matt returned. "But you know about curiosity."

The Judge drew in on his cigar, blew out the smoke gently and said, "They're outlaws. Every one of them."

"Outlaws?" Steve echoed the Judge.

"Yes. You see . . . like they said . . . they fought for the South. In their own amicable way, so to speak. They fought with Quantrill's guerillas."

"They said thet last night," Steve answered, shrugging his shoulders.

"Quantrill. You know about him, don't you? Surely you do."

"Yep," Matt came back. "A young man, school teacher, I believe. Fought for the South."

"Well," the Judge continued, "yes and no. He fought for what he felt was good for his cause. Whatever that was. Jesse got caught up with him through his brother, Frank. Rode loyally beside him. And just before the war came to an end, Jesse got a bullet in his leg and one in his lung. Quantrill took kindly to him like an older brother.

"Jesse got shot up a bit. Thet's why he limps a little. Healed up by now, I reckon. I tell ya, thet kid's one lucky fella for bein' as healthy as he is today."

"He's become a hardened man," Eliza interrupted. "A confused and hardened young man."

"The war came to an end but it didn't stop Jesse. Like my son, Bud, Jesse's mother was killed because of the war. Right on their farm up Carthage way. We all came from Missouri. Every man and woman of us. May, Eliza, Cole's mother. We came here and set up our inn and saloon."

"And from what I see, Judge," Matt replied, "most of the men we met up with last night are still in their teens, like your daughter. They work for you?"

"Oh, no. Like I said, they're outlaws."

"Well, to me, thet don't mean too much. Like Steve and me, we've come back from the war and have to work for a living. Thet's why we're headed to Waco. We'll have a job there."

"How much would you make?"

"Don't know yet. Ain't been told. But it'll be a rewarding job, working for the General."

"These boys all dress nice, don't you agree?" the Judge asked, flipping his ashes in a tray stand by the desk.

"More than nice. Don't think we didn't notice. Even thet horsethief"

"Reed? Yeah."

"We don't care too much for him, either," Eliza interjected. "We did for awhile. We gave him a room on the farm so that he could take care of it. Instead, he took care of May."

"That's another story," the Judge remarked.

"He told us he was goin' to marry May," Steve replied as he leaned on the desk and looked at the Judge straight on. "Is he?"

"I hope not," Eliza answered.

"We're doing our best to discourage it. But what can we do? She welcomes every outlaw here in our inn," the Judge added.

"Welcomes them," Eliza continued. "All because those Yankees came in and caused our city to be burned. They ravaged our business in Carthage that took the Judge a life time to build and make a name for himself. He worked hard, let me tell ya."

"Sit down, Eliza!" the Judge ordered as he arose from his seat and walked to the window. "Those cowardly Yankees. Not more than teenagers, the lot of them. 'Wouldn't listen. Just rode in and destroyed all that I'd built up."

He turned and paused for a moment. His face had grown red from anger. He threw the cigar into the ashtray.

"That's why we've taken a strong liking to Jesse," Eliza added as she nervously played with her fingers.

"Jesse is about the same age as May. Oh we know about him bein' in love with his cousin up in Missouri. But, we kinda think he's got a likin' for May, but she sure hasn't shown any affection towards him as we see it. And we don't want that *horse thief* as you called him for a son-in-law."

Matt rose and joined the Judge at the window. "What does that have to do with us and why are you telling us all this?"

"Because you came along and stood up to that miserable snake. And I think if anyone can best him, you can."

"Do what?" Matt asked, towering the Judge at the window.

"Chase him out of town."

"Kill him!" Eliza came back.

"No, Eliza! No!" the Judge barked as he pounded his fist on the desk.

"He's no good, John. No good. Not for our May." She looked at Steve and said, "Get him in a gun fight. You're fast, too, ain't cha?"

"You called us in here so that we would do your dirty work, Judge?" Matt asked, lighting his cigar.

The Judge turned and looked at Matt. "No, son. Eliza's just crazy with anger because I've lost my temper too many times in front of her. No, son, we don't want him killed. We just want him to leave Sycene and May and go somewhere else."

"Maybe then she'll marry Jesse," Eliza continued.

"Or even Cole Younger," the Judge continued. "I know she likes them both. One or the other would be a whole lot better than that Reed fella."

Steve sat on the edge of his chair as he listened to them talking about the goddess he had become enamored with all in one night. "She's a beautiful lady. She certainly deserves more than a horse thief for a husband." Then he thought for a moment and asked, "What could Jesse or Cole offer her?"

"Jesse," Eliza came back. "Jesse would be just right for her."

"Why?" Matt asked.

"Because they are alike. The two of them. Because they're the same age, and they like the same things, and he has money."

She blurted out the real reason behind her scheme. *Money!*

"Jesse has more money than he knows what to do with, gentlemen," the Judge revealed as he returned to his seat behind his desk.

"Looks to me like all of them have more money than they have sense," Matt agreed. "Are they professional gamblers?" Then Matt thought for a moment. "Jesse certainly wasn't last night. He lost more than the rest of us."

"No, he's not a gambler," the Judge answered, clasping his hands together on the desk. "Like we said, they're all outlaws. They just recently robbed a bank."

"A bank?" Steve asked, almost laughingly.

Matt's mind quickly went back to when his brother Lucas and a bad guy named Jeff robbed a freight office in Montana just a few years before the war broke out. Both men were gunned down and Matt had to flee for his life, never to return home, never to see his father or mother again. To live with the awful truth of seeing his brother killed right in front of him. His brother; only eighteen like Jesse.

"Who robbed the bank?" Matt asked, taking a smooth draw on his cigar. He looked outside the window and through the shade saw Reed and Blackjack talking with a few of the Younger boys. He left the sight and returned his thought to the room. "Who robbed the bank? He asked again.

"Those men you saw in the saloon last night," the Judge answered softly and slowly. They became Jesse's gang. He took them to his home town where he knew about the bank and how they cursed his family when they needed help so often. He did it more for vengeance, I 'spect, than for the money. 'Tho he keeps talkin' about the South rising again. "

"But he's a good boy," Eliza chimed in, wiping her eye with her dainty handkerchief she removed from her sleeve. "And he can do so much more for May. She is so talented."

"How does Reed enter into all this?" Steve asked, as if hoping he could come up with a viable answer to getting rid of him.

"He's a horse thief!" Eliza blurted out, and then covered her mouth with her handkerchief. "A dirty horse thief. Nothing to live for," she whispered from behind the cloth.

"Now that's not exactly all there is to it," the Judge resumed. "May fell for Reed because he knows horseflesh. He has a good nose for good horses and May loves good horses. She loves to ride. And, of course, he made certain that she had the best horses to ride, and then she'd sell the rest. They make a hefty profit off each one.

"It was easy, Matt. So easy. He'd go to Dallas, look for a good horse, wait for the rider to ride out, follow the man out of town. When the man camps, he'd steal the horse pretty much without a fight. Most of the time, that is."

"Well, thet's not exactly how he come about stealin' our horses." Steve suggested.

"Had we heard them, we'd a killed them," Matt told them with grit teeth. "We've always been alert to handle such things, but never considered it thet night. We were jest too tuckered out. A long hard ride, a good meal, and no moon made for a good night's sleep."

"He's never got caught," Eliza added. "He shoulda. Maybe he'd been hung by now and we'd have our worries behind us."

"Not too much of a law here in Sycene, boys," the Judge offered, taking another cigar from the cuspidor. "And now that he's with Jesse's gang, no one wants to go up against Reed. They know they'd be up agin' Jesse, too. They sorta grew up together in Carthage. But one of these days, and that's what we're afraid of; he's going to get hung."

"Ain't thet what ya want?" Steve asked.

"I don't want May to go around with a horse thief for a son-in-law. Him giving us grandchildren and having a no-good 'un for a father. No!" Eliza clamored louder. "And then him getting himself hung and leaving behind a bad reputation for May and her young uns to follow. No, sir!"

Matt looked out the window again and saw the men looking a little edgy as if waiting for him and Steve to come out.

"Well, it looks like trouble is awaitin' for us outside, Judge."

242

The judge rose, walked over to the window and looked out. "He's got Blackjack with him. Maybe too much for you right now."

"Maybe," Matt returned, taking another puff on his half-smoked cigar. "Seems like trouble always follows us. Huh, Steve?"

"There's the back door, if'n you want to use it," the Judge motioned with his hand.

"Never use it, Judge," Matt returned and offered the Judge his hand. He tipped his hat to Eliza and then placed it back on his head. "Ma'am. We'll be bidding you good day."

"What are you aimin' to do?" the Judge asked, opening the door for the men.

"Don't know, Judge. Let's jest see what develops."

The two men walked over to the front doors and meandered out onto the porch. Matt took his last puff on his cigar and slowly let the smoke drift into the air. He threw it out into the street, took out his Navy with a fast draw and split it before it hit the ground.

Blackjack and Reed reacted to the action and before they could respond with their pistols, Matt had his pointed in their direction. Steve backed him up with his .44.

"I've killed men for less," Blackjack returned, holding onto the butt of his .44 still in its holster.

"I don't like ya Blackjack. I jest don't like ya. I've seen too many of you in the war and you just make my belly crawl with anger. Now, if you want to try me," Matt continued, as he slowly backed away from Blackjack while putting his Navy back into its holster, "get out in the street right now!"

Blackjack looked at Matt, turned to Reed, looked at Steve and said, "If I kill you, he'll kill me. That it?"

"Put it away, Steve. This is between these two men and me."

"Why put me in this with him?" Reed returned, shaking like a leaf on a tree. "I ain't got nothin' agin' ya."

"Yeah. Yeah, I think ya have. Else you wouldn't a been talkin' with this scum about us behind our backs."

"We ain't been talkin' about you. Honest."

"I'll deal with you after I'm through with this vermin." He looked intently at Blackjack with his strong fists yearning for a fight.

"Out in the street, Blackjack. Out in the street with this varmint."

Blackjack backed into the street, facing Matt while Reed nervously attempted to join him, walking forward.

Reed attempted to reach for his .44 when Steve threw his cigar at him.

"I'm throwing it down," Reed cried out. "I ain't in this fight."

"Use your left hand and gently, gently toss it towards me," Steve warned.

Matt saw Blackjack reach for his pistol and was quickly on top of him like a leopard to his prey. He backhanded him and slapped him until he lost his balance and fell to the ground.

Blackjack attempted to reach for his pistol, but Matt's boot kicked it out of his hand. Matt brought him up to his chest and then Blackjack found extra strength to hit Matt in the stomach, hard enough to drive him to the ground. As Matt hit the ground, Blackjack brought his boot up under his chin that threw him across the road.

Matt rolled and tumbled, shook his head for a moment and looked at his opponent coming toward him at full speed. Matt dodged Blackjack's body plunge, causing him to run into the hitching post behind Matt. Dizzy from the kick, Matt reeled around, backhanded him again, knocking him against a horse hitched to the post.

Blackjack fell under the horse, barely missing the horse's hooves stomping the ground around him. He rolled out from under the horse, looked for his pistol and fell prey to Matt's hand as it came under his rib cage, causing him to cough up from deep inside. He fell to the ground where his hand came within reach of a loose board in the walkway. He picked it out and swung it towards Matt with all his might with the nails protruding from the end of the board. It missed Matt and hit the horse instead. The horse reared up and knocked the board from Blackjack's hand.

Matt took the advantage and brought Blackjack into his body where he hit him hard with his right fist that sent Blackjack face down on the sidewalk.

Then a shot rang out behind Matt followed by another one. Matt turned around with his Navy in his hand and saw Jesse with Cole and his brothers behind him.

"Put it away, Mr. Jorgensen, or I'll be forced to kill you!" Jesse ordered as he cocked two of his pistols. The third one stuck out of the belt in his pants. "You, too, Steve. Be a nice man."

Matt looked at Jesse and his company and immediately he and Steve holstered their pistols. Without showing any signs of nervousness or backing down, Matt answered, "You want to talk?"

"You're good, Mr. Jorgensen. Real good. With your fists as well as with pistols. We need you with us. But we also take care of our own, if you get my drift."

"I didn't see too much love in your eyes for either of these scums last night," Matt returned. "I sensed their wanting to kill us, so we kinda turned the tables."

"Well, now, Matt. It's not for me to make decisions about the actions of my boys. But, because they are my boys, I see to it that they are protected. You go up agin' any of them, and you go up agin' me. Now, you ready to talk about in comin' with us?"

Blackjack came up behind Matt, grabbed his throat from behind and placed a knife against it. Matt's arm was swift to sink his elbow into Blackjack's rib cage as he grabbed his head with his hands and threw him into the street to slide face down into the dirt. Matt walked over to him, and as Blackjack started up with his knife in his hand, Matt stomped on it hard with his boot and then kicked it away. He pulled him up by his coat collar, turned him around and held him with iron strength as a hostage against Jesse's guns.

"He might be a killer when no one's a lookin', but he's nothin' but cow dung now. You tell him, Jesse. You tell him now to stop it, or I'll break his neck and feed him to the vultures."

Jesse knew he had met his equal with Matt, if not his better. "Put up your guns, boys," Jesse ordered, holstering his own pistols. "You willin' to work with Matt, Blackjack?"

Blackjack's face had turned red and his eyes were bulging out. Blood had splattered from his nose and mouth, and mixed with street dirt, he looked every bit the varmint that Matt saw in him.

"Yeah! Yeah! Anythin'!" he choked. "Just let go of me!"

Matt released Blackjack and threw him back into the dirt. "I don't play for fun, gentlemen," Matt said as he stood strong, looking Jesse and his company down. Wiping his mouth with his gloved hand he said, "Now let's talk."

"Some of you men take care of Blackjack and bring him back into the saloon."

CHAPTER 34

JESSE ASKS FOR MATT'S HELP

Once inside the Shirley House, Jesse took a table in the saloon with Cole and offered a chair to Matt and Steve while the rest of the men took Blackjack to the back room to clean him up.

"You're just like I want to be, Matt," Jesse confessed while he took his makings, rolled a cigarette and lit it. "I'm good. Not as good as you right now. But, I'm good. Look around you. These men are my gang. Thet makes me their leader. We jest came from my home town where we robbed a bank in broad daylight. Everybody knew it was me. I want it that way. Jesse Woodson James. I want to blaze the country with my name 'cause I know the South is gonna rise again, and I've got plans on how to help it."

Matt took his makings and rolled a cigarette while he watched Steve and Cole eye each other. "Then what do you need with us?" he asked.

"Like I said, we robbed a bank in broad daylight. But I knew the bank; the people. The countryside. I grew up there. I want to do it again and again, until the South gets enough money and takes over."

Jesse watched the startled looks on Matt's and Steve's faces, and then continued. "But I don't know if I can do it by myself"

Jesse examined Matt's face closely and then asked, "D'ya know what I mean?"

Matt looked closely into Jesse's eyes and then said, "I suppose so. Like robbing from your own family. Now you want to put fear into others so they won't fight you. Right?"

"Somethin' like thet," Jesse answered, twirling his .38. "I like this kind of livin', but I don't want to have to stay here in Texas all my life. I want to ride out to places like Kansas, back to Missouri and Arkansas. I know thet kind of countryside. Here in

247

Texas, shucks, they'd find me and get me in a minute and hang me. There's no place to hide, except here at the Shirley House. And one of these days, this place won't be too healthy for any of us, either. If'n you get my drift."

Matt looked over at Steve and then back at Jesse. "Sorry, Jesse. No dice! We're not outlaws. I can't see living this kind of life with you."

"This kind of life?" Jesse yelled out and walked out into the middle of the floor, swinging his arms as he twirled around. "Look at this place. My clothes. I've got money, Matt. Lots of it and I'm going to get more. It's Yankee money. Hell, I've given lots of it to my friends in Missouri jest 'cause they needed it. I like you two. You both can share this kind of life with me."

"Jesse,' I just came back from a war. I lost my family. I lost my girl."

"He's been searching for her ever since the war began," Steve interrupted. "He just won't heart when people tell him she's . . .."

"Not yet!" Matt said defiantly, slapping the table with his hand. "Not by a damn sight, Steve!

"I'll search for her 'til I die," Matt continued. "Some how. Some how I know she's still alive."

"Where, Matt? Where is she?" Jesse asked.

"She was shot by a Yankee boy somewhere in Tennessee. I've never found her or her body."

"And since I've knowd him, he's never conceded thet she just plain might be dead," Steve continued. "Some times he drives me mad with his quest to find her." Then he

"Then, Matt, let's find her together," Jesse offered, putting his arm around Matt's shoulder. "You're goin' to Waco isn't goin' to help you find her if she's somewhere in Tennessee. Together, with my gang, we can comb the countryside."

Matt walked back to the table and sat down and thought, *Steve's half right. Maybe she is dead. But for some uncanny reason, I feel thet she's not. I'm tired of looking. Going to Waco and helping a friend is my way of resting awhile from thinking about her. Maybe, jest maybe she is dead, I'm a thinkin'. If she is, then I shouldn't waste my life away.*

He took the bottle that sat in the middle of the table and poured himself a drink. Jesse, Steve and Cole sat at the table and each man joined him in a drink.

Matt drank two glasses of whiskey, wiped his mouth and looked over at Jesse.

"Wull, Matt?" Jesse asked, sipping his drink.

"I've been thinkin', Jesse. And I've been listenin', too. I can't join up with you. Steve can do as he well pleases, but I can't."

Steve stood up and replied to Matt, "We're in this together, friend. We've come this far. We'll continue."

"Matt, friend," Jesse started in. "Me and my gang will be all over this country from Kentucky where our friend Quantrill was killed to Missouri where we all were raised. While moving about the war trails, we can look for your Ginny. We'll do this for you. And when we find out anythin' about her, or if we find her, we'll raise up our flag and let ya know."

"Quantrill? Killed in Kentucky?"

"Shot in the back like only a coward would do."

"Not knowing the man, but you seem to have a lot of Quantrill in you."

"He is Quantrill!" Cole interjected. "Better'n the man himself."

Matt rose from his chair, stared down at Jesse and then looked at Steve.

Steve opened up and said, "She's your girl. I'm with you."

Matt wiped his mouth with his hand and slowly said, "Then, all I can offer. All *we* can offer is this. If you and your gang will keep us posted as to any information you find about her, then it'll be worth our while to train you to be a fightin' company like we done trained Terry's Texas Rangers." He looked at Jesse for awhile and, seeing he wasn't getting an answer, asked, "Agree?"

Jesse looked at Matt, then at Steve, and then at Cole and finally said rather jubilantly, "Hell, yes!" He took a hold of Matt's hand and shook it. "When do we begin?"

The next few weeks found Matt and Steve riding herd over a band of outlaws. Every now and then, May would ride over and watch from the sidelines.

"You still got a crush on May?" Matt asked Steve as they rode in close formation with Jesse's gang.

"Heck of a time to ask me, now thet she's sitting over there on her beautiful horse a lookin' at us, and us a trainin' her boyfriend."

"Well, do you?" Matt asked again.

"Sure. I'd like to kiss her jest like you and Carol."

"Well, why don't you ask her some time?"

"Uh uh! Not on your life. I'd have Reed and his partner along with Blackjack on my back real fast. I like living. I'll be content with leaving her alone." Then he added under his breath, "for now."

He felt he would never get the chance to see how far he could get with May because he sensed her eyes were intent on getting Reed for a husband at all costs. He also noticed that Jesse seemed to have eyes for May. His training skills proved useful, not only in making good men out of Jesse's gang, but by keeping his thoughts from going astray.

Their worst fear was not the law, but Blackjack Kellum and John Younger. John was a fast draw and often gave Matt and Steve a run for their money. Eventually, Matt won John over to their side, but never Blackjack.

"Tighten up your girth, mister!" Steve ordered in a yell as he inspected the men and their horses. When they did what he ordered, he told them, "Unsaddle your horses!" And when they did, he rode past them and yelled out, "Now, saddle up! Tighten your girth!" He used all the good language he learned from his cavalry sergeant, Sergeant Major John Foster O'Riley.

CHAPTER 35

JESSE'S PLAN FOR THE SOUTH TO RISE AGAIN

Each morning, Jesse's gang went back into the field, practicing their horsemanship.

"All right," Matt yelled out to Jesse's gang, "you've got the hang of riding and shooting down to a good level. Now let's go over to the Shirley House, have a drink and go over one more tactic or two thet I ain't told you about, yet."

Jesse put his hand on tall Matt's shoulder, winced at it pulling on his chest where the wound kept paining him, and the pair walked into the saloon together with the rest of the gang following. Steve brought up the rear.

When they had settled down at a table where several corked bottles of whiskey sat along with glasses, Jesse stood with Matt while the rest sat down and poured.

"Reed." Matt brought Reed's attention right away, making him think again that something wrong still filtered the air. He looked at Reed as at any other man who shot at him, but saw no sign of him being shot. He eased up in his thinking it could be him.

"It pains me to say this, but . . ." The room got deathly silent for the men saw nothing but hate and distrust between the two men. "I have to admit, you're a good man when it comes to horseflesh."

Reed's eyes opened wide and he shook his head in disbelief as to what he just heard. "Wull . . .!"

"Don't mean nothin' else, jest thet you're gonna be the key man in this operation."

Jesse looked at Reed's expression, grinned and blinked his blue eyes. "How's thet, Matt?"

"Think about it, Jesse. You and your gang ride into town on good thoroughbreds. What's the first thought that would come to your mind if'n you were a sheriff?"

"Someone has good taste."

"If all of you did, it would tip the law off thet something was a goin' to happen where someone would want to get out of town fast. Especially if there were several thoroughbreds in town at the same time."

"I get it. Some of my men would ride nags and only two or three of us would ride the best."

"Good thinking. Maybe even all of you on nags at first."

"Also," Jesse continued, "we'll pace our coming into town. Spend a few days apart and get acquainted with the town."

"That's your business, Jesse. Not mine. Mine is telling you about horses."

"I get it," Reed interjected. "How many good thoroughbreds do we need?"

Matt could see readily that Reed liked his teaching. Reed had followed Matt's training from day one with much reluctance, but now it seemed that he was the man to lead, and he liked all the attention that was being paid to him.

"You have a dozen men. You'll need at least two dozen, I figure."

"But you said some would ride nags."

"Yes, to start with. When you're on your way out of town, you'll drop off the nags and pick up good thoroughbreds, which . . ." Matt continued, drawing a bead on all the men. "Some will be placed strategically on the route out. So, you've got maybe six thoroughbreds and six nags. Pick up another six on the way out, that makes twelve."

"Then we'll need twelve really good horses. Thet's a cinch." Reed was already taking stock at which horses he would be taking.

"Not so fast, Reed," Matt returned. "Your horses are only as good as they can last running. Before they tire out, you'll need twelve more horses to keep you going. Somewhere along the route, you'll have your horses with one or two of your men guarding them. Take your saddles, change off and ride."

Steve stepped in and reminded the men, "Now you know why we kept you saddling and unsaddling your horses, and cinching up every time I saw a loose cinch. Thet's the Rangers style."

"Now, if you have a weigh station along the route where stagecoaches change horses," Matt continued, "you need to take it over and plant fresh horses there, too."

"Wull . . ." Reed came back with an astonished look on his face. "Thet'll mean at least three dozen horses."

"Now you're beginning to understand why all the training in riding your horses *cavalry* style. Ride your horse until he can ride no more. If you come down easy on your horse, it could mean your demise. Think on it, fellas. Hate to tell you this, but you are only as good as your horse."

"Think you can come up with three dozen horses, Reed?" Jesse asked, straddling a chair and sitting.

"I ain't got thet many in town. I don't know."

"Well, I guess our work is cut out for us," Cole interrupted. "We're gonna have ta help ya round up some good ones."

John Shirley walked into the conversation from his office and addressed the men. "I've been listening. I've got some friends who can sell me some good breed. You don't have to steal horses. At least for the most part. I think I can come up with a dozen or so to throw into the pot."

"Judge? You?" Jesse asked.

"I'm just as much a part of this gang as any of the rest of you. We're all in this together. You helped me before by giving me back my house and stables. The least I can do is get you some good horses."

"It'll take the fun out of it," came a feminine voice from the top of the stairs. May came down the steps in her elegant manner and walked over to the men. "The Judge can get you as many horses as you need. And Reed here," she continued as she put her arm around his neck, "can get us the best. If you catch my drift."

"Then by all thet lives, get them!" the Judge returned. "And I'll supply the rest of what you need."

When the whiskey was gone and the conversation was spent, Jesse took Matt and Steve aside to talk with them in private. "You sure you don't want to come in with us on all this? You'll get rich."

Matt looked at Jesse, frowned and exclaimed, "I thought you said it was for the cause of the South!"

"It is, Matt, indirectly," Jesse answered with a big smile. "Something I learned from Quantrill. Keep a little for ourselves. That way we can keep a-goin'."

"We've fought enough war, Jesse," Matt answered, searching for a cigar from his vest pocket. "For us, the war's over. We're your friends. We like you." He turned to Steve and asked, "You smoke cigars?"

Steve looked startled for the moment and then answered, "You know I do."

"Then how about giving me one."

"Make it two," Jesse joined in with a smile.

Steve reached in his vest pocket and pulled out three cigars and gave each man one. "You don't mind if I smoke one with you, do you?"

"Our proposition to you was to train you to fight one last fight for the South. In return for which you will diligently help me in searching for Ginny. In case you find any evidence of her whereabouts, dead or alive, you'll get word to me."

"But you're goin' to Waco to work for an ex-general who'll pay you cowboy wages. You can work with me and be rich, wear fine clothes like me and my men wear. The Judge was right when he said we helped him get his saloon back, with the inn and all these buildings. The North owes us. And we're collectin'."

"The war's over, Jesse!" Matt continued, lighting Jesse's cigar along with his on the same match. "You're right about Quantrill. Quantrill had fine clothes, too. He lost, and now he's buried in a grave some place. A young man and now a lost soul." He looked in disdain at Jesse and added, "We have no more cause to fight, Jesse."

With this, Jesse became angry. "No more cause? No more cause? Matt, we've no good money but their money. They took all ours. All we're doin' is takin' back what they owe us; Yankee money."

Cole sidled up to Jesse and added, "He's right, Matt. We came south to regroup. The South will rise again. Thet you oan bet on."

Matt looked at Cole and his brothers as they walked up to them, and then at Steve and lastly back at Jesse. "When thet time comes, you'll be ready. But not until. What you're doin' now is nothin' more than . . ." He looked at Steve and shrugged his shoulders. ". . . robbery.

"Yep. Plain and simple. Robbery."

"To you, Matt," Jesse reeled back. "To you. But to us, they owe us! And the war's not over until I say it's over!"

"And when will thet be, Jesse?"

Jesse bit the end off his cigar and lit it with a match he struck on his holster. "When I become the President of these heah Confederate States of America, Matt. When *I* become President." He pounded his chest with his pointer finger, exhaled the smoke and gave out a loud Rebel yell; one that shook the rafters.

Matt stood speechless for a long moment as he looked into the faces of cheering men, talking with one another and raising their fists.

And then he joined in. "Jesse! You mean to tell me that you really believe that the war ain't over?"

"Not by a long shot, mister," Jesse came back, taking a swig of whiskey and then, placing the cigar between his teeth, he echoed his sentiments, "Not by a long shot!"

CHAPTER 36

J. G. PEMBLETON'S SINGING PARTY

And then one Sunday night, Jesse's gang, absent Jesse, traveled outside of Sycene where a singing party was taking place. The Younger brothers went in first with loud boisterous singing, not at all complimenting the singing that was going on. Blackjack Kellum and Jim Reed joined in with a few of the other gang members and began to make fun of the Youngers' singing. Then the rest of the gang made foolish remarks about the others singing and began singing as well, demoralizing the good singers and making fun of the Youngers.

"Whose place is this anyway?" Reed asked, looking around the floor.

"Mine, sir," a voice came from around the corner. "This is my place and my people have come to sing. If you'd like to sing, join us. But don't be rude and make fun of us."

"And jest who is you?" John Younger asked.

"Someone got a jug?" Blackjack yelled out over the noise.

"Some punch on the table over yonder, Blackjack," Reed yelled out.

"I am Mr. J. G. Pembleton."

"You are who?" John asked, making his way over to the punch bowl.

"Mr. J. G. Pembleton. And please don't drink all of our punch. It's not much and it's all we've got."

Before anyone actually noticed the men, several of the members spiked the punch and got themselves drunk as they attempted to drink, sing and dance all at the same time.

"I'm not feeling any too good," one of the members yelled out and gave up his early morning breakfast on the host's floor.

"We've got ourselves a cutie," one of the members bragged as he began dancing with one of Pembleton's singers."

"Please, sir. I beg you to leave her alone," came the pitiful cry of Pembleton. "She's my sister."

"Your sister?" asked the man dancing with her. "Well, you can have her. She don't dance any too good anyway. Hey, Jim, (referring to Jim Younger), don't hog the punch."

Slim, a tall skinny man in his sixties, made a wrong step on the back porch, fell and hit his head on the ground; knocking him unconscious. Several of the members came to his rescue only to find him totally out.

"Can't get him to come to," Jim said with glass in hand and slapping him with the free hand.

"He dead?" Reed asked with a rough tone.

Cole bent down and examined Slim closer. "Looks like."

"What we gonna do, Cole?" Jim asked, looking frightened.

"Well, the party's much over. Let's put him on his horse and take him home."

It was night when the men clumsily climbed into their saddles and headed for home with Slim draped over his horse.

On the next day, Monday, Mr Pembleton went to town and filed charges against the James gang.

"Who was there?" Deputy Constable Ben Tanner asked as he looked over the warrants.

"You must know, sir," came Pembleton's reply. "The entire James gang."

"Jesse? You sure?"

"I don't know Jesse from Bessie. All's I know is they were the James gang cause they called themselves thet."

"Well, all right. I'll serve the warrants. But don't blame me if I can't get them all in for trial."

Tanner went to Sycene and dismounted his horse outside of the Shirley house as if he knew exactly where to find the boys.

He walked through the saloon doors and caught sight of none of the James gang, but the bartender behind the bar.

"Who ya lookin' for?" the bartender asked, wiping a bottle of whiskey with a cloth.

"Jesse," came the answer from Tanner.

"Ain't here. You want to see him, ya'll have to go north of town where he's doin' some special riding with his gang."

Tanner was not a big man, except in his belly. He was not a strong man either. But he was a prudent and determined man. He knew to go against the James gang would be foolish. But at the same time, he knew he had the responsibility to carry out and would have to serve the warrants against them.

He mounted his horse and rode out to the north end of town where he found the men running their horse skills under Matt and Steve's instructions. He never gave it a thought as to why they were practicing so much riding, only that he had to bring them in for trial.

"Mr. James!" he called out from his horse as he stood at the south end of a prairie field.

"Whatcha want, Deputy?" Jesse answered from his horse.

Tanner rode out to Jesse and answered him. "Got some warrants; yours included."

"What fer?"

"Well, it seems that you and your gang broke up a party of singers, got drunk and vomited all over Mr. J. G. Pembleton's good house. One man was kilt."

"My boys did thet. Yep. And a good man was kilt. I knowed about it."

"That's what the warrants say, and my job is to bring you in."

Matt and Steve stayed out of the trouble being brought upon Jesse, but Matt could hardly restrain himself.

"Whatcha laughing at, Matt?" Steve asked.

"Don't you see. This reminds me of the time you arrested me in Nacogdoches. He's one man up agin' Jesse's gang. Now what chance does he have?"

Steve shrugged his shoulders as he and Matt watched the scenario being played out.

"Well, Deputy Tanner," Jesse addressed him with a straw between his teeth. "It seems to me that you've got some mixed up notions that I was involved in something that I say I wasn't. 'Cuz, I wasn't there. I was here."

"Now Jesse. You let me know who was there and I'll take them with me."

Jesse looked at Tanner and then laughed real loud. "Boys! Listen up. We've got ourselves a lulu. This here deputy says we were at a J. G. Pem . . . What was it?"

"J. G. Pembleton's singing party."

"Anyway, he says he's a goin' to arrest all o' you'ns' ." He looked around at the gang's faces and no one showed any guilt. "Matt! What do you think?"

"I'd like to stay out of it, if you don't mind, Jesse," Matt answered astride his horse. He rode easy towards Jesse and the deputy with Steve following.

"I'll have to take you in with me, Jesse," Tanner informed him as he waved the papers in front of him.

"Are you prepared to take me in, Deputy?"

"Hold on, Jesse," Matt came back. He rode over to Jesse's side and whispered in his ears. "Steve here was a deputy and he has an idea."

"What Steve?"

Steve rode over and talked low with Jesse and Matt. "Well, it seems to me thet all he has is a minor offence, and thet ain't nothin' to get excited about with guns. I know. I've done the same thing when I was a deputy. Jest hear him out and go along with it, and we'll all get through the day just fine."

"What about the man thet got killed?" Matt asked.

"He was one of Jesse's," Steve came back. "Got drunk, from what I heard, fell off the porch and hit his head. Plain and simple. Shouldn't effect nothing atall."

"You agree, Matt?" Jesse asked.

"Yep."

"Cole? You agree?"

"Not me, no way. No way, Jesse," Cole Younger came back. "I was there. He'd have to arrest me, and you know my temper."

"You were there. How many of you were there?"

The other Younger brothers rode up. Jim spoke for the rest. "Us'ns. Blackjack. Reed and a coupla others. We were jest havin' some fun until I got all over the floor and table and all, and

Slim fell off the porch. I think thet's what caused his wantin' to arrest us."

"Well, shucks," Jesse came back. "Mr. Deputy, sir. What will it take to get this thing over with so we can continue our work here in the field?"

Tanner took out his handkerchief, removed his hat and wiped his forehead along with the sweatband. "A simple fine, I reckon. Jestice Lauderdale is mighty lenient, especially if'n I tell him we had no fuss or bother."

"Well, boys," Jesse came back. "We've can do thet. Let him arrest ya and we'll see you in the mornin'.

"Go with him, boys. Have a good night's sleep and come on back tomorrow. I'll have the fines paid in the mornin'."

The Youngers, Reed, Blackjack Kellum, and some other members of the gang followed proud Tanner back to the city where he put them all in one cell. On the morrow, they appeared before Justice Lauderdale and pled guilty.

"I understand that one or two of you threw up your breakfast at the party and never bothered to help clean it up," the Judge charged the gang.

"Shucks, judge," a young man from the back stepped up. "I wasn't in any condition to clean up anythin'. I even had it in muh hair."

"Me, too, sir," another young lad confessed. "They had to put me on my horse, I was so sick."

"The rest of you the same?"

"Thet's the truth, sir," John Younger came back. "None of the rest of us did any damage except to our lungs tryin' to sing *Sweet Adeline*."

Lauderdale looked at the men standing in front of him and leveled the gavel to the podium. "Seein' how one of you got hisself kilt, I reckon I'll go easy on the rest of ya. But as fer the two of ya who gave up your breakfasts, eighteen dollars for the two of you – each! And fifteen dollars a piece for the rest. Pay it now and get out of my court."

Jesse stepped up and paid the fine. "Thank you, judge, or your honor. We'll jest pay up and leave. Thank you."

Lauderdale looked at Jesse and said, "You're Jesse James, the leader of this bunch of whatever?"

"Yes sir, and mighty proud to say so, sir. Jesse Woodson James at your service. Your honor."

"You buried your man, yet?"

"No, sir," Jesse answered with a frown and his hat over his heart. "We got him laid out on the kitchen table at home. Gonna have a wake for him as he was part of family. Know what I mean, sir?"

"Well, bury him. And take your gang and take my advice. Don't come back here on any charges whatsoever. Hear me?"

Jesse felt a little perturbed at the Justice's comment, but smiled just the same, blinked his eyes, turned on his heels and left.

"Did I do all right, Matt?" he asked as they left the building.

"You did fine, Jesse. Proud of you."

"You know, Matt. If'n thet happened a few weeks ago, we'd of had a deputy's scalp on our door post. No one talks to Jesse Woodson James like they did. Yes sir, had it not been for you . . ."

Cole sided up to the pair along with Steve and added, "He don't know the half of it. We've had killings up til now that would make me want to puke."

"Sure, we've had," Jesse added as they walked to their horses. "Fights and brawls all the time. You see these men, Matt. We had some more. Killers, they were. We got rid of them, fast.

"My fault, too, I suppose. We had a sheriff one time. Sheriff Moon as I recall. He did the same thing this deputy did, except he caught some of my men, the ones we chased out of our gang. Well, sir, he caught them while they were eating dinner. Kinda like with their pants down."

"What'd they do?" Matt asked, stopping by his horse. He took out his makings and lit a cigarette. "Or am I allowed to ask?"

"Nothing more than these boys did Sunday. Had some fun with some girls. Maybe they went overboard. They got drunk and didn't care what they did."

"So the sheriff got the drop on them and locked them up?"

"No. Not that way at all. Moon got them to surrender, only they asked if they could finish their supper first. He was a good sheriff. Pretty much like this here Tanner fella. Nice and easy goin'." Then Jesse looked at John Younger and added, "Maybe thet's why Tanner was so jittery about arresting us. Ya think, John?"

John knew the ending of the story and agreed.

The men got upon their horses as Jesse continued his story.

"Well, sir, Matt. Like I said, he agreed to let them finish their meal and they would go along with him peaceably."

"And . . .?"

"And, they up and shot him. Killed him dead."

"And . . .?" Matt got uptight and Jesse sensed it.

"Well, my boys came back to us and told us what they'd done. Bragged about it, they did. They were drunk, jest like my boys last Sunday night. 'Course they had no call to kill the sheriff. But they did.

"And, Matt, jest like I said. We take care of our own."

"Oh?" Matt pushed back his Stetson.

"Yes, sir. We take care of our own."

"Meaning?"

"Yep. Simple as it is. We told the rest of 'em to get out of the state. They did and we ain't seen any of 'em since. Don't ever expect to either." They laughed, but they sensed that Matt knew the rest of the story.

Matt sat straight up in his saddle and stretched in his stirrups. "You jest up and . . .?"

"Yep! We don't like killers. He'd a got his sometime down the road, but hopefully not while riding with me."

Jesse looked intently at Matt, showed his smiling teeth, winked one of his blue eyes, and said, "It's our code, Matt. Get my drift?"

Matt tilted his Stetson, held tight to the cigarette between his teeth, smiled a bit and said, "Yeah! Guess so." He remembered times when he rode with General Nathan Edwards Forrest while serving with Terry's Texas Rangers in the Civil War, and knew he'd probably have done the same thing. But that was war. And this, he thought to himself, is *war?*

He spurred Skeeter and rode back to the Shirley House with Jesse's gang.

"Ya gonna bury your man in the morning?" Matt asked, looking at Jesse as they rode together.

"He's been on the table for the last day. Yep. We'll have a wake for him tonight when we get back and bury him first thing."

The wake went on into the early hours of the morning, and just before the rooster crowed, a sound was heard from the kitchen that every member heard; drunk or sober. Then they heard a thud like something fell in the kitchen; except this something had to be big . . . real big to make that kind of noise.

The men carefully sauntered into the kitchen and found their friend on the kitchen floor face down.

"What the hell?" Jesse asked. "Well, just don't stand there, men. Someone pick him up and put him back on the table."

"How'd he fall off?" one of the men, standing behind the rest asked, quivering.

"How should I know?" Jesse came back as he watched two men pick the body up.

Just as they raised him up, another sigh came from the body and the two men dropped him. In a moment, the kitchen was empty except for the body; and he rose upon his feet. Scratching his head, Slim looked around at the empty kitchen and said loud, "Hello!"

The house was emptied as the screen door slammed shut. Jesse ordered, "Jim. John. Cole. Matt. Anyone. Go see what's goin' on!"

Matt looked at Jesse and burst into a laugh. Steve joined in and so did the rest of Jesse's gang. Jesse threw his hat down and said, "Hell. I'll go in."

Matt joined him and Steve and Cole sided them. Once inside, they saw the man standing up, drinking water out of a ladle in the bucket on the kitchen counter.

"Sure am thirsty," he said.

"You all right, Slim?" Jesse asked, feeling the man's head where the blood had dried.

"Yep. Hurt a little right here on the side of my head though."

"It's a superficial wound, Slim," Jesse said. "You bled a lot. Thet's why you passed out."

"Passed out?" Cole returned, looking Slim eye to eye. "He was stone drunk and passed out from the liquor. The head wound made us think he was kilt."

"Well, I'll be swankered!" Slim replied, slopping water down like a hog at a trough. "Real thirsty. I am."

"Hey boys!" Jesse called out the door. "Come on in! Slim's alive."

The news did not settle any too easy among the boys who *knew* Slim was dead. Each man inched his way into the room to see for himself about Slim, and none was any too eager to confirm such. But, however reluctant each of them was, they did sashay in. And when they witnessed the miracle, they rejoiced and almost killed Slim with hand shakes and hugs.

Slim was alive and back into the ranks of Jesse's gang. The men had at first thought they had seen a ghost. They were relieved that they had not, but continued the party the same as if he were dead.

Matt thought and laughed to himself. *A ghost? What would I have done had I seen a ghost of my girl, Ginny? Wow!*

CHAPTER 37

A VISIT TO SEE CAROL

The next night, after a turn at the gaming table and like many nights since his first midnight visit, Matt's thoughts went to Carol at the livery stable. *If I never see Ginny again,* he thought, *I'm wasting my time doing without a girl.* And then after losing a fifth hand, he gave in to his thoughts, turned the cards back, took the little money he had left and made another visit to the stable.

When he got to the stable, he found that the side door was locked. He went around the back of the stable where her house was and looked at the windows to see if there was any sign of life. To his dismay, there was none. In case he was spotted, he picked up a hackamore and a curry comb in the stable as an excuse to visit Skeeter in the night.

Setting them aside, he took out his makings and lit a cigarette. Leaning against the livery stable door, he took a break for a smoke, hoping that she would notice that he was in the stable. But she didn't. Feeling alone he began sizing up the situation. *It's a foolish thought. What am I doing here? Making a fool of myself.* He flicked the butt into the yard, turned and started walking back to the inn.

Suddenly he heard the sound of bare feet running towards him. He turned and saw Carol, her face all aglow in the moonlight as if she had found a lost treasure.

"I was hoping you'd come back," she said, stopping at the end of the livery stable. She waited a moment for him to the make the next move and walk towards her.

"I . . . I, eh, had a hackamore I wanted to leave for Skeeter. And, well, I thought since I was here, I'd, eh, comb his mane. Don't get a chance out in the field to keep him fit, you know."

"Want to go inside?"

"If it's no bother."

To his amazement, the back door was unlocked. She opened it and, picking up the lantern, entered the stable, lit it and walked over to Skeeter's stall. "Go to it."

Matt strung the hackamore on the gate post, took an apple out of his pocket, gave it to Skeeter. Then he took the curry comb and started combing Skeeter's mane. "He likes apples."

"This time of night?" she asked, laughingly.

"You're laughing at me?"

"Yep. You know you didn't come here to comb his mane." She walked back to the opened door and closed it. Then she hung the lantern on the wall and turned the wick down. Her shadow stretched over to Matt's as he stood there watching her.

Her back-lighted figure excited him with a passion he had wanted to feel for some time but never gave into the opportunity until now.

"You are one beautiful lady," Matt informed her as he leaned against Skeeter's stall.

"Like I said outside, I'm glad you came back."

"I've been here each morning, picking up my horse."

"Not what I mean and you know it."

Matt felt uneasy about wanting to quit the small talk and just take her in his arms, but he felt uncomfortable.

"Are you looking at me, or seeing Ginny?" she asked, standing still in the middle of the stable.

"You . . . you remind me so much of her."

"Won't do." She turned and walked some steps down the stable into the darkness where her presence was barely seen by Matt.

"You're young, Carol. You will find a man and love him and give him all your love."

"And have babies and cook suppers and clean house. I'm not looking for a man for that."

"Most women are. Don't you think?"

"Most women aren't me."

"Then what the heck are you lookin' for in a man?"

She walked a little back into the lantern light and stopped. Straddling her legs, she placed her hands on her hips and looked intently into Matt's eyes. "I'm looking for a particular man who will love me. Me. Carol Jenkins. A girl from nowhere in Texas wanting my man to take me to somewhere I've never been. Set me up in a mansion some place on a high hill and treat me like a Greek goddess."

Matt looked at her denim pants, plaid shirt, messed up hair, and then looked down at her bare feet. "You've got an imagination that runs wild with excitement. But I ain't thet man."

"Didn't say you were. Just said that's what I want. You asked me. I told you."

"Then why are you here in the stable with me at midnight with the lantern turned down? Why?"

She kicked some hay between her toes and walked slowly circuitously towards him. "Because, Mr. Jorgensen, I don't think our meeting is by accident. Sure, I would love for you to take me into your muscular arms and kiss me, and even make passionate love to me. But you won't. And I won't let you. Not now. Maybe never."

Matt's stomach ached with a yearning for her that never existed since he had his affair with Ginny several years before. His mind kept remembering that day and the last time he saw her as he rode off to chase a killer out of Tennessee. He thought, *Would I be betraying Ginny if I made love to Carol?*

He asked himself over and over again ever since, *What kind of man am I? Will I ever find Ginny? Will I marry her if she is still alive? Do I go on living an empty life, not knowing another woman?* And now he was faced with a barefooted Carol Jenkins on a warm night in a stable in the middle of Texas.

He took her into his arms and looked into her face as the lantern played shadows upon it. He gave into his impulse and gently kissed her. He felt her body giving in to his as the kiss lingered and her fingers found their way through his heavy head of hair.

Breaking from the kiss, she looked up into his blue eyes and closed hers. He looked upon her beautiful, youthful face and again placed his lips gently and softly against hers. The warmth he felt gently penetrated his soul as well as hers and the two acted as one and then their lips parted.

After a moment, he broke away and smiled at her. "I haven't felt this much love in a long time."

"With Ginny?" She smiled. Looking at his child-like face that he portrayed for the moment, she quickly added, "Just kiddin'."

He continued to stare into her soft eyes and then kittenlishly said, "Well, maybe there was thet girl in Louisiana who . . ." and he laughed. She sensed that he was teasing her. Their lips met again and he brought her closer into his body where she let him feel her warmth, hoping he would lay her down on the hay-strewn floor. Her hands reached up inside his shirt and massaged his back. He knew that she was ripe for the taking and he brought her down with him to the floor, sparking their souls from within. The shadows illuminated from the lantern continued to play upon their bodies almost in rhythm to their love. Both of them let their fantasies play out to the fullest as they slowly and tenderly drew from each other's love.

Afterwards, the two lay there and looked up into the stable rafters as their eyes drew heavy.

Within moments, two quick shots rang out through the night, making the doors of the stable shake like they were hit with canon balls. Matt pushed Carol gently against the stall out of danger and then ran to the rear door and fell outside on the dirt. Looking around, he could see nothing.

Carol came around the stable to where Matt was and held onto his waist. He pulled her up close to his side and held her tight.

"Who was it?" she whispered, looking down the road.

"Don't know." He looked down at her and asked, "You got a boyfriend out there thet don't like me?"

Carol broke from Matt and turned around. "You know, I've had dates before. None serious. I can't think of anyone who would do this though."

"Well, Miss Jenkins. I think we'd better get you home before the city talks."

He wrapped his arm around her and led her back to the house where a bedroom light was lit up. A man ran out the door and up to Matt and Carol. It was Carol's brother, Russ.

"You all right, sis?" Russ yelled out. "Who are you?" he asked of Matt.

"Matt Jorgensen."

"You know him, Russ. He's the man whose sorrel I'm taking care of."

"Jesse's friend? Yeah. I know. I fixed your horse up with some shoes."

"Yep. Thet's me."

"What happened? Why all the shooting?"

"Some one shot up the stable. I went out and whoever it was seemed to take a shot at me. I fired back at what I could, but he rode off."

Some of the town people looked out the window for a while and, seeing nothing in the streets, turned and went back to bed. The city went dark again except for the Jenkins' house.

"That's odd," Russ shot back.

"Yeah. Even more so because there were a lot of 'em. All a firin' their weapons like they were goin' to battle somewhere."

"Here comes another one," Russ added, pulling his hogleg from its holster. "Watch out, Matt! I'll get him."

"Hold up, Russ!" Matt took a firm grip of Russ' gunhand. "It's my partner, Steve."

Steve bounced around back of the stable where he saw the light and found the trio staring at him as if he were a ghost.

"They got May!" he yelled out, holding his boots in one hand and slipping his galluses on with the other.

"What?" Matt reacted with his hand ready to draw his Navy. "Who got May?"

"They took a ladder and climbed up the back of the saloon to her bedroom and kidnapped her. I saw them as they rode off, a firin' their guns and ridin' into the night. Then I saw the ladder up to her window."

"Let's ride, friend!" Matt ordered, with Carol by his side to help saddle their horses.

Then Russ looked at his barefooted sister and added, "What were you two doing out at this time of night?"

"He came to take care of his sorrel, Russ. I heard him and came out to help him."

Russ rubbed his thick head of hair, smiled and then joined them. "Well. Hope you don't get shot at again tonight."

"Me, too," Matt answered. "Me, too."

Russ turned, escorted Carol to the door and the two went back into the house as Matt and Steve saddled and rode out into the street.

"Another time?" she asked softly, clinching her hand as if holding onto Matt's.

Carol looked on until she could see him no more, and then went back into the house and turned down the lantern.

CHAPTER 38

AN ELOPEMENT

Matt and Steve rode into town in the night when they saw a ladder leaning against the upstairs window of the Shirley House stretching to May's window. The Judge was on the sidewalk, walking back and forth, while Eliza stood shivering in her house robe.

"Get her back!" the Judge ordered Matt and Steve, and watched them as they spirited their horses out of town.

It was not too far into the woods that Matt and Steve reined up when they saw Jesse, Cole, Reed and the others with a prettied-up gal with a smile on her face.

"Well, hello, Matt. Steve." Jesse shot at them with his winning personality. "See you made the wedding, too."

"Wedding?" Matt asked, being totally confused. "What wedding?"

"Yeah!" Steve echoed. "What wedding?"

Of course, Steve readily knew that the wedding included the only female in the group; one May Shirley. "You, May?"

"Thanks for coming, Steve. And, Matt," May said with a beam in her eye. "I'm getting married. Me and Jim."

"Reed?" Steve shot back. "Reed! You marryin' up with May? Why? Why May?"

"Why not?" Reed returned, watching Steve slide out of his saddle and approach him. "I'm the better man than you."

"Who says? She didn't!"

Reed stopped his intruder by taking a hold of his shirt collar, only to realize that he should not have done so. Steve took Reed's hand from his shirt, twisted and threw Reed to the ground in one swift movement.

Reed came up with his tight fist that knocked Steve across the field and under a couple of horses. Steve came up on the other side of the horses, regained his senses and, moving the horses with his strong arms, went after Reed with his rushing body. The two fell to the ground with Steve's body crushing Reed. Steve hit Reed twice before Jesse and Cole pulled them apart.

"You better keep your friend away from Reed before someone gets hurt," Jesse advised Matt.

"Yeah!" Matt agreed, taking a hold of Steve by the neck. "Hold on, partner. You licked him good."

Reed arose and started in on Steve again when two of Reed's friends held him back.

Jesse went to Reed and straightened his shirt and vest. "Ya gotta look neat for your weddin', Jimboy. Can't do anythin' fer thet shiner." He took a handkerchief from his pocket, spit on it and wiped the blood from Reed's cheek and lip. He looked into Reed's eyes and asked, "Ya ready to get married now?"

Reed straightened up, looked at an irate man who knew he had been bested by another man in a wedding scheme he had no privilege to be a party to, and now he was pinned down from beating him up by his best friend.

"She must love him, friend," Matt came back. He looked into Steve's eyes, released his hold on his neck and asked, "You seeing things a little better now?"

Steve took a deep breath, exhaled, and loosened his body while he looked at a beaten up groom. "I've never felt jilted before, Matt. Now, I know what it's like."

"Jilted?" Matt returned. "You never even asked her, did cha?"

"Well, no. But I would have."

"You would have?"

"Kinda. I think. I don't know."

May went to Reed's side, took the handkerchief from Jesse and continued wiping Reed's bloodied face. "You should have seen the other guy," she told him and laughed.

"I can't see him in the dark. Did I do good?"

May looked over at Steve, saw that he was in much better shape than her beau, and answered Reed, "You did good, my lover."

While Jesse helped Reed spruce himself up for the wedding, May sashayed over to Steve, squeezed his hand and gave him a wink.

"See thet, Matt?" he asked, as Matt restrained him again with a hold around his chest.

"She's spoken for, friend."

Reed resumed his position at which he was when the two rode up, and May joined him.

"Why does she want to marry him when she loves me?" Steve asked Matt in a low voice. "Tell me."

"Can't, friend."

A tall, gaunt man with an unkempt beard stood before them. His name was John Fischer, a member of the gang and not a minister of any sort.

He looked at the couple with wide eyes that could be seen in the dark from a distance of a hundred feet or more. Then he looked down as if looking at a book in his hand; possibly the Bible, so dirty that no one actually knew whether or not it was.

"May Shirley. Do you take this man, Jim Reed to be your husband. Answer *yes* or *no*?"

"I sure do, John."

"Ain't he supposed to ask the man first?" Steve asked Matt who still held onto him with a strong grip. Matt just grunted.

"And you, too, John. Do you take May the same?"

"Yep," was all that Reed could say, as he rubbed his jaw that pained him a great deal.

"Kiss each other and I'll call you man and wife."

"Easy, May," Reed said, as he leaned into May's red, puffy lips that poised to be kissed.

"You're hitched!" Fischer exclaimed. He closed his dusty book, put it back into his pocket and walked over to his horse.

"They are?" Steve asked Matt as Matt released his grip.

"I suppose so, friend. I'm not goin' to argue any."

"Well, what do we tell the Judge?"

Matt walked to his horse and climbed on board as Steve sided him. *"Judge!* I'll say. *You've got a son-in-law."*

Steve climbed into his saddle along with the rest of the gang and the pair followed the rest back to town.

"Matt," Steve said as he watched the married pair ride in the opposite direction. "You saw her. She took a hold of my hand and squeezed it and winked at me."

"Ah, pal," Matt answered. "Hate to tell you this, but she winked at me, too."

Steve reined up, looked at Matt's back and then spurred his horse to catch up to Matt. "She did?"

Matt snickered under his Stetson and said, "Yep."

Steve pulled back and, while walking, asked, "Were it legal, you suppose?"

"What *legal*?" Matt asked.

"Thet there marriage. You know. May and thet Reed fella?"

"All I know, friend, is that Reed got a bunch of boys together and kidnapped her from her bedroom window. Took her out to the groves and ol' John Fischer up and married 'em on horseback."

"But, thet weren't legal, were it?"

"Maybe. Maybe not. They got half a dozen witnesses says it were. Who's crazy enough to say it weren't." He reined up and Steve followed. He put his leg over the saddle horn, pulled out his makings and rolled himself a cigarette. "You gonna give up on her?"

Steve watched the silhouette of the newly weds disappear over the horizon as the sun lit up the woods in her full glory. He took off his Stetson, dusted it off on his trousers, looked over at Matt and answered, "Yeah! But she shore was pretty. And . . ."

Matt reached over and gave Steve's horse a smack on the rear and rode off towards town. "Let's go get drunk, friend."

CHAPTER 39

A GHOST ON THE TRAIL

<u>29 June 1867</u>

The Louisville and Nashville Railroad train pulled into Nashville on a warm afternoon. A couple prepared to meet Ginny sat in a buckboard parked alongside the road. When the train came to a final halt, the middle-aged lady, finely dressed with her salt-and-peppered hair coiffed inside a small bonnet stepped from the buggy and walked up the platform to receive Ginny. She was Sylvia McBride, her stepmother and widow to her father, James McBride. .

Carrying her satchel, Ginny was quick to exit the passenger train and saw the lady from a distance as Sylvia walked up to her.

"Ginny?" Sylvia called out to her.

"It's me, Sylvia." It did not take much time for Ginny to recognize Sylvia's voice and realize that it was her. They embraced and exchanged greetings, and then walked towards the carriage.

Olaf had left the buckboard and was at the baggage area when the ladies joined him. Once there, he doffed his hat and greeted Ginny with a big smile. "It's been a long time, Ginny. It's certainly good to see you again. I hardly recognized you."

"Me, too," Sylvia added. "Excuse me for looking, but you're . . . not the same person."

"The clothes?" Ginny asked, twirling around to show them off. "Haven't you heard? I'm a refined lady of society. I wonder what would Papa would say if he could see me now?" She laughed and had the Gustafson's laughing, too.

Ginny pointed out her luggage and Olaf took them in hand to the buckboard.

On the ride to the plantation across the Green River and finally over the Tennessee River, the trio brought each other up to date on what had changed since Ginny had left.

"As you know, Olaf and I are married. I'm a step mother to two fine gentlemen. You'll like them."

"I'm certain I will," Ginny returned. "I remember Sam and John. We used to rough-house on occasion as kids. Boy, did the schoolmarm have a time with us. I'm sure they've grown into civilized men."

"How's the plantation doing?"

"With Olaf moving in with us, we have more acreage, more workers and more cotton. That's why you're here, isn't it?"

"One of the reasons. We're starting up another mill; my family and I. And we're going to need every bit of cotton directed our way."

"You'll get it, by golly," Olaf chimed in. "It'll be ready to harvest by the time you have a place for us to send it to. Also we've got a couple of neighbor plantation owners. They'll be ready, too; them that's got enough workers to keep their places going. It's not what it used to be with slaves and all, Ginny, but the colored folks are working for some of us that can see it that way and save parts of the plantation life we knew."

"Yes. I've been keeping track of your progress. Keep it up, now that you've got both places going. My brothers thought that I'd be best at discerning the progress going on here. "

The talk carried on into the evening when they reached the plantation. Two horsemen rode out to meet them as they came around the bend and into view of the house.

"Sam and John," Sylvia introduced them to Ginny. "Sam's the younger one. The big one is John. Boys, I want you to meet your boss, so to speak."

"Miss McBride," John said as he removed his hat. "We remember you. Jest never got to meet you proper."

Sam joined John and greeted Ginny in like manner. Then the two sided the buckboard back to the house.

The lights were on in the main house and a couple of black servants stood on the porch waiting for their arrival. The house was completely made of logs with a tall ceiling inside for the front room. A large fireplace adorned the north wall but was quiet as the evening was warm.

"Olaf his sons built it. You might remember. They'll take your luggage to your room, Ginny," Sylvia informed her as Ginny looked at the huge house.

"This isn't mine, is it?" she asked, stepping from the buckboard. "It's gorgeous."

"No. It's mine and Olaf's. Yours is down the road. Remember? And just as beautiful."

Ginny looked down the country road towards the south where her plantation connected with the Gustafson's.

"It's beautiful," Ginny observed. "Even in the twilight of the evening. Oh, this is where I belong. The warm air. The scent of the peach trees and the apple trees. Like the time I met my Matt the first time."

"Matt!" Sylvia remarked as she led Ginny up the porch and inside the house.

The evening meal was rather festive for the occasion as the Gustafson's wanted to make a good impression on Ginny. After the meal, they left for the large living room with a drink in their hands. There was talk of John's fiancé and coming wedding and maybe refurbishing Ginny's mansion for the newlyweds. Ginny felt it would be good for someone to live there again and be closer to the work being done. There was some talk of possessions that were still there, left behind when Ginny rode off to find Matt and also of compensation and other small details of renewing and making new acquaintances.

"If you ladies don't mind, my boys and I have some chores yet to do. We'll leave you lovely ladies to get reacquainted." He stood with his sons in the hallway of the big room and then added, "It is certainly good to see you again, Miss McBride."

"Thank you, Olaf," Sylvia replied, and then sat down with Ginny.

"About Matt, Ginny," Sylvia started in. "What do you want to know?"

"Everything," Ginny returned.

"I've received all your letters and I can tell that you are one love-sick lady."

"But you've seen him? Tell me how he looks."

"Like I said in my letters. Handsome. I have to say, he's very handsome. But thin. You know; the war and all. And I have to say, it seems that he's sure been riding every where trying to find you."

The conversation led into the night when the ladies had to call it bed time.

On the following day, Sylvia drove Ginny to her plantation where she watched Sam and John work with the lead men and their workers. Then when the sun began to set, she walked up the hill to Blue Moon Ridge, the resting place of James McBride, her father.

"We laid him to rest beneath his favorite tree up on the hillside, Ginny. That way, he could always look over his plantation."

Ginny looked at the cross that bore his name, *James McBride*. She knelt down and prayed. Sylvia watched on with head bowed.

The conversation about Matt carried on into the next four days as Ginny examined and re-examined the land and inventory. She was pleased at how the Gustafson's had kept the land and grown the cotton. Sam and John had managed the workers well and she was pleased.

On her last day at the plantation, Sylvia told her, "Steve's got a sister in Texas. If anyone's kept in contact with Steve, it would be his sister. I'm not sure what her name is."

278

"And Matt would be with Steve," Ginny interjected. "Anything else you can tell me. Where did they go when they left here?"

"Oh, my, of course! Of course! They headed to Nashville to visit a Reverend Bunting. I don't remember his first name. But, I think he's with the First Presbyterian Church there in Nashville."

"Bunting. Nashville. You've been a big help to me. Sylvia. Now I know I must visit with this Reverend Bunting."

"He probably knows Matt better then anyone except Steve, Ginny," Sylvia suggested. "Sam's driving you back to Nashville. He can take you to the church."

She hugged Sylvia in a long embrace and bade a fond goodbye to her ex-stepmother and Olaf as Sam drove her to Nashville. Her thoughts were on her planned visit with Reverend Bunting. *How much could he tell me about Matt? I wonder.*

CHAPTER 40

BUNTING SEES A GHOST

Sam stayed with her as he drew the buckboard up to the First Presbyterian Church. It was still daylight when they were welcomed into the church by the secretary.

"Reverend Bunting," she replied to Ginny's question. "Do you have an appointment?"

"No. But if he's the same man, he will know of Matt Jorgensen."

"Matt Jorgensen? We don't have a Jorgensen with us."

"Allow me, Miss McBride," Sam interrupted. "Was the reverend a chaplain in the war? If he was, this Matt served with him and they knew each other."

"Well, yes. He was a chaplain for Terry's Texas Rangers."

"That's him!" Ginny exclaimed.

"Let me see if he's available for visitors," the secretary replied. "Please be seated." She disappeared out of the doorway

"Within a short while, Bunting came into the office to meet with Ginny and Sam.

"I'm Reverend Bunting."

"I'm Ginny McBride and this is Sam Gustafson, my step-brother from Tennessee."

Sam rose and offered his hand to Bunting.

Bunting's jaw dropped as he loosely shook Sam's hand. "Did you say? Ginny? Ginny McBride?"

"Yes. You know Matt Jorgensen?"

"Yes. Oh, my yes. Matt Jorgensen. And you're Ginny?" Rev. Bunting took Ginny's arms in his hands and with a huge smile threw back his head and chuckled, saying, "Praise God! You are real and very much alive. Matt was right! Praise the Lord. He was right!! God bless you, Matt, wherever you are. God bless you!!"

"So you don't know where he is?" Ginny asked.

"He rode east to try to find you some time ago; like two or three months. Haven't heard from him since."

Then he interjected, "I would love to talk to you about Matt, but I'm late for a council meeting right now. Where are you staying?"

"We're not. I'm sure we can find some lodging."

"Could my secretary show you to my home? I have two extra rooms and I could meet with you first thing in the morning."

"We'd love that. Thank you."

"You've had a long ride. Rest up and we can talk in the morning, Miss McBride."

"Thank you. I shall, and we do appreciate it. Thank you."

They were made comfortable by the secretary while their buckboard was stabled for the evening

She looked at Sam later and said, "See you in the morning."

"Yes'm," Sam replied. "Good night, Ginny."

She saw Sam walk down the hall way, then closed her bedroom door and settled down for the night.

At breakfast, Bunting was all ears as to the other side of the spirit world as he saw the lovely Ginny McBride; not a ghost, but a real and beautiful lady.

"Tell me everything, if you will, Reverend Bunting," Ginny said with a smile and a cup of tea in her hand.

Sam sat next to her at the table and enjoyed the breakfast. But when it got into the conversation about Matt, he said, "If I may be excused, I'll tend to my mares." He rose, and with Bunting's and Ginny's consent, left the table and headed for the stable.

"I must tell you," Bunting went on. "I have seen and heard many weird tales in my life, but I have never experienced one as unexpected as this."

"How do you mean?" Ginny responded.

"Matt talked about you for five years. All through the war you were all he ever talked of. I have never in my life expected to meet you. And when you showed up here to visit with me, I was beside myself. I thought you might be a . . ."

"A ghost?"

"Yes. A ghost," Bunting returned. "Matt has talked about you; talked about seeing you in visions and such."

Ginny's eyes widened. "Visions?"

"Yes. He told me about the visions he had about seeing you."

"Like dreams?" she asked.

"No. Visions. Can you believe that?"

"Yes. Yes, I can. For you see, I have had visions about him."

"Interesting. Then as an afterthought, he asked, "Care to see the church?" Bunting was seeking a way to keep the conversation going on a comfortable level without losing thought as to what the two of them were sharing. Bunting stood up, pulled the chair out for Ginny and escorted her outside and across the courtyard to the church.

Once at the church, he showed her the sanctuary, walking her up to the podium.

"I talk about the spirit world from here," he informed Ginny.

"Spirit world?"

"Well, yes. Christianity. Christ. His Spirit. Angels and such."

"And you are suggesting that Matt and I have a spiritual connection of some kind?"

"I do. After counseling with Matt for five years and now hearing your story, I'm convinced that you both have experienced something extra special. And I'm so glad to know both of you."

He offered her a seat on the front pew and then joined her.

"He told me about one of his visions; it was about some letter."

"A letter?" Ginny asked.

Something about reading it and then seeing you in your bedroom. Which, of course I discounted at the time."

"My bedroom? Why . . . yes. I was in my bedroom when I saw him. Why, he was standing there just as plain as . . . Did he explain it to you?" She blushed slightly.

"That's all I can tell you."

"That's odd. That's one of the times that I saw him. He was reading a letter to me. I could hear his voice, and I could see him, but I couldn't make out all of the words. And . . . That was shen I had amnesia and I didn't know my name. And . . . I couldn't recognize him. Who he was?"

Bunting stood up. He walked towards his podium, stopped turned around, and faced Ginny.

"What about a bullet?"

"A bullet? How do you mean?"

"Never mind. It never happened. Most of what he said was kind of wishful thinking on his part."

Ginny looked at Bunting and then stood up, walked close to him, turned around and said, "I saw him in a vision ready to get shot. I flew to him like in a split second and startled his horse. He reared suddenly and threw Matt to the ground. Didn't hurt him any." She stood up and threw open her arms in gest. "Somehow, I saved him from getting shot by a Yankee."

Bunting's jaw dropped. "What?"

"He told you, didn't he?" She sensed it from the expression on his face.

Bunting stood as if beside himself. "I took it as a spiritual happenstance. Perhaps an angel, but . . ."

"And Matt let the Yankee boy go." She looked at him as he stayed in sort of a shock mode. "So, he told you it happened?"

Bunting took his handkerchief from his pocket, wiped the sweat from his upper lip and said, "Exactly. Just like he said."

He thought to himself, *how will I ever explain this to my parishioners? They'd never believe me. Nobody will. I don't even know if I do.*

And then he quickly added, "And you never saw him since?"

"More in visions?"

"No. In real life?"

"That's why I'm here. To find him. I know he's alive somewhere."

"How do you know?"

Ginny thought for a moment, walked away and then turned back. "If I knew the answer to that, I'd know where he was, now wouldn't I?"

"I suppose so. All I can tell you is that he's searching for you." Then he looked as if lightning struck him. "I know who might know where he is."

Ginny's eyes widened again as she turned into Bunting. "Who?"

"Steve Andrews' sister, Brenda."

Ginny stared at Bunting for a moment and then repeated what he said, "Brenda?"

"You know her?"

"Nope. Who is this Brenda, Reverend Bunting?" Ginny asked with tight lips.

"Well, you might just as well hear it from me as anyone. She was in love with Matt."

"I figured. Hmmm!"

"She visited him while we were in Rome, Georgia."

"Interesting!" Ginny returned. "Very interesting!"

"I've said too much, I know," Bunting returned. "But, I felt you would want to know and would need to know if you put all the pieces together."

"And you counseled with him for five years?"

"Not counseled. We were good friends and we talked a lot of the time we were together in the cavalry."

"You don't have to tell me more about this Brenda."

"But, she is one who could help you because she's . . ."

"Steve's sister," Ginny finished the sentence for him. "I know." Then she straightened her composure and apologized. "I'm sorry."

"What for? For being a woman in love with a man? You're only human."

"Thank you, Reverend Bunting."

"She lives in Nacogdoches, Texas. She's a school teacher. Or was."

"Was?"

"Well, she got married. When Matt and Steve came home from the war she'd had a child. Her husband's name is Clem something or other."

"Clem. A schoolteacher. Nacogdoches. I have to find her."

"One more thing, Miss McBride," Bunting added.'

"Yes?"

"He and Steve said they were heading out to Richmond, Virginia to find you. Kind of sentimental to him. That's where she, uh, you told him that you would see him in a parade.

"Richmond?" She thought, *I'm here and he's in Richmond. That's one for the books. But I've got to make sure.*

"I haven't heard from them since. I guess I didn't help him much when he was here. The things he was saying. Well, you have to admit, they're just not ordinary happenings. But, I'm so glad you came to see me. I can't explain it anymore now than then, but this is the best ghost story I've ever heard and Matt sure is one blessed fellow!

"Be sure and give him my best when you find him. And, you will find him. Of that I'm certain. This has to be God's destiny for you. By Golly, it sure is!

"Thanks, Reverend. I'll check that out after I meet with Brenda." *And God, how I hate to have to see this Brenda.*

Sam helped her step up into the buggy for the ride back to the depot. *Well, Matt,* she continued thinking to herself. *I'm getting closer to finding you.*

CHAPTER 41

A GHOST MEETS THE PAST

And finding Brenda was her intention as the train pulled into the Nacogdoches depot where no one was there to greet her. Ginny left her luggage at the depot as she searched out the sheriff's office.

"Main Street, ma'am," the railroad telegrapher replied to her. "Right in the middle of town. Can't miss it."

She took her satchel and walked to the sheriff's office, dodging unruly cowpokes, riding to avoid the wagon ruts. She felt many eyes burn into her back as she approached the office, and she heard some remarks like, "That's one hellofa good-lookin' lady!"

"Yep!"

And another, "Wow!"

"Are you the sheriff?" she asked the man behind the desk as she walked in. When he stood up, she saw that he was of short stature and sported a salt-and-peppered beard. There was a tell-tale star on his vest and he picked up his well-stained, wide-brim hat from the desk and plopped it on his bald pate.

"Yes, ma'am. Happy Jones. What can I do you for?"

"I'm looking for a school teacher. I just have the first name of her and her husband."

"And what would they be, can I ask?"

"Her name is *Brenda* and his is *Clem*. Know of them?"

"Oh, yeah. The Conleys. Not too far from town. I've got a wagon," Happy suggested. "Might be too fer a piece to walk in that get-up of you'rn."

"Thank you. I'd be obliged." Then she remembered. "My luggage is on the platform at the depot."

"I'll get Hank to fetch it for ya." He turned to the man on the other side of the room with a broom in his hand and asked him, "Can you run over and fetch the lady's luggage, Hank?"

"Sure 'nuf," came Hank's reply as he dropped the broom and headed out the door towards the depot. "What's it look like?"

"Probably the only one there," Ginny answered. "It's got my name on it. Virginia McBride. Could you please take it to the Hotel across the street and tell them I'll be in later"

"Well, Miss Virginia McBride," Happy said as he escorted her to the wagon outside the office, "hop on board."

The house sat on a slope three blocks from town on the west side. It was the same farm house that Matt found when he was offered a meal by the then deputy, Steve Andrews, Brenda's brother. Because of Clem's work around the farm, it became a much improved sight for the town.

"That's the place, miss," Happy informed her as he pulled the team up to the hitching rail. "She should be home. School's out, you know."

Happy offered his hand to Ginny and escorted her to the door. A man was in the barn lot and walked to the house as the buggy approached it.

"Howdy, Happy!" he yelled out as he walked up to the porch. "Who's our company?"

"Howdy, Clem," Happy returned the salutation. "Your lovely wife home?"

"Brenda!" Clem yelled out, climbing upon the porch with hat in hand to greet Ginny. "I'm Clem. Brenda's husband." He was a pleasant man of medium height with dark brown hair and dark eyes. He wore a plaid shirt with rolled-up sleeves and overalls.

"This is Miss McBride, Clem. All the way from . . ." He looked at Ginny and continued. "I never did find out where you're from, Miss McBride."

"Richmond, Virginia."

The screen door opened and Brenda stood in the frame, as lovely as the day Matt met her. "Hello. I'm Brenda. Come on in Happy, and bring your guest with you."

"Thank you," Ginny returned. "I'm Ginny McBride . . ."

"From Virginia," Brenda continued with a slow and determined unpleasantness. "Yes, I heard you."

"I'll be gettin' back to m'office, Clem, Mz Brenda, Miss McBride." Happy doffed his hat and hopped back into the wagon. Driving off, he said, "Nice to have met you." And then quickly added, "Say. I'll be headin' fer home in 'bout an hour. Should I swing by and take you back to the hotel, miss?"

"Thank you, Sheriff. That would be very kind of you." Ginny returned and walked cautiously into the house behind Brenda. Clem followed.

"So! What brings you to Nacogdoches, Miss McBride?" Brenda asked in a very curious and subtle manner.

"Do you have something cool to drink?" Ginny asked, removing her cape. She immediately sensed a little hostility in Brenda's tone of voice and knew it would be a battle of wits between the two of them about Matt. "It's been a long trip, and I didn't stop in town for a drink."

"Heavens. Where's my manners?" Brenda asked as she turned and walked into the kitchen. "Make her comfortable, Clem and I'll bring out some lemonade." She stopped, looked back and, almost indignantly, catching herself as she asked, "Hungry? We'll be having supper soon."

"No. Just thirsty." Ginny made herself comfortable with the help of Clem to sit her down in a comfortable stuffed chair in the front room. She looked around the room at the photos on the table and wall as if looking for Matt's picture.

"You've a lovely home."

"Thank you," Clem answered as he sat on the divan opposite Ginny. "Brenda's work. I do the farmin'. Got some cattle, few horses, a roost of chickens and three hogs."

A black Labrador Retriever came in the kitchen door and plopped his head on Clem's lap, and a Border Collie quickly followed suit. Taking hold of them, Clem shooed them out the front door. "And a couple of dogs with no manners."

He returned in time to help Brenda with the lemonade. After Brenda sat in her favorite rocker, Clem sat and stared at Ginny.

Clem sensed the feminine atmosphere and quickly excused himself outside to finish his evening chores. He called to his dogs, "Come on Coot and Holler."

"I'm happy you came," Brenda said, still showing her curiosity while joining Ginny in a drink.

"I've been looking for this moment for some time," Ginny informed her as she quenched her thirst with the lemonade. She smiled and placed the glass down on the end table next to her. "I understand you knew Matt Jorgensen."

"Matt?" Brenda countered. "Matt Jorgensen?"

"Yes."

"Do you know Matt?" Brenda asked, pretentiously.

"For a long time. I'm looking for him."

"Yes. We know Matt. But . . . "she added, "he's not here."

"I figured. The Reverend Bunting in Nashville informed me that he was heading for Richmond. That's where I'm from."

"I see. But you're here in Texas."

"It's a start. I haven't seen him since before the war."

"He and my brother Steve stopped by here on their way to see the Reverend. May I ask. Why the interest in Matt?

"*Ginny*. Of course. He mentioned you many times. And of course all throughout Steve's letters." Brenda rose from her chair and shook hands with Ginny. "You were the reason he had a hard time just getting to know me." She grinned and almost laughed. "You see, Steve tried to match make us, but never succeeded."

As Ginny stood and shook hands with Brenda, she looked her over carefully and said, "I don't know why. You are a very pretty . . . no, no. You're a beautiful lady. If I'm allowed to say so."

"I always thought so. I always believe it is the duty as a wife and schoolteacher, I should pride myself to look my best.

"Clem and I met during the war. Fell in love and got married."

A bushy-hair boy toddled in from outside through the kitchen and into the front room.

"Well, good afternoon, Junior," Brenda acknowledged him as she beckoned with her hand for him to come to her. "Are you finished with your chore?"

"Yes, mother," he answered politely.

Ginny watched with amazement and wonderment. "Your son?"

"Yes. Junior. Say hello to Miss McBride, Junior," Brenda said, gently coaxing him.

"Hello, Junior. I'm Ginny McBride."

Junior accepted Ginny's hand, rubbed his eyes and went back to Brenda.

"Would you like to run back outside, son?" She wiped his eyes with her handkerchief and escorted him to the door, and then returned to her chair to continue their conversation.

"He's three, or better yet, three-and-a-half, as he says." She looked at Ginny's surprised face.

Ginny was taken by surprise and answered, "I did have a question or two. Reverend Bunting told me you had visited Matt at the end of the war."

"The thought was in Ginny's mind that Junior could possibly be Matt's son."

"Let me assure you, Ginny. I was somewhat in love with Matt and missed him sorely during the war. When I met him in Georgia, we showed affection for each other; but that was all. I knew it. His love for you kept us from going any further."

"He tell you that?" Ginny asked.

"He didn't have to. I just knew. We spent several days together in Georgia. Took walks. Talked a lot. I could tell his mind was still on you. Same as it was here in Texas. But, never a letter. No kind of response."

"So . . . how did you and Clem meet?"

"Now, *that* you may not believe." Brenda finally felt at ease, now that she felt she had control of the conversation. She loved to tell the story and took pride in doing so. She opened up. "But I'll tell you. He and his brother came here towards the end of the war. Dirty, filthy, and hungry. I was intimidated by their appearances. I was definitely concered for my safety, even though they were weak and exhausted."

"What happened?"

"You can see. We're both alive. They passed out because of starvation and dehydration. I fed them and got them cleaned up a bit. Clem's brother was the worst. He didn't care for me. Fought Clem over me."

"He wanted to . . .?"

"Yep. Afraid so. Clem stopped him and chased him off. They left and Clem went back to serve his duty. And then he returned. He wrote to me on an almost weekly basis. That's when I knew he truly loved me as Matt never could.

"When Clem returned, he stayed here and tended to the manly chores of the farm, with my permission. After a short courtship, we fell in love and got married. Junior came along and that's that."

"Have you seen Matt since? Ginny asked, finishing her lemonade.

"My brother and Matt stopped by before they went to see Reverend Bunting. That was their chaplain during the war."

"And now?"

"I got a post from Steve saying they were headed for Richmond. I got a package for Junior from him shortly after that. It was postmarked *Tennessee*. So who knows where he's at by now. It was a small pair of walking shoes that Steve had made for his nephew. "

Ginny rose and said, "Well, I guess you've answered all my questions."

"I trust they've been good answers, and that I've helped you some."

"You have," Ginny replied, pulling her cape around her shoulders.

"May I say something, Ginny?"

Ginny stopped, looked at Brenda and answered her. "Yes. By all means."

"I can see you are in love with him."

Ginny smiled and then answered her, "You bet I am. More than you'll ever know."

"You're quite a lucky woman, Miss McBride," Brenda said.

The two ladies exchanged smiles, shook hands and parted company as Happy came driving up to the porch and offered to drive her back to the hotel.

Brenda waved to them as she watched the wagon drive away.

Bouncing on the front seat of the buckboard, holding tight to her umbrella, Ginny threw her mind to the wind. *I'm gonna find you after all, Matt.*

CHAPTER 42

ESCAPE FROM JESSE'S GANG

9 December 1867

Matt and Steve saddled their horses and led them out of the livery stable before the sun came up the next morning with Carol walking by their sides.

"Sorry to get you up so early, Carol," Matt apologized.

"It's good thet you did, Matt," she returned, putting a package in Matt's hand. "Jesse would never let you go."

"I feel uncomfortable leavin' him, but there's nothin' else we can do. He's set in his way and we ain't a goin' to change him none."

"I've packed you boys a nice meal inside your saddle bags," Carol informed them. "You're gonna be hungry."

Matt turned and looked into her hazel eyes and said, "Kinda reminiscent of some time ago when the war began and we were in Nacogdoches."

"Texas?" Carol asked as she put her arm around Matt's waist.

"Yep. Gonna miss ya, kid." He pulled her into himself and kissed her hard on the lips.

Steve watched as the moment lingered. He finally pulled the brim down on his hat and climbed into his saddle. "Sun's comin' up over the horizon, friend."

Matt and Carol broke and he could see the tears swell in her eyes.

"I wish you didn't have to go." she said weakly, letting Matt wipe the tears from her eyes.

"It's either thet or become an outlaw. We're not cut out to be outlaws."

"Will you ever come back?"

Matt gave her another hug, broke away and smiled at her. He turned and climbed aboard Skeeter; bent down again and kissed her one more time. "I'll stay in touch."

"I'll be married."

"Who to?" Matt asked whimsically as he turned Skeeter away from the sunrise.

"I'll find someone. Don't cha worry none."

"Don't name the first one *Junior* when you do." He spurred Skeeter and the two men rode away.

Keeping his eyes on the horizon as the two men rode westward towards Waco, Matt asked Steve about his infatuation with May Shirley. "Did you sleep with her?"

"Well, no. But, she's beautiful, Matt. I fell in love with her."

"You fell in love . . .? Pal, what could you offer her? Thet Reed fella at least had good taste for horse flesh, and she loves horses."

Matt pulled Skeeter into an easy walk and then took out his makings and rolled himself a cigarette, lit it and watched the smoke drift out onto the prairie as the sun came up.

Steve looked out onto the prairie as if in deep thought. After a moment, he answered, "She's sure pretty. But, I guess you're right." Then in added thought, he said, "You know. We coulda been sittin' mighty pretty right about now, had we joined up with Jesse."

Matt said nothing but showed that he enjoyed his moment of smoking a cigarette.

"Ever think we might go back and join up with them? It'd make sense. You and Carol. And maybe, maybe . . ."

"You and May. Friend, Reed is gonna live to be a grandpa. So get it out of your head."

"Ok. Ok. But maybe, you might think, we could share some wealth like Jesse some day? He got to be a rich man over night, so to speak.

"Sixty thousand dollars! Whewee! Sure beats a lot of dusty trails, not to mention running a ranch and keeping it from rustlers, thieves and cutthroats. You thinkin' about joinin' up with them, Matt? Maybe? Some time down the road?"

Matt looked sternly towards Steve, took his cigarette and flicked it to the wind. Watching it sail out into the wind, he answered, "Not on your life, friend. Not on your life. This life can't be beat." Then he looked towards the west in the direction of the Mitchell ranch, still a good long ride, kicked his spurs into Skeeter's side and said, "Do what you like, friend. As for me, I'm headed for Waco." He spurred Skeeter forward into an easy gait.

"Thet's jest what I wanted to hear you say. Yahoo!" And the two saddle buddies rode west towards Waco where a ranch and peaceful dreams awaited them.

CHAPTER 43

THE BRAZOS RIVER BAR M RANCH

<u>14 January 1868</u>

The day was rather cool but the air was clean and refreshing for two weary ex-Confederate soldiers when Matt and Steve rode up weary to the Brazos River Bar M Ranch.

The owner was Ted Mitchell, an ex-general in the Eighth Texas Cavalry of the Confederacy, known as *Terry's Texas Rangers*. He was seeking the office of governor of Texas when he was severely wounded in the Civil War, losing his right arm. With his career path changed, he was left to be a rancher. Not just any rancher; his dream was to own the largest spread in Texas. In order to do this, he needed the right people doing the right jobs.

He was still pretty good with a gun as a southpaw, but not nearly fast enough. Now he had called upon two of his officers who fought under his command in the Eighth; Lieutenants Matt Jorgensen and Steve Andrews.

The ranch had seen the ravages of the war with the buildings partially ruined by fire, and the ground molested by rustlers, wagons and range free cattle. Since General Mitchell returned home, his help and that of neighbors turned the house back into its original style.

The ranch house was a two-story Victorian with a picket fence completely surrounding it. To the back, and away from the river, stood another house; smaller but of the same style. It had remained in better shape than that of the first building; therefore it required less effort to restore it. This was for the ranch foreman and some of his key ranch hands. Around the yard were the other wranglers' bunkhouse, summer kitchen, the cook shack, a few out houses and a barn. These buildings had lain in various states of disarray but were for the most part in fair condition now, needing slight mending or a coat of paint here and there.

The busted corral posts that once stood in the midst of a large land mass with nothing around it for miles except ranch land had been repaired. The land was rich with good topsoil for grazing and farming, though few farmers were around. Cotton farming was now gaining popularity, especially around the river. Still, the rolling hills in Texas were meant mostly for cattle. A few clouds speckled the beautiful blue sky and oak trees dotted the prairie. The land was a perfect Western portrait except for the few broken pieces. Before the war, the Brazos River Bar M Ranch had thousands of head of longhorn roaming the hills with a couple dozen cowboys keeping them together.

Matt and Steve were volunteers in *Terry's Texas Rangers*. As cavalrymen, they furnished their own Colt revolvers, carbines, and Bowie knives. The regiment furnished the horses. Mitchell knew of their prowess with weapons and horses. He knew these men, above any and all else, could salvage his ranch and make possible his dream.

The Brazos River Bar M Ranch was General Mitchell's pride and treasure to be a legacy he would hand down to his children and on to theirs in time. His only son, Seth, was his first born and rightful heir. But it was his daughter, Leisha who, in Mitchell's eyes, should become heir to it along with his niece, Jamie. Both she and Leisha grew up to know as much about horses and cattle as any ranch hand.

Leisha was the General's daughter, a beautiful lady slightly under eighteen. She had a good figure and a full head of blond hair that hung down her back. She also had a good sense of responsibility ingrained in her by her parents, but mostly by her mother, a pioneer woman of the plains.

During the war, her mother had held onto the plantation as well as she could without the general's presence. Her servants were already working for wages and stayed with her, but were working less and less each day, hoping to see the Blue Coats some day soon.

Just before the war ended, the general's two-year old niece, Jamie, came to live with them after her mother died of complications resulting from a vain attempt at childbirth on her own. Her father, the general's brother, had been killed in the war.

Jamie was a cute little thing with long brown hair that she usually kept stuck inside her Stetson; and blue eyes that made her the darling of the ranch and a pudgy face. She still carried a full belly to match her face. She tried as she could to stay away from fat food, but she loved her beef and potatoes. Some day, she knew she would have to make the sacrifice and bear down on her diet to make herself look more like her cousin Leisha.

General Mitchell and his wife Emily had cared for Jaimie as their own daughter, and Leisha treated her as a sister. Jaimie was now a striking young lady going on fourteen. Emily died from a horse fall a year after the general retired from the war.

Mitchell and his girls walked out onto the porch and watched the two riders as they rode up and stopped at the end of the porch.

"General Mitchell?" Matt called out as he removed his hat and waved it as a tip in the presence of the girls.

Mitchell had a small wooden pipe in his mouth, which he removed as he answered Matt. "Captains. You've made it. All the way from . . .?"

"Virginia, sir," Steve answered, waving his hat to the ladies, also.

"Well, dismount troopers and come on in."

Matt and Steve alit from their horses, tied them to the hitching rail and followed Mitchell and the ladies into the house.

"Quite a good looking ranch," Matt said as he walked into the house.

"You've a keen sense of observation, Captain," Leisha answered, leading the gentlemen down the hallway and towards the front room which sat to the right. "It took more than a year to get it back into shape. A lot of barn raisings, if you know what I mean."

"My daughter Leisha and my niece Jamie, gentlemen," Mitchell introduced them. "The one who answered you is *Leisha.*"

"Ladies," Matt recognized them.

"Leisha. Jamie. These are the gentlemen I've been talking to you about. Matt Jorgensen."

Matt smiled at the ladies.

"And Steve Andrews," Mitchell continued.

Steve smiled and was quickly enamored with Leisha.

Leisha recognized the warmth in Steve's demeanor. Jamie had little to say and kept quiet for the moment with a timid smile on her face.

The men were escorted to the front room where they were met by Mitchell's wife, Emily who waited in the front room.

"Matt. Steve. This is my lovely wife, Emily."

Emily was a beautiful woman in her late forties, shapely with light blond hair and blue eyes. She looked as if she could also be Jamie's mother; her sister who had passed away.

"Mr. Jorgensen," Emily said, recognizing her guests. "Mr. Andrews. I'm charmed. Please. Welcome to our humble abode."

"Thank you, ma'am," Matt returned.

"Yes, ma'am," Steve added with a smile.

A black woman entered and stood at the front room doorway.

"Yes, Laomi," Mitchell addressed her.

"I can take your hats, gentlemen," she said as she held out her arms.

Steve and Matt gave them to Jamie who gave them in turn to Laomi.

"I'm almost ready for dinner, Mistah and Misses Mitchell," Laomi announced, curtsied and went back to the kitchen with the gentlemen's hats.

Emily sat on an over-stuffed divan while the men took straight-back chairs and sat down. As the girls left for the kitchen, Mitchell stood by the fireplace mantel, relit his pipe and talked straight to the men.

"Well, gentlemen. You've seen the ranch."

"Parts of it," Matt answered, looking around at the spacious front room

"At least we have a roof over our heads. We patched that up the first day. We've done the rest in the last year. Slow work."

"And your neighbors helped?"

"The Davidson's. The Roger's. And the Freidman's." Mitchell brought up names of the nearby ranchers.

"But not the McDaniel's," Leisha added as she and Jaimie brought some lemonade and cookies on a tray for the everyone. "Gentlemen. You must be tired and hungry. Our cook is fixing us up something. In the meantime, we thought you'd like some refreshments."

Jaimie deliberately served Steve as if to say, *this one is mine.* Leisha showed no favoritism, but saw a gleam in Matt's eye that pleased her.

"Oh, yes. The McDaniel's. It seems all of them have had as much if not more damage to their ranches than we have. We helped put each other's main ranch houses and barns together. Ours was last. We just need another corral."

"What about the McDaniel's?" Matt asked. "It seemed to be important to Miss Leisha's mind."

"Oh. Nothing really," Mitchell answered, blowing smoke into the air. "It is just too bad. Mr. McDaniel is a proud man. Maybe a little too proud.

"His ranch isn't as large as mine, but it too was devastated. He wouldn't accept help from anyone. And the ranchers around here offered to help him several times. He refused. He was really hurt about the war. His ranch was hurt worse than any of the rest of ours. But his pride has turned into jealousy, and jealousy into hate."

"Where is he now?" Matt asked, looking out at the vastness of the Bar M Ranch. "Maybe Steve and I could ride out and have a talk with him."

Mitch looked at Matt and slowly answered him. "No use. Let him stew for awhile and maybe later you and Steve can talk with him."

"What about his wife?" Steve asked.

"She's a pretty woman in her late forties; my age I suppose. She's a right pretty woman." His eyes turned towards the prairie. "Her face is slightly rough, but tanned gracefully by the Texas sun. Her eyes are a grayish blue, but one could tell the spark of youth still remains. Her hair is auburn; and I know this even though she keeps it tucked tight under her Stetson. She dresses meagerly but neatly, not a hole or a wrinkle in her clothes. One could readily tell she was a proud woman"

Matt smiled and looked over at Steve and smiled.

"Now I know what you boys are thinking, but you're wrong. She's a close friend of Emily's here."

Emily Mitchell walked over to Mitch and put her arm around his waist. She had heard the conversation.

"Nellie is sweet as honey. We all love her. Mitch was just describing what we all see in her. Nothing more. Nothing less."

"Sorry, Mrs. Mitchell," Matt apologized.

"No need to, boys," Mitch responded. "If you ever saw her, you'd describe her the same way."

"But," Emily chimed in. "She's a bearcat when she wants to be. Tells' it like it is. That's another reason we like her so much." And then she added, "Even if she is married to that . . ."

"Now, Emily," Mitch comforted her. "Norman will come down off his high horse one of these days and be one of us again."

"Well, I certainly hope so. He makes me so mad at times. Stubborn as a mule, he is."

"So, we've had a few barn raisin's, and fence mendin', and such," Emily added. "She didn't come over. Don't ask why."

"Once we finish building another corral," Mitch continued, "then we'll need stock. We have some wranglers that signed on with us, and my son Seth is learning the ropes. He's still green behind the ears, though."

"You'll meet him," Emily interjected. "I saw him riding towards home when the two of you rode up."

Seth was a young man, full of energy and quick to do anything that needed to be done. He was a sandy-haired youth with blue eyes and stood five-ten. He was slow on learning the ropes of being a leader, and chose instead to being a wrangler. He was sixteen, friendly demeanor and freckles to boot. It seemed that most of the time he appeared to be cocky as if it were a way to hide his ineptitude of being a good wrangler. He needed someone to show him the ropes. Mitchell hoped it would come from these men who sat before him

"Well, gentlemen," Mitchell continued. "Will you help us?"

"We're here, General," Matt answered with a smile and a gleam at Leisha.

"First of all, forget titles. I'm Mitch to you."

"And I'm Matt," Matt replied.

"And I guess you can call me Steve," Steve answered.

"You're both fast guns and have good horses. Either of you know cattle?"

"I was foreman for a ranch while I was a deputy in Nacogdoches," Steve answered. "It wasn't a big ranch. Five hundred head; give or take."

"And you, Matt?"

"Nope. Don't want anything to do with cows. No, sir."

"He grew up on a ranch in Wyoming, Mitch," Steve came back. "His father was tough as nails and he never wanted to be like his father. You kinda understand?"

"That's all right, son," Mitchell replied, packing his pipe again. "I can use you, Steve, to hire and train wranglers. Think you can do it?"

Steve's eyes widened and he gulped. "How many?"

"Well, I'm going to need ten times the number of cows that you've been used to. Say five thousand head to start with and get ready for next Spring. That means we'll need a couple dozen cowhands, wranglers and all."

"It's a tall order. Where do you suppose I can find cowhands?"

Mitchell lit his pipe and looked back at Steve from the mantle where he stood. "Waco. There's plenty of men there with experience. Hire what you need. Train them and use them. Get rid of the ones you can't use."

"He can do it, Mitch," Matt interrupted.

"And you, Matt," Mitch returned, pointing his pipe in Matt's direction.

Leisha stood beside Matt and watched Mitch as he dictated to Matt. From the side, she kept a keen watch on Matt's expression.

"You're the gunfighter that I see you destined to be. Go with Steve and hire some gunslingers."

"You're telling me that you need gunmen to keep this ranch going?" Matt asked. He stood up and walked around the room. "And you want to hire out my gun?"

"I'm here to hire out both of your guns," Mitch answered. "Steve will handle the stock with my son, Seth. You will handle the gunfighters to keep the ranch from being taken over by cattle rustlers and such."

He looked down at where his right hand used to be and continued. "I wish to God I didn't need either of you."

Matt watched the anguish that built up in Mitchell's face, and he knew he had to be Mitchell's right hand.

They walked outside to continue their conversation so that Mitch could show Matt more of the ranch. As they walked on, Mitch pointed to a man sitting on the opera seat of the corral.

"Got a surprise for you, Matt. Recognize him?" Mitch pointed to the man.

When they neared him, Matt recognized him as Thatcher McTavett; a sergeant from his command in Terry's Texas Rangers during the Civil War.

"Sergeant!" Matt called out.

Thatcher hopped down and shook hands with Matt.

"Captain," Thatcher greeted Matt. "I saw you and Steve ride up. Could hardly wait to see ya again."

"Good seein' ya, mister," Matt came back. "You're here with the General?"

"Yep. He said he needed a gun, and I offered him mine. But to tell you the truth, I'm the one thet told him to get you two. Hello, Steve."

"Thatch!" Steve greeted him.

"Thatcher will be your right hand man, Matt, next to Steve. I figure with the two of you as guns, and Steve and Seth with the cattle, I can bring some semblance of a ranch back together again."

"Have you had any trouble, yet?" Matt asked.

"We had five thousand head. We're down to two hundred, maybe more, counting the ones on the fringes." Mitch knocked out the ashes from his pipe on the heel of his boot. He turned and looked at the men. "I'spect there are thousands out on the open range."

"I'd best get back to my chores, Matt. Steve." Thatcher said. "See ya later."

The two cowboys returned their comments with a wave of their hands.

"Thousands?" Steve repeated with much enthusiasm. "Let's go get 'em!"

"Not so easy, Steve," the General interrupted his enthusiasm. "Open range means just that; *open range*. The ranches around us have been out there . . ."

"And?" Steve asked.

"Rustlers."

"Rustlers?"

"Yep. They wait until the ranchers gather the cattle together then ride down on them and take them away."

"Are the cattle marked?" Steve asked, taking his makings and rolling himself a cigarette.

"They're branded every day, but that doesn't stop rustlers. They'll move them and put their brand over them so neatly that it'd defy you to tell their cattle from ours; the *Bar M.*"

"So what do we do?"

Matt looked on with much interest but waited out the conversation to see where Mitch was taking them.

"Our ranchers around here have scarce hands to tackle them. Most of them would rather run than shoot it out. That's why I need you two men. Will you help me?"

Matt and Steve looked at each other. And then Matt said, "We haven't talked about pay, Mitch."

Leisha turned around and stomped back inside the house with Jamie following her. "Harrumphed!" is what the men heard her say as she rounded the corner.

"I can't pay much, Matt," Mitch continued. "But I figure this time next year we'll see some good money."

"Of course, you'll both live in the foreman's house just beyond the river there; it's in good shape with plenty of room. You'll join us in the main house for dinner each evening. I do have a cache. And more later when the stock comes in and we sell the cattle. And, like Thatcher said, much of what you do now will depend on how rich we become a year from now."

The two men looked at each other. Matt drew his Colt, spun it and returned it to the holster. Steve grabbed a hold of

Matt's shoulder, turned him away from Mitchell and whispered to him.

"It's a job."

Matt rubbed his chin.

"Matt. We've looked all over for Ginny. Let's give it a rest for a while and live a little. My backbone is aching and I'm yearning for a good piece of steak. And to tell you the truth; I kinda like this place."

Then the two of them smelled the aroma of steak cooking from the house. They looked at each other and smiled.

Matt replied, "Yep. It's a job."

The two men turned and faced Mitchell and threw out their hands. "You've got us, Mitch. We rode all this way to help you. When do we start?"

"You've already started."

From the back porch came the sound of a dinner bell. "Dinner's on! Come and get it!"

And come and get it they did. Emily led the gentlemen to the kitchen where Matt pulled out the chair for her to sit.

Seth bounced into the kitchen from the back door, letting it slam behind him. "Dinner?" he asked. He'd been washing up out on the porch, his hair still damp and combed neatly. He placed his hat on a nail beside the door and unrolled his sleeves as he walked in. He took a chair and sat at the table.

When Seth came into the dining room, Mitch introduced them.

"Seth. This is Matt Jorgensen and Steve Andrews. They are ex-officers from my company and, like Thatcher, they've come to help us."

"The fast guns you talked about, pa? Nice meeting you, gentlemen." He took his knife and stabbed himself a slice of beef from the platter as it was set down by the black cook.

"We're going to need your help, Seth," Steve suggested "I've got to hire some drovers and wranglers."

"Yeah. Pa told me. I've been waiting to help out. I want to learn this business so some day I can take charge."

Steve looked at Seth and felt good about his honest talk, that here was a young man who just might want to learn the business, and he could help him.

Leisha and Jamie stared at the four men while the cook looked over his shoulder. The men smiled and then Steve said, "I'm starved. Let's eat!"

"Ahem!" Mitch cleared his throat as he looked at Emily. "Excuse me, gentlemen. Seth." He gave a look of disdain over at Seth, watching him put a piece of meat on his plate. "It's our custom to always say grace before the meals." And with that he and Emily and those gathered around bowed their heads as he asked a short, but reverent prayer, blessing the meal.

It was a good start for the men, and the ladies were pleased.

CHAPTER 44

A CATTLE BUYER

4 April 1868

Steve sat at one of the back tables in the Steer Horn Saloon in Waco for three days, talking with men needing jobs when Matt rode up and dismounted out front. Steve caught Matt's eye as he sauntered toward the back.

"How's it coming, friend?" Matt asked, pulling out a chair and straddling it with his long legs.

"Got a dozen; more or less. They'll be ready to ride come mornin'" He took out a cigar and offered it to Matt. Taking a second one, he accepted Matt's lit match to light up. "You gonna hang around?"

"Thought about it." He looked around for a game and found one at the opposite side of the room. "Can we catch some fun while we're here?"

Steve picked up the bottle of whisky on his table and led Matt over to the table. "They've been playing for a while. Let's see what they've got."

Once at the table, Matt introduced them to the players. "I'm Matt Jorgensen and this is . . . "

"Yeah," came the reply from the dealer. "He's Steve Andrews. "He's in to us for a few pots. There's two empty chairs. Sit in if you care. Name's Jack Barton from San Antonio here to buy some cattle."

Matt's cars lit up. "Buy some cattle? Hmm. This game might get interesting. You know about this, pal?" Matt asked Steve as the two men joined in the game of chance.

"Yep. Told him about the General."

"I'll be out in the morning," Jack informed Matt.

"How many head you lookin' for?" Matt asked, placing the cigar between his teeth as he watched Jack deal.

307

"At least two thousand for now. Steve tells me you have less."

"Yeah. How long you gonna be in town?"

"Figure until I get my cattle." He finished the deal and looked at the players' faces. Matt and Steve made it a five-party game.

"I'm pat," Matt came back.

Jack filled the hands of the other players and continued the conversation. "You thinkin' you might be able to come up with more?"

"You thinkin' about callin' my hand?" Matt asked with a smile.

The raise was up to ten dollars and the dealer called Matt.

"Four aces!" Matt answered. Turning the cards over, he raked in the pot.

The pot came to Matt four times in a row while they continued their conversation over cattle. "You know, Jack. For a card player, you ain't."

Jack smiled. "I know it. Just like the game for what it is. I'm a buyer. I also have a ranch, but I'm buying for three of us up in San Antone." Then he smiled broader and added, "Give me time. I'll catch up."

Jack pulled around the inn the next morning in a black carriage and joined Matt and Steve in a ride to the Bar M Ranch. When they reached the ranch, they were met by Seth at the gate who rode back to the ranch house with them to meet Seth's dad, General Mitchell.

"This is Jack Baron, Seth. Jack.

The General's son, Seth Mitchell."

"Good to know you Seth. You're the son. I thought *you* were the foreman, Steve."

"I am. Seth here is learnin' the ropes, so to speak."

Mitch met the three men from the porch as they approached the house.

"Got a buyer for ya, Mitch," Steve yelled out. "Jack Barton. This is the general, Jack."

Jack stepped down from the carriage, tied the reins on the hitching rail, and walked up to the porch where he shook hands with Mitch. "Good to know you, General."

Bessie, Mitch's house Negro, walked out with a tray of lemonade.

"Gentlemen. Make yourselves comfortable and let's do some horse trading."

The men continued their discussion about cattle for the next hour when Mitch led them out to the corral where they carried on their talk. "Got two hundred now."

"I need at least two thousand." Jack was disappointed at feeling let down as to why they got him out to the Bar M. "Any other ranches close by that can make up the rest?" Jack asked, looking around the terrain of the large Bar M Ranch.

"I'll pull in at least four hundred from three other ranchers. There's the Davidson's, the Roger's ranch, and the Friedman's. I know they'd be glad to ride along." Mitch answered, spreading his left arm out to indicate ranchers beyond the horizon. "That's six hundred."

"Yep. I can count," Jack came back. "But I need two thousand. Any ideas?"

"I have, Jack." Steve stepped up on the opera seat of the corral. "I just hired a dozen men."

"And . . . ?" Jack returned. "How's that make me happy?"

"Well, sir, there're strays out there. We can round them up and hopefully have the rest for you . . . say within ten days? Give or take."

"I've got the time, Steve," Jack explained, spreading a grin from ear to ear. "Are you sure you can deliver?"

Mitch looked over at Steve and gave a strong look of concern. Then he affirmed, "If Steve says he can do it; he can do it."

Matt held back a laugh, broke out his makings and rolled himself a cigarette. He said nothing.

"Well, gentlemen," Jack continued, walking back to the carriage. "I'll give you two weeks. I'll be in Waco. Got some earnings to catch up on. If you know what I mean. You know where to reach me."

As Jack's carriage drove over the ridge, the three men headed for the ranch house.

"How're you going to do it, Steve?" Mitch asked, rubbing his chin as he sat down in a chair on the porch. "Just how in the world are you going to get a thousand head within two weeks?"

"Yeah!" Matt joined in. "This I've gotta hear."

"You know, Matt. I showed you back in town. I done hired a dozen men."

"And . . .?" Matt asked, looking around. "Where are they?"

"They promised to show up today, Matt. They will."

At the same time, riders appeared on the ridge riding towards the ranch.

"He might be right, Mitch," Matt said, pointing with his cigarette at the riders.

"Well, I'll be!" Mitch exclaimed excitedly. "Seth. Ride to meet those men."

While Seth rode out towards the riders, Mitch looked over at Matt and Steve and said, "Here's where you men earn your pay,"

"How's thet?"

"Weed them out. If there's one in the crowd that's not fit to join us, make it known. We can only afford top ranch hands. And, fellas, we want only men who know how to use their guns and won't be afraid to use them in a fight."

The message was clear to the two men as to what Mitch wanted. They walked over to the corral to meet the men as they rode in.

Steve greeted the men as they rode up to the corral. "Welcome to the Bar M Ranch. Tie up your horses."

Once the men had settled in, Steve herded them into the corral and talked with them as he had done many times over to the troops of Terry's Texas Rangers. "This is Matt Jorgensen. He has a few words to talk over with ya." He looked at Thatcher and smiled.

"I won't take long. My job is to make sure this ranch is protected from encroachers and outlaws. Sometimes one or two will hire on under the guise of being ranch hands. If you fall under that description, it's best you let me know now and we'll have no hard feelings. Else, if I find out later, I'll come down on you like an anvil to an ant. Get my drift?"

"Who are ya?" one of the men yelled out, sucking on a straw. He was a tall man, heavier than Matt, and wore his hat low over his eyes.

"I'm your best friend when you need me," Matt answered with his hand on the butt of his .45. "I'm your worst enemy when you cross my path."

"Ya tryin' to say you're a fast gun or sumptin'?" a burly man standing next to the first man asked. He was a mean-looking cuss, reminiscent of a hog gobbling up his slop with large jowls.

"Fists or guns. Makes no difference." Matt answered.

"Let's see how fast ya are, mister," the first man suggested.

"Don't have to, son," Matt replied, walking over to him. When he got within two feet of the man, Matt planted his fist across the man's jaw, sending him to the dirt.

When the man turned over and went for his gun, Matt kicked it out of his hand. "Get on your horse and head out, mister!"

"You had no right to hit me," the man yelled back at Matt as he rose from the dirt. "I jest called you out to see how fast you were."

"And I said, no need. When I have to draw, I do it for one reason. I don't see the need right now. Do I?"

The burly man stepped up and planted his fist across Matt's back, knocking him off his feet before Thatcher had a chance to stop him. Matt rolled over, brought his legs under the man and brought him to the ground. Rising, Matt picked the man up by his coat collar and brought his right hand across his mouth, bringing blood

Steve and Thatcher watched that no other man got into the ruckus, while the first man stayed out of the way of Matt.

The burly man brought his fist towards Matt with a violent swing and missed him as Matt moved out of its way. Matt's fist came fast into the man's stomach, causing him to cough up part of his breakfast. He bent low, caught his breath, turned and came back to Matt with his fist to Matt's face, only to miss again. It gave Matt the opportunity to take a hold of his jacket collar and shove his head against a corral post. The man went down for the count.

"Who's next?" Matt asked, picking up his hat that fell to the ground during the fight. He dusted it off on his pants and put it back on his head.

"Well, I apologize, Mr. Jorgensen," the first man admitted. "Give me a chance and I'll do right by ya."

"Pick up your buddy and ride outta here!" Matt ordered.

The two men licked their wounds, mounted their horses and rode out while the rest of the men continued to stare at Matt, wondering what he was going to do next.

"Well? I asked you. Now's the time to find out if you want to ride for the Bar M or not. Evidently that pair of galoots didn't want a job bad enough."

"They were bad ones in town, Mr. Jorgensen," a red-headed Irishman informed him. "I'm Tom O'Riley. I'm a good man with a rope and I can use me fists when I have ta. Not too fast with the gun, but ain't afraid to use it when I have ta."

"I'm Phil Johnson, Mr. Jorgensen," a tall and lanky man in his twenties spoke up. "I need the job. I jest got married."

"We all need the jobs, Mr. Jorgensen," another man spoke up from the line up. "I'm Todd Harrison. Abilene. I fought for the South. I heard you two were with Terry's Texas Rangers. Thet's why I'm here."

Matt and Steve looked at each other as each man introduced himself to them. When the last man, the eleventh one, was finished telling briefly of his past experiences, Matt said to Steve, "My job's done. They can be your men if ya want 'em."

Steve looked at the men and said with excitement, "O.K. You're all hired. Phil. Go get your woman and bring her in. Any one else married?"

"I were. Twice", Tom answered. No more. No sirree."

The men laughed together and Seth headed them to the bunk house while Matt and Steve walked away towards the ranch house.

"Two weeks, pal," Matt said, rolling a cigarette. "Two weeks."

The next morning, Matt and Thatcher rode out to the other three ranches and got the commitments from them to have their drovers round up with them. It was up to Steve and Seth to work with the ranchers, getting them ready for the roundup.

Two days later, fourteen men from the Bar M Ranch rode with twenty-two others from the other three ranches. Steve and Seth led them out towards their first encounter with cattle on the open range.

On the twelfth day, Matt, Mitch, Thatcher and the girls watched as the men brought their first fruits over the ridge. It was a beautiful sight for them to see as they opened up the corral gate to welcome them in.

"We've got more'n a thousand," Steve yelled out to Matt and Mitch as they stood at the gate. "Yee haw!"

But, unbeknown to them, behind the ranch house on the horizon sat some forty plus men ready to ride down on them. Each one was an expert with his pistol and not afraid to use it for good wages. They were rustlers; predators for the Bar M herd.

CHAPTER 45

RUSTLERS AND JESSE

The drovers pushed the herd towards the corral with the loudest whooping, yelling and whip-cracking heard on the ranch since it first began. Mitch stood on the porch and watched the men bring the cattle into the valley..

Then, a sound of guns popping from a distance sent a chill inside him as he turned and saw the rustlers riding down on them. Matt quickly mounted his horse and rode towards the gun shots. He reined up and Steve joined him.

"Rustlers?" Steve asked.

"Afraid so, friend."

"What's our plan?"

"Get the cattle in the corral. I'll take some of the men and hold them off to give you time to close the corral gate. Then join us."

As Steve turned and started to ride to the corral, he stopped and turned to Matt. "We've got double trouble."

Matt turned to look at what Steve was talking about. What he saw was several of the ranch hands chasing the cattle away from the corral.

"I was afraid of this. They're in with the rustlers. Ride, Steve!" Matt ordered as the two men rode back to the cattle.

"What's happening?" Mitch yelled out as the two men rode past the ranch house.

"Rustlers, Mitch. Get inside!"

Matt looked at Leisha and Jaimie and ordered them. "Get Mitch inside! And stay there. Don't come out! Hear me?"

When they rode past the corral, several of the outlaw ranch hands left with part of the herd, firing their guns at the other ranch hands. Two and then three of the other Bar M ranch hands fell to their gun fire.

Matt returned the gunfire and fell one rustler off his horse, only to have another of the gang ride back and successfully pick him up.

"The cattle and dust are keeping us from returning their gun fire, Matt," Steve yelled out, covering his mouth with his bandana.

"I know." Matt rode into the corral and checked on the other men. "How're we doing?"

Thatcher rode up to Matt and answered. "One killed, Matt. Two others wounded. Here they come, Matt. They're too much for us."

"You gonna run?" Matt asked, looking towards the rustlers riding down on them.

"Hell, no! Never did with you before. I'll die right here with you if I have ta. I've seen battles worse than this before."

"Thanks. How about the rest of you?"

"We're here, Matt," Tom answered for the rest. "Nowhere else to go. Jest get us outa this."

"Don't know how, but keep shootin'."

"Matt!" Steve yelled out. "They're on top of us!"

Two more of the rustlers were felled by their bullets. Tom took a bullet in his shoulder and spun to the ground off his horse.

"Drive the cattle, Steve! Stampede them towards the rustlers!"

Steve looked at Matt and yelled back. "We're jest gonna give them to those bast . . .!"

"Do it, Steve! Jest do it!"

Steve knew somehow Matt's plan would work. He did not know how, but his years of riding with Matt gave him the confidence he needed to obey him.

"All right, men. You heard him. Take your slickers and drive 'em towards those rustlers. Yah hoo!"

Mitch stood by the door while Leisha and Jaimie stood by his side, holding onto him while watching the fight.

"Get my rifle, gal," Mitch ordered Leisha. "Get it now!"

Leisha obeyed and not only got his rifle, but one for herself and for Jaimie as well. Both girls were expert shooters.

"I'll stay here. You two girls cover the back door!" Mitch ordered as he stepped out onto the porch.

"Stay down, Pa!" Leisha yelled back as the two girls ran through the house towards the back.

The cattle spread out and ran amuck towards the rustlers with a fury of fiery hooves. The sky was darkened by the dust drummed up from over a thousand cattle on the dusty ground.

Another bunch of riders came up over the opposite ridge from the east and reined up. The leader looked intently towards the ranch, raised his Stetson and scratched his wavy hair. It was Jesse James.

"What do you make of it, Jesse?" Jim Reed asked as he sided Jesse.

"I don't rightly know. Looks like cattle running one way. A gang waitin' up for them . . . kinda' gettin' outta their way. Funniest thing!"

"What do we do?"

"Dang if I know."

"Looks to me like this heah ranch is being attacked by a bunch of rustlers, the way I see it," Cole Younger joined in.

"We mind our own business, Jesse?" Jim asked.

"Now, Jim. When did we ever mind our own business? Could be thet Matt and Steve are down there," Jesse suggested. "If so, we come to see them. Now, it appears to me thet if they were to get killed, we couldn't talk to 'em."

"But we came to kill 'em," Jim returned.

"In a fair fight, Jim. In a fair fight. Now thet there don't look like a fair fight. Do it to you, Cole?"

"You wanna go up agin some outlaws jest to save Matt's hide, Jesse?"

"Well. Let's jest say, I don't like the odds. Let's have some fun. O.K. guys. Let's ride!"

Like thunder, Jesse's gang rode down the slope towards the rustlers who were at this time attempting to stop the stampede. When they saw Matt, Steve and riders from other ranches, the rustlers stood their ground for a fierce battle. And then it happened. They witnessed Jesse's gang riding with guns blazing at them.

In the confusion, figuring they had the odds on their side, the rustlers from inside the ranch rode out to join them only to be met by the rustlers in a stalemate situation.

Matt and Steve rode towards the rustlers when they recognized Jesse and Cole riding to meet them.

"Jesse?" Matt yelled out.

The other ranch hands rode along with them, totaling over thirty men altogether, not counting Mitch who stood on the porch, waving his rifle in mid air; along with the girls in the back.

The rustlers kept firing aimlessly towards the approaching group, mistakenly thinking they still had the advantage; it being up-hill climb for them among stampeding cattle and the dust that filled the air.

The leader of the rustlers took careful aim at Jesse's horse, bringing it down hard, throwing Jesse to the ground. Jesse looked around and saw the cattle charging in his direction.

"Get me a horse somebody!" he yelled out, running in circles while the dust filled the air.

Matt rode hell-bent-for leather towards Jesse. He reined up, slipped his boot out of the stirrup, reached down and picked Jesse up just before the horns of a cow brushed against his pant leg. Jesse threw himself onto the back of the saddle.

"Whew!" Jesse let out a loud yell. "Let's get the hell outta here!"

"You o.k., Jesse?" Matt asked as he turned his horse and moved out into the open.

"Well, I don't have to open my pants for you know what," he answered, putting his hand into the cut at the back of his trousers where the cow's horns had taken a swatch out of them.

Steve rode up to the pair with a horse and an empty saddle. Jesse slid out of Matt's saddle onto the mare and the three men rode back into the battle.

Shots were fired in all directions as Matt led the charge directly through the rustlers, scattering both the cattle and the rustlers.

"Use your shotguns!" Matt ordered as the men fought in close quarters.

"I am!" Thatcher answered back with his shotgun in the air.

Because of Matt and Steve's earlier training of Jesse's men, they knew exactly what Matt was ordering and followed them, breaking heads and blasting the rustlers out of their saddles.

When the battle was over and the cattle corralled, the rustlers knew that they had been hit hard and word spread throughout the Brazos region that later developed into a legend as to how the *Brazos Kid* came to be.

The injured were carried to the bunkhouse and looked after.

"Well, Matt," Jesse said as they reined up at the ranch house later that evening. "You saved my life."

"Well, Jesse. You saved ours. So, we're even. We coulda been wiped out without your help." Then he looked intently at Jesse and asked, "And just why and how you came to our rescue?" Matt asked, lighting from his saddle.

Jesse threw his arm around Matt's waist as they walked up the porch to the house. Because of Matt's large frame.Jesse could not reach his shoulder. "Came to kill ya, Matt."

Matt stopped short of the opened door that Mitch held for them, turned into Jesse and introduced him to Jesse and the bunch.

"Mitch. This is Jesse. The rest of Jesse's bunch is with the horses at the corral."

Mitch shook hands with Jesse and Cole

"Huh? You came to kill me? Why?"

Cole stepped up on the porch between the men and walked into the house.

"Thet's Cole," Matt acknowledged to Mitch.

"We felt you'd tell some Texas Rangers where we were and what we done," Jesse continued. "Didn't want thet to happen."

Mitch stood there with the door open while Jesse entered. Steve followed last with his arm around Seth. Thatcher waited outside for Matt to go ahead of him.

"You fellas oughta know better'n thet," Steve added as he patted John Younger on the back while he passed Matt.

"You brought your whole gang to get me?" Matt asked, standing strong as he faced Jesse.

"You bet! I wasn't taking any chances."

"And now?"

"Hell, compadre. You done saved my life. I can't shoot ya now. I owe ya! Besides, I don't think you'd rat on me, after us doin' what we did to save your general's ranch."

The men went into the house and were introduced to the Mitchell family while the wranglers from the ranches brought the cattle down, herded them into the corral and cleaned up the area.

That evening found Matt and Jesse walking towards the corral while the others stayed in the house.

"What's on your mind, Jesse?" Matt asked, taking his makings to roll a cigarette.

"You always thinkin' something's on m'mind. Don't cha, cowboy?"

"Usually is. Thet's what makes you the leader of a gang. Always a-thinkin'."

Jesse walked ahead of Matt and joined him at the corral where they watched the wranglers settle the cattle down. He, took out his makings, gave the sack of tobacco to Jesse and rolled himself a cigarette. Matt struck a match on his gun butt and lit both his and Jesse's cigarettes.

"Well, Matt, I've got me a big headache."

"How's so?"

"I'm in love. Really, deeply in love."

"Zee?"

"Yep."

"So, what's your problem?"

"Don't know how to settle down with her."

"How's thet?"

"You know. Get married. Raise some childrun. Be respectable."

"Uh, huh. And jest what would you do for a *respectable living?*" Matt asked, watching Jesse blow smoke rings.

"Thet's the problem. Dunno."

"Get a job in some city where they don't know you? I het what you're a-thinkin'?"

"Somethin' like thet."

"And your problem then is the gang.," Matt suggested.

"You hit the nail right on the head, Matt. The gang." Jesse looked out onto the rolling plains and then continued. "Hell, Matt. All of your training. I liked it. But the gang."

"They didn't?"

"None of them. They're from the old school. Don't like changes. Don't like bein' told what to do. Kinda figure they can do it their own way."

"And . . .?

"And, I know I'm askin' for trouble down the road. They won't listen to you, and they sure as hell won't listen to me. If'n I tell them to use your tactics, they'll go and do jest the opposite for spite. And, to tell ya the truth, I liked takin' orders from you and Steve. Made me feel like I was army again. Know what I mean?"

"Well," Matt started in, titling his hat back and looking up to the sky. "The way I see it, thet is, if'n ya want my advise."

"Thet's why I brung you out here, Matt. Fire away. You always seem to know what to do."

"Not always. Else, I wouldn't be sittin' here with a man who's a killer and an outlaw and wants to kill me."

"Naw! Not any more. And I only kill to prevent gettin' killed. Come on. What's the answer?"

"Dang if I know, Jesse. Your gang can always do without you. They know how to make it alone." He looked intently into Jesse's blue, blinking eyes. "Who're your friends?"

"What cha, mean? They're all my friends."

"I mean, true friends. Real friends."

Jesse took another drag, exhaled and blew the smoke to the dry, whispering wind. "Real friends?"

"Yeah. Real friends."

Jesse threw the cigarette away, looked at Matt and answered him slowly. "Cole. Maybe Jim."

"Cole is his own man. He'll go out on his own one day. Jim? He's a married man hisself now. He don't have time to wet nurse ya."

"Then I don't know if I have a real friend. Outside of Zee and her ol' man. Of course, there's my brother Frank. I always did like May, as a friend, but she's not part of my gang. I'd have to say, I jest don't have a real friend. They'd all pretty much shoot me in the back for a reward . . . if'n they thought they'd get away with it "

"Maybe thet's the answer."

Jesse looked consternated towards Matt as if thought for the moment that Matt was serious or out of his head. "How's thet?"

"If'n it were me, and I'm glad it isn't . . . but if'n it were, and I couldn't' jest up and leave the gang . . . Well, Jesse, I'd fake my death and light myself and my wife some place where no one knew who I was and take up a new life. Yep. Thet's probably what I'd do."

"Fake my death? Now how, jest how in the hell am I gonna do thet?"

"Not for me to say, but I'm sure you could come up with a way . . . ifn't thet were what you'd want bad enough. Thet way, no one, not any member of your gang, would know anything about it."

Jesse thought for a long moment, then hopped down from the railing. Matt dropped down beside him and tossed his cigarette out on the road. "Just a thought."

"Ya got me a-thinkin', Captain," Jesse returned with a smile and a pat on Matt's back. "Whewee!" He let out a long, loud yell. "Yes sir. Ya got me a-thinkin'."

Jesse looked at Matt for a moment and then viewed the ranch. "So this is your home, now? Wow! You coulda been with us. And the Brazos River." He looked hard at Matt and said, "The Brazos. Fits ya. *The Brazos Kid.*"

The two men strolled back towards the house. With the sound of Jesse's yell and the two men singing, Jesse's gang came out on the porch to see what was going on.

"You alright, Jesse?" Cole asked with his pistol raised and cocked.

"You bet we are, Cole," Jesse yelled back. "Me and the Brazos Kid here. Break out the jug 'cause we're goin' home and I'm a-gettin' married. And I feel like gettin' drunk with my friend here. Ol' Brazos."

The gang, along with Matt now nicknamed *Brazos,* and Steve frolicked that night, and certainly made fools of themselves. The night passed away as fast as it came.

Jesse and his gang rode out sober the next morning towards the sun rise.

"Where to?" Matt asked as he waved Jesse off.

"Got to catch a train, Brazos."

"Catch a train?"

"Yeah. Now don't go tellin' no one. It's gonna be a surprise for m'darlin'. Then I'm a-gonna go home to Zee and we're a' gonna get hitched." He let out a Rebel yell and rode out with the rest of his gang.

Give her our best!" Matt tossed his voice, waving his Stetson.

Steve followed suit, waving his hat. He looked at Matt, still waving his hat, and asked, "What brought thet on all of a sudden?"

"Well, pal of mine, I think our outlaw friend jest got hit with a change of heart. He's gonna become a family man."

"Yeah? You think it'll last, *Brazos?*"

"Hey, pard. Don't knock my new name. Kinda like the handle."

"All right by me. Any way, whatcha think?"

"Give him the benefit of the doubt, Steve. He's a damn good man. I know it'll last."

The two men stood there, waving their hats in the wind and watching Jesse and his gang ride out to catch a train.

Matt thought, *To catch a train? Like to know more about thet one.*

CHAPTER 46

NELLIE BECOMES A WIDOW

Nellie McDaniels drove up to the ranch in her buggy the next day and was met by Steve and Thatcher who were out by the corral.

"Who could that be?" Steve asked as he walked towards her.

"Never saw her before, Steve," Thatcher answered.

"Mitch!" she cried out as she reined up the horse at the hitching post.

Mitch came running out the front door with the girls and Brazos following.

"Nellie! What's the matter?" Mitch asked, taking her by her hand and escorting her into the house.

"Norman."

Emily came into the room and took Nellie into her arms, helping her sit in an overstuffed chair where she attempted to comfort her.

"What about him?" Emily asked.

"They killed him, Emily."

"Who?"

"Rustlers. They raided our ranch and took all our cattle. Norman. You know how he is. He went after them and they shot him. Killed him, Mitch. Those stinking bastards killed my Norman." She covered her face with her hanky and wept.

Thatcher gripped the handles of his twin Navies and gritted his teeth.

"What do we do, Mitch?" Brazos asked.

"He didn't want to side in with us," Mitch said, putting his arm around Emily as she continued to caress Nellie. "And this is what he gets for it. I told him we needed his help as well as he needed ours."

323

"It's too late, Mitch," Nellie sobbed. "He's gone."

"How do we get them, Mitch?" Brazos asked.

"When did this happen, Nellie?" Mitch asked as Leisha took Nellie from his grip and dried her eyes and handed her a clean handkerchief.

"Last night. They rode west."

"Right after they left here," Steve said, looking towards the west.

"I kinda know where they might be," Seth added. "There's a hollow this side of the river. They'll cross the river there and head north."

"Let's ride, men!" Brazos ordered.

They gathered their wranglers and rode fast. Because the cattle the rustlers were stealing were slow in moving across the terrain, Brazos and the others caught up with them just as they entered the water.

Brazos, Steve and Thatcher rode ahead of the men, leaving the rest of the ranch hands to wait with their rifles aimed at the group of rustlers.

"If there's a showdown," Brazos advised his men, "which there probably will be, fire into them. Else, we'll see if we can't figure out who and what they're doin'."

"Let's get them now while they're in the water, Brazos," one of the ranch hands yelled out.

"And what if they're not the men we want?" Brazos came back with grit teeth. "I want them just as bad as you do." He looked at Steve and then at Thatcher and said, "Let's ride!"

They never got the chance to talk with the rustlers, for as soon as they saw Brazos coming, one of the rustlers started firing in their direction. Brazos heard the men yelling. "The sons-a-vipers found us!"

Another man turned back towards shore and hightailed it for his life. Two others hesitated, looked both ways at Brazos riding towards them, and then at the one who hightailed it out of the water. "Let's git!" one of the varmints yelled out.

"Rangers, ride!" Brazos yelled out as if he were still in the cavalry. Steve and Thatcher opened fire as they neared the rustler.

Thatcher opened fire with two Navies and then put them in his waist band, took out his shotgun and waited for the moment he closed in on the rustlers. The nearest man, firing blindly at Thatcher, felt the buckshot rip into his skin as he flipped over backwards off his horse and into the water. His body was carried down stream in a ripple of red.

The leader of the rustlers was already on the other side of the Brazos with the first head of cattle that had already reached the other side. "Let's get the hell out of here!" he yelled to the four other rustlers with him. They spurred their horses south and rode hell-bent for leather.

The Bar M ranch hands moved hard and fast towards the river, firing at the rustlers, causing havoc with them in the middle of the river.

"Take 'em boys!" Brazos yelled back as he and Steve doubled back and crossed the river down stream in an effort to catch the leader and the remnant of his gang. "Thatcher. Go with Steve and drive the cattle back!"

"We're with you," Phil Johnson, the tall, lean twenty year old said, as he and two others rode with Brazos.

"Well, quit jawin' and ride!"

The river was deeper where Brazos and his group rode. Brazos was counting on the current taking them faster down stream. He knew he could control his horse, and figured Steve could do the same. But he was concerned about the other cowboy who followed them. He looked around and found that the lean cowboy had stayed with him.

"Let him have his head, Phil," Brazos called out. "He'll get you to the other side all right."

Brazos was right. The horses swam their best with the current, and when they found sure footing on the other side, they dug their hooves into the silt and sand and rode up the bank.

The leader of the rustlers was a mean-looking cuss, not too tall in the saddle, but a wiry varmint who kept kicking his horse with his spurs to stay ahead of Brazos and his group. He took the reins and headed his horse westward with the remnant of his men following close behind. They rode like the dickens to stay ahead of Brazos, firing wildly behind them with hopes of stopping one of Brazos' men.

When the bullets ran out, the rustlers departed their leader; three of the five giving up while the leader and another man kept riding. Steve and Thatcher took charge of the three men while Brazos continued the pursuit. The man with the leader stopped his horse, pulled out his rifle and aimed it carefully at Brazos. Sensing the immediate danger, Brazos zigzagged towards the man with the rifle, causing the man to miss three and four times.

Brazos pulled his pistol out from its holster and, aiming from the waist, knocked the man down with two shots; one dead center through his forehead, killing him instantly.

The leader continued to ride and climbed a bluff that slowed him down, which gave Brazos an edge. Brazos spurred Skeeter on into a faster run, hoping to reach the rustler while his horse was testing terrain. When he was close enough to the horse, Brazos took his rifle and, using it as a club, knocked the leader from his saddle, which caused the horse to fall, throwing the leader down the slope.

Brazos brought Skeeter to a fast halt, did a quick dismount, ran over to the leader, picked him up by his collar and brought his fist hard against his jaw. The leader fell backward and rolled further down the slope and Brazos followed. The rustler stopped at a bolder, rubbed his jaw and rose quickly to his feet to meet Brazos head on. He brought his fist around as he sprung upward and landed a hard right across Brazos's face, sprawling him across the hard, rocky ground.

Brazos saw enough stars to form his own galaxy, but rose in time to feel the impact of the leader's body as it slammed into him, knocking him further down the hill. With the leader's head in a headlock, Brazos tossed him further down the hill, ran after him, reached down and picked him up by his hair. He slammed his head downward into the soil, brought it back up and, sitting on top of him, brought his fist down hard against his face, breaking his nose. The blood spilled onto Brazos' hand and onto the ground. Wiping it off onto the leader's pants, Brazos then brought the leader to eye level.

Seeing the man was out stone cold, Brazos dropped his hold on the man and let him flop to the ground. He took his lasso and tied the man tight and then whistled for Skeeter. Once Skeeter was at his side, Brazos mounted him and rode after the leader's mare. He brought it back to the leader who was stirring but stilled tied.

"Git up!" Brazos ordered as he grabbed the man by the lasso. "Git on your horse!"

The two men rode back to where they joined up with Steve, Thatcher who rounded up the remnant of the rustlers.

"Here, Thatcher," Brazos ordered, turning the reins of the leader's horse over to Thatcher as he and Steve held their weapons on the other rustlers. "One dead back on the slope. Take this one in with the rest. Looks to me like Phil and the others did all right for themselves."

"Kinda looks like," Steve answered, tying the three horses together. "Jesse coming in like he did with the whole body gave them the spirit to do it, Brazos."

"Yeah!" Brazos drawled. "Well, get some men and take them all to the Texas Rangers. They'll know what to do with them."

"They'll string us up," one of the rustlers cried out; a rather thin man who wore a dirty, crusty and torn hat who looked like he hadn't eaten in a month. "We were told this was easy work and thet we'd have lots of money and a party in town."

"Well," Brazos answered, clearing his throat as he caught his breath, "ya shoulda thought about thet when ya chose your occupation. You'll have a party all right; a neck tie party."

Brazos looked at the other two men, and then at the leader. "You, mister, should get to hang twice. Get him out of my sight!"

Steve looked over at the rest of his men and yelled out, "Round 'em up, boys and take 'em back to the ranch!"

Later, Brazos joined in with Steve and led the cattle back across the Brazos towards the Bar M while Thatcher and a couple other men took the rustlers to Waco and the Texas Rangers.

"Seems to me, Brazos, thet we're still fightin' the war," Steve said as he twirled his lasso and smacked a steer's rump to keep him moving.

"Yeah! Except, now these are our cattle and we've got to get 'em back to the Bar M. How many, you reckon?"

"Five hundred, more or less. We didn't lose too many. Jack Barton will have his two thousand within the week out of those at the ranch and these we've salvaged. Heck, there'll be some to spare for our trouble."

With the other three ranches, Steve was able to keep his promise. Cutting the calves and the mothers, Steve delivered his two thousand head to Jack Barton. With the money, Mitch and the other ranchers were financially able to hire and replenish their stock from the open range and within the year brought their herds up to a healthy number.

As for Brazos, his attention was still trained on would-be rustlers, outlaws and young 'uns wanting to make a name for themselves by outdrawing the Brazos Kid; Matt Jorgensen from Montana.

Thatcher took a real concern for Widow Nellie McDaniels and hired out his gun and expertise to help run her ranch. Tom, Phil and Todd helped Steve and Seth run the Bar M Ranch with new wranglers and drovers constantly hiring in for a drive.

In the back of Brazos's mind grew the restless thought, *how nice it would be to drive longhorns back to dad's ranch in Montana. But, naw. I jest don't know. I sure hate cows. Wull . . . maybe!"*

CHAPTER 47

EMILY RIDES INTO ETERNITY

<u>22 June 1868</u>

It was later on a warm autumn night, Leisha and Jaimie took a ride across the ranch towards the Brazos with Emily Mitchell. The ride was easy until Jaimie challenged Leisha to a race, which was their competitive nature.

"I can beat cha!" Jaimie cried out to Leisha.

"Not again, girls," Emily shouted out, hoping to stop them. "Let's have an . . . easy ride." Her voice trailed off as the girls kicked their horses into a fast ride.

It was a short distance to the Brazos and Leisha had an edge on Jaimie's paint with her Arabian. She was easily a furlong ahead of Jaimie when she spotted a rattler along side the road. She reined up and Jaimie rode past, only to rein up a short distance further. Leisha saw Emily approach the road where the rattler was and yelled, "Mother! Watch out! A rattler!"

It was too late. Emily's horse spooked, reared up and took off with Emily trying to grasp her loose reins. The two girls kicked their horses into a gallop to catch her. A tree limb caught Emily by the neck before she could duck and threw her to the ground, hitting her head hard in the fall.

The girls jumped from their horses, and Leisha gently put her arm around Emily's shoulder. Emily showed no response. Her head was limp and fell in Leisha's arms, her eyes rolled back into her head.

Jaimie was quick to ride back to the ranch where Matt and Steve followed with a litter to carry her. They placed Emily's limp body on the carry-on and rode her back to the ranch. She slept through the night; never to recover.

The doctor left the room and gave the family a look of despair. "She's gone, Mitch," he said as he looked at the hurt in

Mitch's eyes. "I'm sorry. She slipped out without ever waking up. No more pain. Her neck was broken."

It seemed that God held back the rain until the last shovel was thrown onto Emily's grave and the family and friends of many headed back to the ranch. The day left heavy scars on every one for Emily was a well-loved wife, mother and friend.

To General Mitchell, she was his strength, and now that she was gone, it seemed that his strength had seeped from his soul. He knew in his heart that she could never be replaced but he also knew that she would want him to continue his life as if she were still with him yet.

Leisha and Jaimie clung to each other as they watched the sun set on Emily's grave; each knew in their heart that it was incumbent on them to take up the reins that Emily had left. Again, Jaimie felt the pangs of losing her mother. With this loss, Jaimie and Leisha became as one in the role of sisters. Now, each of the ladies became more proficient in their ranch way of life, but also kept Seth in their circle of responsibilities.

Brazos sat his horse some distance away from the house, rolled a cigarette and lit it. As he exhaled a stream of smoke to the winds of the Brazos, Steve reined up next to him.

"Watcha thinkin', friend?" Steve asked as he watched the strong look in Brazos's eyes.

"Never knew."

"What?"

"This way of life. Cattle ranching. Mitch needs our guns more than ever now. Seems thet we've got to be his backbone for a while, pal."

Steve threw back his Stetson, looked at the ranch, smiled and said, "Yep. Thinkin' the same thing. Sense trouble?"

"Maybe."

CHAPTER 48

PLANS ARE LAID FOR THE NEW MILL

24 June 1868

It had been well over two years since Matt and Steve rode away from Richmond, Virginia. Captain Willoughby left the army, took up his career as an independent engineer and, with the encouragement of the McBrides, hired on with a Rhode Island company to build a new mill.

The Richmond and Danville Railroad took the McBrides to New England and another time of bringing the clan back together. When they arrived in the small town of Spray, Rhode Island, a carriage and driver awaited them. The two McBride brothers and two sisters rode to the construction sight of a cotton mill where they were greeted by three gentlemen dressed in fine clothes and tall hats.

"I'm glad the McBrides could make the trip," a rather portly gentleman said, greeting the clan. "I'm Nathaniel P. Edwards. My partner, James L. Thompson, and our attorney Broderick Lee Hamilton."

Gerald spoke for the McBrides as he shook their hands. "Thank you, Mr. Edwards. Mr. Thompson. Mr. Hamilton. I am Gerald McBride." Gesturing toward each, he introduced them. "This is my brother, Kenneth, and my sisters, Virginia and Annette. We're certainly happy to be here, despite the circumstances."

"Yes," Edwards returned. "The war destroyed most of our mills We've already rebuilt the old warehouse and are using the front office spaces to issue orders of cotton from the plantations that are able to fill our orders. We understand you are considering our plans for what you are calling *reconstruction of the South*."

"Yes, sir," Gerald answered shyly. We're hoping that we don't step on toes between the North and the South now that the war has been over for two years, gentlemen. But, yes we are very much in the throes of reconstructing the South."

"Well, you know, sir that we are competitors, even if we are not in any war?" Thompson interrupted. "It is our concern in how we conduct our business with you this day will to help our nation and not hinder our competitive spirit."

"As you wish, sir," Kenneth added.

"May we go inside?" Edwards suggested as he led the way for the rest.

"May I ask, Mr. Edwards," Gerald spoke up as they walked towards the three-storied building, "what has made your mills so successful?"

"You may indeed ask," Edwards replied with a lilt in his voice. "People! Cotton and people who need work. Simple as that."

Before they entered the doorway, Edwards put his hand on the handle of the door to enter, turned to his guests and continued. "People. Rhode Island is small, but we have people who need jobs. They apply to these jobs as families, leave their farms and go to work as laborers, earning salaries. At first it seems all too demeaning to them. Then, once they receive their salaries, they realize how they can make more as public laborers rather than down-on-their luck farmers. And then, we have our employees.

"Before we go in, I'd like to point out to you the houses under construction around the mill. These are for the employees; their families. This whole mill with the land around it becomes a village."

The McBrides looked around and showed their interest together with their appreciation of what they saw.

Edwards opened the door and led the group into the hall of the mill. There was no noise of looms in operation. The place was quiet. Stopping on the inside of the doorway, he shut the door behind the group.

"May I ask how you expect to reconstruct the South?"

"I suppose you've answered your own question. We have people that have rented farms. Farms like yours that have been destroyed by the war. The families have turned their rifles into plowshares but, because of President Lincoln's Emancipation Proclamation and the war, they are living on bare sustenance.

"Where we used slaves before and gave them and their families there earnings in food and lodging and such, now they will earn it in money and pay their way. A great many of the coloreds have gone north. And now the farmers and their families themselves need jobs to keep living.

"In order to help them make a living, we want to offer them jobs."

"In the mill?" Thompson asked.

"Yes. And from what we hear," Kenneth added, "you folks here are doing just that."

"You are right, Mr. McBride," Edwards answered as he took several cigars from his inside coat pocket and offered them to the men.

"Gentlemen. If the ladies don't object, may we light up our cigars as a sign of truce and of goodwill?" He struck a match, offered a light to the rest and then lit his own. "Sorry, ladies. Don't have a thing to offer you as a symbol of truce.

"That's quite alright, Ginny answered. "We women fully understand, this being a man's world."

Edwards harrumphed and turned a little red, then continued as they strolled down the hallway together. "You have a fine cause, McBrides. A fine cause."

"Well, we can't do it alone, Mr. Edwards," Kenneth said, letting out a stream of smoke that wafted towards the high ceilings. "We need to learn from you."

"It's even grander than I'd imagine," Gerald said to Ginny as the McBrides walked through the empty halls of the new mill with their gentlemen hosts. He was very much enamored at Ginny's gist of Edward's remarks.

Ginny was dressed as the lovely lady that she was; a full navy skirt with many slips, a black silk scarf-tie with a cameo broach at the neck of her white blouse and a matching navy cape over her shoulders. She carried a string purse in her gloved hands and an umbrella over her arm. Her mousy- brown hair was pulled up under a small hat with a feather.

Annette was dressed; in a full burgundy dress, with a high-lace collar and birthstone locket in the center of her chest, a frilly wide sash and bustle and a cape of blue and magenta paisley swirls. She also carried an umbrella over the crook of her arm. Like Ginny, she too wore her light brown hair pinned high on her head but wore a smaller hat with no plume,. One could tell the ladies were sisters thought.

"I seem to remember how our mill looked, Jerry," Ginny explained as she looked at heavy looms being lowered into place. "I helped papa in the office."

They continued their walk when they found Willoughby standing over a table with a set of blueprints on it. He was instructing two other men about their duties.

"Ginny. Hello, Annie. Jerry. Kenny." Willoughby greeted them and then dismissed the two workers who were in conversation with him when they arrived. "OK fellas. Put the plans into work and let's get some more of the looms in place today if we can."

It was not long before Ginny noticed that Annie was all smiles for Willoughby, as she watched her staring at him with her same blue eyes that they'd both inherited from Grand Mama Sarah.

"Hello, Bryce," Ginny greeted him as did the others with a nod of their heads. "We heard that you were working with the Rhode Island Mill. Nice seeing you again. Are you doing well?"

"We're ahead of schedule, if that's what you mean." He looked at the group of men who represented his employers. "Gentlemen. We've had the flooring settled, and the looms for the first floor were delivered on time. So, here we are. You're seeing the mill as it begins to come to life."

"It's about time. It's been long enough without us hearing the beautiful, whirring of spindles and the beating that looms make when everyone's working," Thompson said with a happiness to his voice and a smile on his face. Then he looked at Willoughby and asked, "How long before we're ready for operation?"

"Oh. I'd give another two months at least, sir. Maybe sooner; the weather holding out for the most part. When it rains or snows, we have a hard time hauling equipment in. These past two weeks have been good though." He looked at Ginny, smiled and then returned to greet Edwards. "Then I can turn it over to you. Lock, stock and barrel."

"Yes," Edwards answered. Two months, you say?"

"Yes, sir. Maybe sooner, with the weather warming up like it is and little rain. We've got windows to finish in the bays, plastering, and now hauling and installing the looms on all four floors."

"Then what will you do, Bryce?" Annette asked. "After this is all done."

"I'm an engineer, Annie. And there's a lot of reconstruction going on across the South. These gentlemen have made me a part of their team. And, I've already made plans on working the southern part of the 700 Valley."

"What's that?" Ginny asked.

"That's the corridor between Canada, the Carolinas, Georgia and Alabama. We're going to put in cotton mills all the way throughout the South, Ginny. I've already been contracted to help build more in North Carolina."

"Why are you so concerned with the South all of a sudden, Bryce?" Gerald asked with a smirk on his face. "You being a Yankee and all."

Willoughby stretched out his arms and spanned the interior of the mill. "The war caused this, Jerry. The ever-loving, God blessed war. Since I've been on this project, and ever since I arrived in Richmond I suppose, I've learned more about what the South has done for our country than I ever dreamed of before. And the South is going to reap from this war just like the North. Maybe more. Who knows? Who could ever envision? I can see it."

"Well, Brother Bryce," Annette piped in, "it's about time. Tell some of your other blue suited gentlemen."

"Oh, I plan on it. I've already told my sister Maggie and Richard. They've written that I should go back to Michigan. I've written back that we've got a project here that needs our immediate attention. And from here, the reconstruction of the South."

The Rhode Island gentlemen harrumphed again and smiled. "We are with you McBrides. It's a big project. Bigger I suspect than any of us, or all of us collectively can imagine. But for the sake of our nation, we're in total agreement; we need to build more cotton mills."

Annette was pleased that Willoughby was not simply addressing the rest of the group, but that his eyes looked right into hers when he answered her.

"As I've said before and I'll say it again," Gerald joined in. "The South shall rise again!"

"Yes," Willoughby said, "if we can do it the right way."

"Meaning?" Ginny asked.

"Well, Ginny, what was a mystery to me is that England across the sea also suffered tremendously because of our lousy war"

"Oh, I knew that, Bryce," Annette answered, twirling her umbrella.

"Lousy?" Gerald came back. "That's a good description for it. It was lousy business for both sides."

"I don't think *lousy* is the best word to describe it, gentlemen," Ginny added. "I think *stinkin'* is more appropriate." She smiled.

The group of people laughed together, and Annette kept twirling her umbrella handle.

"No, I mean it. When President Lincoln, our President back then," Willoughby chided. "When he ordered a blockade of Confederate southern ports, it killed the heart of England and the Continent. That's how much they were affected by our war."

Ginny looked with great interest at this man who seemingly was still in love with her, but who she would not give five minutes of her time to be alone with because of her unceasing love for Matt. Now, all of a sudden, she began to see a knight on a white horse; one that would fight for the South. But, looking over at her sister, being goggle-eyed at him, she realized that competition had set in. She was pleased; both for Willoughby and his set goals, and for Annette taking an interest in a man who could offer her a real future.

"I know that we shipped a heck of a lot of cotton to our mill in Virginia from Tennessee," Ginny reported. "We own a large plantation in Tennessee, gentlemen," Ginny addressed the Rhode Island group. "I hope you know that."

"Oh, yes. I've been told a lot about what you've been doing, Ginny," Willoughby pointed to her family. "Maybe some day I'll have the opportunity to see your plantation."

"Some day, maybe," she returned with a sly glint in her eye that did not escape Willoughby's attention. "I was told that cotton made up at least half of all our exports before the war."

"More like two-thirds, I hear," Thompson joined in. "And, we're going to be there again in the next few years. Watch and see. And I'll tell you something else, Bryce," Thompson went on, addressing Willoughby. "We've got the long haul of hiring families. We're past just looking at single women and farmers from the field. We're hiring entire families."

"And that includes children, boys and girls, past twelve years old," Edwards added, watching the expressions on the faces of the McBrides as they smiled almost in unison. "Can't forget them. They'll accompany their mothers."

"Yes," Thompson added. "Kids twelve years old are good workers. We'll have housing on the grounds surrounding the area as you saw outside," Gerald continued as he pointed out the bays. "Textile mills are the answer for the economy of the South.

"It's a great money maker for whole families; especially women employees. It will bring families together."

"But the South's problem is, as I see it," Kenneth interrupted, "like our brothers here in the North, we're up against farms that were ruined during the war, and families split up, and much more. It's going to be difficult to find enough families to fill our quota."

"Will we be able to help these farmers?" Ginny asked, putting her umbrella alongside the side the table. She stuck her hands in the pockets of her dress, walked around the table and looked at the blueprints.

Annette followed suit by placing her umbrella next to Ginny's and folded her arms as if in deep thought.

"You see the need, don't you, Virginia?" Edwards asked, puffing on his cigar. "Yes. Yes you do. And that, Miss McBride, is what will make your project successful."

"Oh, I've got to clear the air with you, gentlemen," Ginny exclaimed, wide eyed. "I'm an attorney, like you, Mr. Hamilton.

My interest is not in building only for money, Mister Edwards, but to assure farmers, laborers and families their equitable rights."

"Hear! Hear!" Hamilton applauded lightly with his gray leather gloves. "And your alma mater . . . ?"

"William and Mary," she answered.

"I heard they were shut down during the war."

"Yes. But I was tutored personally by Doctor Benjamin Stoddard Ewell, the president of William and Mary during the war, received my degree, passed the bar after the war and I've been in practice for over three years now."

"Highly successful, too," Gerald added.

"But, I am here with my family to learn how the South can benefit from your successful operations."

"And we salute you, Miss McBride, for your honesty and your faithfulness to our country," Hamilton concluded with a bow.

"Thank you, gentlemen." Ginny looked over at Willoughby and gave him a slight smile.

"Now you can see why I left the army for this," Willoughby said with a grin that went across his face like a Cheshire cat.

"We're beholden to you, Bryce," Gerald continued.

"Now, if you don't mind, Bryce, we've got to finish taking the McBrides around and show them just what you've done," Edwards suggested as he led the clan further. "Please come with us, Bryce. You can continue telling us more about what we're doing in this mill."

Edwards offered Ginny his arm as she and Annette both retrieved their parasols and walked her down the long corridor as Willoughby followed, sided by Annette.

Willoughby watched Ginny sashay down the corridor, and he liked what he saw. But he couldn't help noticing her beautiful sister by his side and the pretty way she would look around the brim of her hat to see if he was looking her way.

The stroll around the mill with the group was enlightening to Ginny as the mill structure was completely different than what she had remembered, growing up as a child in Richmond.

"How many looms are you putting in the mill?" Ginny asked as Edwards continued to lead the group down the hallway

"Well, Ginny," Gerald answered. "The war was fortunate for us in a way. The old mill was destroyed in a city where we needed to uproot anyway. Because of the war, we can now utilize modern equipment and build a new and better mill, and in a better location.

Willoughby addressed the group to look further down the corridor. "As you can see, we have four floors to this mill and eighteen bay windows to each floor. And the floors are wider than the older mill, and the ceilings are higher. That way we minimize the dust and lint, a strong deterrent for women and children wanting to work in the mills."

The group walked along the corridor until they came to the first set of stairs. "The upper floors are pretty empty, but you'll get a view of how high each floor is. Safety for our workers is our priority."

"What makes women want to work here?" Annette asked.

"Two reasons," Thompson answered. "For one, the work is mostly for the women, and the children love it, too for the fun of it. It seems that men just don't have the knack for spinning and weaving. For baling and carding, which requires heavy lifting and dangerous work, we use men."

"And the second?" Ginny prodded.

"More money than any other job they could tackle on a farm or anywhere. It brings the weary farmer good money that he couldn't make trying to renovate his farm with meager earnings. They hardly made up for an existence."

"So how does it work?" Ginny asked again.

Edwards looked at the two curious women and laid out the plan. "Understand this, ladies. Women who are weavers don't get paid by the hour. They get paid by the piece. A good worker makes much more than a lot of men. And of course, their husbands love to see the money come in."

Edwards looked at Willoughby who had his eyes fixed on Ginny, and asked, rhetorically. Two months, you say?"

"As I said earlier, the floors are settled." Willoughby stomped his boots on the floor. "There are no longer wooden beamed floors like you had before the war. They are made with steel beams and concrete now."

The group reached the second floor and walked the empty halls through the dirt and dust.

"As to how many looms we'll have?" Thompson reminded Ginny of her question before. "I think that should be Mr. Edward's department."

"I see us having six, maybe seven hundred spindles," Edwards answered. "I've budgeted for seven hundred. And that's not an exaggeration."

"Seven hundred?" Ginny came back. "How many workers are we hiring?"

"Not quite that many. Probably closer to five or six hundred."

"The mills are the heavy economical factor in our country. I'm to understand, Miss McBride, that your family has a lot of clout in Virginia as well as other places."

"Oh, how well I know that. Papa kept me informed of that when we worked the plantation in Tennessee. And Grand Mama keeps me informed. She's the backbone of our clan."

Edwards' ears pricked up. "Do you still have slaves in Tennessee, Jerry?"

"Ginny's brought us up to date on our plantation. We no longer use slaves, as you Yankees know. We hired some Negroes, now, along with all the white folk that we can get." He was careful in selecting his words pertaining to the black people for fear that he would cause friction with their gentlemen hosts.

"Who in the McBride clan is running the plantation, now that you're in Richmond, Miss McBride?" Hamilton asked, smoking his cigar.

"Another plantation owner. A neighbor of our plantation. His name is Olaf Gustavson and he has the largest plantation in the surrounding area. Along with his two sons, he's hired men for us who can supervise the plantation, and he has his own supervisors who also overlook the plantation and send in reports to us. I will be making periodical visits to assize the situation as I firmly believe that this is what is going to help the south rejuvenate itself."

"And make money," Edwards interjected. "Lots and lots of money."

"Gentlemen," Ginny gave her attention mostly to the Rhode Island gentlemen, "what it looks like to me is that the North is becoming rather domesticated while the South is becoming more industrialized."

Everyone joined in laughter while Willoughby smiled and answered, "One might say that. Actually, Detroit has already set an example, and more factories are being built throughout the North."

"Oh, I'm certain of that, but that is not what I meant by industrialization. I'm talking about expansion such as the mills are doing, and the amount of jobs being formed for every one across the South.

Then, as she reached the end of the corridor and started traipsing down the stairs, she looked back at the Rhode Island gentlemen and smiled.

Edwards sided up to her and descended the stairs, giving her his arm. "I highly agree, Miss McBride. I highly agree."

Then looking around at the looms, Ginny said, "The spindle mules. I don't see them."

"That's because we did away with them," Thompson answered. "We now have in their place what we call ring frames. They're made with belts and pulleys."

Edwards continued as the group headed toward the front doors. "We're using modern technology; as modern as we can be. We think safety as much as possible, knowing women and children will work the looms while the men will unbale and card the cotton; jobs too tough and too dangerous for women. Like Willoughby mentioned earlier, the ceilings are higher for better ventilation. The bays are ten feet six inches."

"All very impressive, gentlemen," Gerald commented.

After the day's journey to the mill, the Rhode Island gentlemen were ready to bid farewell to the McBride group at the mill.

"So, Mr. McBride," Edwards addressed Gerald. "What will be your next move? Where do you plan on setting up your mill?"

"It's in the planning stages at the present. Our old mill was burned to the ground, and we can't really see building it on the James again. A flour mill was burned just north of us, too.

"We've studied the situation quite thoroughly, Mr. Edwards, and we can't see raising enough employees in Richmond as we could in, say around North Carolina where the farmers would be reticent to such a move."

"If I may add, Mr. Edwards," Kenneth interjected. "A group of businessmen are considering constructing a mill in Danville using the Dan River. It seems to be most appropriate."

"Danville? Isn't that where your President Davis had set up his last capitol, so to speak?"

"Yes sir," Gerald answered proudly. "Afterwards he was captured and imprisoned in the Carolinas."

"Kinda ironic, one would say," Kenneth returned. "Kinda like a place where the South *should* rise again."

Edwards looked at Thompson and then at Hamilton. The three men smiled and Edwards retorted. "Yes. And we want to help you succeed in reconstructing the South. And Gentlemen, and ladies, too; very attractive ladies, I might say."

Annette beamed and looked over at Willoughby.

"It has been an encouraging pleasure to have met with you this fine day. I've had a rather good time visiting with you, as I think my colleagues here have, also."

"We, too, Mr. Edwards. Mr. Thompson. Mr. Hamilton." Gerald complimented them as the gentlemen on both sides shook hands, tipped their hats and bade each other a good day.

CHAPTER 49

GINNY CLIMBS THE LADDER TO SUCCESS

1870 – 1872

$\mathbf{F}$or the next two years, with Gerald's legal advice and under his supervision, Ginny applied her attributes to the mill as its corporate attorney. Kenneth became the president of the firm while Bryce became the vice-president.

"Your forte is contracts, Ginny," Gerald said as he and Kenneth joined Ginny in the south parlor of the McBride Manor. "Mine is more with wills and testaments. Both Ken and I feel that you are much more qualified for the task of corporate attorney than I, therefore we are putting the ball in your court."

"What Gerald is trying to say, sis," Kenneth interjected, "is that our time, his and mine, will be marketing and managing the mill. We need you to set up the legal documents to make this mill work."

Ginny sat as a refined lady and spoke her sentences very eloquently without any mincing of words, "I will do the best I can, Jerry. It's going to require my making several trips to North Carolina and I will need an assistant. I will need your immediate help with much paper work as I know you and Ken have already dug into this up to your elbows. Let me know what you have started and I'll put the rest in order."

"Fine," Gerald came back.

The old mill took shape with offices and Ginny found herself in a nice size office in front of the mill fully equipped with desk and file cabinets and she selected a young man to be her assistant.

Sitting behind her large desk, she stared into the eyes of her siblings as they stood in her office, observing a young lad of nineteen or so. He was a neat appearing man with light brown hair, brown eyes and of medium stature.

"I have chosen Ralph Martindale, a second-year law student at William and Marry, to be my assistant. I've watched his study habits while I visited there and, quite frankly, he's got a good head on his shoulders and he has the potential to grow with our company. During the summer months, he can find permanent residence there. In the mean time, he will be traveling with me."

"Very well," Gerald agreed, standing up and offering his right hand to the gentleman. "Mr. Martindale, welcome to the McBride Textile."

Ken rose and greeted the lad as well. "And Ginny, you certainly have your job cut out for you. Yes, welcome, Mr. Martindale."

The mill grew and progressed those two years, and as machinery wore out, it was replaced with better equipment, and more bodies were hired to operate them.

Ginny was pleased with her endeavors and rightly so, because she spent most of her waking hours making certain that the mill's legal matters in North Carolina were taken care of. At the same time, while Ralph stayed at the mill, she ran her own affairs at her office closer to home in Richmond as a private attorney for many of the citizens. It also gave her the opportunity to keep close tabs on her grandmother.

Ralph passed the bar two years later and stayed with the mill. He followed in Ginny's successful accomplishments that eventually allowed her to succeed with her clients in Richmond. She focused primarily on her personal accounts when she felt the mill was operating quite well with Ralph's management of its legal affairs. Of course, there were times that she was needed at the mill and she never let the family down.

Such was the case when she met with the board of directors at the mill and ended the meeting by saying, "Gentlemen. And my lovely sister and sisters-in-law. We must end our laborious meeting today with a special announcement."

The members looked at one another and then focused their attention solely and lastly on what Ginny was about to say.

"You have something of urgent importance, I take it," Gerald said as he stood up.

"Well, speak up, woman," Kenneth added as he, too, rose.

Ginny smiled and looked at Annette. "It befalls on me to announce that we will be adding another member to our board soon."

"What?" Gerald asked, looking at Ginny with an astonishing stare.

"Our sister is getting married."

Kenneth smiled and said, "Is that all? We've known that for some time."

"To Willoughby," Ralph interjected. "Here! Here!" He raised his glass of water to a toast.

"Well, then, let's dismiss and get ready for the wedding that takes place a week from next," Ginny added as she walked over to Annette. She took a hold of her arm and rose her to the attention of the McBride clan. "Congratulations, Annie."

The Champaign glasses were filled to the brim as the whole wedding party stood up as Gerald presented the toast to the newly weds at their party by Gerald McBride. "Here's to our sister and her husband." He looked at the couple and then asked, quite inebriated, "Just what the heck is your first name? It ain't just *Willoughby.*"

"Jerry, my handsome brother," Annie came back with a stern look in her eyes. "Didn't you pay any attention to what the preacher said?" She whispered in his ear, "Bryce."

"Of course. Here's to Mr. and Mrs. Bryce Willoughby. May their babies all look like Annie." Then he stopped and said, "Bryce! Your name is Bryce." He toasted his glass to Willoughby while the attendees laughed and continued in their merriments of dancing, eating and drinking.

Willoughby walked over to Ginny, took her hand and waltzed her out onto the floor.

"Congratulations, Bryce," Ginny said softly.

"I'll make her a fine husband," he promised as he twirled her around. "That you can count on."

The dancing and drinking kept on through the night until the couple was whisked away unnoticed by all.

The sun rose upon the manor in Richmond, illuminating her rays upon the terrace and the empty plates and glasses that dotted her lawn. A few stragglers walked away, arm and arm, singing as loud as they could. The drapes on the upstairs window were pulled back and Ginny peered through one of its panes.

Her mind on the matter of her lover, Matt, had been put on hold for the while, but now she found herself standing, peering out the window and pondering about where he could be and what he might be doing. After all, this could have been their wedding.

One spring day, 1872, she looked intently through the window of her office at the mill and watched some birds flying around. She was particularly interested in two birds that flew intermittently around a tree, back around the flowers surrounding the tree and through the bushes as they each seemingly chased each other. She reminisced for the moment about how she and Matt had sat on the bank of the Tennessee River and toyed with each other's affections.

Matt, my darling, Matt, she thought. *Have I lost you? Will I ever find you?*

CHAPTER 50

LEISHA'S 18ᵀᴴ BIRTHDAY

5 June 1872

It was a special evening and warm at the Bar M Ranch in Texas; it was Leisha's eighteenth birthday. The skinned cow had already turned to a golden tan on the spit of the bar-b-q as the cook prepared it for the main dish that night. Tables decorated with plates, platters and utensils, along with benches, lined the lawn of the ranch house. The ladies from the four ranches along the Brazos and some from Waco brought their finest dishes; some a lot, others a jug or two. But pride and warmth filled the air as they lined them up to fill the tables. The Bar M cook provided the cake as it sat in the kitchen ready for its deliverance at the right time.

Beer and whiskey poured for the gents and lemonade and punch for the women and children.

Mitch brought in the Brazos string band from Waco made up of one ranch hand on a guitar, another on the bunkhouse bass, a Texas Ranger on the fiddle and a wrangler for a caller. The music was good and the singing was complimentary as the guests for the evening found themselves dancing and slapping their thighs to the tune of the Texas jigs and the ever-popular Virginia Reel.

As guest of honor, Leisha did not disappoint the joyous party makers as she appeared early in the evening, wearing her finest apparel; a floral print calf-length dress, with lace petticoats filling it out, high laced boots and her long blonde hair reverse rolled and tied at the back of her head, with a silk ribbon flower that flowed down her back..

As she stepped out onto the veranda, her eyes scanned the terrace for one certain cowboy. Matt was not to be found. Mitch approached the lovely lady and escorted her to the dance floor where he twirled her around the floor as if they had rehearsed the movements many times before. And they had, for she loved to dance, and her father was well accustomed to dancing from his early days as a youth.

The dinner bell sounded and the plates were filled as the guests circled the cow and sat at the tables. Leisha's eyes kept scanning the horizon for Matt. Steve sat beside her while Mitch continued to host the evening affair with rhetoric about how she had grown up on the Bar M with her younger brother Seth.

"Seth will be a good foreman," Mitch continued, "a man with a gun and an excellent horseman, but Leisha could outride him, out rope him, and outdraw him on his best day from the time she became a teen. Today, she's a full-grown woman. Virtuous and pure. At least, it'd better be so."

The guests laughed and a few of the wranglers fired off their 45's. "If any one disputes that, I'll shoot 'im."

"Goodness, daddy, must we talk of such things in public?" Leisha said, much amused at the reaction of the company.

Mitch continued as Leisha's eyes caught a lone rider dismounting at the corral. The figure of the man took off his hat, dusted his trousers with it and walked towards the party unnoticed except by Leisha. She kept looking his way, hoping that it was Matt. The man stopped by the trough, laid his hat down on the edge, pumped some water into his hands and doused his face with it. He pushed back his hair and replaced his hat.

Leisha knew by the way he handled himself that it was Matt and a broad smile filled her face.

Steve saw it and looked in the direction she was smiling and noticed Matt ambling into the light of the lanterns. His countenanced fell as he had been hoping that for once Leisha might notice him, and not Matt. His hope disappeared as Matt announced his presence.

"Yee Hah! Howdy everyone!"

The guests returned his salute and waved him to the bar-b-q where another young lady held out a plate for him.

Mitch walked over to Leisha, placed his arm around her shoulders and smiled into her eyes. "Well. He finally made it!"

Leisha returned the smile and stood, waiting for Matt to approach her. When he did, the young lady with a plate for him greeted and curtsied before him with blinking eyes.

"Evening, Matt," She was from another ranch and had set her eyes for Matt for some time before. Matt had never paid any attention because he knew she was far too young for his liking. In fact, he had never paid any attention to any of the ranch girls, including Leisha, for he sensed that he must be twice her age, not to mention the fact that she was the General's daughter.

"Thanks, little lady," Matt returned. He took his plate a put slice of beef on it, looked around at the people and walked over to where Steve was sitting. An empty seat next to him looked inviting, and as Steve arose to greet him, he sat his plate down and punched Steve's shoulder. The *little lady* put her hands on her hips and said, "The least he coulda done was offered me a dance."

As Leisha sashayed over to Matt, she answered the little lady, saying, "Missy. He's not tamed yet."

Sitting next to Steve, Matt greeted him. "Howdy, Steve. Looks like a good party." Then he looked over at Leisha and politely said, "Sorry I'm late. Took a rustler into town and had some paper work to do. But, I'm here. Happy birthday, Little Darlin'. I wouldn't have missed this for anything." He took a big bite of beef and looked around for the drinks.

Mitch slapped a mug of beer in Matt's opened hand as he walked behind him. Pausing, he said, "Weren't worried a' tall, Matt." Then he looked down at Leisha who had a half-way look of despair on her face at Matt's seemingly uninterested gaze at her. "How does she look tonight, Matt? All dressed up real purty." He took Leisha by the hand and helped her stand up for Matt to see.

Matt took another quick glance at her, and then at his beer. When he was about to take a sip of beer, he stopped and took another good look at Leisha. What he saw was a beautiful lady dressed in frills with her hair adorned in ribbons and a tinge of rouge on her cheeks. All of a sudden, she was not a little girl he had helped grow up on a big ranch. He saw a lady in full bloom with a broad smile and sparkling blue eyes and pretty white teeth. His eyes never stopped examining the beauty in front of him as he let them trace her outline from her shoulders, across her bosom and down to her hips. She stood as a full-grown lady and he felt a sensual hunger grow inside him for the touch of her.

"Well, Matt. Aren't you going to ask her to dance?" Mitch asked, offering her hand to him.

The guests, along with Steve, saw the matchmaking going on in Mitch's control. He had liked Matt from when he met him during a battle in the Civil War. He liked the way he handled himself in many skirmishes and most of all when he saved his life. It was not the obligation he might have felt for saving his life that made him offer his daughter's hand to Matt, but the man he saw in Matt as a son-in-law of whom he would be proud.

However, Matt was still in love with a ghost; the ghost of Ginny McBride.

"Yes. Yes, of course. Leisha," Matt said as he took her hand. "May I have this dance?"

The band started up and played a Texas waltz and the vocalist sang as the couple cleared the dance floor with their presence. Steve stayed at Mitch's side and sipped his third glass of beer.

Matt's feelings for Leisha at that moment made any halfway thought of Ginny disappear as he sensed her feelings for him also with the way she held his hand.

She felt the same feelings with his hand on her waist.

Jaimie sauntered up to Steve and saw the look in his eyes at the couple on the floor while the rest of the party began gathering to dance alongside the couple. "Wanna dance?"

Steve stared at the young teenager, smiled and said, "Darlin', I've got boots older than you."

Jaimie looked sternly at Steve, put her fists on her hips and replied, "What's your dern boots got to do with dancing? I didn't ask to dance with your boots." and walked off.

When Matt walked Leisha back to the table, Jaimie walked over to him and said with a broad smile, "It's a fast one," meaning the dance. "Think you could keep up with it?"

Matt eyed Jaimie and answered, "Baby Sister, lead on." He took her hand and twirled away with her on the dance floor.

"She's having a good time," Leisha said as she leaned against Steve and laughed. "She always does; and she's only fourteen."

"How about you?" Steve asked, looking at the most beautiful thing he had ever seen in his life. He never knew he had a feeling for Leisha like he did this night, and now that she was by his side, he knew he could not hold her. But he was going to try. "Like to dance?"

"I'd love it," was her happy reply.

Steve began to enjoy himself once again, until a tap on his shoulder separated him from Leisha. A bigger man than he took Leisha across the floor where they sashayed into Matt and Jaimie.

Steve's beer began to act up on him and so he felt it was time to sit this one out. However, before he had time to reach the bench where he had been sitting, one of the wranglers placed a whiskey bottle in his hand and went off dancing himself. Before he knew it, Steve was drinking whiskey straight from the bottle.

Mitch came along and offered him another tall stein of beer, which, being the gentleman that he was, he took it, toasted to the party and drank it down, while holding the bottle of whiskey behind his back.

Another wrangler saw the whiskey, took it from Steve, gulped down a few drinks and placed it right back in Steve's hand.

Mitch caught the eye of a pretty lady and took her away onto the dance floor, giving Steve time to take some more whiskey. At the beginning of the next dance, a wrangler who had finished a dance with Leisha, offered her hand to Steve and said to him, "Our queen said that she would like to have the next dance with you."

Steve had much more liquor in him to even see the dance floor, but he was game as he watched Matt come back with Jaimie whom he had been dancing with for the past two dances. Eyeing Matt walking towards Leisha and seeing Leisha's dainty hand held out for his taking, he made every effort to take it and dance with her even though the band had not started up again.

"I think we should wait for the music, Steve," Leisha suggested as she held onto an unsteady Steve.

"Yeah!" was Steve's reply as he let go of her hand and tried to steady himself, only to bump into his buddy and close companion, Matt.

"Whoa, fella!" Matt cried out as he caught Steve.

As the band resumed playing, Steve escorted Leisha to the dance floor and attempted to dance. He made a few subtle attempts to dance and gave way to the floor.

Sizing up Steve's condition from across the floor, Matt left Jaimie's hand and waltzed over to Steve. "Settle down, son! You've had too much to drink." Matt attempted to pick him up, but quickly found out he had made a wrong move, for Steve came up swinging. He missed Matt, but said as he went back down to his resting spot on the floor, "I can hold myself up. Up I can."

"Well, you're doing a bad job of it, friend."

"He's been drinking all afternoon," Mitch said as he helped Steve back to the table. "It seems that everybody was cheering him on with drinks as he helped put this shindig together. I didn't know he had whisky, too, else I wouldn't have given him more beer."

He helped Steve to his feet and led him out into the fresh night air. Then he walked him to their house where he laid him out on his bed and covered him with a light blanket. He took his Stetson and flung it onto the nearby nail, hooking it on the first try.

"Sleep it off, friend. I'll get you up in the morning."

When he dimmed the lantern and left the house, he ran smack into Leisha, standing just outside the door.

"Oh. I'm sorry, Leisha. Didn't see ya."

"I thought I'd come out and give you a hand, but I see you made it all right."

"Yep. Steve don't usually get thet drunk. But today has been a pretty busy day for him. Seems everyone gave him a bottle."

"How about you?"

"Me?"

"Yeah. You still sober?"

"For now. But another round on the floor with Jaimie and a few more glasses of beer, and watch out!"

"Like to go for a walk?" Leisha asked as she turned opposite the dance floor and walked out into the night. Matt followed.

"Whatcha got in mind?" Matt asked, putting his hands in his hip pockets. He followed like a puppy with his master.

It was a lengthy walk, but the two were oblivious to the time as they talked and laughed together. The moon was bright so they could see the path they were walking along.

"I'm eighteen, Matt," she said matter-of-factly as she walked with her hands clasped behind her.

"I know. You sure did grow up fast, let me tell ya."

"I'm glad you noticed." The couple walked a little further out, this time without talking. She stopped, turned into Matt and said, "Are you going to give me my birthday kiss, Mr. Jorgensen?"

"Huh?" was all Matt could muster up, for by the time he started to say something, her lips were pressed hard against his.

She broke away and said, "I asked you if you were going to give me my birthday kiss, Mr. Jorgensen?"

She kissed him again; this time a little longer. "You're not the first man I ever kissed, you know."

"Oh?"

"No. Of course you don't know." She smiled and continued talking while holding onto Matt's hands. "Not real good, though. Some silly kid kissed me behind the barn one time after school. Didn't mean a thing. He was puny to boot."

"Well, Leisha. I thank you for this privilege. And now, I think we should be getting back to the dance before your father misses us."

"But you still didn't give me my birthday kiss," she said as she puckered up.

"You took two kisses."

"Yes, I did," she said with her hands on her hips. "And I liked them. But you didn't give them to me. I took them myself."

Matt looked around to see if anyone else was looking or listening. Then he took her in his arms and kissed her gently. When he broke away from the kiss, he held her in his arms and kissed her nose and then her forehead.

"Wow!" she said as she melted in his arms. "I've really been kissed."

She took his hat and, with her fingers, tossed it away. She then took her fingers and ran them through his wavy hair as she looked into his eyes.

He looked at her eyes, and then at her lips and kissed her again.

"I'm a big girl, now, Matt."

"Very much a woman, I'm a thinkin', Leisha."

"You've never looked at me as a woman before."

"Never had the cause."

"Do you like what you see?" She broke apart from Matt just a little but held onto his hands. "Well?"

"All the right places."

"You look right to me too . . . in all the right places."

Leisha walked into Matt and placed her knee against his groin as she felt him bring his body into hers. The moon shone down upon her hair giving it a sheen that Matt had never seen before. He tenderly touched her hair with his fingers, catching a wayward strand and, bending slightly, kissed her shoulder ever so tenderly.

The shrill yelp of a coyote in the distance danced with the coolness of the wind in a moment of ecstasy as the couple intertwined their dreams into one. The lovely eighteen year-old lass had found her moment of adulthood as the gentleman tasted the nectar of the windswept prairie.

When the couple returned to the dance, they could see through the moonlit night most of the party goers riding away. Mitch and a few others hung around the punch bowl while some of the ladies cleaned up the food dishes. A few couples still occupied the dance floor. As they left the floor, Matt and Leisha walked over and met with Mitch.

"Did you get Steve bedded down?" Mitch asked, smiling at Leisha's messed-up hair appearance.

"He's sleeping it off, last I saw of him," Matt answered sheepishly as he watched Mitch's eyes look at Leisha's hair.

"Where'd you two wander off to?"

"Down the trail a bit," Leisha answered with a devilish grin.

"Quite a bit, sir," Matt returned. "We walked almost to the edge of the Brazos it seemed."

"Oh, we didn't walk that far." Then she giggled some and added, "Of course, it seemed like it."

Mitch was not fooled that night, and from then on, he kept his eye on his good friend, Matt Jorgensen.

So did Leisha.

So did Jaimie.

And, so did Steve after he sobered up the next day and heard about the infamous night walk of a pair of kids. Kids? "Hah!" was all Steve could say as his jealous laughter wafted in the warm summer wind.

CHAPTER 51

THE SAGE FADES AWAY

4 May 1879

For six more seasons, Ginny and her siblings managed the mill. And for the same seasons, Sarah's health steadily declined. While Henry and his nurse watched over Sarah, Ginny made a hasty but necessary visit to the mill in Danville.

The rain had been steady for two days in Richmond when Ginny arrived back home. Henry met her at the depot with an enclosed carriage.

"You're looking great," Henry noted as he rushed her into the carriage, holding an umbrella over her to protect her from the rain. He placed her luggage upon the back of the carriage, strapping it down with rain gear.

"Only been gone a month. Where's Barnabas, Major?" Ginny asked as she received his lift into the carriage.

"It's good to have you home, Ginny," he said as he whipped the reins over the backs of the two mares and drove out to the McBride Estate.

"Ginny? You've never called me *Ginny*. What's up?"

"Emma and I, well we just figured it's time to call you by your real name."

"Ummm. Sounds rather nice. Thank you."

"Your grand mother has been asking for you. I thought it best that I tell you myself while driving to the mansion."

"Grand Mama? It'll be good to see her again. What's wrong?"

"Not well, I'm afraid, Ginny. She's dying."

Ginny's eyes shot open wide. "Grand Mama?"

"But she's held on until you came home. She needs to see you. I'm glad you came home when you did. It's time, darlin'. You've got to release her in peace."

At the threat of unreleased tears, Ginny said aloud, "Yes, Major. It's time for me to be strong for *her*." Then Ginny fell silent, thinking to herself about how Grand Mama had been the link during the dark years of her memory loss to finally remembering her past. It was her grandmother who gave her the renewed courage to pursue her heart's desire to journey and look for him when she came home, discouraged from trying to find him.

"She's had a heart attack. I've given her a sedative. It might not be too serious, but I'm keeping a close eye on her. As weak as she is, it's beginning to take a toll on her."

"Anything I can do?" Ginny asked, twisting her fingers.

"Just stay with her. Visit with her when she's awake. She could pull through it, but I won't know for how long. No salt in her food."

"Oh, great. She loves salt," Ginny responded. "But I'll keep it away from her."

Henry brought the team to a halt at the mansion and escorted Ginny to the door. Ginny turned to Henry and asked him, "Would you please wait while I go to see Grand Mama?" Barnabas was there to meet them, took the reins and drove the carriage to the stables.

Ginny removed her rain cloak, gave it to Barnabas and ran up the stairs to Sarah's room while Henry waited in the parlor by the fireplace.

Sarah knew her time on earth had come to an end and she wanted so much to speak to her grand-daughter.

"Grand Mama. I'm here." Ginny said in a whisper as she sat in the chair next to the bed. She reached over and took a hold of her pale hand, caressed it with her own and gently kissed it. "Are you awake, Grand Mama? Shall I open the drapes?"

"I'm awake, child," Sarah answered, opening her eyes.

"I'm back."

She looked at Sarah and saw that she appeared to be getting weaker.

What is it, Grand Mama?"

"I'm afraid I have failed you, Ginny."

"No, Grand Mama? No. You have never failed me."

"Yes, child. My time is up. I don't believe I will see tomorrow, and I have something to tell you."

"Don't talk like that, Grand Mama. You're going to live. You've got to live. You've got to keep going. I'm here because of you. I keep going because of you."

"Please listen to me. Don't interrupt. I must tell you this. You must find yourself, Ginny; your destiny."

There was that word again, just as both Reverend Bunting and even Brenda had said, *Matt is your destiny.*

"But, Grand Mama, I can't go anywhere. What about you . . . and . . . what about the mill?"

With her eyes still closed, she harrumphed, "No, grand daughter. There are plenty to run the mill. All the children have their places and their families. Even Annette has married her beau. No, you must go and fulfill your life. He's waiting for you."

"You know something, don't you, Grand Mama?" Ginny stated more than asked.

"Oh, I might have foresight and prophesy now and then. But I also have intuition."

Sarah turned her head to look into Ginny's eyes. "I, too, have dreams. Visions as you may call them. I know who Matt is and where he is. He came here searching for you. He is a tall, good looking man. The man you saw on the street. That was him."

"I told you. I told you that was Matt!" Ginny exclaimed happily. "You've seen him . . . again?

"Listen to me, Ginny. Listen carefully to what I have to say. I can't talk much. I keep falling asleep. Stay . . . stay with me."

"I'm still here, Grand Mama."

Sarah closed her eyes for a moment, which made Ginny think for the moment that she was losing her.

"Grand Mama! Oh. Please, Grand Mama. Come back to me!" Ginny cried, and her tears fell upon Sarah's pillow.

Again, Sarah opened her eyes and looked up into Ginny's hurt eyes.

"He was the man . . . who stood in front of the Purple Garter Saloon. I saw him then and afterwards in a vision. He came to your wedding. He . . . came to your wedding."

"Oh, Grand Mama. I knew it. Somehow, I just knew it."

"Your friend, that Willoughby fellow, made out to you that his sister was the woman he was marrying . . . and made Matt leave. Barnabas told me later, but Willoughby made him promise not to tell."

"He was here? In the McBride mansion?"

"I'm tired . . . so tired."

"I never saw him. Where? Where *is* he now?"

"Follow your heart, Ginny. He's searching for you . . . waiting for you. You will find him. You *must* find *him*. He's giving up and riding in the wrong direction; westward, so *you* must go to him."

Then Sarah took a deep breath, smiled, turned to Ginny and said, "There's something I need to tell you, my dear one. You and Matt have a gift. A very special gift. I know. I had it with my Jonathan."

"What, Grand Mama

"Let me ask you, dear. When you whipped Matt by the Tennessee River, did you feel the same pain that he felt?"

Ginny frowned and looked deep into Sarah's eyes. She thought, *how could she know all that?* And then she answered rather weakly, "Why, yes. Yes, I did. But no one knew. Not even Matt. How did you?"

"It is a phenomenon. A gift, if you may." She looked at the glass of water on the stand and asked, "May I have a sip of water, please?"

"Certainly, Grand Mama." Ginny obliged as she gently held the glass to Grand Mama's lips and watched her as she sipped the water slowly.

Then, patting Ginny on the back of her hand, Sarah indicated that she was through and Ginny returned the glass to the stand.

"I know. I know. That's why you stopped whipping him. And that's . . . why you fell in love with him. And he with you."

"I felt it. But how? How did you know?"

"As I said, I had the same feeling with my Jonathan; although at the time, Jonathan did not know it. I never told him." She smiled.

"But your Matt, Ginny He has it, too."

"Matt? How? What do you mean, Grand Mama?"

"The letter you received on the wall, my child. It was . . . from him. Oh, he did not know it would ever reach you, for you see, he wrote it and then some time later, he tore it up and threw it to the wind. But you . . . you received it all right."

"And, he communicated with me."

"Yes. And you with him. I'm sure he saw you at times in a vision just like you have, but he never really connected it with his gift like you have."

Ginny leaned in closer to Sarah and listened to the whisper of her soft voice and captured every word that escaped from her frail lips. "And . . .?"

"When he was in danger . . . your spirit went to him, immediately. You saved his life."

"You mean, when I saw that he was going to get shot, my spirit . . ."

"Yes, Ginny. Your spirit saved his life. And you will continue to do so throughout your entire life." She smiled, lifted a feeble hand, patted Ginny's cheek and then closed her eyes again. "I'm tired now."

"Oh, Grand Mama. Grand Mama. You've made me so happy. You've answered so many questions for me in just this short period of time. I love you so."

"Never, ever, child, tell any one. Not even Matt." Then she elicited a slight smile and a chuckle. "But then, you don't have to tell him. . ."

She relaxed and sighed. "He . . . some how . . . knows you are his . . . and he is yours by virtue of this gift. And . . . he will never give up looking for you until he finds you."

Ginny stood up, walked to the window and watched the rain pelt against it as heavy thoughts captivated her mind. Without turning around, she asked, "Will we ever find each other?"

"It's inevitable, dear."

Ginny quickly turned around, wiped a tear that ran down her cheek with her dainty handkerchief and asked, "How?"

"Look to the . . . hills of . . . Montana."

"Montana? Why? He's from Wyoming."

"Montana. I just know you need to look there. That's where you'll find him." Sarah closed her eyes again.

"Grand Mama!"

Ginny left the room and met Henry in the parlor. He caressed her and said, "I'll be back in the morning. Nurse Nelson will stay with her."

"Thanks, Major." She watched Henry take his bag and walk out to his carriage. "Love you."

"Me, too, Ginny." He felt more than ever before the father-daughter relationship that Emma was longing for. With a snap of the whip, he drove away, and Ginny returned to take care of Sarah, the matron of the McBride Mansion.

Nurse Nelson gave Ginny a comforting smile and said, "I'll be in her room if you need me" and went upstairs.

"Thanks," Ginny replied and went back to her room.

The hours grew long as Ginny sat by Sarah's side. Then the day came when Henry was summoned to her side.

"I'm afraid she's turned for the worst, Ginny," he said after examining her. "All we can do now is to wait and see how she responds to the sedative."

Ginny remained with Sarah for a while and then went downstairs to visit briefly with Henry in the parlor. He had sent for Emma and they were both visiting and comforting the different family members as they gathered. Each had sat in turn with Grand Mama during the day.

As she had awakened for brief moments, Sarah asked Nurse Nelson for each Great Grandchild to be brought to her and without saying so, gave each of them a final moment. Each grandchild in response seemed to receive a final smile and a word of blessing.

She visited with Jerry last, the eldest son of the family. She talked with him as her grandson, but reminded the lawyer in him of her last wishes they'd planned at length long ago. Just before he left the room, she took his hand and said to him "Jerry, promise me that you'll send Ginny west. Don't keep her here. She needs to go. Don't ask any questions, just see that she doesn't stay here and live an empty life, Jerry, promise me." Jerry kissed Sarah's cheek and promised her without question. He whispered, "We sorely need her here. But, if it's about finding her Matt, I promise, Grand Mama. I promise."

As the family returned to the parlor, they gathered as evening crept in. Ginny assured them that she would sit with Grand Mama through the night and they should each go on home. She excused herself so that Sarah would not be alone and left them to dismiss themselves homeward for the night.

Ginny read Sarah's Bible that she found on the night stand. "I will not leave you . . . nor forsake you." It was marked in the Book of Ruth.

Later in the evening, Sarah once more opened her eyes to find Ginny still sitting in the chair with her hands clasped and her head down as in prayer.

"Child!"

"Grand Mama. You're awake. You're going to be all right."

"No, child. I'm ready to meet my Savior. My time is up. Remember this . . . Go to Matt. Your destiny is with him. I see you riding horses together and traveling together. But, go to him . . . as your name dictates . . . Ginny McBride."

"Ginny! Yes, I know, Grand Mama.

"You are Ginny, child and I love you. Virginia McBride."

Sarah closed her eyes and sometime during the night went to be with her Jonathan.

Sarah passed away that spring. The drapes were closed in her room, but a dimly lit lantern outlined Sarah's body as she lay on the bed. Ginny remained by the bed for awhile with Sarah's Bible in her lap.

Gerald, Kenneth and Annette sat in the drawing room with the members of their families, waiting for Ginny to come down.

When Barnabas answered the door on the Paterson's usual visit to the mansion, they knew by observing his countenance that something had happened. They walked solemnly into the large home and, with Barnabas leading them, wound their way to the drawing room where Lula Belle, in her sorrow, served tea and coffee to the family and close friends who had gathered there. The Patersons went to join Ginny at Sarah's bedside.

The rains soaked up the tears that mournful morning as they laid Sarah's body ever so gently into the grave on the grounds of the McBride Mansion. Emma held Ginny's hands as they led Sarah away. With her other hand, she also held onto Henry's.

The mass entourage of carriages drove down the hillside and away from Sarah and the McBride mansion, leaving her to rest there with her Jonathan.

CHAPTER 52

GINNY LEAVES FOR MONTANA

The years after the war were kind to Ginny; and now she had just celebrated her thirty-seventh birthday. As an attorney, she proved to be one of the best in Virginia. Her practice grew as her clients relied upon her for her knowledge of good Virginia law.

Being the attorney for the mill had carried a lot of weight and credibility for her. At the same time, her brothers were busy in Danville as the mill was running and becoming stable. Her sister Annette had married their chief construction engineer, Bryce Willoughby, who also became an important member of the firm.

Then the day finally came as Grand Mama predicted it would when Ginny realized her dream of finding Matt rested solely on her shoulders because she had never heard from Matt or his whereabouts. That day was particularly a busy day for Ginny as she returned to her home and to meet with some of her clients.

Her main target now was one Norwegian widow in Montana. After Sarah passed away, Ginny put a tracer out through her colleagues to see if they could locate a Norwegian lady by the name of Jorgensen in, of all places, Montana. With the information that Matt had told her so long ago, she knew he was one of two sons who were reported as being killed in a holdup.

The source came back for one Mrs. Anne Andersen, a widow living in Bozeman, Montana. Ginny felt she had struck pay dirt, for through correspondence with her, she had a feeling that Mrs. Andersen could very well be Matt's mother. It was just a hunch, but that was all Ginny needed to start her trek.

"If I'm ever going to put my life together with Matt, I'm going to have to find him," she addressed Emma from behind her desk in her office. Emma and Henry had dropped by for a routine visit with her. "I've figured that out all by myself. Well, with the help of Grand Mama."

"So you're still using the name of *Beth* for your law practice?" Henry asked as he watched her pack her law books. "Why, may I ask?"

"Because, Major Doctor Paterson," she answered in a perky manner, "he knew me as Ginny McBride and I don't want him to know who I am until I find him. He might be married. He might not even like me any more; or remember me. And, besides, my law degree has my name as Elizabeth Paterson, and it will be hanging there in my office."

"Oh!"

"You, boob," Emma came back. "You knew she was going incognito from the beginning."

Ginny then turned and watched Emma appear on the verge of tears. Henry also seemed to be watching as if a spark were to burn out before them with Beth's leaving.

Emma reached out to Henry, letting her tears stain his newly-ironed white shirt.

"Yes. Yes. I'm going as Beth Paterson, your adopted daughter." She pulled herself away and wiped her tears with her hankie, and then she wiped the stains that had fallen on Emma's shoulder. "If I stayed and worked with my family in the mill; yes, there'd be no problems of using Beth as my name. But, no. I'm going to Montana to find Matt. I'll probably always be Beth to you. And to Matt, if ever I find him, I'll also probably be Beth, the attorney." Then she smiled and straightened her dress a little. "That is, unless he sees me as and takes me back as Ginny."

"Do you think he'll remember you as *Ginny?*" Emma asked.

"Do I look like Ginny?" she laughed, even through the tears.

Emma looked gently into Ginny's eyes and replied, "I don't know the real Ginny; I don't suppose. But, no. No. You look like our Beth."

"Then, I suppose that answers your question. I doubt if he'll ever know the difference. I just hope, when I find him, if I find him, that he will fall in love with me, *Beth*. Or the ghost of Ginny McBride. I'll catch him, one way or another."

"And you know pretty much where you are going to start looking for him?" Henry asked, lighting his pipe.

"I remember that he left a ranch and a mother. I've learned that it might be somewhere in Montana," Ginny related. "That's all I know. Oh, something about a . . ." She blushed for a moment.

"A *what . . .?* Henry asked.

"She whispered over at Emma but knew Henry would hear, too. "A set of crushed balls, too." Then she continued the conversation for all to hear. "He told me that was the name of his ranch."

Henry laughed, and Emma frowned, but nothing more was said.

"I just have one question, Ginny," Henry interjected.

"What's that, Major?" Ginny asked, using his title.

"What if he's married to another?"

Ginny stared away blankly. Without turning around, she said, "I've thought about that. Quite often."

"Well, then?"

"Through the visions, I'm firmly convinced that he's looking for me as much as I'm looking for him. I know I'll find him."

"I just don't want you to be disappointed."

"And I have a question for you, too," Emma broke in. "If he is married, or missing, or, God forbid, dead, what will you do next?"

"I don't know, Emma," Ginny replied.

"Will you come home and become a part of the McBrides and take up your place in the mill Industry?" Emma took hold of Ginny's hand and softly squeezed it.

Ginny thought hard on that question for a lengthy time.

"Would you?" Emma asked again, looking into her deep, searching eyes.

"No." And then she added with a laugh, "My little sister's already hitched to him."

That elicited a chuckle from Emma and she said, "We just want you not to be hurt. Just to get what you really want out of life."

Ginny released Emma's hold on her, walked away, and then turned back and answered her. "I've spent the past fifteen years searching for him. A man I only knew for a short span of time. A man that proved to be a man to me.

"I gave up my position at the mill to become an attorney so that I could prove to myself, I suppose, that I am still Ginny McBride. I'm not a ghost. I'm real. I'm going to take my practice to a place called Virginia City, Montana. If I do not find Matt, I . . . I just might settle there to be next to *his* ghost."

"You love him that much?" Emma asked. She walked over to Ginny and took her hand again in hers. "Yes, I can see you do. No doubt about it."

"And the ranch life is going to be what you want?" Henry asked. "After all, you're a refine lady and a very rich and respected attorney now."

Ginny appeared to be somewhat naïve about ranches. Emma looked over at Henry and answered him for her. "I'm sure she'll find the ranch some how, dear,"

Emma took Ginny by her arm and walked her to the door. "When you find your man, bring him home. Hear me. Bring him home. You now have a mansion of your own."

On the next day, Richard and Victoria Jamison's carriage drove up to the front of the house. Stepping out of the carriage, the couple walked up to the house and was greeted by Barnabas. Ginny's bags were sitting by the door. Entering the house, they were met by Ginny whom they found standing just outside the first foyer.

Victoria hugged her and said, "I made it in time. I couldn't let my niece go away without saying goodbye."

Victoria was not as tall as Ginny and showed her age with a little plumpness that she appreciated from her years playing the part of an aunt. She wore her hair up and adorned with colorful pins. She wore makeup that could make one to want to model after her as it appeared natural and yet beautiful, accentuating her light green eyes. She was adorned with a long dark green dress with a shawl around her shoulders. Her neck was adorned with pearls that matched her ear rings.

Willoughby rode up to the mansion on his white gelding, reined up at the hitching post and dismounted.

"Goodbye, Victoria. Richard," Ginny said in a pleasant manner. "I'm so glad you accepted my clients so well. I couldn't leave without your help."

"You're a good attorney, Ginny," Richard returned. "Almost as good as me," he gestured. "Your clients will be well taken care of, and when you return, you can resume your practice here in Richmond."

Richard was one of the wealthiest attorneys in Richmond and now had accepted Ginny's clients which, along with his own firm's, would increase his credibility. He was a proud man, in his late fifties, balding somewhat, sporting a proud moustache, and a little paunchy. His dress as an attorney was impeccable with the best suit ensemble, tie and watch fob.

They were joined by the Patersons who came by to see her off. The entire McBride clan was there, too.

"We'll take good care of your clients, Ginny," Victoria assured her. "When you return, we'll help you set up again."

Willoughby caught up with Ginny as she left the mansion to get into the carriage. Ginny caught the look in his eye and returned it with a smile, and she winked at Annie who sat by Willoughby's side.

"We've already talked about that," Kenny interjected. "I offered her my help, little as it is, overseeing the mill with my brother." Then he looked at Richard and said most assuredly, "I'm glad that you're taking good care of her in my stead."

"Thanks, Victoria, but I don't want to come back to practice."

Willoughby interrupted politely to confirm her decision. "You're really leaving all this? The mansion? The mill? Your law practice? Any or all of which could give you a great living for life."

She looked at the rest and said, "Excuse me for a moment," and walked over to Willoughby. "Yes, Bryce. I told you I was.

Annette watched with jealous eyes as Willoughby still kept pawing at Ginny like a cat.

"I never thought you'd leave Richmond," Willoughby said, taking a hold of Ginny's hands. She smiled and released the hold on his hand.

"You're a married man, Bryce," Ginny answered him. "Take care of my little Annie. Hear me?"

Then Annette watched with a smile in her eyes. Yes, she knew Bryce was hers. All she wanted now was for him to know it as she patted her slightly round belly.

As she stepped up into the carriage, she tried to reassure Bryce. "Go to Georgia on your seven-hundred mile voyage or whatever and make your fortune with Annie. As for me, I'm headed for, who knows where." Then she gestured, "But I'm a goin'." Then she giddily added, "Don't worry; I'll write."

She looked at her siblings, along with Martha and Barbara, and the little ones, and said to them all as she gave them each a goodbye kiss, "But I will return. I'll return with Matt to show him my family. Once I find Matt, I'm going to settle down, wherever he chooses, for good."

As Beth? Victoria wondered to herself. *Or as Ginny?* Ginny saw the puzzled look on Victoria's face for a moment, smiled and walked away.

Ginny settled down into the carriage as Barnabas loaded her bags. Once the luggage was strapped in, Simon whipped the lines of the carriage, getting the mares started down the road towards the railroad depot for the Norfolk-Pacific Railroad to take Ginny to Montana.

Henry and Emma stood atop the hillside with the McBrides in front of the mansion and waved at their adopted daughter. Ginny bade a *goodbye* to all of them. She tossed a kiss to Annie who threw it back with a smile.

"She'll be back," Emma said. "Maybe not by herself, but she'll be back."

"You know everything, don't you, Emma," Henry surmised, gently squeezing her waist.

"Oh, I know she never gave you a tumble, you old fart." Emma laughed and went back inside.

Henry's face fell for the moment. He looked at Ginny one more time riding down the road, turned and walked side by side with Emma to the veranda. "Old?" he cried out, and skipped down the hallway.

Richard and Victoria walked in and met the Paterson's on the veranda where Lulu Belle awaited with tea to serve them.

The ghost of Ginny McBride was set and determined that she was going to find her man. That is, if her Matt were still alive.

CHAPTER 53

ANNE ANDERSEN

As a professional attorney, Ginny knew how to establish her business practice in a northern town called Virginia City, Montana. She went under the name on her degree, *Beth Paterson.*

She had already made many friends throughout the city and the surrounding area. Her dress and demeanor were above the average person in Virginia City as she parlayed her style and experience into a profitable business almost overnight, taking on only the clients who seemed to be most affluent in all areas and the one who truly needed her help. After all, she came from an aristocratic family that had no need for putting on airs. And for that matter, she was financially set for being an attorney in a new environment, although she had already accumulated an experience of over twelve years as a practicing attorney in an affluent section of Richmond, Virginia.

Ginny waited on pins and needles to meet with Mrs. Anne Andersen. They had made arrangements through their letters that they would meet. She had told Ginny that she had one heir to her ranch, *The Double O,* and she wanted to leave it to her only son, Matt Andersen.

The bell rang on the door that led into Ginny's office as Mrs. Andersen stepped into the room. She was a frail woman in her late sixties who had gone through tough times and seen her husband leave her behind for a cattle drive; never to return.

She was accompanied by Jean Wrisley, a friend from a nearby ranch. She was a woman in her early forties and the mother of Danny Wrisley, a wrangler who helped get her husband's cattle to Belle Fousche. It was on that cattle drive that her husband, Wil Andersen was killed. Since before her son's return with the other young cowboys from the same cattle drive, Mrs. Wrisley has been close friends with Annie.

Ginny's office sat in front while her living quarters were behind. The room was warm and comfortable, decorated with a feminine touch. Floral curtains hung behind a small desk that sat to the front to eliminate the overbearing power a large desk. A bookshelf filled with books stood against one wall. An elegant doily and an oil lamp set on top of the bookshelf. Across from the bookshelf set an elegant draped table with a sterling silver tea set on it. A potbellied stove sat off to one side of the room with the teakettle on it.

Annie, as she had been accustomed to being called, felt at ease in the confines of the room and waited for Ginny to enter from the back room divided by a strand of beads that hung from the ceiling to the floor.

Ginny stepped into the room, dressed as every bit the unpretentious lady attorney that she was, and with a smile, held out a gloved hand for Annie to receive.

"Mrs. Andersen," Ginny addressed her. "You're right on time."

"Thank you, Miss Paterson. This is my friend, Jean Wrisley. You remember her from our first visit?"

"Yes. Mrs. Wrisley. Please sit." She offered them the straight back chairs that sat in front of the desk.

"You look beautiful today, Miss Paterson. As usual, I suppose." Ginny had to get use to the idea of once again being called Beth Paterson, this time in Montana.

"That's kind of you, Mrs. Andersen. And may I repay the compliment?"

"After this ride?" Mrs. Wrisley commented. "I'm a mess."

As Ginny conversed with her, she held back the excitement that had swelled up in her veins.

"I have made some tea for your visit," Ginny informed her as she stepped to the side table to pour the tea. "I know it was a long ride. I hope it was comfortable."

The first visit earlier was that of getting acquainted with one another in a comfortable fashion. Today was a confirmation of Annie's last will and testament.

"They appear alright to me, Miss Paterson."

"Marvelous. Then I'll get the papers together and have them ready for your signature. Why don't I bring them out to you? Say Monday around noon?"

"Fine. Fine," Annie answered.

And Mrs. Wrisley, if you will be so kind to be there, I'll try and bring another guest as a witness, and everything will be finalized."

"I'll make it a point to be. Thank you, Miss Paterson. It's been a pleasure."

The ladies bade Ginny a good day and left. She sat still for the longest time after the two ladies left, feeling deep inside that she was getting closer to Matt.

On another warm and sunny day, Ginny slept in until noon. She dressed in a long, frilly dress that skirted the floor, and a wide brim hat with a small feather. She resided in Virginia City, and she definitely wanted to keep an air of pretense about her that would make the town believe she was someone important, whether they knew anything about her or not. She strolled to the east end of town to visit her good friend, Mrs. Dorothy Phillips.

Dorothy was a woman in her fifties who could wear fine clothes well; being a well-known owner of the only millinery store in town. Her husband, Roger, a retired gentleman in his sixties, worked in the assayer's office in Virginia City. He did this for pleasure and to stay active more than to earn extra income, although he did this rather nicely, too. He was a middle-size Scotsman with balding features and long sideburns. He wore spectacles of a kind, which revealed him as being a man of wealth. Dorothy had first made friends with Ginny while she was shopping in the general store, shortly after she had arrived in town.

A lovely, young black woman answered Ginny's knock and opened the huge door to the Phillips' stately mansion. The aura of the mansion was no problem to Ginny, herself being from the McBride family of Richmond.

"Mrs. Phillips, please," Ginny requested.

The young woman recognized Ginny and motioned for her to enter as Dorothy entered from a room adjacent to the foyer with arms outspread in welcome. "Well, well, well, Beth Paterson," she exclaimed, "how wonderful to have you here again. I see you walked over."

"The walk was not too long, and I rather enjoyed it because the weather had warmed up a bit."

"It's Sunday, Beth. You should have had your buggy?" Dorothy pulled back the chenille curtains and looked out her front window in all directions.

"It is such a beautiful day, I figured I could use the walk and fresh air."

She stepped up into the house and Dorothy led her to the front foyer where they sat to share the afternoon.

"With too many things on my mind, I gave up trying to work with my clients, and thought I'd visit with you awhile. That is, if you have some free time."

"Most certainly, darling. Please sit. I'll have Ellie get us some tea, if that's all right with you."

"I could certainly use something hot."

"Ellie, would you bring the tea cart out, please?"

The afternoon passed quickly as the two women chatted about what was, what is, and what was to come with the townsfolk of Virginia City.

"You are planning to spend the evening?" Dorothy asked rather rhetorically. "I won't let you out of this house."

Since Dorothy was a wealthy woman, greatly admired by the citizens of Virginia City, she welcomed many an overnight visitor of an esteem nature.

"Certainly," Ginny answered. "I planned on it."

"So," Dorothy started in. "We need to talk about you for a change. How's your practice coming along?"

"Better than expected. I've few clients yet as it is, but I'll make out alright."

"What's the latest news?" Dorothy asked, leaning her elbows on her knees.

"Well, this I can tell you. I've done a lot of investigative research into the whereabouts of one Matt Jorgensen."

"And? Who's he?"

"A very special friend. I think I've traced him to this area and I'm sure I've located his mother."

"You're lover? You've found him?"

"I don't know. Not for certain. I've discovered that a man of his description was killed in Bozeman and that his mother lives here"

"Do you think it was him that was killed?"

"No. But, if it was his brother, he could still be alive. That's why I'm so excited."

"How do you know? How will you know for sure?"

Ellie came in and interrupted them for a moment with her standing in the door way, wanting to know about supper.

"Not now, Ellie!" Dorothy spurted, waving her hands at her. "Not now!"

Ellie curtsied and scurried away, leaving Dorothy tied up in knots over the news that Ginny was revealing to her.

"Well, the stars fell on me this past week and I'm too excited to hold it in."

"Well. Well, let me in on it."

"Nothing to jump to conclusions about, yet. After all these years, I've just about given up. Well, this certain lady from up the Bozeman Trail visited me the other day and we talked. The more we talked, the more I believe I've found my Matt."

"What'd she want?"

"She had a special request."

"Tell me!" Dorothy said with enthusiasm as she fidgeted with her fingers.

"Don't get your tail feathers in a ruffle, Dorothy. I'm not real certain, yet. But . . ."

"But? But what? Go on!"

"You know I can't divulge who this person is or about what, but I can tell you this much. She wants me to handle her last will and testament."

"And . . .?

"There are particulars that are leading me to believe I may be on the right track for finding my Matt."

"I can't tell you, now. Not now. But I just wanted to let you know how excited I am."

"Excited? You've got me on the edge of my seat. What's next?"

"When I know, I'll certainly let you know. Are you comfortable with that?"

Dorothy wrinkled up her nose and smiled. "It'll do; for now."

"Now, may I ask a favor of you?"

"Certainly," Dorothy agreed. "What?"

"I need you to go with me tomorrow out to her ranch to act as a witness to her will. Nothing more."

Dorothy felt excited and readily agreed. "You bet I will." She was chomping at the bit to meet Annie.

It was a long ride for the two ladies in Dorothy's carriage as her black servant drove her to the Double O Ranch the next day, Monday, to meet with Annie and Jean once more.

Annie sat in a rocker on the front porch with Jean standing beside her as they awaited Ginny's arrival.

"Mrs. Paterson," Jean called out to her as Ginny's carriage pulled up to the hitching post. Assisted by the servant, Ginny and Dorothy stepped down from the carriage and walked up to Annie and Jean.

"Mrs. Andersen. May I introduce my good friend, Miss Dorothy Phillips?"

Dorothy was polite and shook hands with Annie.

"This is Annie, Dorothy. Dorothy owns a millinery in town."

"Yes. I'm familiar with Miss Phillips' store," Annie remarked, looking hard at Dorothy. "Though I've not been there for some time."

"Well, Mrs Andersen, although I can't recall seeing you, I'm certain we've met before. You do seem familiar."

"We can all go inside, Miss. Paterson. Miss Phillips." Jean invited the guests in as Annie rose and walked feebly into the house.

The ladies entered the house while Dorothy's driver stayed with the carriage.

The room in the house was the same as it was when Wil left it; bare pine walls and a fireplace against the far wall. Two hand-made overstuffed chairs and a straight back sat in the middle. A lit lantern decorated the kitchen table to the right with four more chairs opposite the fireplace. The ladies made themselves comfortable in the front room.

"I've had Ellie make some lemonade for us and your driver," Jean said as she retrieved some glasses. Ellie came in and in turn gave one to .the driver who came upon the porch.

"Thank you, Jean," Ginny returned, readily taking a sip to cool her parched throat from the trip. "And, Jean, please call me Beth. I'd feel better about that."

"Yes . . . Of course. Beth."

When the formalities were over, and the client and attorney had become comfortable with each other, Ginny opened her brief case and withdrew Mrs. Andersen's file folder.

"I've had the papers drawn up for you as you requested."

"Thank you," Annie answered as she looked weakly into Ginny's soft eyes.

I might look too excited about handling your last will; and I apologize for that."

"Why?" Mrs. Andersen returned.

"Well, as you know, this is an attorney-client confidential relationship, which we discussed on your first visit."

"Yes. Yes, I'm aware of that. And I certainly appreciate your keeping it that way. I have heard a lot of good things about you, and that's why I selected you to handle my affairs."

"Mrs. Andersen, as you know, is rather weak and tired," Jean Wrisley informed Ginny.

Ginny looked at Dorothy and Jean and asked, "Would it be alright with you ladies if I talked with Annie alone?"

With the ladies' consent, they walked out on to the porch with their glasses and left Ginny and Annie to be alone.

Ginnie looked at Annie with compassion and asked quietly, "May I ask you an important question concerning your son, Annie?"

"Yes."

"Your son, Matthew. It is recorded that he was killed in an attempted freight robbery. Yet, you are seeking to leave all you have to a dead son."

Annie cringed and Ginny knew that she needed to put her arms around her shoulders. She rose, walked over to Annie and did just that.

Annie took her handkerchief from her waistband and wiped away her tears, and then confirmed, "What I tell you here goes no further. Right?" Annie asked,

"Absolutely. My solemn word."

Ginny was so excited she could hardly restrain herself. She knew deep in her soul that this was her Matt that Annie was revealing to her. She wanted to know more, much more, and here was the truth.

"My son, Matthew Andersen, is alive!"

Ginny sighed. She had one more question; the all important question. "Where is your son?"

"Oh, my land sakes," Annie returned. "I didn't tell you?"

"No. No. In our first visit, you simply stated your son's name is Matt Andersen. I failed to ask you at that time, but when I examined the court records, I find that your two sons had been killed."

"Yes."

"But you say one is still alive."

"Yes."

"Where? Where does he live?"

"In Texas."

"And, does he still go by his birth name?"

"No. No."

"Then he has another name, I presume."

"Yes."

Ginny waited a long moment and watched Annie's eyelids flutter as she fidgeted with her hands. Annie's story about her two sons in a hold up and one killed and the probability of the other being on the run had a lot of merit in it that made Ginny feel hopeful that Annie's son Matt was her lover.

Then Jean stepped back inside the house. "I'm the only one that she has revealed this to, Miss Paterson," Jean interrupted. "Just my husband, Roger and I know the truth." She looked at Ginny's startled look and continued. "We could hear through the open window."

"And . . .?" Ginny looked wantonly into Annie's eyes.

"His name is Matt Jorgensen!" Jean revealed with a passionate look into Annie's eyes. "He's a hired gun on a ranch south of Waco, Texas across the Brazos River. It's called the Brazos River Bar M. and run by a General Ted Mitchell."

Ginny held her gloved hand to her upper lip to calm herself from fainting.

Through the course of conversation, the ladies enjoyed each other and revealed as much as they could to help bring the pieces of this jigsaw puzzle of one Matt Jorgensen together. Ginny learned then of the botched-up freight company robbery and how Matthew escaped.

"I'm suggesting something that you may or may not like, Annie," Ginny opened up to Annie.

"What is it, Beth?" Annie returned, accepting a fresh glass of lemonade from Jean.

"Well, it might seem that there is sort of an egotistical motive behind my request, and there is."

"Well, Beth. Let it out."

"First of all, wouldn't you love to have your son exonerated from all the things being said about him? Give him a clean slate?"

"Why, yes. Of course. But how?"

"If what you have told me about the robbery is true, then Matt can be cleared of the charges. We can bring him back to Virginia City, have him stand trial and . . ."

Before Ginny could finish, Annie interrupted. "They'll hang him, Beth! They'll hang him!"

"Yes. There's no guarantee about anything. He's your son. I'm your attorney. I know I'm good. And I would like the chance to have him exonerated."

The two women faced each other with a moment of truth staring them in their eyes. Dorothy sat motionless, waiting for the scenario to play out. Annie showed fear and consternation about the awful possibility of causing her son's demise by revealing the truth to the world that her son was alive. Ginny showed excitement and enthusiasm about her seeing Matt again. She thought, *Would it be worth it to see him if it could also cause him to possibly be hung? Could she get him exonerated?*

Of course, she thought, *if Annie refuses to have Matt brought back for trial, then I can still go to Texas and meet him. But he needs to see his mother before she passes on. And,* she concluded to herself adamantly, *he needs to be set free.*

She looked steadily at Annie for an answer, which seemed an eternity coming.

"How sure are you that you can get him off?" Annie asked.

"With your consent, I'll start right now to build my case. The first thing I want is for him to come back to you. Not as Matt Andersen, but as Matt Jorgensen. It's been a long time. Things are forgotten and gone by. People have died. We've a good case, Annie. I can do it! I know I can."

"How are we going to get him to come back?" Jean asked, sitting on the edge of her chair. "He won't just up and come back, unless . . ."

"Unless we tell him that his mother wants to see him," Ginny added. "Of course. And forgive me, Annie, but this is what you would want, isn't it?"

"To see my son again. Yes. Oh, yes."

"Then we'll need to go after him."

"You?"

Ginny stopped and took a deep breath. Then she said, "No. I couldn't bring him back." *I want him to see me on my terms and as I am,* she thought to herself. *I don't want to lose him again.*

"My son," Jean opened up quickly. "Danny. He was on the cattle drive with Wil Andersen."

"Danny?" Annie asked. "Alone? He's no match for my son. It's gonna take more than Danny to bring him back."

"Then," Jean came back, "he and a couple of others can go to Texas together and bring him back. Surely three men can bring back one."

Without any hesitation, Ginny said, "Done! Let's talk with Danny.

"We're going to bring your son home, Annie!" Ginny exclaimed. Slapping her hand on her lap, she stood up. "With all God's help, we'll bring him to you!"

She took the papers from her briefcase and handed them to Annie. "I'll make this fast. Annie. These are your papers as you requested. I'm notarizing them now. I'll keep a copy for my files.

After putting her seal to the papers and signing them, she put them in a folder and turned them over to Annie. Annie took the folder in hand, caressed it to her chest and uttered low and slowly, "Matt! My son, Matt!"

CHAPTER 54

MONTANA COWBOYS TO WACO, TEXAS

12 June 1882

Several days later, the Waco and Northwestern train eased to a stop at its destination, Waco, Texas, and three good-looking cowboys dressed in chaps got off. They were sent by one Beth Paterson to bring Matt Jorgensen back to Montana.

Charlie Honeycutt, tall and gaunt, with auburn hair, was twenty and known as "Slim." Because of his age and height, he assumed the leadership role of the trio of cowboys. Attributing to this, also, was his patience in paying particular attention to things that were happening around him, which kind of made him a polite sort of person.

Dan Wrisley, once known as "Four Eyes" because he wore a pair of family heirloom glasses at an early age, was a few months younger than Slim. He lost those glasses when a rustler named Long Hair took and broke them.

Slim carried a guitar, which he played expertly, and every once in awhile, when things were quiet, he would bring it out and play a tune.

At nineteen, Homer Bickerdyke was the youngest of the three. He was called "Shorty" because of his height, but he had broad shoulders and knew how to take care of himself.

The sun was just past high noon, and the day was unusually warm for three cowboys from Montana this time of year. Looking around, they caught sight of the livery stable and ambled over to rent some horses. After they picked them out, they saddled up and rode into town.

Their hungry stomachs demanded they find a place to eat. Coming across a small restaurant, they tied up their horses, walked into the empty restaurant, and settled down at a gingham-covered table for a meal, and ate like three hungry wolves devouring a prairie dog. They cleaned their plates with swabs of biscuits.

As the waitress picked up their plates, Dan asked, "Know of a Matthew Jorgensen in these parts, ma'am?"

Stopping for a moment with dishes in her hands, she replied that he was working the spread across the river. "I think he's the foreman or ramrod; something or the other."

"We're from out of town, ma'am," Dan continued. "How do we get there?"

She put the dishes down on an empty table and pushed a ringlet of hair from her eyes, looking at the men in a flirtatious sort of way. "Gonna join 'im?"

Slim answered, "No, ma'am. Just need to talk."

"Wouldn't be staying?" She threw a look back at Dan as she picked up the dishes. She paused for a moment, then said, "No, guess not." She gave them directions and pointed out the window with her long fingers. "End of the road, there's a fork. The road to the left leads to the Brazos River. There's a bridge. Cross it, and follow the river. You'll find it." She disappeared into the kitchen, her voice trailing after her. "Or they'll find you."

"Well, let's go," Dan said, getting up from his chair.

Slim tossed a couple of golden eagles on the table and called out to her, "Gotta stop by the rangers' office."

She returned and picked up the eagles with a smile and said to Dan, "Few doors down on opposite side of the street. What's your hurry?"

Dan stopped and stared, but Slim and Shorty took him by his arms and dragged him out the door. Not too far down the street they found the rangers' office. The cowboys turned into the doorway and found two rangers standing, and the captain behind his desk.

Captain Ralph Johnson was a gentle-looking man in his sixties and had a salt-and-peppered mustache. He was a little overweight for a man under six feet tall, but that was evidence of his wife Maggie's good cooking. He was reading the *Waco Gazette.*

Slim spoke for the three cowboys. "We're from the Double-O Ranch up Montana way. Is any of you Capt'n Johnson?"

Captain Johnson answered, "You must be the three cowboys I heard about. Been waiting for you. Suspected it was you up at the stable. See you got some horses." He looked the three over and waited for someone to speak, but no one did. "Welcome to Waco, Texas. Just got in on the noon train, I take it? Well, come around and have some Texas-style coffee. It's free."

Dan spoke up, "No thanks, Capt'n."

Shorty took off his hat and sat down. "We want to get some riding hours in before the sun goes down."

The captain grinned and poured himself a cup of coffee. "Well, sit for a spell. At least you can stay a little while. Texas hospitality, you know." He sat back down himself.

The two rangers introduced themselves as Tom Elliott and Floyd Douglas. The former was at least six foot tall, trim, and in his mid-twenties. Douglas was shorter and a little older. He was rubbing down a rifle barrel with an oil-slick cloth.

The three cowboys examined the interior of the rangers' quarters with their eyes. Rifles and shotguns decorated a wall cabinet and pictures of numerous rangers hung on the wall. A flag of the Lone Star State covered most of the back wall and a sign, "Texas Rangers," hung just above it. A flagpole with the American flag stood to the right.

Slim spoke again, "Thanks, Capt'n. But we gotta get to this Brazos River Bar M Ranch where Matt Jorgensen is staying."

"Matt Jorgensen?" Tom asked. "If you're talkin' about the hired gun on the Bar M, he goes by the handle of the *Brazos Kid.*"

"He's right. Better call him, *Brazos.*" He poured himself another cup of coffee and then added, "Wish one of us could ride out with you, but it's a good jaunt. Don't know what else I can tell ya, except good luck."

Slim opened the door and said, "Thanks, Capt'n," and the three cowboys stepped outside.

The captain walked out with them and began giving them directions. "You stay t'other side of the bridge and head south. Take the first fork and stay with the river. Day and a half, you'll find some longhorns. That'll be the beginning of the spread. Keep riding 'til ya see some cotton fields by the river. You'll see a trail heading east. Follow it 'til ya come to a large estate. That'll be General Mitchell's place, the Brazos River Bar M Ranch."

"We better get movin' then," Slim said, and the captain watched the three step into the street, mount up and head out to find Matt.

CHAPTER 55

A TOUGH DECISION FOR BRAZOS

21 July 1882

Jaimie sat on the porch, watching General Mitchell cleaning his shotgun after a day of hunting. She was always concerned about her uncle's safety. After all, he was in his mid-sixties and not as spry as he once had been.

Mitch stood up in the doorway of his ranch home with his shotgun in hand.

Jaimie stood up with him, looking at the strangers approaching the ranch. "They've dismounted. Just waiting."

"Keep an eye on them, Jaimie," Mitch ordered, eyeing the men intently with a steady and cautious stare.

"They're back on their horses," Jaimie yelled out. "They're riding around back."

Mitch quickly inserted two shotgun shells into the chambers and clicked shut the piece. He turned, faced the end of porch and waited with his finger on the trigger.

Slim and Dan came to the back of the ranch at full gallop.

The General defensively pointed his shotgun at them and yelled out, "Who the hell are you?"

Seth quickly reined up in front of Mitch and stopped the General from raising the shotgun. "Those are three cowboys from up in Montana, lookin' for Brazos. Said they came twelve hundred miles to find him."

"Brazos?" Jaimie asked. "Our Brazos?"

"Well, yeah," Seth continued. "Don't ask me why . . . I don't know."

A band of riders led by Matt Jorgensen rode up from the corral.

He yelled out while holding his excited horse back, "Steve, and get Mitch and Jaimie into the house. Now!" He looked at the scuffed-up cowboys, tightened his jaw, then looked back at McDaniel's' group riding in. "Seth, get the rifles on the roof and in the barn."

Seth obeyed immediately, getting the other wranglers situated with rifles.

Brazos drew his gun, twirled and cocked it at the same time. He then pointed it at Slim and Dan.

Steve yelled out, "We can use 'em, Brazos. They killed a couple of McDaniel's' men out on the plains." Steve paused and looked at Brazos, waiting to see if he would shoot them. "But it's your call."

Brazos holstered his pistol. "Use 'em, then. But get 'em the hell out of my sight. I'm tempted to shoot 'em." Brazos then whipped his horse around. "Fasten down the windows, General. Steve, take five of my best," he said as he motioned for one of the riders to check the barn. But he noticed Leisha was missing. "Seth, go look for your sister."

Seth ran as ordered, stopped by the corral, then headed for the barn.

Steve and the rest ushered the General and Jaimie into the house.

The young cowboys' feelings of awe at Brazos's presence passed as Steve gave them orders. "Grab your rifles and take cover with the others behind the hay bales."

Dan blurted out, "You're Brazos."

Brazos reeled his horse around into Dan and looked at him angrily. Steve came down the steps. "Brazos, same as last time?" He was referring to their last gun fight and how Brazos used a special tactic.

"No. Little different," Brazos returned, looking out at the motionless group. "McDaniel's' men want me to come out now. We'll give them sometime to cool their heels. Kinda play according to our rules, not theirs. Keep an eye on 'em, Steve. Let me know if they stir any. And tell Seth I want him right away."

Brazos climbed down off his horse and walked over to Dan and Slim, still looking angry. "Son, if you know something about me that I don't, spill it."

Slim answered, "We're from Montana, and we've been looking for ya. By your looks and all, you match your dad's."

Brazos's angry look dropped from his dusty face, and he began to hang onto every word these strange cowboys were saying. His palms became sweaty, and he wiped them on his chaps. He couldn't stop the wetness swelling up in his eyes, so he looked away at the group in the distance.

He asked, "Where'd ya see my dad?"

Dan answered, "In Montana on his ranch. We worked for him."

Brazos turned quickly as if to collar Dan, but instead kept his hands palm down on his chaps. Gritting his teeth, he said, "He's dead!"

Slim agreed, "Yes sir. Been five years now. We were there when . . ." He stopped, looked at Brazos and then finished. "We were there."

"When he got killed, why don't ya say it?" Brazos snapped quickly. "You knowed I knew. Why'd 'ya come down?"

The three cowboys looked at each other and then concentrated their attention on Brazos. Dan answered. "To take you back to Montana. To see your mama one last time; she's not well, Brazos, sir."

Brazos' jaw dropped as he stared at the three young men. He knew the time had come for him to return to Montana. But for now, he knew he had another battle to win at the Brazos Bar M Ranch. All three of the visiting cowboys from Montana joined him.

When it was all over, only two of the cowboys lived to take Brazos back to Montana. Shorty was gunned down on the bridge, across the Brazos at Waco.

CHAPTER 56

THE GHOSTS OF MONTANA

7 August 1882

T he Northern-Pacific pulled into Virginia City, Montana because Bozeman did not yet have a rail siding. Disembarking the train, they were met by Russell, a wrangler for the Double-O who had been wired of their coming. He was a strong looking man, and appropriately chosen for the task of helping with Shorty's coffin. Russell was a Norwegian with muscles that bulged out of his shirt sleeves. He was one man that Brazos sized up real quick and decided that he was one that he wouldn't want to pick a fight. On the other hand, Russell was also a tame man of a gentle nature, with blue eyes and blond hair.

"I'm Russell, sir," he said, in a strong voice which impressed Brazos. "Most jest call me Russ."

"You'll do."

"He means, he thinks you're okay," Dan said.

"That your wagon, Russ?"

"Yes sir."

"Well, we've got our friend Shorty on board. He got killed down in Texas during a range war. Good man. Wanna give us a hand?"

They set to work getting Shorty's coffin out of the baggage car. Once the coffin was loaded aboard with their other gear, Dan climbed in back with the coffin. Russ took the reins.

Once aboard, Brazos took over the lines.

"Just show me where to go, Russ, and we'll be all right."

Russ was a little put off at first, but relinquished the reins and settled back for a long ride, as the three men headed towards the Double-O Ranch with Shorty's body.

"Take a turn at the end of the road, and it'll head us out into the country. We've a long ways to go."

"Just let me know which way to go," Brazos answered, "It's been too long a spell for me to remember much of this country, as pretty as it is." Brazos paused. "Tell me something."

"Yes, sir."

"You say 'yes, sir' one more time, and I'm liable to dump you out."

"Yes – uh. Sir, I'm not comfortable at calling you anything. Can I just call you, Brazos?"

"Fits." Flipping the reins loosely across the backside of the team of horses taught them to keep the gait and follow their new leader's commands. "Get up, there." Then, looking straight ahead, he asked Russ, "How's my ma?"

There was a long pause as Russell stared into the Montana horizon.

"She's gone, Brazos. I'm – I'm sorry."

There was a quietness like the wind had quit, and the sound of the horses' hooves and the turning of the wheels was oblivious to the moment. The shock took several moments to sink in, and when it did, Brazos was slow to say anything.

"When?"

"She passed away just a week ago in her sleep. Had no way of tellin' ya. She tried to stay with us. Poor soul. Her heart jest couldn't keep a beatin'."

The wagon kept going, as thoughts spun around inside Brazos' mind. *Why am I coming back? What good can I do her, now? Why do't I just turn this horse around and get on the next train for Waco?*

The wagon kept going, and he received no answers to his silent questions. It was a while before any one spoke.

"Can I say somethin', Brazos?" Russ asked.

"Go ahead. It's a free country; isn't it, Dan?"

"As far as the eye can see," Dan answered.

"You really Wil's son?" Russ asked.

"Yep."

"Then, how come you left, and now you're coming back, all a sudden for your ma and all? But what will become of the ranch?"

"Didn't anyone tell him, Dan?"

"Nope. Thought it best to keep it among just a few of us. The ones who were raised by Wil, so to speak."

"Well, Russ. Let's just say, I got homesick and decided to come home."

"Most of us figure you came back and you were going to take over the ranch. And, we don't rightly know what will become of us?"

"First things first. If I take the ranch, and I say 'if', cause there's a lot of attachments to that idea; then you'll have a job there. If you're good enough to earn your keep, that is."

"I'm good, Brazos. I can throw a rope around a horse further than any of them. And I have the strength of three men when it comes to dogging. And I can shoe faster than any of them."

"Then, my good friend Russ, I don't think we have anything to worry about."

"He's good, Brazos," Dan informed him. "One of the best hands we got. One of the reasons they sent him by his self, I'm thinkin'."

"Another thing, Russ. Does anyone suspect I'm Wil's son; outside of the ranch hands?"

"Not that I know of, sir, eh, Brazos. We were told not to talk it up. You're supposed to be buried next to the house. And, now you're supposed to be buyin' the ranch. Too many supposin's."

Brazos whipped the reins over the horses' rumps and yelled, "Yo. Get up there." Then without looking at Russ, he asked, "Who's they?"

"Your ma and your ma's lawyer lady."

"A lawyer, eh? A lady? I never thought they had lady lawyers. Not in Montana, anyway."

"Yes sir. Just recent like. And she's all lady, Brazos. Real nice lady."

"Well, whatcha thinkin' now?"

Brazos said nothing but stared straight ahead.

The trip across Montana's land towards Bozeman was long and hard; nothing like the flat prairies of Texas. The road was narrower and filled with ruts from the constant rains and winter snows. Brazos kept the team at an even trot, sometimes just letting the reins go, and sliding himself back against his seat to close his eyes. At other times he would whip the horses for a fast walk, and even a faster trot. Then, when appropriate, the riders would get out and walk the horses; something he learned while in the cavalry. The other two had no qualms about how he drove the team of horses. He seemed to know better than the rest about how to get along with horses.

He sensed uneasiness in Russ, so he kept silent most of the trip.

Russ finally broke the silence and said, "The boy in the box. His parents are waiting for us."

Slim answered, pushing his hat back on his head. "Shorty got killed in a range war. Almost made it. Stuck his head out from behind a tree. I was right beside him. Caught one right in the forehead. Good man. Good friend. Real good."

Along the roadside, every once in a while, he would eye a cow and give it a blank stare. His thoughts were still not favorable towards ranching. His thought returned, "Why the hell have I come this far?"

Finally they approached the hill which would give him a glimpse of the Double-O Ranch. The same house was sitting slightly on the hill and away from any gully where the rains and snow would gather. It had changed though; it was larger, with an expansion for two more bedrooms, and a larger den. When he was alive, Wil was not accustomed to too many rooms. He never acquired the taste for a den.

Where there was one barn, now there were two, with storage for more hay and fodder, and more stalls for the horses. The corral was much larger than the one Brazos had ridden in before. In fact, there were three. The other two were smaller than the main one. However large it seemed to him now, over what he remembered, it was still no Brazos River Bar M Ranch. He would perhaps occupy one of the bedrooms in the main house. However, he was curious to know who would acquire any of the others.

He asked, "Who sleeps in the main house?"

"You will, now, Brazos," Dan answered. Your mother had two more bedrooms added in case you returned and got married. Your mother had a den added. She knew you would want to read, being an officer and such."

"You an officer, Brazos?" Russ asked quite inquisitively.

"Capt'n," responded Dan.

"The South?"

"Any problems with that?"

"No, sir – uh, none."

"Good."

Brazos pulled the team into the ranch and stopped in front of the ranch house.

Russ leaped out and tied them to the hitching post.

All of the wranglers were outside to meet them.

Brazos' eyes scanned the lot of them as if he were trying to recognize any, but they were all strangers to him.

They were at a loss as how to react to the new boss. The stories about him were many and strange. Mostly, they had heard that he and his brother, Lukas were wild boys who drank, shacked up with prostitutes, and gambled. When they lost their money, they went on a robbing spree. The story about the freight office was blown out of proportion. They came in with a gang and shot up the town. It was the brave sheriff that gunned down most of them, including him and his brother Lukas.

Now that Brazos returned, the mystery had spun an even wider web. No one had been told the truth. They only speculated that, somehow, Brazos escaped the guns of the sheriff, or was only wounded and came back to life, broke jail, and ran north to Canada. The tales were almost messianic in nature.

Some heard that he fought on the side of the Confederacy. Knowing Wil's allegiance to the North, this rumor was quickly played down by most.

Now, looking around at these men, he saw that a few were older than him, but most were younger.

They were looking for a strong boss. They knew they had found him in Brazos. No one dared to walk up to him and ask him about the truth. They continued with their work.

As his eyes caught theirs, he saluted them with the two fingers on his right hand as if to say "everything was okay". He, too, wondered how many of them fought on the side of the North.

"We'll take the team now, Brazos," Dan said, adding, "Russ, you and some others take care of the coffin. Put it in the front room. We'll be burying him in the morning, first thing."

Brazos turned quickly and asked, "Where?"

"Up on the hill, Brazos?" It was more of a question. "If it's all right with you." His words trailed off.

Brazos looked up to the hillside where he knew his mother would be lying. He also remembered Wil had marked two graves with crosses there. One was his.

When the ranch hands returned to their duties and prepared Shorty for the night, Brazos walked up the hillside to the top. Her grave was fresh. He opened the gate to the yard and entered. Taking his hat in hand, he knelt beside her grave and looked at her marker as he stopped a tear's attempt to roll down his cheek. The marker read,

"ANNIE ANDERSEN
1817 – 1882
WIFE – MOTHER
THE COWBOYS' MA"

Slowly, he drawled inwardly to himself. "Ma. I missed ya something terrible. I've kept most of your letters. They kept me going through the War. Made me feel good on the porch, down in Texas, when I'd look up in the sky and knew you were under the same sky, just further north. I tried, Ma. I tried to get back before .... Ma. I love you."

He turned his eyes briefly to the marker next to hers, and recognized it belonging to Wil. It was not the same marker the boys put in the field, and his body was not in the grave. But, just the same, a marker stood next to Annie's because they never located Wil's hastily dug grave that they made somewhere on the plains between Bozeman and Belle Fouche.

"He was a good man, Ma. Good father. His sons jest disappointed him. Wish I coulda come home and done him proud. He wouldn't have it. Had I stayed here, he would still be alive."

He stood up and looked at the other markers. The two crosses were still there. They were old and weather-beaten, but he could make out the markings.

"LUKAS ANDERSEN
1838 – 1858"
"MATT ANDERSEN
1836 – 1858"

His thoughts quickly raced back to that morning he left with Anse. He looked back and saw Wil digging the graves with Annie by his side. He never dreamed he would be back again, standing by the graves of his parents; Wil and Annie Andersen.

A short distance away was a marker of one Charlie Nightlinger, they used to call "Black Charlie". He got his name from being black, and older than the night. He was their cook on the trail, and boss, after Wil was murdered. Now he was with Annie on the hill.

Brazos's eyes returned to his parents' graves. He looked upwards, closed his eyes, and whispered a prayer.

He stayed there for hours, just sitting, while the rest of the men continued their work. Dan and Russ left him alone.

Suddenly, the figure of a woman climbed the hill to be beside him. When she reached the gravesite, she stood in silence and watched her man. It had been too many years since she last saw him, and now he stood in front of her. She feasted her eyes on his physique, his rugged looking face and then his blue eyes.

It's Matt, alright, she thought to herself in those precious moments. *My Matt.*

She had spent days, months and years, thinking about what she would say when and if he found her, and now the moment was here and she found herself at a loss for words. She didn't want to act like some giddy kid at a birthday party, but at the same time, she didn't want to act too prudish as if to ignore him completely.

Afterwards, when she felt it appropriate, her gentle, womanly voice broke the silence and startled him. "I'm truly sorry about your mother."

His gun whipped out of its holster, cocked and pointed in the direction of a young lady dressed in riding clothes. Her hair was swept up under her Stetson, and she wore a light jacket to keep out the Montana chill.

"I suppose I deserved that, Mister Jorgenson. You are Matt Jorgensen, are you not?"

"I'm sorry. I didn't hear you walk up," Brazos apologized. In his heart and mind, he felt he was in the presence of extreme beauty. And for a moment, he thought . . . *naw, it couldn't be. But* . . . For the moment, he was frozen in thought and space.

He answered, "You can call me *Brazos.* I'll answer to thet. But, yes, m'name's Matt Jorgensen. And you are?"

Brazos was convinced that what he saw was the loveliest woman he had ever laid eyes on. It was as if every pretty girl he had ever met were rolled into one. The voice was not exactly angelic, as it had a slight roughness to her tone, but it was crystal clear and melodic to listen to.

"You were concentrating. I apologize for disturbing your time of mourning. My name is Miss Beth Paterson", she said, trying to hide the girlish smile of delight as she recognized the blue eyes and rugged, handsome face from all her dreams and memories. And then she thought, *Can he recognize who I really am? Why not just tell him? No, I can't. I've got to wait for his move.*

She continued, "I'm the attorney for your mother's estate and I asked the cowboys to bring you home."

He was convinced that he was seeing the most beautiful angel ever, standing in front of him, and his thoughts melted into one. *It's Ginny!* And before he could stop himself from saying anything, he blurted out . . . "Ginny!"

In a moment of fantasy, he walked over to her in slow motion, grabbed the crop out of her hand and threw it to the wind before she could react. In one felt swoop, he grabbed her, whirled her around, picked her up in his strong arms and kissed her hard on the lips. She reciprocated with a long and passionate kiss, throwing her arms around his neck without any resistance. He broke from the kiss and returned to reality. He looked deeply and intently into her soft, moist blue eyes.

"I said, I'm Beth Paterson. I'm the attorney for your mother's estate."

Brazos' jaw dropped and his brow furrowed while he recovered from his feeling of ecstasy and replied, "Yes, ma'am." He smiled and said to himself, *and I'm Buffalo Bill.*

He turned into her and stuttered, "Yes, ma'am. And I'm Matt Jorgensen."

"I'd . . . I'd like to meet with you at a proper time," she replied, straightening up her wind-blown hair. "This is your time to be alone. May I call upon you some time tomorrow . . . say noon time?"

He gave a frozen look at her and answered shyly, "Yes, ma'am. You're . . ."

"Beth Paterson. You're mother's attorney for the estate." She noticed Matt's hesitant drawl and cupped her hand to keep from laughing. She knew she had found her man and she wanted so much to tell him, but she thought to herself, *Not now, Ginny. Play it out until you're sure about each other's love.* "Is noon, tomorrow alright?"

"What? Oh, yes. Yes, noon tomorrow."

Her eyes gleamed as her whole entity wanted to be wrapped up with his as one, but she turned and walked away. Her steps were high and light as she sashayed down the hill with the wind blowing wistfully through her clothing.

Brazos' eyes trailed her down the hill and watched her as she met Dan at the ranch house. He followed her slowly and saw her leave in her carriage. Dan waited on the porch for Brazos to return.

"So, you met the lady lawyer," Dan recognized as Brazos stepped up on the porch.

"Nice lady," Brazos returned.

"Yeah! We kinda think so."

Brazos took his makings and, as he watched Dan through the side of his eyes, he asked, "Notice anything different about her?"

Dan smiled and answered, "Yes sir."

"What?"

"She looked a lot prettier when I helped her into the carriage."

"Yeah?"

"Yes, boss." Then, feeling more at ease, he added, "Told you she was cute."

EPILOGUE

Brazos stood anxious on the porch of the ranch house in Montana the next day, waiting for Beth to return. He observed the goings on of the day where a few of the wranglers were busting broncs in the corral. Homer, Russell and some of the wranglers were riding fence on the hillside, making sure that no strays were hurt or missing.

Dan sauntered from the backside of the house with a half-eaten biscuit in one hand and a cup of coffee in the other. "Post came yesterday. Forgot to mention."

"Oh," Brazos responded, walking over to the well. "Anything important?"

Dan took one last bite of the biscuit, then reached in his back pocket and pulled out an envelope. "Just one came in; from Steve."

"Steve Andrews," Brazos acknowledged. "He's been my partner for these many years and now he's the ramrod for the General's ranch in Texas. Wonder what he's got to say? Here. Let me have it."

He took the letter and read through it. "A Mrs. Rudolph Dusselhoffer. Something like thet. "Dusselhoffer? Don't ring a bell. Says she dropped by with her husband and two young boys" He looked at Dan. "Who is she?"

"Oh, here it is. Her name's *Carol*."

"Carol?"

"Know her?"

"Yeah." He read a little to himself. *Two young sons. Blond and blue eyes like their German father. They're beautiful.*

"Blond boys. Germans. Ha."

He continued reading parts of the letter aloud again *I'm sorry I missed seeing you in Waco . . . but cherished the time we spent together in Sycene.*

He looked over at Dan and said, "We were kinda good friends."

Another thing, Brazos. Jesse was killed this week. You probably already heard, but just in case you hadn't, he was killed by some dirty coward.

"Jesse?" Brazos muttered to himself.

"What?" Dan asked. "Who's Jesse?"

Brazos took a deep breath as he stopped walking. "Jesse James. He was killed. Says *by some coward . . . shot in the back.*

"Good man, thet Jesse. He'll be sorely missed. Not only by me, but by hundreds of others." He took his bandana and wiped his nose.

"The outlaw?" Dan asked. "What for? Being bad? A killer? A bank robber?"

Brazos looked at Dan and said softly, "Yeah. All thet. But the real man was the man inside. Like me, he had a destiny in life.

"Let me tell you a story I heard about him a few years back. He held up this train. Yeah. A real train robber. I would guess he robbed more than just a few, from what I hear. Anyways, he was walking down the aisle of this here passenger car, taking money from the men and stealing jewels and kissing all the ladies when one man objected; vehemently. One of the ladies in the car who hadn't been robbed and kissed by Jesse yet looked over at the man and, as she waited her turn to be robbed, said, *Shut up, you ol' Coot and let Jesse rob this train.*

"He helped others who couldn't help themselves. He loved people. I suppose you wouldn't know thet."

"You knew him?"

"Yep," Brazos said with pride. "We rode together."

Dan's jaw dropped. "What? You rode with the infamous Jesse James?"

"The infamous? Remind me to tell you more about him some day."

Brazos left Dan standing there, wondering how he and Jesse rode together. Then he caught up to him again. Brazos paid no mind to him as he thought back to the segment of time when Jesse's gang messed up a bank robbery without Jesse and some of the gang got killed.

He whispered to himself but Dan could make out a few words. *Had that part of his gang paid heed to our training, they'd probably be alive today and so would Jesse. But, no. Just because they had a grudge against us, they had to ride into town on the best geldings, with slickers to boot; a dead give-away thet something was goin' to happen. I'll bet the whole dang town was a-waitin' for them, not knowin' who to look for. It was like hanging a lantern around their neck as a beacon light. And then they had no fresh horses waiting for them outside of town. The gang was destroyed, the Youngers were captured. All gone except for Jesse and Frank. And now Jesse . . . dead. Too bad.*

"You were a good man, Jesse," Brazos said aloud, looking up into the sky. "Yes sir. You'll be missed."

Hearing Brazos, Dan removed his hat, rubbed his hair and then said, "Brazos, you're a man of mystery. A real man of adventure."

"Yeah! A man of mystery and adventure, Dan!" Then Brazos remembered telling Jesse to fake his death if he wanted to live a peaceful life with his wife Zee. He thought, *Umm. I wonder!*

Brazos read the rest of the letter to himself as he walked away. He reinserted the letter into the envelope and stuck it in his back pocket. Then the two walked on out to the corral.

The day was good for the two men as they climbed upon the top of the corral to watch some broncs being busted by the Double R wranglers. Brazos' rugged-looking face broke out into a smile as he reminisced about Carol, married with two boys.

He looked back at the ranch and caught Beth driving her carriage his way. He immediately jumped down and walked over to the house to welcome her. He smiled at her, grabbed the reins of the horse and brought it to the hitching post. As a gentleman, he helped her out of the carriage and walked her to the door.

His thought kept going through his mind. *She shore do look like my Ginny. Dang if she don't.*

He took off his Stetson, brushed his hair back and asked, "What do we do next, Miss Paterson?"

The End

An excerpt from one of the chapters in the next thrilling
story of the Brazos series

BRAZOS

By

Ermal Walden Williamson

FINAL EPISODE

A BIG CHALLENGE FOR BRAZOS

"Tries it on, Miss Beth," Haciola said, holding Beth's new
dress up to her.

"Oh, it's beautiful," Beth said, thrusting her two arms into
the sleeves while Haciola helped lift it over her head.

"Fills out thet skinny body of your'n with your tight
bloomers and corset. My, my, my, my my. I cain't never see why
a woman like you wears a corset no how."

"It makes me look just right in the proper places, Hacci," she said, poking her head up through the neck of the dress. "It's just like the dress I wore to the dance with Brazos; back in Tennessee. That was before he became *Brazos*."

"He's gonna like you when he sees you in this heah dress, I'ma thinkin'. Youse gonna be the best lookin' gal at the dance."

"It's been too many years, Hacci. If he does, well, we'll just have to see."

"My, my, my. You sho' is a mysterious woman."

Haciola went into her bedroom in the back of the house, took something out of the dresser drawer and returned to Beth's bedroom.

"I'se got sumptin else for ya, Missy," she said, holding up a strand of blue glass beads.

"Oh, my!" Beth responded with widen eyes as she retrieved them gently from Haciola's hand. "These are beautiful. Where did you . . . ?"

"If'n I tells ya, I 'spect you gonna hafta' keeps it a secret for me?"

"Why . . . of course, Hacci. Of course. But why?"

She put the strand around her neck, turned and allowed Haciola to fasten them to her neck.

"Oh, my," Beth exclaimed as she looked at them through the mirror. "They're simply beautiful."

"They's belonged to Missy Andersen."

"Oh! Then I can't accept them, Hacci. I just can't." Beth reached up to unclasp them when Haciola stopped her by holding her hands.

"You jest hold on there a minute, Missy Beth. They's yours cause she woulda wanted you to hab 'em."

"But, why? She never told me anything about them."

"Thet's cause she held them dear to her bosom. Ya see, they's from her dead husband."

"Wil Andersen?"

"Well, in a way, yes."

"Tell me more, Hacci."

"I learned from them boys there thet Mistah Andersen, he was told by Missy Andersen to get a strand of blue glass beads when he finished the drive in Belle Fouche."

"But he never reached Belle Fouche," Beth reminded her.

"Yes. But the boys did, and they too knew what Missy Andersen done told Mistah Andersen. He told them afore he done passed away that he was gonna get 'em. On his dying day, he told them."

"And they bought them in Belle Fouche?" Beth asked, looking back in the mirror at the strand around her neck. She rubbed them gently with her fingers and smiled. . "Yes, ma'am. And they done got them and brought them to Missy Andersen. She told me about them, too," Haciola added. "She done told me to find someone who I thought would love them as she did and to give them to her. Didn't know it at the time thet it'd be you, missy Beth. But . . . well, here you is and here they is and . . . You sure do look pretty with them on youself. Lordy. Lordy. Lordy. And youse does, too. Youse sure do make them look real pertty. Yes, ma'am. Real pertty."

Beth twirled around in her gown and then sat down.

"Youse gonna find out real soon, missy, jest how pretty you really is," Hacci said, watching Brazos stride towards the house from out the window. "Your fella's a'comin' in the house right now. And he's all duded up, too. My, oh my, my, my."

"Quick. Help me get out of this strand and gown. I don't want him to see me in this dress before tomorrow night. We're going riding right now."

Haciola took gentle care helping Beth slip out of her new dress. She hung it up in the closet, then curtsied and went to the door. "I'll be in the kitchen if youse needs me, ma'am." She passed Brazos at the foot of the stairs. "My, my, my, my, my. Youse does look sharp, Mistah Brazos, suh. This is a special occasion, it is."

"Why, Hacci, what on earth do you mean?"

"You comin' courtin' Miss Beth with your new set of britches and cowboy boots."

"Just goin' for a ride, Hacci."

"Yes, suh, Mistah Brazos, and have youse sho have got yoself a purty lady to ride with." She smiled broadly.

"Get your ridin' britches and come on with us," Brazos said humorously.

"No suh, not me. I don't ride those big animals." She smiled and walked towards the kitchen as Brazos tipped his hat.

A knock on the bedroom door caused Beth's heart to beat fast. When she opened it, Brazos filled the frame with his physique, holding a cigar in his mouth.

"If you come in here, you'd best be getting rid of that smelly old thing," Beth said as she quickly slammed the door.

Brazos pushed the door open again with his two hands and walked in. "This is my house and this is my room. No one keeps me out of my house or my room."

"Ohhh!" Beth exclaimed, allowing her Scottish temper to flare up as she pushed him back out and slammed the door. "I'm not dressed, yet."

Brazos took his cigar out of his mouth and stood there. "The least you coulda done was to have told me. No need hitting me in the head with the door." He took his smashed Stetson and walked back downstairs and waited by the fireplace. His cigar smoked up the room as if to relate his anger.

After awhile, Beth opened the door slowly and stepped out into the hall way. She wore a new black outfit that Hacci made for her, reminiscent of the one she wore when she first met Brazos.

His face lit up and, with a Texas smile he said, "Ginny?"

Hacci overheard him, giggled and said, "He ain't seen nothin' yet."

RESOURCES

Piedmont Valley, VA = Southside is traditionally defined as the region south of the James River, east of the Blue Ridge, west of Tidewater, and north of No' Carolina

http://ncatlasrevisited.org/History/histTitle.htm#histfg14#of
spindles quadrupled starting 1870 in NC
isolated villages

Piedmont region = VA, NC – SC – Ga – Al
Carolina Piedmont – mill workers followed the "Rhode Island Model"

http://piedmontwanderings.blogspot.com/2009/10/heres-interesting-description-of.html

http://docsouth.unc.edu/southlit/chesnut/ill9.html

http://www.suite101.com/content/the-confederate-white-house-a179819

http://www.google.com/search?q=textile+mills+1865&rls=com.microsoft:en-us:IE-SearchBox&ie=UTF-8&oe=UTF-8&sourceid=ie7&rlz=1I7GGLL_en

About Bunting and the First Presbyterian Church:
http://books.google.com/books?id=kZ1uqscl51AC&pg=RA3-PA315&lpg=RA3-PA315&dq=robert+bunting,+first+presbyterian+church+in+nashville&source=bl&ots=Zt9ErNXJ2R&sig=bhz-ornjlyIgoIyzmVDLb6nLd5E&hl=en&ei=gTNeS9OTDsSztgfimLSnAg&sa=X&oi=book_result&ct=result&resnum=7&ved=0CBgQ6AEwBg#v=onepage&q=robert%20bunting%2C%20first%20presb yterian%20church%20in%20nashville&f=false

Belle Starr:
httphttp://en.wikipedia.org/wiki/Belle_Starr#Early_life

http://www.texomaenterprise.net/page12.html

http://en.wikipedia.org/wiki/Belle_Starr

Scyene:
http://freepages.history.rootsweb.ancestry.com/jwheat/scyene.html

http://www.lkwdpl.org/wihohio/star-bel.htmher lips.

http://www.civilwarstlouis.com/history/jamesnorthfield.htm

RESOURCES

Piedmont Valley, VA = Southside is traditionally defined as the region south of the James River, east of the Blue Ridge, west of Tidewater, and north of No' Carolina

http://ncatlasrevisited.org/History/histTitle.htm#histfg14#of spindles quadrupled starting 1870 in NC
isolated villages

Piedmont region = VA, NC – SC – Ga – Al
Carolina Piedmont – mill workers followed the "Rhode Island Model"

http://piedmontwanderings.blogspot.com/2009/10/heres-interesting-description-of.html

http://docsouth.unc.edu/southlit/chesnut/ill9.html

http://www.suite101.com/content/the-confederate-white-house-a179819

http://www.google.com/search?q=textile+mills+1865&rls=com.microsoft:en-us:IE-SearchBox&ie=UTF-8&oe=UTF-8&sourceid=ie7&rlz=1I7GGLL_en

About Bunting and the First Presbyterian Church: http://books.google.com/books?id=kZ1uqscl51AC&pg=RA3-PA315&lpg=RA3-PA315&dq=robert+bunting,+first+presbyterian+church+in+nashville&source=bl&ots=Zt9ErNXJ2R&sig=bhz-ornjlyIgoIyzmVDLb6nLd5E&hl=en&ei=gTNeS9OTDsSztgfimLSnAg&sa=X&oi=book_result&ct=result&resnum=7&ved=0CBgQ6AEwBg#v=onepage&q=robert%20bunting%2C%20first%20presbyterian%20church%20in%20nashville&f=false

Belle Starr:
http://en.wikipedia.org/wiki/Belle_Starr#Early_life

http://www.texomaenterprise.net/page12.html

http://en.wikipedia.org/wiki/Belle_Starr

Scyene:
http://freepages.history.rootsweb.ancestry.com/jwheat/scyene.html

http://www.lkwdpl.org/wihohio/star-bel.htmher lips.

http://www.civilwarstlouis.com/history/jamesnorthfield.htm

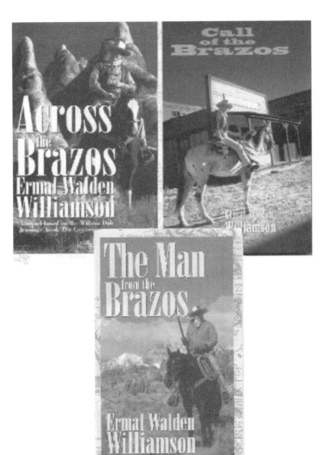

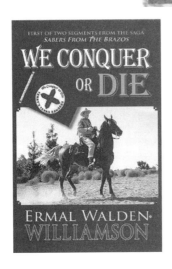